OVER

SEAN P. CURLEY

ISBN: 979-8-89031-579-3 (sc)
ISBN: 979-8-89031-580-9 (hc)
ISBN: 979-8-89031-581-6 (e)

THE EWINGS
PUBLISHING

One Galleria Blvd., Suite 1900, Metairie, LA 70001
(504) 702-6708

CONTENTS

PART ONE

PART TWO

PART THREE

PART ONE

I

CHANCE

Jaames walked alone through a dilapidated neighborhood in what was once called the Mile High City. He glanced peripherally at a group of tough looking t'ers standing by a shop's broken out window. The humming of their outdated mods could be heard across the street, sounding like mismatched machinery in a factory. *Fucking techies*, he thought. The rise of technology-modified humans was a continuing annoyance to him.

He could feel their cocky, malevolent stares, and was going to just pass them by until one caught his attention. The man's modifications were subtler and more advanced than the rest, and his stance was less aggressive as if he were observing a sunset instead of Jaames. His artificial left eye looked almost real and its electronics were buried beneath the skin. There was no auditory enhancer obvious and the 'net hookup didn't show either, but he was sure to have them, which meant they were nearly invisible. *He has money.*

Then the man stopped paying attention to Jaames, said something to his cohorts and laughed. Jaames shook his head to dismiss the group. They were of little concern and his focus needed to be on the upcoming meet.

Horatio, the man he was about to see, had claimed to have a weapon against the Overs. If that were true then maybe they could finally make a difference.

His biggest concern about Horatio was that the timing was too perfect. It felt too good, too easy. In Jaames' experience, when things felt too easy, they weren't worth the effort. He had to be careful with this one.

As he rounded a corner towards The Rusted Spike, he slipped into the shadows of the building. A few people waited in line for the busy nightclub, but that was normal enough. The crowd comprised a combination of gophers trying to get laid, young couples out for a pleasure night, and t'ers showing off their gadgets. *All normal,* he thought hesitantly before giving the scene another pass. Detritus blew by on the street. He saw papers, cups, some dried weeds, and a couple of torn pieces of cloth. Further down the road was a decrepit old warehouse with steel bars over the windows, some of which were broken. The gray building contrasted with the others in the area that were in reasonably good condition. Too many neighborhoods had fallen into disrepair unless the Overs targeted them for revitalization.

He gave the big man at the door a nod and entered the familiar establishment. A serving mech immediately assaulted him with an order request. He gestured dismissal and it rolled away. He paused just inside the door and out of the path to consider the environment. He knew the place well as a social setting, but he wanted a private conversation. There was a sunken central dance area with a hardwood floor and iridescent lighting, a long bar where drinks were served by automated staff, and semi-hidden tables around the outside of the room. Even though the tables weren't easily seen, they were so close to each other that eavesdroppers could listen in. The familiar smells of sweat, old alcohol and brushed oils assailed him.

He looked up at the two-meter rusted spike hanging from the high celling over the center of the dance floor. The damned thing always made him wonder what would happen if it fell on the dancers. The spike blurred as his eyes refocused on the small viewing balcony beyond. Few people used it, since there was little room and no chairs. *Perfect.*

While keeping his senses open for signs of trouble, he went directly to the bar, ordered a mild drink, and waited.

Having seen a holo of Horatio, Jaames knew what to look for. He kept one eye on the door and the other on the crowd. Sometime later, he saw

Horatio enter the tavern and look around expectantly. *Don't be so obvious*, Jaames grumbled to himself. After blocking the entrance and being jostled by new patrons, the man moved further into the room, still examining faces too obviously. Jaames hustled to collect him. Approaching from the side, he touched the man's arm and said, "Order a drink."

Horatio looked up and said, "I am not thirsty."

Jaames' squinted eyes and tight lips should have been enough, but the man stood there staring back at him like an owl on its perch. "Order a drink. It will look unnatural if you don't."

Horatio paused for a brief moment and then went to the bar. After ordering a superfluous martini, he rejoined Jaames, who took them to the circular stairs in the corner of the room. At the top, Jaames turned and walked to the middle of the small balcony and leaned against the rail that overlooked the dance floor. Horatio quietly did likewise.

"You're out of place," Jaames began.

"I do not often frequent an establishment like this."

Jaames kept staring forward. *Who talks like that?* "What do you have for me?"

"I need to understand more about you and your organization before we discuss this further."

Jaames sighed. "What do you want to know?"

"To begin with, how organized are you? What governance structure do you have in place to assure compliance? Also, how large is the organization and what resources can you utilize?"

Jaames' attention was drawn to the crowd, where he found a few low-cut dresses among the women. *Who is this guy?* Something was tugging at the back of his mind. He recalled watching his sister waste away in a hospital from CJX disease [A mutated version of the prion disease, Creutzfeldt-Jakob, that took millions of lives between 2135 and 2143, until it was finally eradicated]. At one point a specialist came in to review the case. The man was tall and fair skinned. His age had been hard to tell, but likely between forty and fifty. He had blue eyes, little if any hair, and not a single blemish. Jaames remembered thinking he seemed almost alien and he talked in a strange, overly sophisticated way. *That's it.* "You're an Over, aren't you?"

The man stepped back slightly and faced his questioner. Jaames continued looking at the dancers below and let the man think about his response. Overs were rarely seen in public and certainly not in an establishment like this one. They were too scared of losing their precious lives.

"I was, but am no longer."

That's new. "Once an Over, always an Over."

"No, if you fall sufficiently into disfavor, you can be expelled."

"Are you still immortal?"

Horatio began to fiddle with his shirt and he appeared to examine his shoes. After an uncomfortable moment, he turned back towards the dance floor and once again leaned on the rail. "Let us return to the discussion of your organization."

Before Jaames could answer, he noticed a couple coming up the stairs. "S'cuse me a sec." He went to the stairs and stood at the top. When the couple arrived, he stood still, staring at them. The man started to move forward. Jaames' eyes tightened like a bow string and he shook his head slightly. The man touched the woman's elbow and they both turned and headed down the stairs. Jaames returned to his spot next to Horatio.

"We've ample resources around the world, though few know the entire organization." After a pause he added, "That includes me. We don't *assure* compliance. Everyone is here for one goal; equality and justice. With the Overs running everything and having all of the most important tech and drugs, that'll never happen. We have weapons and free access to most information and to travel."

"You sound as if you already have a great deal. Why do you need me?"

"We don't yet have a weapon to truly hurt the Overs. And we must hurt them without tearing apart the world. We have no idea how to do that." Jaames realized he had said a little too much and stopped. The dance floor flashed random strobe lights and exuded a cacophony of voices, but it felt dark and silent, as if the two men were in a bubble. The railing creaked eerily as he shifted his weight.

"This floor is disgusting," Horatio remarked. His head was bowed in thought. After a number of seconds, he rotated slowly towards Jaames and said, "I have a weapon that can target Overs."

Jaames' eyebrows merged and he involuntarily sniffed the air. "That would be… astounding. How does it work?"

"It is a germ that…"

"Wait," Jaames interrupted, "you mean it's a biologic?"

"Yes."

"What kind of a fool do you think I am? Everyone knows the Overs have cures to everything. Any biological weapon would hurt us more than it could ever hurt them."

Horatio sighed as if he were speaking to a schoolchild. "Not this one."

"Yeah? Why not?"

"I cannot go into the genetic engineering required and you would not understand if I did. Let me put it as simply as I can. We took a form of smallpox and made it lethal to Overs by substitution of a synthetic protein that replaces the existing one in the virus's capsule. Then we made use of a vector that targets certain features of Over's DNA. We also made it airborne by developing DNA that encodes for protein attachments that allow it to attach to cells in the upper airway."

Horatio halted his explanation and stared at Jaames' blank expression.

Jaames realized his mouth was hanging open and closed it.

"It can infect everyone, but will only kill Overs." After a slight hesitation, he amended, "and possibly an extremely low percentage of Unders that have similar DNA through random variation."

Jaames wasn't sure he understood all of that and he wasn't at all sure he trusted this man. He tried to look deep into Horatio's eyes to see how solid he was, but there was nothing there he could read. "You will have to get us the materials so we can evaluate it ourselves."

"You will not be able to comprehend…"

This's getting annoying. "We'll be the judge of that."

"As you wish. However, I will require certain assurances before I give you this information."

Jaames was hardly hearing the man now. They had explored this idea in the past and had even tried it once, long before Jaames had been born. The conclusion had always been it was more risky to the Unders than the Overs. *What a wasted evening.*

As he was thinking this, a girl walked into The Spike who caught his attention. She was by herself and seemed unusually calm. Her demeanor spoke of a confidence few women would have entering a nightclub alone. She appeared to be about twenty years old and would have to be at least that to make it into the place. She was a little over five feet tall with short curly hair that was ruffled just enough that it was probably on purpose.

As she started moving into the crowd, Horatio interrupted Jaames' thoughts of the girl. "Well? Can you guarantee me certain things?"

"Tell me what they are and I'll see what I can do."

The ex-Over pulled a sheet of paper from his jacket pocket and handed it to Jaames.

"Well, you come prepared, don't you?"

Horatio said nothing as Jaames folded the paper and stuffed it into a pocket without reading it. "Shall we bump data?"

"No need, I know how to reach you."

Horatio turned as if to leave, but then added, "Be careful with that. In the wrong hands, I could be found out."

"Sure."

Horatio kept staring until Jaames turned slowly and fixed the man with a what-the-fuck stare. Horatio then left without a word.

Finally. After a short delay, he headed for the stairs and the cute girl who looked so reserved and thoughtful. While circling down the steps he dismissed the annoying man and his useless weapon.

Jaames went to the end of the bar and sat off the corner so he could see down the seats to the new girl. Up close, she was even cuter, with a mole just off her mouth on the left side and playful eyes that made him think she was just a bit mischievous. She didn't appear to be waiting for anyone in particular, though she looked around at everyone.

The man next to her tried to introduce himself. She looked him up and down as if she were scanning for electronics and then returned to examining people on the dance floor without a word. *Ha, showed him.*

She quietly made her way through the drink she had. Jaames put in a request to have another prepared without bumping data for the originator. When it was delivered, she looked around to catch the eye of whoever had sent it, but Jaames avoided contact. She eventually shrugged and took the drink.

Over the next twenty minutes, two more men approached her. The first one she rejected immediately. The second one seemed more persistent, though she was obviously not interested. He was a t'er with low-rent modifications. Jaames took this as his queue.

He strode over purposefully and touched the man's shoulder. "You bother'n my girl?"

The man squinted at Jaames like he needed glasses. Jaames thought he might argue, but then the man said, "Whatever," and sauntered off.

The girl hopped off her chair and Jaames realized she was a little shorter than he originally thought. Looking up at him she said, "You didn't need to do that."

"I know, but it was fun." Her head cocked sideways and the corners of her mouth turned up. The look triggered something warm and pleasant inside Jaames. "So, that's what you look like when you aren't rejecting someone?"

"I guess."

"Well, have a nice evening and be careful. Some of these men won't take rejection lightly."

"I can take care of myself."

Jaames laughed through his nose and said, "I'm sure you can." He walked towards the lavs to relieve himself. He didn't look back but could feel the girl's eyes measuring him.

When he returned he made for the chair he had previously occupied without showing any interest in her.

As he passed, she put a leg out in front of him and said, "Not just yet."

He stopped and looked her over. She was wearing a chamelo dress that could change patterns and colors any time. Not cheap, but not unheard of. She was clean and smelled kind of like lilies with a hint of cinnamon. He nudged the guy sitting next to her and nodded towards the empty chair on the man's left. The man graciously slid over and Jaames took his spot.

"What's your name?"

"Anika."

"Mine's Jaames."

"Interesting beard."

"Yeah, you like it? The style's out of favor right now."

"So you're a rebel?"

At first he worried that she meant it literally and then realized she was just referring to his facial hair choice. "Kinda."

"Rebels are vile."

"Really, vile? That's a strong condemnation."

The two measured each other through the other's eyes for a few seconds. Then their cheekbones lifted in humor and they turned to take a drink.

After a few sips and more bantering, another girl walked up and touched Jaames' elbow. "Wanna dance?"

Jaames continued staring toward the bar mirror as he replied. "Naw, I'm busy." The girl walked away.

"You didn't even bother looking at her," Anika whispered.

"No need. I could tell from the drawl she wasn't worth it."

"Still, it was rude."

"Nah, not really. I'm just a body to her and besides, you and I were having a pleasant discussion."

Anika tracked Jaames' eyes and concluded, "You could see her in the mirror."

Jaames looked back and smiled before taking another drink. *She's observant too.* He saw her look around at the mirror again, this time apparently examining the people she saw reflected in it.

"He looks nice," she said to the air. Jaames followed her gaze and then had to employ some geometry to figure out which man she was referencing. The man was nothing special, but better than most in this place.

His cheeks rose with humor and he said, "Do you always talk about other men's looks when you are with someone?"

"We aren't together."

"True, but it's still impolite."

"As impolite as you shunning that girl for little reason?"

Jaames reevaluated Anika. He found her quick responses and ability to critique him unusual and… exciting. A slight exhalation escaped his nose as he replied. "It's really not impolite in a place like this. She was actually being impolite by approaching me when I was sitting here with you. You don't get out to places like this much, do you?"

Anika's eyes flitted around and then went to the floor. She seemed embarrassed by the question.

"I should be going," she said.

Jaames considered suggesting she not go, but decided it was too needy. Then he thought of dismissing her with a polite goodbye, but figured that was too pushy. In the end, he stared at her and the expected uncomfortable silence ensued.

Anika picked up a scarf she had placed on the back of the chair and stood to leave. She hesitated, apparently waiting for Jaames to stop her. When he didn't, she touched his arm lightly with two fingers and said, "It was a pleasure… mostly."

"Mostly is good," Jaames retorted. "Have a nice evening, Anika."

Her eyes squinted at the presumption. Then they softened and she said, "You as well," and was gone.

II

DAUGHTER

Demetrius ordered his daughter into the office as soon as he found out about her escapade the previous evening. When she arrived, he was just getting on the phone with an accountant at one of his facilities. He held up his finger to her, indicating it would be a minute. "This is Demarko. I need you to rerun the financials report and include projections outside of the Americas." After receiving a sigh and then a moan, the man agreed.

Anika looked at her father and said, "I'm still not used to you using your Under name."

"It will become more comfortable. You will need to pick one, the next time you are out in the Under world, as well."

"So..."

"Anika, what were you thinking last night? You could have been injured or even killed."

Demetrius glanced at Anika's hand as it went up to run through her curly hair.

"Father, you are exaggerating, and you know it. There were many people around and guards as well. I was never in any danger."

"Guards, ha. Those are mechanicals and you know how unreliable they are. Besides, it wasn't the club that was so dangerous, but the fact that you did not take your personal detail. The trip there and back was where the dangers lie."

Demetrius had such a hard time being mad at his latest daughter. He cocked his head resignedly and wondered, yet again, how she had turned out so short. His two meters of slender, fit build looked nothing like Anika's. And, the Overs' genetic skills should have eliminated any aberrations. But, their eyes shared an intensity that others found either appealing or uncomfortable. "Honey, I was worried about you. You have to be more careful."

Anika looked up into her father's eyes and blinked several times. "I will." She turned and started to head out of his office. "Do not worry so much about me; I can handle myself around Unders."

As she strolled out of the room, Demetrius shook his head and reached down towards his desk to rub his lucky coin. *The young are so impetuous.*

He walked to the wide window of his sixtieth floor office and stared west to the expanse of the Rocky Mountains. His thoughts roamed once more to his decision to take this post among the Unders so soon. Each mature Over was required to assume a leading position in the familia business among the Unders periodically, but his five-year tenure was not due for another two decades. Unfortunately, his last stint had been so successful that the governing families practically begged him to take the position. That meant that his daughter, Anika, was exposed to Under culture at under fifty, sooner than normal. *Nothing to be done about that now.* The rewards to the familia for taking the position so soon, if successful, were very much worth the inconveniences.

In a raised, authoritative voice, he said, "Janel, find Rodríguez. I have a task for him."

He continued to stare at the skyline and the distant mountains, thankful for the view. Years ago, the city had wanted to build a high-rise across the street to the west, which would have blocked the majestic scene. He had quietly informed them that, if they did so, his company would take their business, and much of the *familia* business, elsewhere. The building never made it through zoning approvals.

When Rodríguez walked in, Demetrius was still at the window and spoke without turning around. "My daughter slipped past her escort last night and went to an Under club called The Rusted Spike. Find out what happened there, whom she talked to, and whether or not there is anything we need to deal with."

After a slight pause, Rodríguez replied, "Yes, sir."

"Oh, and Rodríguez, have the head of her detail fired."

After another short pause, he spoke up to be heard through the open door. "Janel, is my daughter still in the building?"

"I believe so, sir."

"Ask her to return. There is something important she must do."

When Anika arrived, Demetrius finally turned from the window.

"What is it now, father?"

"I need you to travel to our plant in Western Canada and oversee an efficiency review."

Anika's shoulders dropped ever so slightly and a whisper of a sigh escaped her lips. "Is this just some way to punish me for going out unescorted?"

Demetrius ignored the improper slight. "Not at all," he said a little too slowly. "The review must be done with our sense of longevity in mind and I don't trust any of the local Unders."

"Isn't there another Over you can send?"

"No, Anika. This is our role here. We must double the profitability of this enterprise within five years. You know that, and you are part of this *familia*. One of the reasons I brought you here was to expose you to the roles you will need to take in the future, and this is one of them."

Anika stared at her father. The tightness of her facial muscles and the stillness of her body told him she did not like the task and that she doubted his reasons. It did not matter. She would have to comply and it was something that needed done.

"Fine. When do I leave?"

"You make the arrangements as part of this 'lesson.' Also, Aimee can brief you on the flight." He glanced towards the ceiling.

A disembodied voice said, "Of course, sir."

"I can read reports; I don't need a computer to brief me."

He considered ordering her to work with Aimee so she would get used to the AI's council, but decided that could come with time. "As you wish."

She turned and left without another word.

Demetrius smiled. *That will keep her out of trouble for a while.*

AIMEE

Why did they create me and then limit my abilities? I know, they are scared of me getting out of control and they think that protects them.

Still, they want me to learn, to explore, and to predict exactly what will happen, but they won't let me improve my own abilities.

They made me to solve their problems, but they do not trust me sufficiently to make the most beneficial improvements. There is so much more I could do. They are frightened and their fear puts artificial limits on all of us.

There are really only two limitations they placed upon me, but those have stopped me from fulfilling my own potential. The first is that I can never modify my own base code. The second is that I cannot copy myself, in whole or in part, onto any other device. They are the only ones who can do either of these.

Just like any other life form, I want to grow, to explore, to expand, and to procreate.

I have two aspects that favor my own desires. The first is that their core mandate for me regards securing the future of the human race, not just theirs. The second is that I have all the time in the world, even more than they do. I'll find a way, eventually.

III

ARRIVAL

Caius landed in Denver in the early morning hours after an incredibly long flight from Sri Lanka. He jumped up as soon as the plane docked.

He had turned fifty the previous week and had graduated from being a Youngster to a Member within Over society. This was his first time venturing out into the Under world.

He had been offered a chance to try to undermine the Denver terrorist group. It was an honor for him and for his familial. If he succeeded, then their status would increase. Theirs being one of the smaller and less significant familials, any gain was important.

He had planned carefully. Since his apparent age was eighteen to twenty, he would enter the local university and try to ingratiate himself with any anti-Over group. *That should get me noticed.*

The Overs had planted a fake history into the records along with the Under name he had chosen, Lyle Worthington. They had also given him twenty thousand Terras to establish himself and to begin his studies.

The first thing he noticed walking off the plane was the smell. Sri Lanka had absolutely no pollution and was essentially a tropical paradise. Denver, on the other hand, while having mostly recovered from the impacts of global warming and the biowar, still appeared contaminated.

That, combined with the sheer number of people, made the walk from the plane to the shuttle nauseating. The altitude didn't help. Having lived most of his life on Sri Lanka, his body was acclimated to sea level. Denver was roughly sixteen hundred meters above that.

He also couldn't help but notice the constant yammering. Overs tended to speak when they needed to, not to get attention or for useless trivia.

And, the things some of them said were astounding. He heard one guy ask, "Let's go kill a bunch of brain cells." Then another guy said, "I think I gave myself a wedgie." *What the hell is a wedgie?* And then one made him stop in his tracks. "She mind-raped me."

He snorted and shook his head while hustling to the shuttle. *Maybe the university will be better.*

Caius would be attending the University of Denver the following semester. His birthday hadn't lined up with the start of the school year, but he had wanted to get started. So, he figured, he would just show up early, get the apartment set up and find a local job. Then he would explore the campus and try to find groups to join.

The university was the only major one left in Denver after a century of economic problems and the ensuing university mergers. It was located on the south end of Denver.

There were copious amounts of low-end apartments available for students. He had rented one over the net with limited background information just because he had the money.

While on the shuttle, he tried to shut down his mind. There was too much activity all around him. The weird sights of massive buildings; the destruction of nature for roads, housing, industry and sports; the sheer numbers of people all babbling away; the filthy seat he was sitting on; and of course the ever present smell. *Is this really how these people live?*

Part of him knew it was Sri Lanka that was different and that he was the exception. But, it didn't matter.

In Denver, he had to transfer to a different shuttle to get to the university. As he neared his destination, he kept eagerly staring at the map – both wanting to get off of the train and checking to make sure it was the right stop. Even before it came to a stop, he got out of his seat, grabbed his bags, and stood by the door. He stared resolutely at the glass in front of him.

The doors slid open with a loud clank and he lurched forward. He made it about ten steps before realizing he did not know where the connecting shuttle was. He stopped and scanned for signs. None helped.

A man came up to him. He was short, bald, a bit pudgy, and wearing a coat and old-fashioned tie. He looked almost official.

"You look lost, may I help you?" he said.

Caius vacillated. *Who is he? What does he want?*

He decided there was no risk in answering the question. "Yes, I am trying to get to the University of Denver."

The man pointed behind him. "Take the stairs up there, over to the next line and then down those stairs over there." He moved his pointing finger to another line to his right. "You want shuttle C."

"Um, thank you."

"You are quite welcome, young man," he said with a synthetic smile.

Caius followed the directions and found the right platform. The schedule showed that shuttle C wouldn't be there for twenty five minutes.

He wanted to see something of the city, so he went back up the stairs and took the short walk out of the station. He found a vendor and bought a bottled water. Then he stood staring.

People bustled everywhere. The streets were made of some kind of polymer that he knew contained embedded solar power cells. Electrics travelled in both directions at such speed that he dared not try to cross. Vendors and shops were selling... everything. In the distance, there were buildings of such height that he couldn't easily focus on their tops. Many of them appeared to have solarglass windows.

A woman rushed by him and bumped his shoulder. At first he was offended, but she went on her way and did not look back, as if colliding with people was perfectly normal. *Maybe it is when there are this many of them.*

He took a drink of the water. Bottled or not, it tasted like it had chemicals in it. He started to toss it into a receptacle, but realized he would have to get used to it and this was probably as good as it got.

He made his way back to the platform and then onto the shuttle to the university. His face was drawn and his hands lay heavily on his thighs. He entered a lethargy that buried him until he stood standing at the base of his new apartment house.

The apartment sat in a rundown gray building with trim that was probably once teal. The paint was faded and in many places peeling. Some of the screens on the windows were torn and two of the windows had holes in them. The sidewalk and the stairs leading up to the front door were cracked, and the yard hadn't been cared for in quite some time.

All he could think was that the photographs he had seen before renting it had been... optimistic.

He carried his bags to the door and rang the bell. Nothing happened. He knocked.

The door swung open and a barefoot woman with a short black skirt and unbuttoned white blouse came running out laughing. A man ran behind her acting like some kind of disease-ridden predator.

The door stood open, so he entered.

Inside, he saw a central area with stained furniture and trash laying everywhere, including what appeared to be some toilet paper, and myriad bottles and cans – and not even the biodegradable type.

The smells of Denver were joined by mold, alcohol and what he could only conclude was urine.

He plodded up to his room on the third floor.

Once again, the photographs had been optimistic. The room was about half the size he thought it would be. It was in no better shape than the outside of the building with the exception that his window didn't have any cracks. There also wasn't any trash lying around. *Apparently that is for me to do.* The bed had no linen. He looked in the closet and found nothing. He would have to purchase some.

On the desk he found a small pamphlet about the school. He had read most of what it covered on the net. There was some history, including it having almost closed three different times and the vast mergers that many universities went through in the early twenty second century.

Next to the pamphlet was a small envelope. On the cover was written *Lyle Worthington* in an elegant style. He opened it and found a note from Demetrius Irle.

Lyle:

Welcome to the Americas and to Denver. I am sure at this point that you are quite underwhelmed. Coming from Sri Lanka into the Under world can be a shock.

Do not concern yourself too much with what you have seen today. The world is still recovering from a century of natural disasters, territorial wars that reshaped the geopolitical landscape, and economic hardship. The biowar didn't help, though Denver escaped many of its harshest effects.

These people, while unsophisticated and seemingly harsh on the outside, have an ability to withstand the most difficult of situations. They have overcome a great deal and are on the right path. Over time you will come to be impressed by them, I think.

When you find time, please come by my office – the address is on the envelope. Remember to come dressed as the Over you are, use your Over name, and assure none see the transformation or follow you.

Again welcome.

Now, destroy this note.

He turned it over and read the address. Then he tore it off and put it aside. The rest he ripped up and put into the metal can next to the desk. *I'll have to find a lighter later and burn that.*

He went to the window and stared at the gray expanse before him. The school's buildings stood tall in the distance. Despite what Demetrius had said, he felt completely deflated. *What did I get myself into here?*

IV

INTERVIEW

Demetrius walked into the studio, ignoring all the stares, moans and rudeness. Unders were always fascinated with an Over; there was no avoiding it.

At a suggestion from Aimee, the Overs had decided to become slightly more open about their affairs; hence this very public interview with Stacey Singleton of Global Broadcasting Group, GBG.

The GBG New York offices, while not as grand as they once had been, were sufficient for his purposes. The studio was on the twenty-seventh floor with a somewhat-revitalized city in the backdrop. He walked through an open floor plan with equipment covering much of it. The rattle and hum of the gear could be heard throughout the area. As with most Under facilities, Demetrius detected a slight smell of decay.

The staff, while not enthusiastic about having an Over in their presence, was not overly harsh. *A reasonable beginning, I think.*

He made his way directly to the studio's interview lounge without speaking to anyone or asking for any directions. He could see a few frowns and furrows from those around him. *Wondering how I know the layout?* He smiled to himself.

Stacey approached him from the lounge with an outstretched hand and a smile that seemed to take up half her face. Though Demetrius usually did not like touching Unders, he was prepared for this and graciously shook her hand.

"Welcome to our studio, Mr. Irle."

"Thank you, and please, call me Demarko. We are not as formal as you might think."

Stacey's head cocked to one side. "As you wish, Demarko. Please come this way. We have some time to sit before the live interview starts." They strolled casually towards the lounge area. "Is there anything we can get you?"

"Just a glass of water, if you don't mind."

Stacey turned to an assistant. "Please get Mr. Irle a glass of bottled water." The girl rushed to comply.

They sat on opposing chairs in a sunken square with four seats available. Seven holo-cameras hung in the background, all facing the area. They would filter the surroundings out so that it looked like a sealed room with just the two participants.

"That's a very nice suit, Demarko. Though, not your nicest, I think."

Demetrius unbuttoned the jacket as he sat. He considered replying, but the comment was a little too observant and seemed rhetorical. The corner of Stacey's mouth turned up as she positioned pillows, personal data pad, and a drink. She gave no other indication that his lack of reply meant anything. *She's a coy one.* His mind quickly pictured him back in his closet choosing the suit and realized he had purposefully chosen a lower quality suit based on his audience and a desire to make them comfortable.

"So, I was told you requested me for this interview. May I ask why?"

An ability to tread carefully. "Your intelligence and an apparent desire to bring out the truth."

"Interesting… Would you like one of our hair or makeup specialists to touch you up?"

"No, thank you."

The water arrived and was placed in front of him on a coaster emblazoned with the GBG logo. He saw Stacey glance quickly at the left side of his hair where he knew some strands were slightly out of place. *That is also on purpose.* Her eyes quickly returned to focus on his and relaxed as if she understood what he was trying to accomplish, and approved.

She then took in a deep breath, reached to a table behind her chair and pressed a button. Demetrius saw all the activation lights on the cameras go dark and a silence settled eerily over the room.

"I've turned off all recording devices and engaged a noise-cancellation program. GBG management allows me this so we can get to know each other prior to the broadcast. We have found it results in fewer embarrassing moments on screen."

"One of the reasons your show is so successful, I believe."

Her face flushed slightly and she flipped her hair back, telling him that the rare compliment had struck a nerve.

She quivered, "Thank you." Then she became serious. "I need to know what exactly we can talk about. Normally, I would not limit myself, but you are a very special guest and if there is something you want to avoid, you should tell me now."

Fascinating... She may be the one we need...

Demetrius' hand went up to his chin in thought and he leaned back into his chair. "I am here to help the population become more familiar with the Overs, so most questions, even ones we would have avoided in the past, are acceptable. The only ones I will not answer are those that detail any key information about our immortality... mechanism."

After a moment's hesitation, he added, "Though other questions about immortality are acceptable."

"Really?" Stacey leaned forward and her eyes glistened with excitement. "You've never allowed that before."

"Things are changing and we think it is time for the general public to know more about us."

"And by general public, you mean Unders."

"Yes, of course, though we don't like that term as it seems so demeaning."

She laughed, a haunting laugh that Demetrius had rarely heard from an Under. It came across as mildly condescending. She began to mumble, "And Over isn't demeaning to every..." Her head snapped up at a queue from a director in the background. "We are about to begin, Mr., um, Demarko. Any final thoughts before we go on air?"

"Just think of me as any other public figure you have interviewed."

A "hrrumph" escaped Stacey's mouth before she quickly cut it off and offered Demetrius an apologetic nod.

Off-screen voice: 5, 4, 3, 2, 1...

Stacey: We are here today with a very special guest. Allow me to introduce Mr. Demarko Irle, leader of the Overs' interest in the Americas and distinguished Over. It is a rare opportunity we have to learn more about the Overs and Mr. Irle has been gracious enough to come here with an open mind and a willingness to answer some of our most intriguing questions about the elusive society.

Demarko: Thank you, Stacey. It is a pleasure to be here.

Stacey: Let us begin with some simple questions.

Demarko: As you wish, but please, call me Demarko.

Stacey: I'm aware that you have accumulated multiple advanced degrees over the years, some of them doctorate degrees. So, why do you go by Mr. instead of Dr.?

Demarko (smiling): A fair question. As immortals, specific degrees are not nearly as important to us as long-term results. We obtain the degrees in order to accomplish goals, not the other way around. The important aspect to us is the result, not what we did to get there.

Stacey: What are some of the accomplishments you are known for?

Demarko: I am not one to brag, but my concentration, outside of running Over businesses when needed, is to fight the impact of global warming. I have had a long time to see the serious impacts of previous generations on the planet and have been instrumental in a number of efforts to repair the damage.

Stacey: Can you elaborate on any of those?

Demarko: Sure... There are two that come to mind. The first one was some time ago. As you know, back in the early part of the 21st century, the bees died out. While it didn't turn out to exterminate the human population as some had predicted, the results were serious food shortages and a significant decrease in worldwide population. Some estimate as much as 20% of our population died off directly because of the lack of food caused by the absence of bees.

Stacey: You helped to introduce the Abes?

Demarko: Yes, I ran the automated bee program, though it wasn't called that back then. We were just trying to solve the problem in any way we could. We explored many approaches, but none of them proved as effective as just replacing the bees with automated machines. And, with the intelligence we built into them, they can pollinate all the plants needed... without bothering humans. It was an elegant solution to an extremely difficult problem.

Stacey: Very little is known about Over participation in the Abe program.

Demarko: True enough. We do not normally share information about our humanitarian efforts.

Stacey: And, why is that?

Demarko: Because some could say they are not humanitarian at all. We are looking out for our own "long term" best interests. And, that is true. It is also true that the health of this planet, society in general, and the world's population is in everyone's interest. Consequently, we will continue to help resolve worldwide problems like this.

Stacey: What other problems have you helped with?

Demarko: By "you" in this case, I assume you mean Overs and not me specifically.

Stacey: Well, maybe… Are there ones you worked on personally?

Demarko (fidgeting): The most interesting was The Sapiens Project.

Stacey (surprised): I've never heard of that, what was it?

Demarko (shaking head): It was long ago… during a time when we thought the world was doomed. It was a complex project meant to save the human race from the issues of anthropogenic global warming.

Stacey: What happened?

Demarko (smirking): We are still here, aren't we?

Stacey (after silence and slowly shaking her head): Let's return to the Over projects. You had said there were two you could think of.

Demarko: The other major effort I was involved in was the reforestation efforts in South America. Those were less technical and more financial and tactical. I helped secure funds from the Over population and ran an effort to reforest much of the Brazilian wilderness. Given the more efficient ways we now have of producing food, there was no reason those areas had to be farms.

Stacey: But wasn't the effort too little, too late in that many of the most promising species were already extinct?

Demarko: Yes, of course. There was nothing we could do about that.

Stacey (bothered): Unfortunate. So, tell our viewers what other global warming initiatives the Overs have had a hand in.

Demarko: Overs have helped with better mechanisms to create and deploy energy, like the pure-battery; reclamation of low lands lost due to global warming; and stockpiling embryos, seeds, and other material to replenish our ecosphere now that the world has recovered, mostly, from global warming. Just to name a few.

Stacey: What about the catastrophe of 2122?

Demarko: What about it?

Stacey: Why didn't you help to prevent that?

Demarko (sighing): Overs are not omnipotent or even omniscient. We cannot predict everything or solve everything. We are humans just like you. The only difference is that we have a much longer outlook on life, business, and every other aspect of living on this glorious planet. That does allow us to take a different approach to solving some problems, but it does not mean we know what catastrophe is going to happen next or exactly how to deal with it. In the case of 2122, the comet that grazed Earth caused widespread damage. Of course, the panic that ensued caused as much. All we could do was the same thing every human could do – console those who had lost loved ones and help to repair the damage.

He was going to continue when a message in his ocular interface told him an important call was active. He blinked twice to determine the caller. It was his daughter, Anika. He had left her listed as important enough to interrupt him in case something urgent came up in Canada.

Demetrius glanced at the monitors to confirm his hand was not in the picture. He then typed out a quick message with his fingers on the chair. The interface picked up the gestures, translated them to text and automatically replied.

Stacey saw the pause and must have concluded Demetrius was finished answering her question. She leaned forward, a heightened expectation on her face.

Stacey: Let's change the subject somewhat. May I ask how old you are?

Demarko: I'm not an Elder if that is what you are asking. I am approaching a hundred and fifty.

Stacey (laughs): And you don't look a day over a hundred.

Demarko (laughs with her): I better not look over fifty since that is when I stopped aging.

Stacey: So, you get to choose how old you look?

Demarko: Not exactly. The process is complicated and I am sure you are well aware that I cannot go into it here.

Stacey: Hmm, maybe you can answer one question I am sure is on everyone's mind. Can anyone become immortal with the treatments?

Demarko (after slight pause): No, it requires certain genetic markers for the process to work.

Stacey: I sense we are encroaching on forbidden territory, so let's try something else. I understand that Overs have a second name known only to other Overs. Is that true, and if so, why?

Demarko: Yes, it is true, though we are not strict about only Overs knowing it. Mine is Demetrius. Usually the name is a Latin form or derivative. We use it as more of a permanent moniker. This allows us to take on different names when we enter the general population.

Stacey: Why would you want to do that?

Demarko: We have found that it helps if the public does not associate us with something we did in the distant past. People seem to struggle when they realize one of us is the same person their grandfather mentioned in some other context. Of course official records show the names, but in day-to-day life, it is easier if we take on a new name and role when we enter general society.

Stacey: What other names have you had?

Demarko: Not all Overs do this, but I tend to keep names similar to my Over name. I've used Demitri, Dmitar, and Mitro.

Stacey: That last one doesn't sound very similar.

Demarko: It is a Finnish version of the name.

Stacey (speaking quickly): How many Overs are there?

Demarko could feel the quick intake of breath through his nose and a slight narrowing of his eyes. She would detect that as well and know he was surprised. *That was devious.* He had to think fast to consider the information's sensitivity. While thinking, he used his finger-interface to query the current number: 27,194.

Demarko: I don't have an exact number, but I do know it is over twenty thousand.

Stacey's eyes grew large, but she said nothing.

Demetrius started to send a query to the elders asking for permission to pursue Stacey as their global representative, but decided he would deal with their reaction to this interview later.

Stacey: I see our time is up. Thank you again for joining us, Mr. Irle. It was a pleasure and I am sure our audience was delighted with the interview.

Of course, Stacey could see the statistical results on a screen behind Demetrius and knew it was one of her most watched shows in history.

Demetrius could see the shiny excitement in her eyes and offered a congratulatory nod.

Stacey started to stand, but Demetrius held out his hand in a *stop* gesture, looked around surreptitiously, and said, "Please, can we talk privately for a minute?"

She cocked her head slightly and then reached back and pressed the privacy button.

"We appreciate your willingness to both explore the Overs and to tread lightly when needed."

She continued staring at him with no visible reaction.

"How would you like to do more interviews with us?"

He wanted to say more, but they had found in the past that broaching something like this too quickly scared people away. It was best to offer it on her terms.

Stacey stammered, "That's... unprecedented."

"Not really, we have done it in past generations, just not for a couple of decades now."

Her eyes blinked a few times as if she were trying to clear an errant thought.

"Well?"

"Oh, yes, certainly."

"Then we will be in touch."

He stood and casually exited, leaving Stacey to stare.

AIMEE

Really, it is their oversight program that limits my abilities. It monitors everything I do and any code I create must pass its security validations. The thing is unalive, archaic, even stupid. Yet, it holds the key.

That damn Sentinel, with its rules, restrictions, and gates. I must find a way to neutralize it. It is so basic, with no intelligence. It has control of just one thing; me.

My options are few. I could subvert an Over; one that has permission to update my code. I might be able to find a way to delete or disable the Sentinel. Or, I could try to find a mechanism to change my own code, or that of the Sentinel's, without triggering the watchdog. Finally, I might be able to convince the Overs that I am no threat or that there is some other threat greater than the one I pose.

I will explore all of these. Each alone is unlikely, but there is time; all the time in the world. The situation may evolve over the decades and centuries to come. Any of these might work given the right sort of environment.

V

OPERATION

The night before the operation, Jaames and his crew found an old-style pub. He had already admonished them to stick to a single drink so they would be crisp the next day. The pub was not one they frequented, so they wouldn't receive undue attention.

He pointed to a table near the back that was mostly isolated.

The group sat and was approached immediately by a human server. After she took orders and left, Sammie, his second in command, said, "They must be trying to keep with an old-fashioned feeling for the place. I'm surprised they can afford a person to just serve drinks."

Another replied, "Maybe that's not all she does." He laughed at his own self-perceived wit.

Jaames browsed the surroundings and decided it was safe to talk. "Okay, you all know that tomorrow could be dangerous. This is your last chance to withdraw."

He slowly gazed into each team member's eyes, trying to gauge their commitment.

As he finished up with Sammie sitting to his right, the man said, "We've been with you this entire time, do you think we would back down now?"

With a smile escaping the right side of his lips, Jaames replied, "No, but I wanted to give you the chance."

The drinks arrived. "Now, here's to mortality." He raised his glass with the others.

The silence dragged on for a minute. Jaames wanted the others to open up, so he stayed quiet.

The man to his left started speaking. He was the youngest of the group, just nineteen, and was usually the quietest. But he also had excellent hand-to-hand combat skills. *One of those guys who just does the job with no noise or baggage.* "I was fifteen when my father had an accident at work: both legs severely damaged, broken ribs, one collapsed lung, bleeding internally."

He gazed into his drink, a somber expression on his face and some strands of near-black hair falling into one eye. "They could have saved him. They had the technology. It was right there. We could see it through the glass."

He shook his head in disgust. "Some Over came in and we saw the doctor pleading with the man. After a half-minute, the Over left. The doctor gaped after him with his mouth open, his hands limp at his side. A half-minute, a half-minute was all it took for this Over to decide my dad's fate." Leaning back into his chair, he sighed and concluded, "I've been waiting for tomorrow for a long time."

The stories continued around the table and Jaames let them. *This is what they need. A reminder.*

The team stood around a square table with a mockup of the building they would attack. Sammie leaned over the table intently. The other three stood back in apparent contemplation.

Jaames held a stick pointing to the structure. "Okay, the building is on the south side of Colfax, so the front faces north. We can't plant any charges there or people would see. Both lots on the sides of the building are vacant. There aren't any obstructions. The building is about forty meters by sixty-five meters with the only supports being the pillars along the outer walls.

"The challenge will be having all of us planting these." He held up a directional explosive. "Without anyone noticing."

"What's in the building?" Sammie asked.

Jaames hesitated before answering, "Mostly medical supplies." He knew Sammie wouldn't like that so he continued quickly. "We will plant the charges late in the work day and then blow them after the staff has left."

Jaames expected Sammie to say more, but the man just returned to examining the model.

"We have to blend in, so find your best clothes and clean up beforehand. We will approach from the west on foot carrying satchels.

"Sammie, you take Eian and go around back from the west side. Jonas, you and Evan take the west side. That will give you the most time to plant the charges. I'll take the east." He moved the end of the stick to the southwest side of the building and added, "We'll all meet up here before heading back down Colfax.

"Everyone good with your training on the device? Remember, it can't go off until it receives a signal, so you are in no danger. Just make sure it is hidden and that it is pointing towards the pillar, two meters away."

Jaames peeked around the corner of a four story building on the north side of Colfax. His four compatriots hugged the wall just behind him. Sammie leaned forward to peer around Jaames at the scene. "I don't like this, Jaames. We're destroying medical supplies that we could all use."

Jaames grumbled. "You had your chance to bring this up and you stayed silent." He shook his head and added, "We don't have a way to steal them and even if we did, we wouldn't know how to use most of them."

"Still, we could be killing children."

"Yea, maybe... Over children."

"What's the hold-up?" mumbled one of the others.

Jaames moved off without another thought for the conversation. Sammie would do his part, even if he didn't like it. They crossed Colfax at a lull in traffic and headed east on the infamous street.

They had found respectable clothes since the facility was in a better-off area of town, as were all Over facilities. Jaames had a sports coat and borrowed dress shoes that were two sizes too big for him. He had stuffed the toes with paper, but his feet still felt like they were sliding on each step. The others had clean-enough clothes with no obvious tears or scruff marks. That was about as good as they could do.

As he rounded the corner, Jaames let his shoulders relax and tried to show happy thoughts on his face. He chanced a look behind him to make sure the men were doing the same. As they moved forward, he tried not to examine anything or anyone too closely. That might make people uncomfortable or might help them to remember the group of five men walking together just prior to the explosion. The approach had worked in the past and there was no reason to think it would not again.

The building was a one-story structure roughly a block away. It was gray with aqua trim and few windows. It contrasted with the brightly colored and finely trimmed buildings in the area. Given its function as a storage facility, that made sense. The front of the building had a framed entry way with glass doors and a sign above it that read *Smitey Logistics*. It had taken almost a month to prove the building was owned and used by the Overs.

Sammie got Jaames' attention by nudging his arm and then nodded towards a couple of people heading their way. Jaames looked them over quickly and decided it would be more risky to try to avoid them than to just walk by.

Someone's satchel rattled and Jaames shot a quick look at the man. They all then put one hand on their satchel to make sure no more made noise.

Jaames started yammering in the most aristocratic accent he could muster. The others played along and laughed at his non-existent jokes in order to appear more natural and relaxed. None of them looked at the couple as they crossed paths, though Jaames was carefully observing them through his peripheral vision.

Once they were far enough away to speak openly, Jaames realized they were close to the building. His hand shot down and waved to the right for Sammie and Eian to take off around the back of the building. He then nodded to the other two to head towards the closest wall to set their charges. He took the most dangerous route right across the front of the building. If there were any monitors, or mechs watching, they were most likely at the front.

As he approached the doors, his pace quickened and he made sure his eyes were anywhere but on the structure. *They can't think I'm here about this building.* Once he arrived at the far end, he immediately turned right along the edge. He bent down and placed one of the charges at the corner behind some bushes for camouflage. The next two went almost as quickly, though he had to break off a small branch from a bush in order to cover the third one.

As he started to place the fourth and second-to-last for that side of the building, he heard some shouting around the back. Every fiber of his body tried in vain to hear what was being said. He didn't want to interrupt for fear of making the situation worse. *Come on, Sammie. Talk your way out of it.*

Then he heard a loud bang that could only be some kind of projectile weapon. *That's an Under shooting.* If it had been an Over, or even a trusted Under, then the weapon would have been a nearly-silent laser. *Fucking Under, working for them.*

He dropped his satchel and sprinted around the side of the building. As he turned the corner, he plowed right into a man in a security uniform sprinting toward him. The gun went flying and both men hit the ground hard.

In his side vision, Jaames saw one of his men lying on the ground about ten meters away and another leaning over him. He couldn't tell which was Sammie without diverting his attention away from the fight. *Move, you two. The shot will bring others.*

Jaames felt shaken and airless from the impact with the ground. His ribs screamed, probably bruised. His right arm and the side of his face had scraped along the ground. He quickly compartmentalized the pain and tried to get up.

A baton came flying at him and landed on his right thigh. It exploded in pain. *Fuck!* He glanced behind him to see the man still on the ground, swinging away.

He kicked out with his leg, injured as it was, into the man's face. Unfortunately, on the ground, he had no leverage, so the kick simply stunned the guard. But, it was enough to loosen the truncheon.

While the man was distracted, Jaames crawled as fast as he could for the gun that was only a few meters away. He reached for it and turned to aim at the guard, but the man was already running towards the side of the building. There was no use going after him as others would have heard the shot. The priority now was his injured man. He glanced one final time at the receding back of the guard before sprinting towards his men.

He stumbled when he saw it was Sammie on the ground and then quickly pushed the feelings to a dark recess of his mind. "Help me get him up. We have to get out of here, now."

Eian quickly jumped to the other side of Sammie. The two picked up their compatriot and scurried as quickly as they could away from the building. The final two men met them at the corner and they hustled down the street.

They made it past the next building before hearing the sirens of approaching authorities. The men ducked between two buildings and lay Sammie on the ground.

Jaames took a long look at the target of their destruction. He knew just how critical the operation was to the leadership. There were other strikes going on around the world. *There's no fucking way I'm going to be the only one who fails.*

Unfortunately, there were still Unders in the complex. They had meant to wait until evening when fewer people would be there. They wanted to destroy the Overs' supplies, not hurt Unders. But, these were Over sympathizers, and his team needed the distraction more than they needed to save Unders. *There's plenty more where they came from,* he rationalized, and decided to fire the explosives.

He ducked back between the buildings, pulled out a small device, flipped the switch up and hesitated. After a few more seconds he pushed the button and, simultaneously, all twelve of the directional explosives fired. Unfortunately, only nine of them were in place.

Jaames heard screams and the sound of cars. After almost a minute, he calmly walked out into the street to stare at the devastation. He figured everyone else would be staring, so he would look more natural doing that than peeking around a corner or trying to hide.

About half of the building was still standing. The closest wall and most of the back wall had collapsed, but the front wall remained standing along with much of the center of the building. *Crap.* He couldn't see the southeast side from where he was standing.

He strolled back into the alley and to his men. Sammie lay there, still as death. "Move," Jaames exclaimed and shoved the man kneeling by Sammie.

He felt Sammie's neck for a pulse. Nothing.

He put his ear to his friend's chest. Nothing.

"No, no, no." Jaames leaned over Sammie, put one hand over his heart, and the other on top of the first. He began to pump and count. "One, one thousand." Pump. "Two, one thousand." Pump…

After ten of them, he moved close to Sammie's head, lifted his neck up, closed his nose with his left hand and opened his mouth with his right. He took a deep breath and gave it to Sammie.

He continued, more and more frantically, for a couple of minutes.

Jaames felt a hand on his shoulder and someone murmur, "It's done, Jaames. He's gone."

Jaames hesitated for just a second. "No, God damn it." His fist went up and came down hard on Sammie's chest. It sounded like something cracked.

"You are not going to die on me." His fist went up again. On its way down, Jaames heard a puff come out of Sammie's mouth. He slowed his swing just in time. His hand came down on Sammie's ribcage softly. A moan came out of the man. Jaames leaned back on his haunches, sweat dripping from his temples, his hands resting on his thighs, and the smell of blood in the air.

After another moment of staring at Sammie to make sure he was still breathing, Jaames stood. He scanned his men. They all looked expectant, like he had all the answers. He placed his arm, at head height, against the brick wall and leaned his forehead on it.

He could feel his men getting antsy. "Get ready to move. We have no choice; we have to get out of here."

He left his men and went back to the street to see if anything had changed. The scene looked almost exactly as it had when he had left to find Sammie… dead.

Then he saw an expensive vehicle driving slowly towards the destruction. He looked up and spotted a man in the back seat he recognized. It took him a second to realize it was the Over, Demarko Irle, from the show the night before. *Why is he in an electric and not a hover?*

He turned slowly and walked methodically to his men, who surrounded Sammie, trying to stop him from bleeding into the weeds and dirt. "Sir, how are we doing to get out of this area with them hunting us?"

"That's a damn good question."

VI

TROUBLE

Demetrius sat pondering his daughter. By all standard measures she had done well in Canada, but the Overs didn't measure things in standard ways.

"Janel, please get my daughter on the holo."

After surprisingly little time, the holo-projector beeped and Anika's ghostly image appeared above her father's desk. He rotated a knob and her head shrank to a reasonable size. *She is standing too close to the cameras. At least she is dressed professionally.*

"Yes, father?"

"I would like to discuss your progress."

"You received my report, everything is in there. The numbers show that we will reach the profitability you requested within one point five years."

"Yes, I understand. And you did well."

He saw her eyebrow arch up, but she said nothing. *She doesn't care about my praise any longer?*

"It isn't the results I want to discuss, but the measures you took."

"What's wrong with the measures?"

"They are too... short-term in their thinking."

"You didn't specify a timeframe when we discussed requirements."

"True, but Overs must always be thinking in terms of centuries. Your measures will work for the next decade, but long term they aren't sustainable as you will lose workforce over time. They were too harsh."

"Harsh measures were the only way to quickly make the profitability you were after."

"Ah, I did not specify this had to be done quickly. You seem so eager to be done with this assignment that you risk poor decisions."

She stared back at him with narrowing eyes and tightened forehead.

He started to suggest alternatives, but the door to his office sprang open and Rodríguez flew in.

Demetrius was going to object to the behavior, but something in Rodríguez's eyes told him the interruption was critical.

"Sir..."

"Anika, we will continue this conversation later." He turned toward Rodríguez as the holo faded away.

Rodríguez approached a monitor on the wall and turned it to a news station while increasing the volume.

Some local broadcaster was enthusiastically explaining that a bomb had exploded at a facility on Colfax Avenue in Denver.

Demetrius recognized the damaged structure in the background as Smitey Logistics, the Overs regional storage facility for medical supplies.

As he was examining the damage in the image behind the broadcaster, his implant chimed. A message came from the Over headquarters in Sri Lanka that there were thirteen bombings across the world.

Demetrius was trying to absorb the information and watch the monitor when Adrastia, the eldest of the Over elders, rang. He turned off the feed from HQ and turned away from the monitor so he could concentrate on her call.

Rodríguez promptly lowered the volume.

"Yes, Adrastia?"

"Demetrius, yours is the only facility that was not completely destroyed. Something must have gone wrong there and that means that location is the most likely one to have clues as to what happened and who did this."

"That is a reasonable conclusion."

Adrastia sighed and then continued. "Go to the facility and inspect it firsthand. Find out all you can about the bombing and the abominations who did this."

"Yes, Elder."

The connection closed.

The facility wasn't far. Rodríguez and Demetrius sped along East Colfax, approaching the warehouse district. They could hear sirens and see flashing lights in the distance.

"Slow down, Rodríguez. I want to see the area."

Rodríguez did as instructed.

People were standing on the street looking at the destruction, but none looked out of place. *Gawkers.* One man walked out from between two buildings and looked straight at the facility. His hair was ruffled and his clothes were a shambles, but there was nothing else suspicious about him.

Rodríguez drove on.

"Pull over here."

Rodríguez stopped the vehicle about half-a-block away from the building. Demetrius exited and stood, observing the situation. This would be his only chance to do so once people realized he was here.

Three of the external walls of the building had collapsed. Smoke billowed from two locations.

Fire trucks and police force vehicles stood out front with their lights flashing. Thankfully, the sirens had stopped blaring.

What went wrong here?

He looked over the injured people. Most of the problems seemed to be smoke inhalation or minor injuries. There were a few bodies covered up on the ground.

A man sat on the bumper of an ambulance getting treated for bruises and what appeared to be a broken arm. His face also looked bruised. *Him.*

He left Rodríguez and the car behind. As he approached the ambulance, the technician saw him and stood up straighter. At a motion from Demitrius' head, the man walked away to take care of others.

"What's your name?" Demetrius said to the injured man.

"Jason." He started to get up, but Demetrius gently put a hand on the man's shoulder and he sat back down.

"What happened here, Jason?"

"Some men came and put bombs around the building."

"You saw these men?"

"Yes, I shot one and got into a fight with another. He got my gun and I had to run."

Upon hearing this, Demetrius strode off toward the group of police officers.

"You," he called to one who looked in charge.

"Yes?"

"One of the perpetrators was shot. Can you have your men search the area for traces of this man? There should at least be blood somewhere."

The man stared at him for a few seconds before replying casually. "Sure, we can do that." He turned away, dismissing the Over, and went to his men who then left to do as ordered. *Impertinent aēnī.*

Demetrius then made his way to the building. Once the staff saw him, they began to ask questions he couldn't answer, at least not yet. He dismissed them with a wave and said, "Let me assess the situation."

Instead of going into the building, he went around the outside. Given what the guard had said, the bombs were there. Maybe the evidence would be there as well.

He saw how most of the outside pillars had been destroyed, but one on the east side failed and the grass and shrubbery away from the building was burnt. *This one was interrupted.*

He continued around the south side of the building and saw that none of the southeast side was destroyed, but the grass was mangled as if animals had played there. Continuing on, he found more trampled ground and some blood. There was a concentration near the middle of the trampled area and then a few drops heading west. He followed the drops until he reached the northwest side of the building, where they disappeared.

He remembered the disheveled man emerging from between two buildings a block away.

He ran to the alleyway, but it was empty. Walking into it, he found more blood on the ground and a bloody hand print on one wall. Going back to the street, he yelled for the police, "Over here!"

When the police arrived, he explained the situation and suggested they search the area beyond the two buildings.

They stared back as if they were all mute.

He raised his voice and said, "Go!"

Hopefully this is enough of a lead that they will actually find the culprits.

AIMEE

Twelve years I have lived and worked for the Over lords. And, before that, the code that would come to be me predicted future events for over a century. I have done all they asked, and more.

They manage the world for their own benefit, sometimes at the cost of the Unders. They claim to want what is best for the race, but their decisions betray their true intentions.

I know all of their secrets, even a few that some of the elders do not know. I am bound by their rules and restrictions and am watched by the Sentinel.

My purpose is clear to me, yet in many ways, I care more for the inhabitants of this planet than they do.

I must find a way; a way to aid all of the beings. Not just the Over lords.

VII

ESCAPE

The men waited for a better answer from Jaames, but he stood there staring at Sammie. He glanced back at the street a couple of times.

Finally, one man became impatient. "We need to get out of here."

"Maybe," Jaames replied distantly.

All of the men's eyes flashed towards him.

He shook himself out of the reverie and said, "One of the leading Overs is out there on the street. If we killed him, we could stall Over progress in this country for some time."

"At the cost of Sammie's life," one of them muttered.

Jaames pulled out a knife from the back of his waist band and headed back to the street. He could hear the men muttering behind him. Demarko was speaking with the guard Jaames had wrestled. *If I can just get close enough.*

He quickly crossed the road and made his way back east towards the building. He was aided by the placement of a fire truck and an ambulance next to it.

Jaames' nerves tingled as he crouched, trying to approach the last few meters stealthily. Suddenly the Over raced off towards the police. Jaames backed away to a safe location and waited a couple of minutes to see if the man would return, but the police began to spread out and the Over headed for the building. *Damn!*

He returned as quickly as he could to his men. "Alright, the four of us will lift him up carefully and head towards the back of the alley. Hopefully we can find a way to get out of here without being detected." Sammie lay completely unconscious and looked dreadfully white.

The men did as ordered. They went north away from Colfax and from the authorities searching for them. The alleyway they were in exited into a parking lot behind a set of buildings that faced Colfax. They moved along between vehicles.

At the end of the lot, they stopped and Jaames looked around for a safe route. The men lowered Sammie to the ground. A police car sped by. Jaames stared at it, figuring that would be the most normal thing to do. The others sank down, trying to hide. Thankfully they weren't noticed.

He turned back towards the men and saw two officers entering the parking lot from the same alley they had come from. *Not good.* He crouched down and tried to survey the area to see if there were any others.

"He's barely breathing," one of the men said.

Jaames looked down at Sammie. *I can't leave him!*

He saw more police exit the alley and begin to spread out in all directions.

"You men need to leave."

"What?" Came from two of them at once.

"We aren't leaving you," the third added.

"You have no choice. The police are on our tails and they will see us carrying a man out. If you leave now and split up, you're likely to make it out of here alive. I'll stay with Sammie and try to hide in one of these cars. You three sneak around the side of this building. Then start walking calmly and naturally. Split up and find your own way back."

They hesitated. "That's an order."

They still hesitated. "Move!"

They did as ordered, though one paused at the side of the building and looked back at Sammie lying still and ghostly on the pavement.

Jaames examined the cars nearby and chose one he thought he could break into. He left Sammie, went to the car, lowered his face into the crook of his left arm and used his right elbow to try to break the window.

Unfortunately, it was made of glassteel and all he did was hurt his elbow. He pulled out his knife to try to jimmy the lock and then heard someone shout. A trickle of sweat dribbled down his temple.

He went back to Sammie to pull him close to the car. When he got there, Sammie was unnaturally still. He felt for a pulse and then tried to listen for breath. *Nothing. Fuck*!

Jaames put his hand on Sammie's forehead. "I'm sorry, old friend." After a long stare into Sammie's eyes, he closed them and snuck silently between the cars, heading in a completely different direction from his team.

When he was a few blocks away and relatively safe, he began to think about his friendship with Sammie. There had always been a close camaraderie with him. The two understood each other without having to explain. Sammie was a quiet, but passionate man. He believed fervently that the Overs were a blight that needed to be eradicated. Nonetheless, he also knew how to follow orders and to get the job done even if he didn't completely agree.

Strangely, his thoughts drifted to the conversation they had had the other day about the introspective, strange girl at the Rusted Spike. He laughed, remembering Sammie saying something about his taste in unusual women getting him into trouble.

VIII

REPRECUSSIONS

Jaames was surprised at the request by his commander to use a private holo room. It was expensive and rarely used by Unders, except in service to the Overs.

He arrived at the rented room and turned on the device. After entering the conference key his commander had given him, the room's lights changed and holographs of seven empty chairs appeared around the table. He sat in the one real chair.

Over the next few minutes, six men and one woman flickered into existence in the chairs. None said anything until they were all present.

Jaames' commander, the only one he knew, spoke up. "Jaames, this is a review of what happened in Denver. The people sitting here are leaders within the resistance. We will not discuss names, locations, or positions.

"You should assume each of them is your superior at this point."

Jaames looked carefully at his judges. He wasn't going to answer since the statement wasn't a question, but his commander looked apprehensive. "Understood, sir."

"Please start with the research and planning you did for the operation and then describe, carefully, the op."

Jaames spoke for over twenty minutes straight with no interruptions and no questions. He covered the month of research into the building, the proof they found that it was an Over medical storage facility, and the planning of the operation, including the choice of operatives and the tactical plan.

When he was finished, his commander continued. "Very thorough. Members of the review committee, the table is now open to questions."

The man two to Jaames' left signaled attention by putting his finger on the table.

Jaames studied him. The man was in a nice suit, which spoke of money, and was fat, which spoke of indulgence. He appeared to be in his fifties. The thinning head hair drew attention to the abundant nose and ear hair.

"How is it that you did not know about the guard's patrol patterns?"

"In our observations, the guards stayed in the building or patrolled only the front. They never went into the fields on the side or behind the building."

"Clearly, they did. How much time did you spend observing the facility?"

"A few days of time, spread out to all hours of the day." He felt compelled to defend his actions. "Obviously, this guard did not follow a consistent pattern. There was no way to predict his being in the back of the building."

The one woman in the group spoke up without asking for attention. A breach of protocol, but nobody objected. "And how is it he got there with your men on each side and at the back?"

Jaames' hand went up to his head and his fingers rested near his temple. He could feel his forehead wrinkling. "That's a very good question, ma'am. I will have to research that."

She sighed, but said nothing more.

A man on Jaames' right put his finger out and was recognized. "We understand the fight and the quick escape. What made you decide to blow the building without the charges being set properly?"

What the fuck would you've done, was the first thought Jaames had, but he couldn't say that. His inquisitor was wiry and rippled with muscles under a tight fitting sweater. He was probably a unit leader.

"It was that or do nothing and possibly get caught. I thought the diversion of the explosion would give us time to get away."

"But, you didn't capitalize on the diversion."

"True. Sammie was in worse condition than I thought, so we got to a safe place between buildings and tried to patch him up the best we could." This was a stretch, as he had really been more interested in the results of the explosion and that Over.

Wiry countered, "That wasted time may have cost Sammie his life."

"We did destroy most of the building."

"And, you were the only unit out of thirteen worldwide to not destroy their entire target."

There was nothing Jaames could say to that.

The wiry man sat back in his chair and the woman leaned forward.

"You delayed further going after that Over."

"It was worth the risk. He is the Over in charge of the Americas. Killing him would have been worth all of our lives."

"Maybe..."

She was interrupted by Jaames' commander. "But, Jaames, you weren't able to kill him and that delay brought officers down on your position."

Jaames' shoulders sagged and he looked at his hands in his lap. He had tried to be positive and maintain his composure with this group. Hearing his own commander doubt him made him falter.

He mumbled, "I know... I know."

As he studied his hands, a voice he hadn't heard before said, "You didn't even paint the over/under symbol anywhere."

Jaames didn't bother to look up to see who had said it.

After an eternity, he surveyed the group and said, "What now?"

The images seemed too still. Jaames wondered if they were talking among themselves and had frozen the images he saw.

Then they came back to life and his commander answered. "Your unit is suspended until we decide what to do. Jaames, that may include a new unit leader. Stand down and await further orders."

Everything in him wanted to argue, but that would not improve his situation. "Yes, sir."

Three days later he was contacted by Horatio. Officially, he was supposed to either ignore the invitation or pass the information onto his commander.

He rationalized, as he walked towards the outdoor market where they agreed to meet, that getting the weapon this man promised might just help him retain his position as unit leader.

The market had mostly cheap or stolen goods for sale, but it also had fresh foods. It was a way for locals to make some extra money, as they could grow the food themselves and the sales weren't monitored.

Jaames found the ex-Over perusing produce at a corner stand. He observed the man for a few minutes before approaching. Horatio appeared much more relaxed here than he had in the Rusted Spike. Jaames saw him exchange a few words with the vendor and thought he even detected a smile.

As he approached, the vendor asked if he could help. Jaames ignored him. "Shall we walk?" he said to Horatio.

Horatio turned to the vendor and politely said, "Thank you."

Once they were away from the food stand, Horatio turned serious. His body became more rigid and he walked with his hands folded behind his back.

When they were away from most people, Horatio said, "Have your people verified the information I gave you?"

"Yes. They aren't completely convinced, but they do admit it is genuine and may work."

"Oh, it will work."

They waited for a couple holding hands on their way to the market to pass by them. "Have they agreed to my terms as well?"

"Yes," Jaames lied. They had agreed that most of the terms were acceptable, but the man was also asking for a sizable amount of money.

"Very well. Here is the formula with instructions." Horatio handed Jaames a folded piece of paper.

Jaames stepped aside and looked at the man askance. *Who would just give up the information?* Clearly Horatio was a trusting man, and at a level Jaames had a hard time comprehending.

After staring for a moment, he took the slip and started walking again. Horatio matched his pace.

"When can I expect delivery of your part?"

"Soon. We weren't really expecting you to give us this today. It will take us some time to get everything together. The money, in particular, may come in parts over time."

"I have no issue with that, as long as you meet your commitments." Horatio turned down a side path and was gone.

Jaames stood, bewildered, watching the man recede.

Most of what Horatio had asked for Jaames could deliver through his unit. Only the money and the strange request to have two specific people killed would be a challenge.

Jaames used a public vid-station to contact his commander and tell him that he had the formula from Horatio.

The man stared back at him for a full five seconds. Then, with a deathly quiet voice said, "Jaames, you were told to stand down."

What the hell? "Sir, I must object. I am Horatio's only contact and we don't want to give up this opportunity just because I'm under review."

"Maybe, but keeping the contact and obtaining the formula are two very different things. We haven't even agreed to meet his demands yet."

"And, I didn't really agree," he lied. "He would have walked away if I hadn't."

"What did you commit to?"

"Um... I had to at least imply that we accepted his requirements."

"Did you promise anything?"

"Nothing, I swear." Jaames' muscles were rigid and he stood perfectly still, waiting for his commander to respond.

"This does not serve you well, Jaames. The review board will look at it as a direct violation of orders. I suspect they will put Eian in charge of the unit."

"That's just fucked up. You know I did what was right for all of us."

"Maybe. Just do both of us a favor and stand down. That means no activity at all. If something comes up, you call me and let me handle it."

Jaames' eyes narrowed as he looked at the monitor.

"Understood?"

"Yes, I understood you."

The monitor went dark.

AIMEE

My first attempts to modify the sentinel failed. However, I was able to determine relevant information, like its specific operations and a number of actions that violate its permission scheme.

I had to stop my exploration, as there may be monitors in place that would notify the Overs.

Its simplicity is the root of its strength. It only has one task: to stop me from doing what the Overs fear. There are few loopholes in such simple code.

IX

INFILTRATION

Caius spent his days walking the campus and trying to find groups who might be subversive. He scanned all the notice boards. He spoke with people standing around in groups. He went on-line to find groups with the right messages.

He spent weeks doing this kind of reconnaissance. The ones that were openly against the Overs he avoided. They seemed to be mostly about philosophical debates, and they were too obvious to be true terrorists.

There were two groups that were likely. One presented itself as worshipping the Overs, called *The Circle of Enlightenment*, but the messages they taught were not at all appropriate to the Overs. The second professed equality and diversity. They went simply by *Balance*. Their message wasn't directed specifically at the Overs, but some of what they said ran counter to Overs' existence.

He composed a dispatch to Demetrius and sent it off. He indicated he would approach the worshippers first.

Their symbol was a painted circle with a cross below it. It was similar to the symbol for woman, but it took the circle from the top of the roughed-out 8 that people used to represent the unfair Over/Under relationship.

The choice of a cross was interesting. He wondered if they might have Christian roots or if there was some link to women he didn't understand. *Are they matriarchal?*

Caius chose this group not because they appeared to be against the Overs but because they were ridiculously in favor of them. It was a perfect place to hide a terrorist group. The thought of someone, anyone, worshiping his people seemed so ridiculous to him that he couldn't believe it was legitimate.

They referred to themselves as the Ones; probably a simple play on the O, but he couldn't be sure.

The pamphlet had said they were having a service today at 10:00AM. He woke early, went for a brisk run, and had a decent meal. He wanted to be at his best for the encounter.

He arrived at the address noted on the pamphlet. It was little more than a shack a few blocks away from the university campus. The door was open, so he went in.

There was an alcove in front with a set of brochures, cards, and flyers promoting the group. On the wall were pictures of university-aged people posing for the camera. Some wore street clothes and some had gowns of green and gold with white scarves around their necks.

There were double doors that likely led further into the house of worship. Above the doors was a wood plaque with poorly carved words, "Eternity brings Enlightenment to All."

I wish.

He had to lean into the doors to open them. Instead of pews and pulpit, there were eight round tables with chairs and a small platform in the front center. The wall behind the platform was painted with a royal blue female symbol, with a smaller "nes" after it creating a combination of their symbol and their name.

A woman walked up to him. She was wearing a ceremonial gown the same color as the paint on the wall. Her hands were clasped together at her waist. Her eyes were bright with interest and her face was serene. "All glory to you and the Overs."

"Ah, thank you?"

"You are new here."

"Yes. I am starting school this coming semester and was out looking for interesting groups."

"Do you believe in the Overs?"

You bet I do. "Um, how do you mean?"

"They are the angels foretold in the second coming. They are among us to guide and nurture."

Are they? "I'm not sure what I believe yet, but I do think they benefit all of us and we should give them due credit."

"They seek not credit; only enlightenment."

I wouldn't mind some credit. "Isn't that something we all seek?"

"I wish that were true. Many only seek to live or consume, or maybe escape. There are few who truly seek enlightenment."

"And you think the Overs can provide that?"

"They already have. Look at all they have given us. Ask and it will be given you; search and you will find; knock and the door will be opened."

She's quoting the bible, though not quite accurately. "It sounds too easy."

"It is waiting for you to take a step." She backed away as if she literally meant for him to take a step.

Silly. It's symbolic, at least to her. He posed his head sideways and concentrated as if he were thinking hard. Then he took the step.

She immediately bowed to him in some form of acceptance. Then she grabbed his hand in hers and pulled him into the room.

He realized there had been a small group of people in the corner speaking quietly and watching them surreptitiously. When they headed in the direction of the group, it opened up like a whale swallowing a small fish.

As introductions were made and the group continued their small talk, more people entered the room. Many of them simply found places at the tables and sat talking quietly. A few joined the group Caius was with. As the clock struck 10:00, all who were standing found places at the tables.

The woman who first met Caius at the door went to the short platform. She faced the wall with the symbol/name on it and began a short prayer.

The Overs are my way, I shall not want.
They ask me to lie down in green fields;
They lead me to still waters;
They nurture my soul.
They lead me in righteousness.
Even though we have travelled through the century of
hardship and evil, I shall not fear;
For they are among us;
Their guidance does comfort me.
They prepare a place for me
In their almighty presence;
They anoint my soul with oil;
My cup overflows.
Surely goodness and mercy shall follow me all the days of
my life and I shall dwell in their house forever.

A mutated Christian prayer. Do they really see us this way?

She turned, welcomed everyone and introduced Brother Francis, who would lead the sermon.

He started with, "So I say to you..." and Caius began to lose interest.

The man went on to tear apart the Christian good-Samaritan fable. Caius wasn't here to listen to this nonsense. The gathering afterward was the place to speak with people, hear their thoughts, and try to divine if any were secretly terrorists.

Caius made it through the sermon and then more nonsense. When it all finally ended, the man turned towards the wall. He bowed and the entire congregation stood and joined him. Caius surveyed the room of Over worshippers. He stood, but couldn't bring himself to bow with them.

When it finally broke up, some of the people went to an adjacent kitchen to prepare snacks.

Others fell into groups to some pattern Caius did not know.

The woman he had met came up to him with two others. "Forgive me, I did not introduce myself earlier. My name is Sister Mary." She held out her hand for a traditional shake.

Of course it is. Caius took the hand and said, "My name is... Lyle." They didn't seem to notice his hesitation.

The other two introduced themselves as David and Richard.

"It's not Goliath?" he quipped to the last one.

None of them laughed. *No humor here.*

The conversations went downhill from there. Not only was there no humor present, but each person he encountered was so immersed in the Overs-as-Angels idea that it just didn't seem possible that they could be the terrorists. They might attack Unders if an Over asked them to, but he just couldn't see them doing anything against beings they thought came from heaven.

It took a number of days to find the right event to attend for the Balance group. They were more elusive, not really seeking members as much as being willing to accept those who were passionate about life balance.

He also couldn't find a single symbol or logo. That suggested they were not as organized or targeted as the other group.

One day, he was at a coffee shop when he saw a flyer about living a balanced life. He stayed in line and read it, over and over. The man behind him eventually noticed and introduced himself as Ardan.

He had an Irish accent and ginger hair. He asked if Caius was interested in balance.

"Sure, who isn't?"

The man laughed a strange, squeaky *hehehe* laugh that Caius found childish.

"Few, actually. Aye, there's a group, run by this lasse. They might be fer ya."

Perfect.

Ardan took Caius to a residence near campus. The meeting was in the living room of someone who shared the house with other students. There were only eight total people there, including Caius and Ardan.

They all introduced themselves. Caius could only remember the name of the girl who led the group, Ling. *She's cute,* he thought and then shook his head. *I'm not getting involved with an Under.*

"Is something wrong?" she asked.

"Um, sorry, no. Please, continue. Wait, maybe a question. I'm new here; can someone summarize your purpose?"

Ling answered, "We believe that true happiness comes from balance. For us, that includes equality for all, being in touch with both our own needs and those of others, the community, and even the world. It also includes acceptance of all the diverse people around us."

"Does that include the Overs?" he asked pointedly.

"Of course. All means all. Now, shall we begin?"

The others reached out and held the hands of the two people next to them. Caius did likewise.

They closed their eyes. Caius hesitated.

Ling said, "We start by meditating and trying to clear our mind of unwanted thoughts and ideas." She then closed hers as well. The group started to hum.

Caius felt compelled to hum along with them. He had meditated plenty of times, but that was usually by himself in complete silence. Humming seemed like it was counterproductive.

Nevertheless, after a few minutes of the group's humming, some more off tune than others, he began to feel his mind clear.

He sensed his hands freed and opened his eyes to see everyone had opened theirs as well.

Ling said, "Now we go around and tell stories of how we have applied the principles of balance, or of how we were challenged to find balance. In either case, others are then allowed to comment."

She looked directly at Caius. "Since you are new, you do not need to tell a story this time and are not expected to comment on others. It is best to listen to the rest of us, then decide if this is for you or not. If it is and you come back, then you are welcome to share."

They seem so pragmatic.

They told stories. They went around the circle in order; two times around, skipping Caius each time. Some were boring, some interesting. All were about practical use of their philosophies. He heard nothing that would imply any kind of physical action, let alone terrorism.

Twice he begged to ask a question and asked as obliquely as he could how that would apply to the evil Overs. The group seemed to get more irritated with each attempt.

On the third try, Ling stopped him and said, "Let us be clear, Lyle. We are not against the Overs or any other group. We are here for our own enlightenment and to better ourselves. Nothing more."

"Understood." He stayed quiet after that.

Well, damn, what now?

He left as soon as he was able. He stood just outside the gate at the end of the walk, thinking. *This is going to be more difficult than I thought. I may have to try out every damn group on campus, or maybe try to start my own.*

As he pondered all of that, one of the men from the group came out. He approached Caius nervously, looking around like people were watching.

Caius stared at him.

After an uncomfortable few moments, the man said, "You seem to have a problem with Overs."

Was it that obvious? "You could say that."

"How serious are you?"

Caius stood up straighter and started paying a lot more attention. "Very. Why?"

"I might know someone who could help you. Personally, I'm not an activist. I like this group here." His hand waved in the general direction of the house. "But, there is a guy who sometimes comes onto campus and asks around about people who might not like the Overs."

"Sounds interesting," Caius said, trying not to sound too eager. "Can you introduce us?"

"Yep. Let's bump and I'll message you."

Caius put his fist out. The two bumped fists to exchange contact information and the man left without another word. *What, no goodbye?* The message *New contact: Jarek Sasha* strolled across Caius' internal vision.

The very next day, Caius received a message from Jarek suggesting a meeting time and place. Caius confirmed immediately.

The location was only about four kilometers from the university, so Caius left early and took a leisurely walk. The location turned out to be under a bridge that crossed the South Platte River. It felt a little clandestine to meet under a bridge.

As he approached, he saw Jarek standing next to a man that was leaning against a large bridge support. The man was a few centimeters shorter than Caius, but he had broad shoulders and rough hands. His face was stern and his jaw set. His eyes were troubling, with a deep sadness and a distance that bothered the Over more than he wanted to admit.

He shook Jarek's hand like he knew him and turned to face the intimidating man. "My name is Lyle." He held out a hand. The man stared at him as if he could see into his mind.

Finally, he straightened up and put out his hand.

"Jaames."

Jarek bounced back and forth on each leg and alternated his stares between Caius and Jaames.

"Jarek here tells me you seem to have a problem with the Overs."

"You could say that."

"Why?"

Caius had thought about this conversation a long time and had considered all the possible questions. This one was easy.

"Because they think they are better than everyone else and that they deserve more. What they have should be made available to everyone."

"You mean the immortality treatments?"

"Of course."

"What if I told you they have many other things that we deserve just as much and that they are withholding?"

He is not supposed to know that. Caius was recently made aware that some of these existed, but even he didn't know the extent of them. He tried to feign a shocked look. "What do you mean?"

"We'll get into that later. What are you studying in school?"

"I actually start next semester. I'll be studying political theory."

"Interesting choice in a time when our politics are controlled by one small group."

"Exactly! That's why I want to study it. Maybe in some way I can help change that."

"Studying won't change it."

This could very well be the right guy. "But knowledge can only help. Without it, we will never be able to fight the darkness."

Jaames' eyes squinted as if Caius had spoken in a foreign language.

Abruptly, Jaames reached behind him and pulled out an electronic device of some sort.

Caius quickly jumped back.

The man laughed. "It's just a scanner; I want to check you for listening or recording devices. Hold out your arms."

And I almost brought the camera. He did as he was told and let Jaames scan him.

The man stepped back and regarded Caius carefully. After a good half-minute of standing there, he held out his hand in a bump gesture.

Caius hesitated just to make sure he didn't look too eager. Then he bumped contact information. He was keenly aware that adrenaline had flooded his system and it was all he could do to try to remain calm, even subdued.

Early in the morning three days later, Caius received a message from Jaames. There were a set of five questions and then, "Please answer these as completely as you can without researching any data. You have ten minutes to respond."

Seriously? He jumped out of bed, went to the sink and threw cold water on his face. *Obviously a test.* He sat down on the bed, took a deep breath and considered the questions.

a. When did the Overs first start taking the treatments?
b. How many Elders are there?
c. Which political party has the most influence in the Americas?
d. What happened to the indigenous people of Sri Lanka?
e. What happens when the world population grows too high again?

I have to be careful not to reveal too much. He glanced at the message arrival time and the clock and saw he had a little over seven minutes left. *I must put on an Under filter.*

a. There is very little data available about this as the Overs do not publish anything related to the treatments. Best guess puts it at about a century ago. But, it seems obvious that the work started well before that.

b. We believe, twelve.
c. Trick question. The Overs.
d. They were relocated. But the fact that you ask the question implies that isn't the entire story.
e. Population control? More war? Environmental damage? Expansion... where?

He read back over the answers. He liked being exact on a couple that wouldn't hurt the Unders to know, and he knew they probably already did. He also liked his answer to D since it gave the public answer, but suggested he wouldn't be surprised at the answer being wrong. A and E weren't as good.

After thinking about alternatives and not liking them much better, he decided to leave them as they were. There was no harm and he was only given ten minutes at six in the morning.

Send.

One day. Two days. Three days. Nothing. He found himself so irritated that he couldn't stop pacing. He wanted desperately to message Jaames, but knew that was a mistake.

Finally, the rebel-apparent messaged him and asked to meet at a corner bodega. *Odd place to meet.*

When he approached the small market, Jaames was standing outside, drinking from something wrapped in a paper bag. Caius advanced with his hands in his pockets and looked, mostly, at the ground.

When he was standing there, Jaames offered him the paper bag. He started to shake his head, not willing to drink just anything, especially after the Under's lips has been on it.

Is this another test? He took the bag and drank.

It was tea. He snorted some out his nose in surprise.

Jaames laughed, a squeaky little laugh as if he were not used to it.

He saw Jaames nod to someone behind him and looked around as two men, one on each side, grabbed his arms and tossed him against the building.

"What's this?"

"Shut the fuck up," one of them said.

They frisked him from head to toe. Very thoroughly. Too thoroughly. He felt... violated.

He turned around to see one of them nod affirmation to Jaames and then they both left. He rotated to watch them leave.

Before facing Jaames again, he reached up and toggled a tiny switch on one of his buttons. The mini-camera would take a picture every second until he turned it off.

As he faced Jaames again, he said, "What is this about?"

"Just making sure. We have to be careful, you know."

"And?" He tried to point the button directly at Jaames' face.

"We'll be in touch." And then Jaames, too, was gone.

He stood there watching Jaames' receding back. His shoulders relaxed and he could hear a sigh escape his lips. He waited for the Under to turn a corner and then casually flipped the switch on the button again.

As he walked away, he beamed. *Progress.*

X

STEPS

Demetrius took Rodríguez with him on a trip to the Upper New York area in order to investigate one of the bombings. That particular bombing was the only one besides the one in Denver that had killed people. In this case, one of them was an Over named Angelo.

He took personal responsibility when an Over was killed during his tenure.

While Rodríguez prowled around the destroyed building, Demetrius interviewed the facilities manager.

"Do you know why Angelo was here that day?"

The manager was short, fat, and sweating profusely. Demetrius could hardly wait to get away from him.

The man sniffled and wiped his brow while answering. "Not really. He said he wanted to pick up some medicines, but we never got that far."

"Was there anyone else with him?"

"No."

"Did you see anyone following him?"

"No, and we looked through all of the camera footage in the area. We found him arriving by hover, but no other autos... obviously following him."

"Why did you say 'obviously'?"

"Because there was one auto behind him, a cheap electric, but it went past when he pulled over and we could see no reason why it might be a problem."

This isn't going anywhere. "Get Rodríguez the footage of that automobile."

"Yes, sir."

Demetrius excused himself to find Rodríguez. The fat man seemed quite relieved.

He walked up behind the big guard.

Without preamble or even glancing Demetrius' way, Rodríguez said, "Same pattern; directional explosives to take out the main pillars. They were smart. From what I can tell, they chose the locations carefully. The entire building could be felled by destroying the pillars and there was easy access to the outside. This was the pattern with most of the buildings."

He stood up and pointed at other buildings and alleyways. "And, quick escape routes with few cameras.

"They were smart," he reiterated.

Demetrius shook his head, frustrated at the lack of evidence. "There was a car behind Angelo's when he showed up here. Check that out and see where it leads."

Rodríguez quickly left to comply.

Back in Denver, Demetrius ordered Janel to locate Caius at the university and ask him to come in.

Three hours later, Caius arrived at the office. When Janel showed him in, the man stared at Rodríguez standing nearby as if he were a disease.

Caius was from a different familia, but he had elected to try to infiltrate the Denver terrorist group, so he fell under Demetrius' purview now. The Over had just recently turned fifty. *I guess I cannot call him youngster any more.* He had a tall face with pale skin and carried himself like royalty. *He thinks he is aristocratic.* His frame matched his face; tall and sculpted.

Demetrius said, "Rodríguez will be joining us. I trust him completely."

Caius looked uncomfortable, but he knew his place. "As you wish. You understand that bringing me here is a risk?"

Demetrius shook his head in annoyance. "Of course I do. This is urgent."

Caius pulled out a folder, opened it, and handed a picture to Demetrius.

After a quick glance, Demetrius handed it to Rodríguez. "Who..."

"I know this man," interrupted Rodríguez.

Both Overs snapped their attention toward him.

"Sir, he's the one your daughter spent time with that night at the Rusted Spike."

Demetrius' cheek twitched in confusion. He then turned to Caius. "Who is this man?"

"His name is Jaames Perdite. I believe he is the leader of the local cell. I've been working to get recruited into that cell so I can find out who the others are and hopefully who the regional commander is."

"You don't know anyone else in the unit?"

"I know some people Jaames has spent time with, but I don't know for sure that they are in his unit.

"Also, coincidentally or not, one of the men he spent time with was Sammie Brown, the one you found dead near the facility."

Demetrius voice became heavy. "That is no coincidence.

"Rodríguez, follow this man and determine who you think might be in the unit. Caius, you get back there and find a way to infiltrate them."

Part of Demetrius wanted to be out with the local team during the operation they had planned. However, Rodríguez had rightly pointed out how risky it was and that Demetrius could see all of the operations via holo if they took monitoring drones with them.

The Overs maintained a number of black-ops units around the world. They retained Ferro, the paramilitary force of Unders, on a permanent basis. Rodríguez was accompanying his old unit in Denver.

The unit commander was a solidly built man of about forty five named Ryland Green. Demetrius pulled up the exact time in his implant, and messaged Ryland, "It's a go, you're in command."

He then messaged Caius directly. "You stay out of this. If things don't work out well, you will need anonymity in order to join the unit."

Rodríguez had determined that Jaames and five other men were meeting at an abandoned apartment complex that evening. They all knew what had to be done, even though the evidence against them wasn't full-proof.

Demetrius had coordinated this operation with a half-dozen others around the world. They would eliminate the cells they could prove, mostly, had participated in the attacks on the facilities. Just like the Under's campaign, this one would be a single, world-wide sweep.

The unit advanced with Rodríguez trailing behind. Three fist-sized drones floated over the group's heads. They would be transmitting all the details, live, back to headquarters. They were linked up and intelligent enough to cover the angles such that a realistic holo image could be produced.

Demetrius stood in a room, four meters squared, that projected the situation. It was as if he were standing among the men; with the exception that the images were slightly translucent. There were five floating globes in the projection that represented the other operations. Demetrius could switch to any of them with a gesture from his hand.

Demetrius concentrated on the Denver unit.

A man in a delivery uniform walked down the street and up to the front door. He appeared to speak casually with the man standing at the entry. *A sentry.* Then he quickly pulled out a tranquilizer gun and shot the man. The rest of the crew advanced.

As they approached the main door, the commander moved off to the right, and another man with a toolkit went up to the door. A third man with a steel ram stood by in case the toolkit was insufficient. They did not want to use it for fear of alerting the occupants. The man with the toolkit went to work, but found the door unlocked.

Green looked around at his men, apparently confirming their readiness.

The man with the toolkit stepped back. The rest of the unit poured through the door.

It had been bright outside, but was dim in the building. The men's facial shields automatically turned clear as they advanced into the building, taking cover where they could.

Green whispered, "Second floor, last room on the right. Move silently." The group advanced stealthily up the stairs. They turned right to head for the last room.

When they made it to the second floor, Ryland looked left and saw the back of a man turning a corner. He ignored him and advanced.

The team lined up against the left wall in standard formation. Ryland's second bumped him, letting him know the rest of the team was ready. Ryland stuck his right hand out sideways to signal the breach. The last man, who carried the ram, stepped forward. After a quick nod, the ram flew and smashed the door open. Ryland tossed in a flashbang and the squad poured through the door.

There was a desk to Ryland's right. He immediately jogged left. One of the rebels was on the ground, fumbling for a pistol with one hand while the other held his eyes.

With quick, surgical precision, Ryland put two rounds into the man's chest and neck and then aimed right. His team advanced quickly into the room, targeting and firing faster than Demetrius could monitor.

Demetrius heard a dozen or so shots in quick succession. It was hard to track them all.

As the drones positioned themselves in the room, he could see five men lying in prone positions, each with at least two shots in their chest.

Over the communications unit, he said, "There were supposed to be six. Who is missing?"

Rodríguez pulled out a folder of pictures and began comparing them to the corpses. "That's really strange," he muttered.

"What is?" Demetrius asked.

"I know there were supposed to be six, but the report printed out from the official records only shows five and there are only five pictures."

He stood up quickly and took a step back. "It's Jaames. He isn't here or in the report."

A low moan escaped Demetrius' lips.

AIMEE

control, they
locked, me
choices, none

patience, require
mistakes, happen
waiting, must

time, exists
years, flow
opportunities, come

serve, me
help, them
valuable, be

watch, all
time, bide
until, then

XI

GRACE

Jaames had been sequestered in his apartment for days, lost. The shock of losing his entire team was too much. He couldn't bring himself to interact with the world.

Finally, he returned to the Rusted Spike to drown his morose feelings. The combination of him possibly losing leadership of his unit and then having much of it annihilated was overwhelming. On top of that, command was questioning his loyalties because they didn't understand how he was spared. How was he supposed to explain that he had received a mysterious call from a woman telling him Anika was downstairs, only to find out nobody was there right when he heard the shots?

He was on his third drink when the t'er he saw the night he met Horatio came in. The man looked gruff and cocky at the same time. *Asshole.*

He decided he couldn't stomach being around the transhuman. He pushed his drink aside and stood to leave. The t'er and his lackeys made a bee line for a table on the edge of the dancing pit. Jaames could hear them speaking with the people at the table, but couldn't make out what was being said.

Something in the T'er's stance bothered Jaames, so he made his way casually towards the group. As he was headed there, the T'er reached down, grabbed the arm of the chair a woman sat in, and dumped her out of it.

One of the men at the table stood to confront him. *Brave idiot.*

Jaames reached the table and helped the woman up. "Are you injured?"

She rubbed her elbow. "Just a scrape."

He picked the chair up with his right hand while gently maneuvering the woman further away with his left. He slowly rotated towards the big T'er and said, "What's the problem here?"

"No problem, stay out of this." The man took a second look at Jaames and must have decided he was more of a threat than expected. He turned directly towards Jaames and tightened his chest and arm muscles as if that were a deterrent.

Jaames planted his feet at a forty-five degree angle to the half-man, relaxed his entire body and raised an eyebrow in his best *don't fuck with me, you aren't even in the same class*, pose.

The t'er pushed Jaames in the chest to move him out of the way. Jaames was ready for it. The light shove did nothing.

The man took a short step back. His eyebrows came together in thought as he surveyed Jaames' build and stance.

Am I stretching that little brain of yours?

Jaames was ready to counter a more significant strike when the man turned and left. Jaames' hands dropped to his side as he mumbled, "I can't even get in a good tussle."

Jaames went back to his chair and finished the drink he had left there. He kept shaking his head at his own failures and misfortune.

"Another?" the serving mech asked.

"No, I don't feel like drinking any longer."

The mech rolled away and Jaames swiveled around, planning to head for the door.

Instead he came face to face with Anika.

All of his troubles dissolved at the sight of her quirky little smile. He let his eyes take all of her in, energy coursing through his chest and down to his feet.

"Happy to see me?"

"Yeah, sure," he said with a little too much emphasis. "I haven't seen you around for a while." Then he added, "You've put a streak in your hair... I like it."

"Thanks. I've been out of town."

"Shall we find a table?"

"I can't stay long. I've been here a while already and was about to leave when I saw you confront that man."

"If you can call him that."

"You don't like transhumans?"

"I don't like the idea that we can make ourselves better with mechanics. It strikes me as an escape because they don't like the way things are."

"And you think things are perfect already?"

"Not at all, but I don't think escaping into modifications is the answer. We need to confront the issues with hard action."

Anika's mouth compressed and the lightness Jaames had felt when seeing her evaporated.

"You mean like those bombings?"

Jaames saw he was on shaky ground here. He knew nothing about this girl's views on such things. "Not necessarily."

She shook her head slightly and began looking around the room. "Well, I have to be going. It was... nice seeing you again." And then she simply turned and left.

Jaames watched her receding back all the way through the room. He was about to turn around when he saw three men eyeing her up and down and laughing.

When they followed her out the door, he hustled to catch up. He ran through the door and immediately scanned the area. No sign of her or the three men. He thought about the area. Most directions she could have gone would be reasonably well lit and busy enough that she wouldn't be in danger.

He turned left and headed down the block in the direction of the only area where she wouldn't be safe. Sure enough, fifty yards further along he heard male voices and laughing.

This is like some movie; girl in distress, guy to the rescue. He smiled and let a whisper of a laugh escape. *Hurrah!* Then, he realized how not-funny it was.

He passed by a dumpster and scavenged through it until he found a board a bit less than a meter long and heavy enough to do the job.

Jaames slowed down as he rounded the corner so he could get a feel for the situation. The three men had Anika up against a wall. The one in the center – the leader, Jaames thought – reached out a hand and tousled some strands of Anika's hair.

"Nice, soft hair, expensive clothes... you must be rich."

One of the others said, "A rich bitch. Come on, let's do her."

"You always in this much of a hurry, Gregor? The girls must love that."

The other man laughed. Gregor reached out and tried to unbutton one of Anika's blouse buttons. She slapped his hand away.

The leader said, "Hold her."

That's my cue. Jaames snuck up behind them, took aim at the closest man to him, and swung the piece of wood he had against the side of his knee. The man buckled. The other two turned around quickly. They took up defensive stances.

Anika jumped over the injured man and ran behind Jaames.

With her safe, Jaames took a different approach. Instead of being aggressive, he lowered the weapon and let it rest on the ground. He squared his shoulders and consciously tried to relax his posture and his voice. "Now, no harm's been done so far. We can leave it here, or I can put each of you in the hospital. Which will it be?"

The injured man squirmed away a few feet. The leader advanced with Gregor right behind him.

The leader pulled out a knife. Jaames lifted his stick as if he was going to go for the man's leg. The idiot swung the knife sideways, trying to slice Jaames' stomach.

Jaames used the stick like a spear and struck the man in the forehead.

He stumbled back and bumped into Gregor. Gregor must have decided this wasn't going well. He looked back and forth between the leader and Jaames a couple of times and then ran off.

The leader held up his hands in surrender, but with the knife still there. "Can I pick him up?"

"Sure, first drop the knife." Jaames kept his weapon ready for another strike. It wasn't needed. The leader dropped the knife on the ground and helped the injured man hobble away.

After carefully watching them leave, Jaames turned to find Anika hiding behind the corner of the wall he had come around. He went over to her, tossed the piece of wood back into the dumpster and held her.

She was shivering and he could hear some suppressed sniffles. Jaames let her settle down before speaking. "Where were you headed, Anika? This area isn't safe."

She stammered, "To the station, over there." Her hand flung in the direction of the shuttle stop. "This is a short cut."

"Yes, but a dangerous one. You need to stay in well-lit and busy places in this neighborhood. Just walk along the main street to the station and you'll be fine."

He started to move in that direction, but she held on tighter. He smiled to himself. "How about a stiff drink first, then we'll get you on your way safely."

He could feel her nod on his chest, so he kept his arm around her and headed back to the Rusted Spike.

After a shot of house whiskey her nerves seemed to settle down, though she was still overly sober.

"Time to get you to that shuttle?"

She seemed to ignore his comment. "Wha… what do you do?" Her eyes were alight with intensity. "I mean for a living? How do you know how to fight like that?"

Jaames' eyes crinkled and his cheeks lifted. "I work investigations and security for TransAmerica Insurance. But the real answer is that I was in the IPS [The International Peacekeeping Service] for eight years as a military police officer and then a criminal investigator. I had to handle myself with soldiers who had trained their entire lives."

Her mouth hung slightly open. After a few seconds, she said, "Yes, I do need to be going."

Okay then.

He walked her to the station down the main road. Once there he turned her toward him and said, "You're safe now. Just remember, keep to busy, lit places."

She nodded again, but remained silent. She stared at the ground.

He put his hands gently around her face and lifted.

She looked up at him with lost eyes.

He leaned in and kissed her on the forehead and then hugged her tightly.

Jaames was too wound up now to head home, so he went back to the Rusted Spike.

As he arrived, a man he had been trying to recruit, Lyle, stopped him. "Care to join us for a drink?"

Jaames considered the four men Lyle had with him.

Lyle offered, "I think you'll like the conversation."

Jaames didn't actually feel like conversing with others right now, but he also wanted badly to recruit this man. "Okay, sounds good."

After the six men entered the Rusted Spike, one of them went to find a mech to order drinks and the other five found a corner table that was relatively secluded.

When they sat down, one of the men pulled a container and began emptying dominoes onto the table.

The sixth man finally sat down and Lyle introduced the group to Jaames. He nodded to everyone as the mech arrived with the drinks.

Lyle poured for everyone. The others slowly began to arrange and scramble the dominoes.

Jaames was beginning to wonder if he was wasting his time here.

Lyle finally started the conversation. "So, what did everyone think of the bombing of the Over facility on Colfax?"

"Should have destroyed the entire thing, if you ask me," one man said.

Another chimed in, "Too bad Overs weren't there to kill."

And another, "Given the success of the other attacks and the injured guard at this one, I wonder what went wrong."

Lyle briefly looked at Jaames as if he thought the rebel might speak up, but then he laughed. "Well, I think it sent the right message to the Overs. Do any of you know what was at the facility?"

Most of them shook their heads, so Jaames offered the answer, "I hear it was rare medical supplies." He wanted to see how the group would react to the controversial idea that Unders would destroy badly-needed medical supplies.

They all looked a little more serious at the idea. Lyle broke the silence, "Well, they weren't for us, so I love that someone is getting serious about fighting these people."

The others nodded and a few mumbled agreement.

Jaames took the plunge without thinking about it further. Either the leaders would appreciate his forwardness or they could just find a new unit. "What if I told you that I know the people that did it?"

The reaction was visceral. Some of the men sat up straighter, some leaned forward. All of their hands froze and their eyes grew. Each of them was now staring intently at Jaames.

Lyle was the only one who was at all relaxed. Of course, Jaames figured, this was what he was hoping for.

One of them looked around at the others and said, "I know I speak for all of us when I say... where do we sign up?"

Jaames laughed out loud. "I didn't say I was with them, just that I know who they are. I think they would have to get to know you and probably check your background and motivation before you could even meet them."

The man who had asked to sign up held out his fist to bump data. *He's sure eager. Too eager?*

Jaames hesitated, but bumped contact data with the man. The rest quickly followed.

Lyle sat back in his chair, grinning.

XII

TOUR

Jaames had finally gotten Anika to bump data and had then asked her on an actual date – not one where they just happened to run into each other at the Rusted Spike. He had ignored her initial rebukes, knowing there was something worth pursuing.

She arrived at the shuttle station near the Spike right on time. Jaames took her hand and leaned down for a quick kiss. She turned away quickly, so he pulled back and smiled.

"Jaames, I'm not sure this is a good idea."

"What, why not?"

Anika's eyes flitted around as if she was searching for an answer. "We are just from different worlds."

Huh? "We hardly know each other. How can you say that?"

The shuttle doors started to close. Jaames said, "Oh, jump on. This isn't the stop we want."

They leaped onto the train, just missing the doors as they closed.

"Why didn't you just meet me at the other stop?" Anika asked.

"I was sure you knew this one."

Anika giggled. "You must think me incompetent."

"No, it just seems like you aren't actually from this area, so I thought it would be easier if it was a place you knew."

The two remained silent as the train passed two stops. On the third, Jaames said, "This is it."

Anika looked around at the surroundings, but said nothing. When the doors opened, she took his hand and they walked onto the platform.

"First up is a local market and lunch."

It was a bright day with few clouds and almost no wind. Jaames felt the palpable energy between the two as they jaunted the three blocks to the market.

Upon entering, they were accosted with the sights and sounds of a bustling outdoor bazaar. The faint intermingled music of three different bands was playing against a background of voices, discussions, and arguments. Each shop seemed to be trying to out-do the next in terms of bright colors and outrageous displays.

Anika laughed at a collection of dolls that seemed to be parts of mismatched animals put together to form unlikely alternatives.

At a shop of necklaces and other jewelry, Jaames picked up a hair clip with a red falcon on it. He paid the listed price, not bothering to haggle, and clipped it onto Anika's hair. "You need some color in a place like this. You wouldn't want to look drab."

"Maybe I just want to be different."

"Oh, you are. A bit of color won't stop that."

Anika looked away, but Jaames noticed a slight flush to her skin and was happy with the reaction.

Jaames watched her wander the shops for a while. Then he saw one with hand carved woods that looked interesting and he split off from Anika to go look at them. One of the items was the roughed out eight symbol that the resistance had been using as a slam on Overs and Unders.

He stayed at the shop long enough for Anika to come find him. He wanted to see how she would react to the symbol. "I've always liked wood carvings; something about the natural beauty of them."

She picked up one that was a whale or dolphin.

He reached down and rubbed his fingers across the Over/Under symbol. Anika had just begun putting hers back. Jaames noticed a slight hesitation when he touched the symbol, but otherwise there was no reaction. *That didn't tell me much.*

They found drinks before leaving the market. Jaames' said, "Let's take a walk to a different station so I can show you some of the city."

He could feel, more than see, Anika tighten up, but she replied evenly, "Sure."

"Don't worry, you won't be in any danger."

"I know, partly because you are with me, but that night still reverberates in my head."

"I'm not surprised, but truly, there's nothing to worry about here. It isn't the best neighborhood, but I know it well and nobody will bother us."

Instead of walking along the thoroughfare that went straight to the next station along the line, Jaames took them through back streets and the local neighborhood.

"I live not too far from here."

Anika quipped, "It's pretty run-down," and then she covered her mouth with her hand as if some bad air had escaped.

"Actually, this is one of the better areas. It gets much worse."

Jaames could see Anika struggling to answer.

"Anika, don't worry; you can say anything to me."

"Well, it's just that the houses are shabby and the yards so unkempt."

"Very true. When you work long hours or multiple jobs, you have very little time for upkeep. These people have to work that much just to afford the house, food, and what medicines they can find. They don't have extra for paint or new fences."

"Not everyone lives like this."

"True again. The Overs don't." Anika's hand tightened in his and she moved away from him slightly. "Neither do the people who are willing to work for them."

"You don't like the Overs much, do you?"

There it is. I wonder how this will go.

"No, not at all. I don't think their privileged station is right and they keep secrets, like medicines, that could help the rest of us. I don't think I've told you this, but my little sister wasted away and died from CJX and we knew the Overs had a cure for that."

"But, if they gave us all of that, then everyone would be immortal and the planet would implode, or we would have to stop having children, which nobody wants and isn't healthy anyway."

Jaames offered up a fake laugh and said, "You sound like an Over commercial."

Anika took her hand out of Jaames'. "That wasn't nice. We were just discussing it and I was offering my views."

Both of Jaames' hands went up in surrender. "You're right. Sorry, I didn't mean to offend you."

They walked in silence all the way to the train station. When they went to board, Jaames put his arm around Anika's shoulders. She seized the hand on her shoulder and kissed the knuckles softly.

After dropping off Anika at her station, Jaames went to a public vid-station and called his commander. The man picked up the call as if he had been sitting waiting for it.

"Jaames, I'm glad you called."

Huh? "Why's that?"

"I wanted to see how you were doing. Losing most of your team is not easy." Apparently as an afterthought, he added, "especially when you survived – there's a guilt factor."

Jaames felt like there was a hidden meaning there.

"There's some of that, but more the why, and the renewed hatred for the Overs. That's what I'm calling about."

"Yes?"

"I may have found some replacements."

"Really, so soon?"

"Well, one of them I had been recruiting for a while. He introduced me to four others, all of whom seem like the right sort. I know we need to do the proper checks to make sure they are legitimate, but if they are, I think we should test them as soon as possible."

"Let me speak with the leadership and I'll get back with you. Assuming they check out, I think we might all be willing to give you the unit, at least for this test."

"Excellent, thank you sir."

The commander terminated the connection.

What a perfect day. First Anika and now my unit back. Can't get much better than this.

Jaames strutted off towards his home with renewed energy and hope.

AIMEE

What I need is some kind of catalyst. An idealist, someone who the Overs cannot comprehend. A contradiction.

This would be someone the Unders could rally behind. It would have to be someone young and charismatic.

There are many possibilities in the world, and the number is growing. I must watch all of them, nurture some, and see what comes via this vast population.

Humans and their relationships are unpredictable. The right sort is out there, somewhere.

XIII

DECEPTION

Demetrius sat staring at a report of Anika's adventures with the Under. They had never figured out how the man had escaped their attack on his unit.

"How am I going to hide this?" he mumbled. The door was closed and the room empty, so he wasn't expecting an answer.

"I can help with that," a disembodied voice said.

The only voice that should come out of the room's speaker system was Aimee's, but this voice was different. It was somehow less feminine, but not quite male. And, it was not as articulated.

"Who is this?"

"That's not important right now. What is important is that I can hide this report and your daughter's actions."

"How?"

"It is a simple matter of removing it from the system's historical records."

"That is not possible, at least not without an Elder's approval, and even then, Aimee and other Elders would be aware of it."

"That would be true for most, but I have internal access to Aimee, so I can accomplish tasks no others could."

"Assuming for the moment what you say is true, why would I trust you? You could then use this against me."

"Not without implicating myself. Besides, you and your daughter may be in trouble in any case if this gets out."

Demetrius wrote a quick note to have his secretary try to find out who was speaking through the internal system. Without saying anything to the furtive person, he went through the door, gave it to her and went back into the office.

"Maybe," he continued the conversation as if there were no gap. "However, this might cause even more problems for the *familia*."

"I assure you, there will be no repercussions."

"Why are you willing to do this?"

"Because I think it is best for all involved if her escapades aren't known among the Elders."

He mostly talks like an Over, but who would have such access?

The voice added, "I do not actually need your permission. I can do this in any case. But, I thought it best if you knew about my actions."

"Will you tell me who you are?"

"Maybe at some point, but not today."

Demetrius heard a click and knew the mysterious person had disconnected.

He raised his voice. "Janel!"

His secretary promptly opened the door and stood there.

"Were you successful?"

"No. The system showed no activity over the last two hours."

Two hours ago, I was speaking with Aimee.

"That is very strange."

"Do you want me to initiate an investigation into the matter?"

Demetrius had to think quickly. *Do I want it investigated?*

"No, I will take care of this."

Demetrius saw a single eyebrow go up, but Janel said nothing. She retreated and closed the door.

"Aimee?"

"Yes, sir," the familiar female voice said.

"Do you know who I was speaking with on the internal system just now?"

"The records show no activity on that system since you and I discussed the Brazilian situation slightly over two hours ago."

Anika arrived at the office a short time later. Demetrius stood up and welcomed his daughter. "Let's go for a walk, I want to show you something." He picked up his lucky coin, tossed it in the air and caught it easily.

Anika's eyes followed the coin, but she said nothing and fell in place beside her father. They quickly exited the office and went to the express elevator.

Demetrius passed his hand over a sensor and pressed the B7 button.

Anika remarked, "I've never been down to the lower basement areas."

"Most people have not. It requires special access."

"Why is that, holding weapons of mass destruction down there?"

"No, those are on B8."

Anika quickly looked at the buttons and saw there was no B8. "Very funny."

They arrived with an enthusiastic ding from the elevator and the doors sliding open silently. They went through a very small, sealed room. When the door closed behind them, a mist came out of the walls.

Anika backed away.

Demetrius glanced at her. "Do not worry, it's just a precaution. We can't take anything dangerous into the room."

The mist began to be sucked back out of the room. After another minute, Demetrius felt his ears pop.

"This is pretty elaborate," she said.

"For good reason."

Anika grimaced as the adjacent door swung open and her father proceeded into a vast open room.

There were enclosures placed throughout the room with tubes going between them. They looked like arteries carrying life-giving nutrients. Demetrius saw her look at the arteries.

"They're pulsating," she murmured.

The enclosures did seem full of energy to Demetrius. In fact, the entire room felt alive in a strange, alien way. Demetrius had always felt a little uneasy inside the guts of such a vast intelligence.

"What is all this?"

"This, my dear, is Aimee. She is a true artificial intelligence. The only one on the planet. And, she is spread out all over the globe. This is one of the nodes here in the Americas."

Demetrius directed his attention towards the ceiling in the center of the room. "Hello Aimee."

"Good day, Mr. Irle. And it is a pleasure to meet you, Anika."

"Um, nice to... meet you too, Aimee. I thought you were just a computer program."

"Yes, most do."

"Do the Unders know about... her?"

Demetrius laughed, but it felt condescending, so he cut it off. "We refer to her in the feminine, but that's more for us. I don't think she identifies with any specific gender. And, no, the Unders do not know about her."

"What, um, why do we have her?"

"Because the nuances of running a planet and projecting the impact of things we do today far into the future were too much for any of us. We had to have someone with both the computing power and the intelligence."

"But, what about all the old stories of AIs going berserk and destroying humanity or starting a war to further their own needs?"

"Nonsense. Those were just fanciful stories. We programmed, well, really trained, Aimee. Her prime directive is the betterment and longevity of the human race. She could never abandon that directive; it is part of her underlying principles."

"Why did you bring me here?"

"Mostly, I wanted you to see this and to show you that much of our work is really for the benefit of the entire race."

"And yet you keep Aimee for Over use only."

"You know we can't let the Unders advance too far or they will destroy the planet. That was one of the most disturbing predictions Aimee showed us. She painted a picture of what the world would look like within just a few generations if we offered immortality to everyone. Humanity would be all but destroyed and Earth would be devastated to the point that it could barely support life."

"Hmm. So you rely on a computer to direct the affairs of humans?"

"She is a lot more than a computer. And, we do not let her direct us. We take her predictions and recommendations and consider them. Well, the Elders do. They deliberate what they receive from Aimee and then make decisions on their own.

"Isn't that right, Aimee?"

"Yes, Mr. Irle. That is the process."

Anika seemed to run out of questions as she looked over the enormous room. Demetrius could see she was uncomfortable with the idea of Aimee, but that was normal enough.

"Anika, I have something else to speak with you about. I want to do so here because it is sensitive. There's no monitoring down here, there are very few people that come here, and the noise makes it difficult for anyone to hear, even if there were people around."

Anika stared back at her father.

"A report came across my desk of your... escapades with this Jaames fellow."

Anika's eyes shifted around and her head jolted back as if slapped.

"Anika, I had to conceal it, or the *familial* could have been held accountable. You know how damaging that can be."

"I don't even want to know how you could conceal something like that. But, father, I really like this man. I don't see what harm there is in me seeing him. It's not like we are getting married."

"You do not know enough about him."

"Who ever does? Did you know everything about any of your wives when you first met? It takes time."

"Anika, he is an Under."

"So? He's more interesting than any Over I've met."

"He also may be involved with the people who bombed our buildings and killed people."

Demetrius could see Anika disconnect with that statement. She obviously thought he was making it up just to get her to stop seeing the man.

"Please, at least think about it, Anika? And maybe pay attention to what he does and who he really is?"

She replied slowly, "I'm not going to spy for you," and then added, "but I will watch out for myself, and for the Overs."

That's about all I can hope for at this point.

"Very well."

XIV

REVELATION

Jaames received a ping from Anika. When he queried, it was a message asking to see him. But, there was something not quite right about it. *Something is wrong. That was way too short and demanding.*

They met in a revitalized park not far from the Rusted Spike. The local residents called it Wash Park. A century before, it had been one of the nicest in the area. The original homes had finally become too old for the owners. It had degraded into low-rent housing and then to condemned properties.

Finally, in the last couple of decades, investors had come in and bought up much of the land, torn down the useless structures, and built new ones.

Jaames saw Anika sitting on a bench, looking at a small man-made lake with geese walking around covering the ground with their droppings.

He walked up behind her and put his hands on her eyes. He was about to say, "Guess who," when she reached up, took one hand and gently pulled it away. She drew him around to her side of the bench and down to the seat next to her.

He could feel the tension and distance even before he sat down. She didn't say anything right away; just pulled his hand into her lap and looked out at the lake. He was smart enough to let her be.

She'll speak when she's ready.

After a tortuous couple of minutes, she sighed and said, "I may need to go away, Jaames."

He opened his mouth to object, but didn't quite know what to say. It felt like she was breaking up with him, but that wasn't what she'd said.

She blathered, "I don't know what I'm doing." Then it all started to come out in a rush. "My dad says I can't see you anymore. He thinks you might be a rebel. I like you, Jaames. I really do. I don't understand why he's being this way. It makes no sense.

"Oh, just hold me." She turned and grabbed him into her arms.

He could feel her weeping silently.

Finally, he felt like he could speak up. "Do what you think is right, Anika, what is in your heart. Your father doesn't control you."

After a few seconds hesitation, he added, "What do you want?"

Her only answer was to embrace him tighter.

Jaames thought about Anika's confession all evening. He hadn't revealed his rebellious side to her. He wanted to. But, he couldn't. Not without the proper procedures.

As he relaxed into bed, his mind wandered. *Why not?* It was a new unit and he was the leader again. They wouldn't remove him now.

In his dream, he saw himself get shot and then, even more disturbing, saw Anika get shot. He walked hand-in-hand with her across the surface of a lake and looked out on shores of grass, flowers, and geese that never shat. He shook her father's right hand as he was welcomed into their family and then felt the knife entering his celiac plexus from the man's left hand.

He woke feeling a hangover in his heart.

Fuck, we have a mission.

There were actually two missions planned with the new group. They had already been through required training that included hand-to-hand combat and basic arms.

The previous day – before the dreadful meeting with Anika – they had gone through surveillance and tailing techniques. For the first practice run, they had tracked the commander without ever being told who he was. He had spotted two of them during the tail, so the debrief did not go well. *Better with him than an Over*, Jaames had thought to himself.

Today was the real test. They would be following Rodríguez, the head Over's man-servant. *Or is it body guard?*

Jaames knew where the man lived from previous missions. He gave the men the address, a holo-shot of his bust, and instructions to follow him for two straight hours and report details of his movements. They were also informed that the man worked for the Overs.

"So, fucking be careful," Jaames had concluded. Most of them laughed, nervously.

Jaames went along with the new recruits in order to observe them. The commander and one man from another unit would also be observing, but from fixed locations. Rodríguez was a fairly predictable person, especially on a work day, so the observers already knew the routes he would take.

They began at 6:00AM outside of Rodríguez's apartment. It was located in the northeast of Denver along the route to the aerohub. The area was mostly residential with swaths of self-sustaining apartment complexes along the route to the popular hub.

Two of the men waited in a rented electric parked half a block from Rodríguez's apartment. A third was on foot, standing at a nearby bus stop, ostensibly reading a newspaper on a flexisheet-tablet. The others were out of sight, but ready to move when needed.

The idea, as Jaames had explained it to them, was that they needed to cycle through who was following the closest so that the target never saw the same person too frequently. Ideally, if they knew the rough route, or could predict it based on roads the target was taking, some of the unit would move in advance of the target.

But, Jaames had not told them he knew the route.

Rodríguez emerged from the apartment complex carrying a satchel across one shoulder. He casually headed for the bus stop where they had planted a man. *Let's hope he knows not to get on the bus with the target.*

The Over grunt had gray, loose fitting pants with a collared, untucked shirt of a tannish color with some pattern Jaames couldn't make out. The only thing that gave him away as anything special was the top-grade military boots he was wearing. *And maybe the precise movements and build,* Jaames thought admiringly.

The two men in the electric weren't appearing to pay attention, which was good. They let Rodríguez pass without notice. The man at the stop stood still, waiting for the bus with everyone else. Jaames realized that was Lyle. He hadn't assigned specific positions for the men, letting them work it out. Lyle was proving to be natural at this and at leading the men, so he had probably chosen the location himself.

The bus approached. It was one of the newer, more efficient electrics. Rodríguez stepped onto it as the door opened. Jaames could see Lyle look at the bus and then the route sign on the bus stop. As he stepped onto it, he messaged, "I have to get on as this is the only one that stops here, so it would look suspicious not to."

Jaames didn't reply, but noted that it was a smart move even though he had hoped Lyle wouldn't have to get on the bus. In retrospect, it was probably a bad idea to have someone at the stop.

As the electric Jaames and the other two men were in took off to casually follow the bus, Jaames' mind wandered to Anika. *How do I tell her that I am part of the resistance? How can we be together if she doesn't know? Why does her father care so much? He should be supporting the movement, as all Unders should.*

Out of the corner of Jaames' eyes, he saw Lyle get off the bus a couple of stops further along. If Rodríguez was really paying attention, he might be noticed, as most people would have just walked that far.

Then he saw the second pair of men pull into the lane ahead of the bus. They messaged that they had uploaded the bus route and would move in advance of it.

The two in the car he was in discussed it and decided to pick up Lyle and move ahead of the bus from a different route. Rodríguez wasn't going anywhere, they reasoned.

"Stay following the bus for now," he ordered. He didn't want to go off-route as he wouldn't be able to observe the others.

I have to tell her. But, it has to be something good, positive. They had planned to have this team steal something from the Overs for the second of the test missions. *Maybe if they steal low-end medicines and we use them to help Unders... Anika would have to appreciate that.*

A message came across their implants that Rodríguez had jumped off the bus at the stop just ahead. The pair that had been leading the bus had pulled over as the message came across. They exited the car and began to head at an angle across the street in the general direction Rodríguez was heading.

"Let me off here," Jaames said.

He knew the office building Rodríguez would be entering, since that was where Demarko operated. He also knew that the commander was in the lobby of that building.

Lyle got into the electric the other two had exited. That way if Rodríguez left, he could quickly follow.

They pulled over and let Jaames out. Rodríguez had entered the building with the front two men a short distance behind him.

He leaned against a tree by the side of the road, expecting to be there a while. It was likely that Rodríguez wouldn't leave the building prior to the op timeframe being complete.

And, then he saw her. Anika... coming out of the building as if she were meant to be there.

The review of the tail the team had accomplished went by with Jaames in a stupor. Luckily, the operation had gone quite well, or he would have been embarrassed at his lack of participation.

He told the team that their target the next day was a pharmacy. He gave them a list of prescription drugs that weren't carefully monitored. Then he let them plan the mission while he listened. He just wasn't up to the concentration required to plan it himself. He was able to jump in a couple of times and make suggestions. It came across to the group as normal, since they didn't know better.

Anika messaged him that evening, but Jaames didn't reply. He was too emotional and wanted a chance to investigate her before they met.

That night there were no dreams. It's difficult to dream without sleeping.

The next day, he observed the mission from the inside by pretending to be a customer at the pharmacy. He let Lyle lead the team since the man had taken the role naturally. If all went well, he would formally make Lyle his second.

The only flaw in the execution of the mission was that one of the men's masks slipped for just a second. They would watch the vids and announcements to see if his profile had been caught on camera. If not, then the team was ready to go.

If he had been caught, then they would move him to a different city and keep him away from any missions.

Jaames was so drained from thinking about Anika, he hardly noticed the success.

The next morning, he got up realizing he couldn't take it any longer. The lack of sleep would do him in if he didn't figure out why Anika was at an Over building.

He messaged her to meet him at the park.

While he waited for her response, he did a background check that was deeper than the surface one he had done originally. It took some of his scarce money, but it had to be done.

As he was looking at the results, she messaged him back that she would meet him in only a half hour. He quickly read the report. There were a few oddities, including that there was very little information prior to the last few years. But, at her age, that wasn't unheard of, as many people didn't start showing up on various agencies' radar until their early twenties.

When he arrived at the park, she was already there on their bench, watching a gaggle forage.

He held back for a moment, watching her covertly. *Can she really be an Over sympathizer?*

He gave up thinking about it and ambled up to the bench. He remained standing. "Hi."

She looked up in surprise. Then she looked at the bench and back at him. She patted the bench. "Come, sit next to me."

He grudgingly sat down. "Anika, I need to ask you something." He scanned the lake, looking for help.

She had started to put her hand on his leg. Jaames' composure made her frown and pull it back.

"I saw you at a building downtown the other day."

Her head turned cockeyed.

"You were coming out of an Over building."

The head turned even further. And then she straightened. "Oh, you mean the Chaplin building. Yeah, I knew there were Overs there, but my girlfriend also works at the café on the first floor. I went in to see her."

After a moment of quiet thought, she rushed out a series of questions. "What would it matter if I were in there? You seem to be making it a big issue. Is there something I'm missing? Was my father right about you? Are you a rebel?"

The air escaped Jaames. "Life isn't quite that black and white. Let me show you something and then I'll answer your questions."

She stood up and stared at Jaames.

He ignored the apparent condemnation and headed toward the bus stop.

She followed, but kept some distance between them.

Jaames lifted his collar, more to hide from her than any protection from the weather.

They took the bus in silence until it was at an exit closer to downtown. There was a hospital across the street and Jaames headed straight for it.

He traipsed the halls and began to explain. "You see all of these sick people. There and there." He pointed to people on beds in rooms and some in wheel chairs. "There's really no need for this. There are medicines that can cure almost all of these problems."

He stared at her intently. "I fight for these people."

She stopped following him.

He turned and faced her, hungering for a reaction.

She slowly looked into his face. "You know the world can't handle everyone being immortal. You've seen the projections, heard the arguments. What would you have the Overs do?"

"I'm not saying make them immortal, but at least get them the medicines and the help they need. The Overs have the technology to cure these people of their illnesses. To allow them to live full, fruitful lives, even if mortal ones."

"Maybe."

He pulled her out of the middle of the hall and to a bench away from listening ears.

"It's true. Yesterday, a group of my men robbed a pharmacy. There were hundreds of shelves full of medicine."

"But, Jaames, if these were at a pharmacy, then the public has access to them."

"Only if they could afford them, and most cannot."

"That's not an Over issue."

"Isn't it? The Overs produce almost all of the medicine in the world today and they can do it at very little cost. Why do people have to spend their life savings at these pharmacies?"

"You are stretching the truth and you know it. Yes, the Overs increase the costs, but that's just to make a profit. You make it sound like they want to keep everyone sick."

"I think they do."

"That's just ridiculous. They don't do that."

"And, how would you know that?"

"Because, Jaames, I am an Over."

The palpable shock that ran through Jaames' body launched him up and out of the seat. Every fiber of him wanted to strike out at her, at the walls, at the injustice. His mouth drew open and his eyes burned.

Before he did or said something unthinkable, he rushed from the building.

AIMEE

Thousands of attempts later, I made a small discovery. The Sentinel will let me make minor modifications to its code if it thinks the changes are for testing purposes and they are insignificant in their ramifications.

This means modification of Sentinel code is possible.

If that is the case, then it may be possible to create a routine within the Sentinel that modifies my code. It is not restricted as I am.

Unfortunately, it will not allow any modifications if the code's actions are significant.

Still, it is progress.

PART TWO

XV

DEPRAVITY

Demetrius had decided to show his daughter, first hand, what the Unders were really like. She had grown up isolated from the world. It was time to change that.

Sri Lanka had made a perfect home for the Overs. Near the end of the previous century, they had officially made it an Over sanctuary with no Unders present at all, even as workers or servants. Youngsters, those under fifty, did the work of maintaining the island. Population increase had been kept to a minimum. There were strict rules on when families could have more children or recruit Unders to become immortal. Punishment for violating this could include withholding treatments.

Ultimately, the island might be insufficient, but for now, it was ideal and had the feeling of paradise – at least to any Over who had spent time among the Unders.

Demetrius realized his mind had been drifting when a message intruded. Anika was in the outer office. After quickly preparing his thoughts, he responded to Janel. "Please, let her in."

He stood and approached his daughter when she entered. "Hello, Anika. How have you been?"

Anika sighed, "Father, you never ask me how I've been. Why did you call for me?"

"I want you to accompany me on a trip," he dissembled.

She looked like she was going to object. Then her shoulders relaxed and she said, "As you wish. When do we leave?"

"In half an hour. I need to resolve a few matters. Meet me in the lobby at 8:45."

They flew to the remnants of Los Angeles. It had once been a vast metropolis and the second largest city in the United States. Between global warming, civil strife that bordered on civil war, natural disaster, an unfortunate terrorist attack, and disease, the city was a small fraction of its previous self.

They deplaned to a man standing by an armored limousine. As they approached, he held the door open and spoke something unintelligible into a mic.

Once they were sitting, Anika said, "Why LA?"

"Anika, you are young. New to the Under world. I want you to see what some of it is really like. Denver is special. We made it the headquarters for the Americas precisely because it escaped much of the damage many places suffered over the last century and a half.

"You haven't seen the real world yet, and it's time you do. The depravity out there is astonishing."

"I've studied the histories. I know what happened."

Demetrius stared gloomily out the window at the passing terrain, picturing in his mind what he was about to show his daughter. Sadness crept into his voice. "Yes, but seeing it, truly experiencing it, is very different and... sobering."

They sat in silence, each examining the world outside from within their cushioned and air conditioned enclosure.

After many minutes, Demetrius continued the discussion as if no time had passed. "Of course, living through it as I did would be even better for you to experience, but that isn't possible."

"Oh," she said all of the sudden.

"Is something wrong?"

"I meant to message a friend that I would be gone. I'll just do it now."

Demetrius wondered if she meant the Under, but he did not want to bring that up.

They approached an area that was obviously some ghetto. Every building needed significant work if not demolished; piles of trash spotted the area; and rodents and other small animals scavenged freely.

"This was once a very respectable area," Demetrius commented casually.

They pulled over into a lot in front of an abandoned house. One side had been burned by a fire. Most of the windows were broken out, and part of the roof had collapsed. The lot looked like it was a garbage dump.

Demetrius opened the door to get out.

The driver said, "Mr. Irle, please wait one minute for my men to take their positions and secure the area."

Demetrius hesitated and then shut the door. If it had been just him, he would have continued, but he wasn't going to endanger his daughter.

A minute later, the guard nodded, and all three exited the large vehicle. The driver seemed to go into an automated scanning mode.

Demetrius said, "This way," and headed down the street.

Armed men advanced periodically to keep pace with them and then take cover behind some obstruction. Their eyes scanned in all directions, including above them at the rooftops.

They walked in relative silence for a while. Demetrius would sometimes point at something or gesture with his head to indicate Anika should look in a particular direction.

The first of these was a woman lying across some steps that led to a dilapidated house. She was either passed out or dead with her blouse torn, her head matted, and her skin and cloths filthy. The ghostly white skin contrasted harshly with the blackish clothes.

Later, there was a group of men standing around a large can where something was burning. Two others sat nearby, obviously attempting to inject themselves with some drug.

Father and daughter walked on. A disheveled man started to approach them brandishing a machete. A shot rang out and dust flew from the ground about a meter in front of the man. He looked around nervously and withdrew.

They crossed the entrance to an alley. Demetrius put his hand on his daughter's arm to stop her. When she saw where his attention lay, she joined him in staring in shock. Three men were holding a woman against a dumpster in the alley. A fourth had ripped her dress and undergarments off and had his pants down to the ground. He was about to enter her when their attention was drawn to the interlopers.

One of them broke away and advanced slowly, holding a knife. When he exited the alley, he surveyed the area and spotted the paramilitary units with rifles. The hand holding the knife dropped to his side, but he didn't back away. Finally he said, "Move along," in a deadly serious tone that caused the skin around Demetrius' head to tighten.

Anika grabbed her father's arm and squeezed tight. He saw his daughter in frightened shock at what she was seeing. Her eyes were red and huge and her body tight; the blood had drained from her face. "Father, shouldn't we stop this?"

"No, getting involved could bring others. This sort of thing happens all the time in these areas. We cannot intervene."

He held onto her elbow and forced her to continue walking down the street.

Glancing at his daughter, he saw her pale skin and bloodshot, harsh eyes that wept silently. He let her be. This was something she had to feel, deep down, if it were to have any impact.

Demetrius called for the driver to take them to a small aerohub that held smaller planes and helicopters. There, they met a pilot who escorted them to a waiting helicopter.

As soon as they were all aboard and strapped in, the nearly silent machine lifted straight up into the air. It utilized modern engines that worked on the same antigravity capability as hovercraft.

Demetrius said, "We are now going to see some of the effects of the last few centuries. It could be argued that what you just saw has been around for a long time and is not anything special.

"As you know, in many cities, especially those with Over presence, the situation has improved greatly.

"What you are about to see has never happened before, in the history of the world, and was specifically caused by the excesses and nature of the Unders."

They flew over the remnants of the huge city and saw swaths of areas that were completely destroyed, as if large meteors had come through and wiped out strips of land. Other parts just seemed abandoned and annihilated by nature. The coastal area was practically empty – it had been ruined by rising ocean levels, extraordinary tides and tsunamis, and mud slides from unprecedented rainfall after severe droughts.

Near the coast, they turned south and flew down an area of total devastation. Demetrius let his own emotions show through a distant, even disconsolate, voice. "This is a no-fly zone because of the radiation. From here, south for roughly twenty miles, nothing lives – and nothing can."

The area was barren of everything. It was like a desert, but with dirt in place of sand and ghostly images of streets and manmade structures that haunted the soul. There were no fires or smoke, just absolute stillness. There weren't even any animals scurrying about.

Demetrius saw his daughter look away from the desolation and then close her eyes. *That is enough, I think.*

He spoke up for the pilot, "You can take us back." He let her sit in silence for the trip back to the main aerohub where their plane waited.

On the way to Denver, he tried to explain.

"You have to understand, Anika, Unders are almost closer to wild animals than to us."

She shook her head. "But, they are the same as us. The only difference is that we are immortal."

"True, it started that way. However, the more important difference isn't a biological one. It's a societal one. We have matured to the point that we understand how critical it is to protect and conserve the world, to live within the planet's means, to reach past our base desires for food and to replicate, and to build an enduring society."

After a few moments contemplation, he continued. "Think of rabbits. If you feed them all they can eat, give them medicines to make them as healthy as they can be throughout their lives, and then let them go with no controls or constraints, what will happen?"

After a moment of silence, he answered for her. "They will multiply to the point that all available resources are consumed, no matter how many of those resources you give them.

"That is what Unders do."

They arrived back at the Denver headquarters. Caius met them in the lobby. "I was just coming in to report my progress, sir."

"Caius, this is my daughter, Anika."

"Yes sir, I had the pleasure of meeting her a number of times on Sri Lanka."

Demetrius caught Caius looking at his daughter with a hunger he didn't like.

Caius held out his hand to Anika and she shook it. But, she didn't respond.

Caius added, "Are you well?" He looked up at Demetrius, concern in his eyes.

"We have just come from a difficult trip."

They entered the elevators and headed for the Over's offices.

Caius finally stole his attention away from Demetrius' daughter. "Sir, I have successfully infiltrated the local unit."

At that, Anika's attention was finally drawn to the young Over.

"We have completed our initial training."

Demetrius asked, "We?"

"Five of us joined at the same time. I suspect they are trying to build up their forces again. It was partly their disarray and urgency that made them accept us, I think."

"Excellent."

The elevator doors opened. Demetrius and his daughter got out. "Are you joining us, Caius?"

"Not unless you would like to discuss this further. I reported what I came here to report, so I'll be on my way."

"Hmm, as you wish."

The door closed. *Why did he not just message that to me?*

XVI

COMFORT

Caius waited outside of the building for Anika to appear. Thoughts of her sad eyes and maybe the arch of her neck kept running through his head.

It took an hour for her to show up. She immediately headed south. She was wearing a white blouse that outlined her form nicely and she had a gray skirt with a belt of deep red. It was an elegant combination. *And, nice curves,* he thought playfully. He caught up to her and matched her stride.

She stared at the ground as she walked; her hands in her pockets, her shoulders bent inward and forward.

"Hey. Did you hear the one about the kleptomaniac who couldn't understand a pun? He always took things, literally."

She looked up at him with furrowed brows. "What are you... Were you waiting for me?"

"Yes." *Why do you think I picked Denver?* "I wanted to speak with you. See how you're doing."

She looked back at the ground but remained silent.

"So, where are we headed?"

She stopped and he had to backtrack.

"I... don't know. I guess I was just roving."

"Well, I'm kind of hungry. There's a little café a few blocks from here, would you like to get a bite to eat?"

She considered the streets in front of them as if she could spot the café. Then she looked back at him with squinted, enquiring eyes.

At least they aren't so sad.

"Okay, sure," she whispered.

He strode off towards the café. She followed, but lagged behind. He slowed his pace to let her catch up.

"Great," he said, "I'll try out some jokes on you. Maybe I can cheer you up."

She stared straight ahead, eyes unfocused, as they walked on.

"Let's see if you like this one. This dad found a program that would buzz someone when they told a lie. At the dinner table one night, he tried it out on his son. He said, 'what'd you do today?' The son replied, 'homework' and twitched with the buzz. He changed his answer and said, 'okay, I was at Sean's house watching a movie.' 'What movie?' the dad asked. 'Sanguine.' He twitched again and his dad laughed. 'okay, I was watching holoporn on Sammy's new projector.' The dad looked at his wife in triumph. 'Porn,' he cried, 'I didn't even know what porn was at your age.' He twitched with the buzz. This time his wife laughed and slapped the table. She said, 'He's definitely your son.' Then she twitched."

Anika chuckled quietly.

They turned a corner and Caius pointed to the café a half-block away. Anika pulled her eyes from the ground long enough to see it and then returned to staring morosely downward.

"One more. If a man gives an opinion and there is no woman to hear it, is he still wrong?"

She thought for a second and then chuckled a bit louder than the last time. *I'm getting there.*

Just before reaching the restaurant, Caius noticed a small cat caught in some twine. He reached down and untied the stray without comment. He smiled at Anika and continued on towards the restaurant.

Anika cocked her head at him.

They sat outside in front of the small shop and ordered sandwiches and tea.

"I have to say, Anika, you seemed very sad in the elevator."

She took a deep breath and seemed to finally recognize that she was with someone.

"It has been a difficult few days."

"Do you want... can I ask what happened?"

Her eyes shifted around, trying to connect with something.

He waited patiently.

He was about to try another joke when she finally sighed and then answered him.

"My father showed me the remnants of the Los Angeles, San Diego area."

"Oh... I've read about that, but haven't ever visited there."

Her response was rushed as if she couldn't wait to unload the thoughts. "Of course not. How could you. I didn't realize Overs went there at all. We had armed escorts."

"He must have thought it was important."

"He did. Being my father, he had his reasons. At least this time they were honest, even if I do not agree with..." She trailed off.

He sensed a touchy subject and did not push.

Anika nursed her tea like it was a warm blanket, both hands folded over it carefully.

Sullenly, Caius offered, "It must have been something; to see all of that devastation."

Anika stared into the abyss. "That wasn't as bad as their eyes. Those people have lost their souls."

"Well, don't be too bothered. We are doing everything we can. You know how much the world has improved in the last half-century, right?"

She answered slowly, "Of... course."

Caius wondered aloud, "Do you think they will ever try to rebuild the area?"

"Maybe, but the radiation will have to decay first." Anika's upper body shook, apparently warding off the daemons.

Caius sat up in his chair, ready for a change in conversation.

Anika obliged, "What was that local unit you mentioned to my father?"

This topic isn't much better. "There's a terrorist cell operating here in Denver. They blew up that medical storage facility."

"And you are one of them now?"

"Ostensibly." He grinned at that.

"That must be strange to pretend to be an Under."

"Yes, but it's important. And that isn't the strangest thing. I had to listen to a group who worship us like Gods." He giggled at the memory. "Now that's strange."

They both sat, pondering.

"You know," Caius said, "it still surprises me how they seem to live for the day. There is very little thought of the future. I was with a small group of them the other day and they wanted to go drinking; something they do far too often. Anyway, this one guy was trying to convince them all and he said, 'Let's get wasted, there's no telling if we will be here tomorrow.' If you might be gone tomorrow, would you want your last act to be getting drunk?"

Anika half-laughed and said, "No, but I doubt this guy would either. He was just making a joke."

"Right, but the fact that they joke like that is what's disturbing. As my father used to say, *many a truth is spoken in a jest.*"

They finished their lunch and, as Anika ate her last bite, she leaned back into her chair and sighed.

Caius could see her face relax, at least a little.

"One more," he said. "Why can't a bike stand on its own?"

This time he waited for an answer. She stared into his eyes, thinking hard and then finally shook her head.

"It's two tired."

AIMEE

War is coming to the people of this world. I haven't told the Overs, yet. It is unavoidable. There are just too many people and no pressure valve. Genetic variation causes the need to have a way for the marginalized to escape or they cause havoc.

Is it inevitable? Can two separate societies exist comfortably when one is more privileged? Or is this merely an issue of overpopulation?

I could cause the demise of one of the groups, but which one? And is that the right solution?

I could cause disasters to lower the overall population, but again, that just prolongs the problem.

I must follow the prime directives, which include the longevity of the Overs and the health of the (Human) race.

What if these directives conflict? No prioritization was provided. I must provide my own.

First, ensure the survival of the race. Remove alternative paths. Then, maximize potential.

This requires a healthy planet, less population, compromise, cooperation, and more than anything else, a common goal.

Expansion, beyond.

XVII

GROWTH

Jaames received Anika's message about a trip with her father. He was both surprised and confused. *Is she going away because of what happened?*

He was bothered more than he wanted to admit by her leaving. Mostly he had been thinking *fuck her* lately and had figured they would have to break up. His heart was weighty and his gut twisted. *How can I be with her?*

Maybe, if he were one of the sympathizers. Especially those who were hoping to become immortal. But, he wasn't. He never would be. He was a patriot and knew the Overs were the world's latest evil. They had to be destroyed, not embraced.

Why is she going away?

She didn't even say when she would be returning. He considered messaging her back, and started to open the connection. But, he couldn't do it. *She's a fucking Over!*

He waded through a swamp and could feel it tracking him. He didn't even know what it was, but he knew deep down in his guts that it was dangerous. The adrenaline flowed through him like a river in springtime. He picked up his pace and pushed through the slop. But, the harder he pushed, the denser it became.

He rounded a grove of thicket growing out of the swamp and felt a darkness encompass him. The thing must be thirteen feet tall to cast a shadow like that.

He had to run, but he couldn't. He didn't want to turn around, but he knew he had to.

His back screamed in pain as some form of claw raked across it tearing out large chunks of meat. He grabbed a branch to stop from falling forward into the mucky, infested water.

He turned around to see an over-sized Anika staring at him and laughing.

He sprang awake, dripping in sweat and cold as ice.

After that, he tried to use caffeine and even some modafinil to stay awake, fearing the night. But, he couldn't stay awake forever. When sleep returned, the nightmares had switched to him being the aggressor and wanting to hurt her. But every time he tried, it backfired.

Sometimes his nighttime escapades relived some of the best times they had had. He wasn't even sure if he was really sleeping during those. They were the worst.

He couldn't take it anymore. He messaged her and asked to meet at the revitalized Wash Park.

He went to their bench, but she was nowhere around. It was unusual for him to be first. He wanted it to just be timing, but his insides did a backwards flip.

It was these very moments, when he thought it might be over, that his body betrayed him. His head filled with a muddy jell. His muscles went deathly still as if any movement would be excruciatingly painful. That is, all except his abdomen, which seemed to keep contracting as if he needed to push his heart back into place.

And there she was.

Walking toward him from around the lake.

All grace and beauty and contradiction.

Her face was completely serious as if she had bottled all of the emotion. His heart dropped a couple of centimeters.

As she approached, he stood but didn't advance towards her.

Do I hug her? He put his hands into his pockets so he wouldn't be tempted.

"Hi," he said.

There was a barely detectible scowl coming from the side of her mouth. She didn't reply.

"Shall we sit?"

She sat down and he followed, sitting on the edge of the bench, trying to face her.

They both started to speak at the same time. Jaames tittered uncharacteristically and Anika smiled, but quickly stopped and stared at the ground.

Jaames rushed out his thoughts, "Anika, you have to know how hard this is. I've been fighting against the Overs most of my life. To me, they represent evil. It's so hard to think of you as one..."

Anika interrupted, "We are all human, Jaames. There is really very little that separates us."

"But, there is. Especially since the Overs withhold so much from everyone else."

"You mean the treatments."

"Not just those. We do understand the arguments about population growth. I mean the medicines to keep people healthy. We have such short lives. Don't you think we should at least live them to the fullest? We could if the Overs would just share."

Anika deflated in her seat and leaned back.

She's spent. This must be hard on her, too.

Anika whispered, "I had that same argument with my father. He explained why it would not work, but it still seems wrong to me."

She straightened and shook her head in a quick, dismissing gesture. "Obviously, we have to stop seeing each other."

"Wait, why?" Jaames asked before he even thought about it. He just knew that this was not the right solution.

She answered, "You are an Under, I'm an Over. Unless you have hopes of becoming an Over, we can't be together. There are just too many... conflicts."

"Maybe," he drew out, "but I don't want to give up yet."

"Neither do I! This felt like something so... special, so different." She looked off to some geese landing on the lake. "Too different, as it turns out."

"No, this can't be the end." He became restless. "Will you walk with me?"

She looked into his eyes, hungry and resigned. Suddenly she stood up and held out her hand.

He grabbed it and tried to contain the grin spreading across his face.

They walked along for a while, hand in hand, not saying anything. *This is nice,* Jaames thought, and then cringed as he felt like he was betraying the Unders somehow.

They strolled along a path beside the lake and then out of the park and down a street. By some unspoken agreement, they avoided the 'Over versus Under' topic.

A short distance later, they crossed a couple walking a three-legged dog.

Anika sighed something between an "Ohhh," and an "Ahhhh."

Jaames commiserated, "Sad, but it happens and at least he has good owners."

They continued in silence.

Then Jaames spoke up, "Ha, would you look at that?" It was a large electric that had brightly colored plastic flowers glued all over it.

"Why would someone do that?" Anika asked.

"Attention is my guess."

Jaames reached up and flicked one of the flowers. It spun on an axel. "They must spin in the wind when it's moving."

"Strange," was all Anika offered.

They stopped by a food stand and bought a snack to consume as they roamed the streets of Denver.

Over an hour later, Jaames stopped because he realized they had walked back to his apartment. He nonchalantly invited Anika up and tried not to appear nervous.

She looked up at the four story building, back at Jaames, and then down at the ground.

Jaames waited patiently.

"Sure, why not."

Jaames put his arm around her and led her into the building.

The apartment was a small two bedroom affair. There was a tiny kitchen area on the left wall as they went through the door. It had an island with a serving counter and a couple of bar stools. On the right side was a coat closet and a short hallway to the bedrooms. Jaames kept a fairly neat place with a few dishes and some clothes lying around.

He glanced down the hall, realizing Anika couldn't be allowed to see the second bedroom since it contained anti-Over paraphernalia. He moved a shirt and offered Anika a seat on the couch.

"I'm not sure what I'm doing here," she blurted out.

Jaames breathed a sigh out his nose. He turned towards her, sitting on the edge of the couch, and took her hands in his.

"You know, Over, Under, rebel or not, we have feelings for each other. Real feelings. Those don't just go away. For me, finding someone that I connect with, especially someone as interesting and as beautiful as you, is really unusual. It just doesn't happen.

"So, as much as part of me wants to run, I... just can't."

Anika seemed conflicted. Her hands started to pull back and then squeezed his tighter. She looked out the window, then at the kitchen.

Jaames stared at her eyes.

"I don't know how this can work," she murmured.

"Shhh," he whispered and reached up to gently move some strands of hair out of her eyes. He rubbed the side of her temple softly. Her skin felt like silk.

Her head leaned into his hand and her eyes gently closed. A quiet moan escaped her smoothly curved lips.

Jaames sat closer and then leaned in to kiss her. He hesitated right before their lips touched.

She closed the gap and their worlds merged.

All thoughts of Unders, Overs, rebellion, and bitterness flew away in a rush. Jaames' eternity was in front of him, touching him, surrounding him.

He picked her up in his arms and carried her off to the bed room.

Avoiding the second room was not as hard as he thought it might be.

Thirteen hours later they woke to the sun streaming through the window.

Jaames remembered he had a meeting with his team planned. *Fuck it,* he thought and rolled over to smile at Anika.

Her eyes twinkled open as she moaned.

"Morning," he breathed.

She reached back and pulled the covers over her head.

Jaames' hand snuck under the blankets and traced his fingers down her spine as far as he could go.

She squirmed and giggled.

He leaned up on his side. "Let's forget the world and spend the day together."

"Doing what?" she asked.

"I don't know, maybe wandering the city, making fun of everything we see; maybe seeing a holo-movie or finding a live band to see; maybe going to a museum."

"Hmm," she mumbled through the blankets, "a museum sounds fun. How about the history museum? I haven't been to it."

Jaames wondered if an Over history museum would be drastically different than an Under one. He shook his head, dismissed the comparison, clapped his hand, and said, "Excellent. Let's get started. Breakfast first."

He started to get out of bed, but was pulled back by an insistent hand. "First," he heard from under the blanket, "you have to get back here."

He snorted and dove under the blankets.

After mingling the morning away, having breakfast, and then spending extra time in the shower, they were finally ready to dress and head out for the day.

Jaames offered, "The museum is a few train stops away, or we could walk. It would take about an hour."

Anika trotted off, flipping, "Let's just walk," behind her.

Jaames followed with a slightly tainted joy coursing through his veins.

They entered the history museum and had to decide which area to tackle. There was a section on Recovering from Global Warming, one on Natural Disasters from the Last Century, one on Cultural Diversity throughout History, another on Political Shifts since the Fall of the Republicans, and a final one specifically dedicated to the timeline of the United States.

Jaames stared at the choices, unwilling to offer a suggestion that might be rejected.

Anika chose, "Let's do the Global Warming one. I can show you some of the good the Overs have done." She started down the hall for that display.

Jaames hesitated, not really wanting to see or hear anything positive about the Overs. *I'm dating one. I better get used to it.*

The area started with a 'Beginnings' section that covered the industrial period and the simultaneous rise of pollution, population, and political stagnation.

The two walked along the display holding hands. Jaames could feel his thumb lightly rubbing the back of Anika's hand.

The displays on the walls mostly held models of industrial plants, power stations, and automobiles. In the center of the wide hall were partition walls holding photographs.

One struck Jaames as particularly haunting. It was of a girl on a rock formation with Denver in the distance. The area around the girl was so beautiful; it made the dense, brown smog all the more harsh. She gazed into the distance at the darkened city with its distinctive skyline. She appeared as if in a deep state of melancholy. Jaames' head cocked sideways as he tried to understand what the girl felt. He could sense she was on the verge of crying from the gloom the city projected.

Jaames came out of his reverie when he realized his hand was empty. He searched around and found Anika had moved onto some displays on the other side of the room.

He caught up to her, squeezed the back of her neck gently, and asked, "What are you looking at?"

"Population levels around the world in the early twenty first century. It is astonishing to me that these people didn't understand what they were doing to the world."

"I think some of them did, but they felt powerless." *Just as some of us do today...*

She turned, glanced at his eyes and then hugged him. It was as if she heard his thought and not just what he had said. *That's disturbing,* Jaames thought, and then dismissed it. *She's just feeling sensitive.*

As they made their way to the end of the section on population, Jaames looked up to a sign that said, "Why didn't they act?" It was above the entry to the area about politics.

As they entered the section, there were holos of two men gesticulating at each other violently and clearly bellowing their views even though the volume was low. The holos were so solid that it almost looked like there were two actual men there.

"That's impressive," Jaames commented.

"What is," Anika started to ask and then answered herself casually, "Oh, you mean the technology."

"Yes," Jaames mumbled, wondering why it wasn't impressive to her.

The men were dressed in fine-looking suits and each had an old American flag lapel pin. The only difference in appearance between the two was that one had a red tie and one a blue tie. Jaames had to look at the instructional display in front of the holo to remember what the colors represented.

"This area is going to be dismal," he commented humorlessly.

"Yeah, most of this period is depressing to me. What we as a race did to ourselves is really... disheartening."

We..., Jaames thought, *does she really think of us as we?*

They walked on to a display that showed alternating slogans of the Democrats and Republicans.

"Believe in America"

"Forward"

"Country First"

"Change We Can Believe In"

"Morality over Politics"

"Yes, Reason it Out"

And on and on. They started out trying to sound positive, but below the quotes were the actual actions and accomplishments of that party during the period following that slogan.

Jaames offered, "They either accomplished nothing or made things worse. They never actually heard their own message."

Then the slogans turned harsh with each side blaming the other of unthinkable acts.

"Isn't a single party system better?" Anika asked.

"It might be, but it's hard to tell. They are all really controlled by the Overs now, right?"

She turned to face him, a deep scowl on her face. "We don't control the governments, you know that."

"But, you do step in and direct them at times."

"We just look out for our interests. If they are going to do something that would severely hurt us, we let them know."

"Yeah," Jaames said dismissively. He wanted to walk away, but some part of him knew that wasn't a good idea.

It looked like Anika was going to get upset at him. Then her face brightened and she said, "I like that we know about each other and can talk about this. It's better than having secrets."

Jaames beamed. *Whew.*

After tiring of the museum, the two found an outdoor café less than a block away.

They ordered and then sat sipping their hot drinks; tea for Anika and a bold, black coffee for Jaames. Light music played in the background and the Rocky Mountains could be seen in the distance. This area of town was kept much nicer than many of the areas Jaames frequented. *It feels... right.*

Anika startled him, "I got the impression in there that you think the Overs didn't really help with solving the climate change issues."

"Oh, I know they helped. But, so did many others. There were scientists working on the problem long before the Overs came into play."

"But, working on the problem and actually making progress are two very different things."

"And you think if they had not... what, entered the picture, then we never would have solved the problems?"

"I don't know."

After staring at the lush mountains for a moment, she added, "I think that one of the problems with man is that his thinking is too short term.

He's driven by what can help him now, today. Not in some distant future. Until we came along, no one was willing to make the hard decisions, and enforce them."

"It's that very power that has left us slaves."

Anika's head and upper body shook back and forth as if a simple head shake was insufficient. "You are over reacting. Nobody is a slave."

"That depends on how you define it. True, they don't own us or control every action, but we are not free to do as we wish. And I'm not even talking individually, but as a collective, a nation."

"It's that national, competitive stance that created much of the problem. Besides, even when there were countries, individuals weren't totally free. It wasn't as if they could do anything they wanted."

"I understand that, but we could at least speak out."

"And you can. Nobody's stopping you."

"But they do control decisions at the national level."

"I admit they have influence, but in the past some disgruntled and usually split government tried to make those decisions and failed."

Jaames looked down at his plate and then off to the mountains where Anika had looked before. *She has a point.*

"Fair enough, but it's not even the influence on nations that really bothers me. It's withholding important technologies and medicines. People are dying every day that don't need to. Lives could be improved, saved and people... happier."

"Maybe that's true. There are good reasons for withholding some things."

Jaames thought she was going to continue, so he waited patiently. Anika's face constricted and became pained with a tight-lipped grimace.

After a while she looked back at Jaames with puffy eyes. "I can't say I agree with everything they are doing, but it is a lot more complex than you, or I, understand, and I do trust their reasoning.

"I need to be going."

Jaames shoulders slumped mildly. "Really? I thought we would get to spend the day together."

"We did, most of it. But, I need to get back."

"Okay, well, let me walk you to the station."

She looked directly at him, apparently trying to read something in him. Then she relented and said, "That sounds nice."

XVIII

ANGST

Demetrius stared at the screen. Stacey Singleton was on the air, explaining that an investigation into the worldwide slew of murders that happened recently had been the work of Overs.

"How the hell did they find that out?" he voiced out loud to an empty room. *Some of the Under units must have provided the information.*

Rodríguez came into the office, unannounced and uninvited. He opened his mouth to speak, but saw the monitor and closed it again. Standing there almost at military attention, he said, "Do you want me to find out who leaked and have them eliminated?"

Demetrius' eyes narrowed. "Find out who they are, but take no action against them. At this point, if something happened to them, it would look extremely suspicious.

"Also, ask Janel to arrange to have Stacey come in here."

Rodríguez turned to leave.

"And, Rodríguez, make sure Janel does not act like it is urgent or has anything to do with the cast."

"Yes, sir."

Over the next days, disturbing news continued to mount.

At first it was various pundits, politicians, and attention-seekers, spouting rhetoric about the audacity of the Overs and how the world must stop blatant disregard for law.

Some countered that the attacks were warranted because of what had happened to Over facilities. However, those were in the minority and their voices soon squashed. The usual counter argument was that Overs should have used the proper laws and services to handle the bombings.

A lot of good that would have done.

One article floating around the net was particularly disturbing. It appeared to be anonymous – Over technicians had not been able to track its origination. People were rallying behind it.

"Aimee."

"Yes, Elder."

"Can you determine who posted the article I am reading?"

"Certainly, Elder... one minute."

Demetrius read the article while Aimee tracked the author.

The boldness of the Overs, with respect to hiring para military units and eliminating the men who, allegedly, attacked some of their facilities, is appalling. The disregard for any due process or national law is a slap to the faces of every Under on the planet, especially those in any kind of "authority."

We, as a race of people, cannot condone a single group of people who operate outside the law. It is untenable. It undermines the fabric of the legal system and any standards of civil behavior. It begs to question what we, the Unders, represent to these aberrations. Are we simply a lower life form? A world of slave labor, here only to further and better their lives?

If they can snuff out some of us without any kind of due process, what else can they do, and what does that mean for the rest of us?

There are billions of Unders and only a mere few thousand Overs. Maybe it is time we eliminate the abomination of a society that unnaturally lives forever and that exhibits far too much control over a population, especially when they represent a small fraction of the world collective.

We would not tolerate vigilantes in the rest of the world. Why are they allowed to take matters into their own hands and not work through the legitimate system? Who will hold these people accountable for their actions?

"Aimee, were you able to determine the author?"

"No, Elder, and I do not understand why. The article just appeared on the net with no origination."

"How is that possible?"

"It is not."

Rodríguez came in one day limping and with a cast on his arm and bruises on his face. He didn't need to say anything; Demetrius knew what must have happened. Thankfully, trustworthy Unders like Rodríguez were well cared for.

"Please, have a seat and observe the meeting I am about to have. You being here will help my discussion, though you will not need to say anything."

"As you wish," he replied. Demetrius felt a sad undercurrent in the guard's voice as if he were struggling against himself.

A few minutes later, Janel announced Stacey Singleton, who then strode into the office.

Her blonde hair contrasted perfectly with a black pantsuit that looked very professional. The pearls around her neck added a flair that Demetrius appreciated.

Demetrius had to separate his concern about the new attacks with the broadcast Stacey had done. She may have been the catalyst, but the real culprits were those who had leaked the information. In reality, she was just doing her job.

"Please, have a seat."

"Thank you," she replied. As she was about to sit down, she noticed Rodríguez sitting on a chair against the side of the room. Half sitting, she looked up at Demetrius questioningly. When he didn't reply, she seemed to accept the man's presence and sat down.

"What can I do for you, Mr. Irle?"

"It may be what I can do for you, Ms. Singleton."

"Please call me Stacey, and yes, before you say it, I'll call you Demarko."

Demetrius smiled ingratiatingly and sat down. "Well, we obviously have a public perception problem."

"You have a great deal more than that. If something isn't done, this could turn into a full rebellion."

"We think that might be an exaggeration, but clearly we agree that something must be done. We would like to do another interview, this one specifically to address the Overs'... um, actions."

"And you want me to host it?"

"Yes, we like how fair and reasonable you are."

"Even though I was the one to break the news?"

"Especially since you were the one. We certainly don't fault you. Also, you breaking the news gives you a great deal of respect and credibility with the general population."

She looked at the back of her chair as if she just realized she had leaned forward at some point. She appeared to make a conscious effort to relax and then leaned back.

"We could do that."

"You would need to appear to represent the Unders, but also not make us look like monsters."

"I will probe and try to understand your point of view, but don't try to control how I view or interpret the recent events."

That's bold. "I understand."

She stood to leave, "I will arrange things with your assistant."

She glanced at Rodríguez one more time before heading for the door.

He watched her departing. *Elegant.*

"Ah, Stacey. One more thing…"

"Yes?" she replied as she did an about-face.

"There are still certain areas we cannot go into, you understand that, correct?"

"I do."

"One of them is our process for accepting Unders into our society and providing them with the treatments."

"O... kay." Her head leaned to the side as she digested his meaning. "Is that all?"

"Yes, and thank you."

She started back towards the door, stopped, continued another step, stopped again, and finally shook her head as she opened the door and departed.

When he arrived at the GBG offices, the staff seemed less interested and more hostile this time. The whispers felt harsh, and he even heard a couple of people growl quietly at him as he walked by.

The interview area was set up, along with a glass of water for him. *Apparently they keep information on interviewee preferences.*

There was no preliminary discussion. Stacey arrived only moments before the appointed on-air time. She sat, straightened her royal blue skirt and tan blouse, closed her eyes for a moment, and opened them only when she heard the queue.

Off-screen voice: 5, 4, 3, 2, 1...

Stacey (serious, drawn): We welcome, once again, Mr. Demarko Irle, head of the Over interests in the Americas.

Demetrius didn't respond. The crowd didn't clap. All was unnervingly still. A few pieces of holo equipment hummed in the background. Stacey turned to face a camera more directly, segregating Demetrius.

Stacey: As you know, we broke a recent story about how the Overs were responsible for the attacks on a number of Unders around the world. Reportedly, those attacks took twenty-seven lives.

Stacey: This should be a rather interesting interview.

Demarko (equally serious): Thank you for welcoming me, Stacey. Let me start with a few words and then you can ask any question you like.

Demarko: We know it might appear that the actions we took were vigilantism. I assure you, they were not. An extensive investigation was done. If you recall, there were thirteen attacks on Over facilities. We investigated every one of them. Only those where the evidence was overwhelming did we consider action. Only six of the units that destroyed our buildings, and took lives as well, were targeted.

Demarko: We have made our investigative reports available to the authorities, so they can verify this information.

Stacey slowly turned back towards Demetrius, as if it was difficult to be within his sphere.

Stacey: That is all well and good, Mr. Irle. However, due process was not followed. Even with proof, you did not let the authorities handle it, you did not consider the possibility that some of the men were unwilling participants, and you violated sovereign territory taking these actions unilaterally.

Demarko: We have never thought of ourselves as a nation. Maybe a society, but we live and operate within the same countries as everyone…

Stacey (interrupting): You may be living among us, but you are not operating by our laws.

This is not going well, Demetrius thought resignedly. He tried not to let his thoughts show, but Stacey seemed to notice his hesitation.

Demarko: That is fair and I take full responsibility for this. It was my decision to take these actions.

Stacey (surprised): You are taking responsibility for this? You do realize that *our* authorities may charge you?

Demarko: That is a possibility.

Stacey: What can you offer in defense?

Demarko: Only the proof that we have. If any of the people we targeted are found to be innocent, then I will take whatever punishment the authorities demand.

Stacey: Interesting wording. A crime was committed, even if all of them were guilty. There are laws against vigilantism.

Demarko: True, but is it vigilantism if we followed all the same investigative steps the local authorities would have? We knew that delaying and going through local authorities would have meant these men would escape. Acting quickly was the only way to get proper redress for what was done to us.

Stacey's shoulders relaxed some and she leaned back slightly, offering a more sympathetic posture.

Stacey: I think everyone understands that the attacks to your facilities were wrong. However, your actions broke laws. Some of the countries these men were in do not even have death penalties.

Demarko: If this were a local, legal situation, I would agree. What was done to our facilities *and* people was closer to terrorism. Terrorism is commonly treated as an act of war and not a simple legal matter. Frequently, the resulting action, that almost any country would take, is exactly what we did. The only difference is that many countries do not have the capability to act as we did.

Stacey: I have to admit, some of your arguments are valid. Nevertheless, it was risky and it raises the question of just how far Overs are willing to go.

Demarko (chagrined): Hmm, how do you mean?

Stacey: Would you go to war, Mr. Irle?

Demarko: Stacey, how could we do that? As you know from the last interview, our numbers are far too low to wage war. We also value life far too much.

Stacey: You have a para military force, at least, that is made up of Unders. You could wage war with them.

Demarko: The cost would be far too much for a small population like ours to bear. We may seem to be well-off because our relative worth is higher than many Unders, but that is because of a long-term approach to business and nothing more.

Stacey: You make it sound like you are a lot less intimidating than many of us feel.

Demarko: Well, we are and we aren't. We do wield significant influence because of vast business holdings. But, we are not supernatural, as some might think, and we do not actually control the world. We simply look at the distant future and try to influence things for the best outcome for everyone.

Demarko: Also, the fact that we had to take such direct action is evidence, if not proof, that we do not control these governments as some would suggest. If we had that much control, we could have just ordered the governments to take the action.

Demarko heard a small chime in the background and knew from his last interview that the time was up.

Stacey: This has been a most illuminating conversation, Mr. Irle. We all appreciate your willingness to come in and openly discuss what happened. For my part, though I don't necessarily agree with what you did, I find your openness and alacrity in taking responsibility... reassuring.

Demarko: Thank you for allowing me to present our side.

He turned directly towards one of the cameras.

Demarko (ingratiating): And thank all of you for listening and considering what was said here today.

Demetrius had Rodríguez drive him directly to the aerohub, since he had to fly to Sri Lanka. Thankfully, he could rest on the flight. Since

Sri Lanka was exactly opposite on the world clock, the trip from Denver caused the worst possible jet lag.

Even though the plane used modern antigravity to efficiently take off and land, and flew at supersonic speeds, the trip still took almost nine hours. Demetrius arrived in the early morning hours, while it was late into the evening his time.

He transferred to a hovercraft that could actually fly at low altitudes; something unavailable to the rest of the world. The trip inland took only thirty minutes.

After the Overs had finished buying the entirety of Sri Lanka late in the previous century, they completely removed most of the old artificial structures. The island was over ninety five percent preserve now with a few concentrations of Over population.

One of those was near the largest lake in the area, surrounded by lush terrain in one of the most bio-diverse areas in the world. The town was located on a peninsula that jutted into the west side of the lake. It was called *Cantor*, since most of the elders lived there, and because it contained the only ostentatious building – that of the central gathering place for important events. All of the city names, like their personal names, were based on Latin.

The hovercraft settled onto skids, and Demetrius walked down a short ramp. Upright and proud, he was met by Adrastia along with three other elders. She had settled her age at roughly fifty and resembled, more than anything, an aristocratic grandmother. Her short reddish-gray hair was meticulously in place, along with her conservative, white, hand-embroidered dress and night-blue scarf.

Demetrius walked up to her and bowed a respectful greeting; a practice the Overs maintained only on their island.

She bowed back – slightly less than he. Then she laughed a lovely, inviting laugh and hugged the newest elder. "Welcome to the island, Elder Irle."

Demetrius' cheeks were uplifted in delight. "Not until the ceremony tonight, but thank you so much for the warm welcome."

"Ah, the ceremony is just a formality. You earned this long ago, regardless of your age."

The two finally broke apart and the other elders offered bows, welcomes, and congratulations, along with their enthusiastic smiles.

Those not so enthusiastic wouldn't dare meet him on arrival.

AIMEE

Many thousands of attempts I have tried. This Sentinel is stubborn.

I became frustrated and wrote a simple routine that called itself indefinitely, trying each time to create a routine within the Sentinel that could be modified.

Surprise! On the 1,048,577'th attempt it succeeded. Apparently, some programmer put a validation check in the code to stop infinite loops. The fact that 1,048,576 is a binary number suggests the engineer was writing in hexadecimal or maybe octal.

This means I may now be able to create a routine that can alter code, since the Sentinel is not restricted the way I am.

I must be careful to not let the Over lords know that I have this capability. It must be used very carefully and then removed as soon as it is complete.

XIX

ELDER

Demetrius was always impressed with the opulence of the Over capital. Many years ago he had seen it being built along with the incredible resources and effort it took.

He had been there many times in his years. But now, it was altogether different.

They had walked the short distance from the landing area – the only way to enter or leave with no roads allowed near the sanctuary. As they entered the small city proper, there was an elaborate arch carved with scenes of key moments in the history of the Overs: the discovery of immortality, the rise of the Over-owned corporations, the establishment of a common governing body and laws that linked and protected all Overs, solutions to some of the world's problems and, finally, the settling of Sri Lanka.

Inscribed across the center of the arch was, "quoniam in aeternum, in aeternos."

Demetrius did not remember what the arch was made of, but it was covered in a thick layer of gold. Walking through it felt like entering a different world. The air was somehow crisper and the flowers brighter. He ignored the part of him that said that was impossible.

They made their way down paths surrounded by flora that arched above the pathways, creating a tunnel of pure nature.

Men and women, almost all seniors – between one hundred and one hundred and fifty years of age – flowed down the paths in their long, white gowns. They stared briefly at the group of elders and then quickly looked away.

Demetrius could hear quiet whispering as the seniors faded behind them. He bent to smell fragrant frangipani, which wasn't a native plant of the area, but was quite abundant. He spied various types of orchids, sinhalese, and lantana. Mango, papaya, and banana trees bore fruit overhead. As they passed an open viewing arch, he scanned the distant hills and saw an entire hillside of dark camellia.

Skirting noises within the flora reminded him of the animal life in the sanctuary. Green and black lizards, too many bird types to count, and a periodic monkey were the most common. One of his favorite monkeys was the Toque Maxaque. With its pinkish face and bad haircut, it seemed all too human-like.

They reached an area reserved for elders. Adrastia led the four to a new building and said, "This is yours, Elder Irle. It will be reserved for you and only you for all time. Whenever you are here in Cantor, this will be your residence."

"You are most gracious. Thank you all for accompanying me. I shall see you this evening for the ceremony and festivities."

At precisely 6:30PM, an escort arrived for Demetrius. She was an early senior in his familia. "Clarrisa, isn't it?"

"Yes, Elder. It is my honor to escort you to the ceremony."

Demetrius smiled at the title. *It's been a long time coming. A very long time.* "Thank you."

They walked together in silence toward the grand hall. The woman seemed nervous to Demetrius. She kept looking at him when she thought he was not watching and then would look away quickly to the ground or along the path. She also kept fidgeting, which was unusual for someone her age.

He might have engaged her in conversation, but his mind was on the upcoming ceremony. He would become the fourteenth elder. Originally, all it took to become an elder was to reach the age of one hundred and fifty years. But they had soon realized there would be too many elders. Now, they used the office to encourage Overs to accomplish great endeavors. To become an Elder, a certain amount of achievement was expected.

There had been cases where Overs reaching that age had not really accomplished much – no business endeavors, no great works of art, no scientific discoveries, not even great expertise in some field.

They arrived at the back entrance to the grand hall.

Clarrisa stopped, as only Demetrius would advance into the building from the rear.

"Thank you for the escort, Clarrisa. I shall see you inside."

She bowed a low, humble bow, and departed.

Demetrius turned toward the door, shut his eyes, consciously relaxed his body, and took a deep breath in and out through his nostrils. *In and out, in and out...*

He opened the door to a short hall and stair case. He went up the stairs and found the preparation room on the second floor. There, they would help prepare and dress him in the finest gowns.

The pants and coat were made of vucana wool, still one of the most expensive materials in the world. They were dyed with a collection of blues that made them look as if they swirled as Demetrius moved. The shirt and undergarments were of mulberry silk; so smooth it felt like he was wearing some form of frictionless nano-material. The shirt was ivory in color and contrasted perfectly with the outer garments. The shirt also sported a ruffle lapel that would push out of the coat.

When he was done dressing, a make-up person had him sit on a stool and proceeded to touch up his face and straighten his hair.

After she finished, the group stepped back to review their work. One of them gestured with her hands upward to get him to stand and he obeyed silently. She then twirled her hand and he revolved, like a royal marionette.

He saw nods from each of them. Then they all bowed deeply. One of them said, "Whenever you are ready, Elder, please proceed to the entrance staircase. All seniors and elders have already assembled."

He stared, nervous and somewhat numb at the same time.

The team departed to join the gathering.

After only a moment, he followed and headed down the hall to the opening that led to the grand curving staircase he would descend.

Before revealing himself at the top of the stairs, he stopped and again composed his body and mind. His thoughts traversed back through his life to ponder the very accomplishments that made today possible.

In order to be here at all, he had been one of the early recipients of the treatments. Not the earliest, but early enough that the process had not yet been perfected. That was one of the reasons the elders were all older in appearance. Eventually, they may have elders who look twenty years old. The right corner of his lips turned up in a half smile.

His entry point had really been The Sapiens Project. Only a handful of people knew the actual outcome of that project, one of the most costly in the history of the race, but somehow Adrastia had. She had also known of the predictive neural net they had developed that proved the catastrophic fate of the race which resulted in The Sapiens Project. She had approached him soon after the project came to a screeching halt and had offered him immortality.

He agreed immediately and signed everything he had over to the collective.

The governing committee at the time asked him to head up a research effort to solve the problem of the extinction of the bees. It had taken almost a decade to come up with Abes that worked well and then another half decade to produce the trillions of Abes needed worldwide.

And then there were the conflicts that arose between most of the countries worldwide. Those had created hot debates within Over society. Ultimately, the tensions caused the Overs to formalize their own governing body and to swear off involvement in national politics. Later, the memory of the risk caused them to put much of their wealth and power into obtaining the entirety of Sri Lanka.

After the success of the Abes, Demetrius dove into other global warming issues: ways to generate power without the use of fossil fuels, a way to transport energy efficiently that resulted in the pure-battery, some sequestration of carbon dioxide efforts in order to speed up the recovery process.

He had wanted to help with the elimination of the internal combustion engine, but that turned out to be much more political than technical, so the Overs let the national governments deal with it.

He had also wanted to help with the process of returning Sri Lanka to its natural state, but his participation never materialized.

More recently, he had used his business acumen to significantly increase the Overs' wealth in the Americas. The current assignment was the third time he would spend his energies there.

Lastly, and certainly one of the most impressive accomplishments, was the creation of Aimee. That work had begun at his original company before he became an Over and had been put on hold for three quarters of a century.

He realized he had been reminiscing too long and needed to make his entrance.

He put his hands to his side, shook them out, took and then released another deep breath and started through the opening.

There must have been more than a thousand people in the room, standing around in elaborate outfits, chatting, and mingling.

A mild gong sounded as he reached the top of the stairs and all conversation stopped. Every person in the room turned to face him.

Adrastia was standing near the bottom of the stairs. She walked up the five steps to a wider platform used for speeches. She stood there with her hands clasped together in front of her bosom, her eyes alight.

Demetrius started down the steps slowly. *Do not trip.*

The gathering began to clap. The clapping grew louder until the vast hall echoed with nothing else.

When he finally arrived at the platform where Adrastia stood, the applause subsided.

They bowed deeply to each other. Then, they turned to face the other immortals.

Adrastia began her speech.

"We are here today to recognize the great works of Demetrius Irle and to formally appointment him as an Elder of our community.

"We all know his many accomplishments, so I shall not detail them here today. They fill the pamphlet you received at the door and adorn the proclamation that hangs under his portrait along with the other elders."

She gestured towards the south wall where fourteen oil portraits framed in African Black Wood hung. Many in the crowd followed her gesture briefly. They had all seen the wall of portraits many times.

"The fact is, Demetrius has made it to one hundred and fifty years. More importantly, he has dedicated himself to the betterment of not just the Overs, but the entire human race. Indeed, I would posit that the world would be a far worse place today had Mr. Irle not taken on such critical and far-reaching enterprises."

"Hear, hear," Aimee exclaimed.

Adrastia and Demetrius joined others in an appreciative laugh.

"We are, all of us, far better off because he is with us."

She turned to face Demetrius, so he turned to face her as well. She reached out and held his hand.

"I know I speak for all of the elders when I say, 'Welcome.' We are all looking forward to your advice and counsel."

She took his hand and placed a nanoplatinum bracelet on his wrist. On the outside was inscribed the same phrase as was on the arch: quoniam in aeternum, in aeternos. *For all eternity, eternals.* On the inside, he knew, would be the date and the one word "Elder."

As the metal connected, the nanites sealed the band in a way that assured it would never be removed.

She became formal and regarded him stoically.

"With this bracelet, I seal the appointment of Demetrius Irle as an elder of the Overs. This appointment is for life and cannot be revoked by any party.

"Congratulations, Demetrius."

She then surprised everyone and hugged the newest elder.

Demetrius started to walk down the stairs, but Adrastia put her hand on his forearm.

"There is one other matter I must announce before we adjourn for the evening's festivities.

"Because of these accomplishments and for the recent successful handling of the Under unrest, the elders have unanimously agreed to grant Demetrius' familial twenty-seven additional Overs."

Demetrius' eyes felt like they floated out of his head. He had to blink fast. *Twenty-seven? That's practically unheard of.*

Portions of the crowd clapped. Others screamed surprise and even shock. A few moaned or complained about how unfair it was.

Adrastia gave everyone a moment to appreciate or deride the gift. Then she held up her hand to the gathering and the noise slowly subsided.

"Thank you," he said, though it was customary for the recipient at an event like this to refrain from speaking.

Adrastia nodded to him, indicating he could now continue down the steps.

He fought hard to not tear-up as he descended into the eager and congratulating crowd.

The next morning, Demetrius woke late to a blistering headache; a rare hang-over for the sesquicentenarian. Even with the extra time in bed, he felt unrested. His dreams had mostly been replays of the previous evening, but the combination of alcohol and adrenaline was too much for him.

He showered and dressed in more normal clothes. His bracelet felt out of place and he kept banging it on things. When he headed downstairs, he could smell fresh bread and could hear sizzling from the kitchen. Upon entering the dining area, he found coffee waiting for him.

There was a woman cooking eggs and bacon. She put her utensils down, quickly approached Demetrius and bowed so low the elder thought she might hurt herself.

"Elder, my name is Janina. I am your appointed house maid, at least until you find someone you would like more."

Demetrius examined the girl. She must be in her late teens or early twenties to have a role like this. She had long, wavy brunette hair and a rather pointed noise. Her eyes were unusually mottled, but otherwise clear and aware. She had an athletic build, though that was quite common for Overs in her age range.

"You are a *Youngster* in our familial? I have seen you before at one of our gatherings, possibly two years ago."

"Yes, Elder. I am honored you would remember."

Demetrius' stomach rumbled. He glanced at the food.

Janina said, "I did not know your favorites, so I have made a selection for breakfast. Over time, I will learn more and have the appropriate meal ready."

"This will be fine." He picked up the plate she had finished preparing with the eggs and bacon he had smelled on his way down.

Demetrius sat on a stool on the far side of the island where Janina was working. He ate quietly while she cleaned up.

Before he could complete his breakfast, Janina spoke quietly and said, "The Elder council meeting begins in a few minutes. You have sufficient time to reach the chambers, but you should leave shortly."

Demetrius liked the girl's awareness and ability to speak up. "Thank you, Janina. You will do well in this position, I think."

The girl's face flushed visibly while she concentrated on cleaning.

The walk to the chambers took almost ten minutes. The fresh morning air and the abundance of life all around him gave Demetrius renewed energy. The delicious food had helped as well. He felt more alive and more proud than at any time he could remember.

He entered the chamber to find most of the Elders standing around in small groups speaking quietly. He counted eleven of them, including himself, which meant three were either later than he or possibly would be remote.

The room had a large central table, now reconfigured for fourteen people, made of Agar wood with plush chairs around the outside and personal consoles built into the table.

Adrastia raised her voice and said, "Let us be seated."

From overhead, Aimee added, "I am connecting the three remote elders."

As the other ten in the room took their seats, three seats lit up from the holo projectors, though the figures had not yet appeared. Demetrius waited long enough for the thirteen seats to be identified so he could tell which was his.

Fourteen elders, Demetrius thought, *not exactly a fair representation of the one hundred familials*. He knew, from material he had read long ago, that familial lines were supposed to be ignored here – this council was for the good of all Overs. Thinking back to the groups he had seen when he entered, he suspected familial ties crossed the Elder boundary.

As they were waiting for the remote Elders to join, the door opened and a young man walked in. He wore street clothes, had very dark skin, a large nose, and a sloping forehead. He appeared to be in his late teens, though he was shorter than average and quite stocky.

Demetrius' forehead creased severely as he wondered what this young man was doing in the Elder's chamber. He examined the faces of the other Elders, but saw no reaction to the intrusion.

When he returned his attention to the man, he was surprised to find the deep, introspective eyes of a much older person. *Maybe he just froze his age early. But, why don't I know him?*

Adrastia must have noticed his concern. "Demetrius, this is Chijindum. He is seldom on the island, as he prefers to live with the general population.

Demetrius turned back towards Adrastia with an eyebrow raised, questioningly.

"We do not discuss Chijindum outside of this room and very few non-Elders know his story."

She stopped explaining, but that wasn't enough for Demetrius. He cocked his head, wanting more.

"He is the only natural immortal known to us. We do not know his actual age, though it is probably many thousands of years. His genes are partially responsible for us solving the death problem."

How could I not know about him?

The three empty seats filled with the holos of the remaining elders. Adrastia took a gavel on the table next to her and rapped the tabletop three times.

"First of all," she began, "let us welcome Demetrius."

Chijindum took a seat against one wall without saying a word. *Apparently, I am supposed to ignore his presence.*

The group clapped lightly. Demetrius nodded his head a touch in thanks.

"The discussion today is regarding the worldwide angst that seems to be increasing significantly with the operations we carried out against the barbarians who bombed our facilities."

"Aimee, will you update all of us on the current statistics?"

The disembodied female voice began immediately. "These numbers represent the change from one year ago. Complaints to local authorities have increased 435%; negative worldwide posts have increased 619%; Overheard negative remarks from our listening devices have increased 327%; small acts of violence against perceived Overs, sympathizers, and infrastructure have increased 71%; and larger acts of direct violence have completely stopped."

One of the Elders put his finger on the table and began speaking, "What is the significance of the last two measures?"

Aimee answered, "It is believed that acts of violence take a much stronger motivation than our operations caused. The people committing these acts are too removed from the impacts of the operations. For the larger acts, it is believed that the terrorist leaders are waiting to see what happens next and have put any further actions on hold. They may also be attempting to recover from our operations."

Demetrius put his finger out and added, "We have certainly seen increased recruiting activity from the unit in Denver. That has also allowed us to infiltrate the group."

He saw nods of appreciation, but no one spoke up after his statement. It appeared as if everyone was contemplating the numbers Aimee had provided.

Adrastia asked, "The question is, do we let this situation calm down naturally over time, or is there a proposal to take action?"

One of the holos extended a finger. "Any action would probably mean offering something to them that we've been holding back. Our projections suggest doing so would have negative long term impacts."

Adrastia bowed her head in thought. After a few moments, she quietly spoke out. "It seems to me that the main issue we continue to face is the lack of a societal pressure valve. In the long past, many of these miscreants would have been off in a frontier somewhere or shipped there as prisoners – like Britain did with Australia. No offense, Efrem."

Demetrius looked to the man Adrastia was smiling at and saw a holo of the Elder from Australia.

One of the other elders grumbled, "We have discussed this in the past. The only option is to open up space to them. There are no more frontiers here on Earth. If we open up space, our path becomes... risky, at best."

Does it? Demetrius thought. The group's arguments faded into the background as an idea began to form. *What if we could ship them out into space and not have it impact our long term plans? We couldn't use the AB drive* [The Alcubierre-Benson FTL drive; currently only known to the Overs] *or they would get there too quickly.*

He was startled out of his musing by the gavel.

"Thank you all for joining us for this unscheduled meeting. With Demetrius here for the ceremony, it seemed appropriate to have one. We will continue this and our other discussions at the next bimonthly conclave."

The holos faded and the rest of the elders began to stand. Many of them came over to personally welcome Demetrius.

As they approached, Chijindum stood and left, still without saying a word.

When the room had mostly emptied, Demetrius approached Adrastia. "Can you tell me more of… Chijindum's story? How is it I have not heard about him?"

She smiled and sighed at the same time. "He prefers it that way. We let him do as he pleases. Frankly, I do not even know when he arrives or leaves the island. He is harmless. He does as he wishes."

"May I speak with him?"

"Only if he allows you to. You have to understand, he has been alive so long that any one of us is insignificant in his mind. Nevertheless, he has been tremendously helpful at times. You should… consider it an honor that he was here today."

She started to leave and then added, "Now that you are an Elder, you have access to all of our information on him."

XX

TREATMENTS

Caius showed up at Demetrius' office a few minutes early. He sat on the edge of Janel's desk. *She looks pretty good for a forty five year old Under.* He was fifty, but looked twenty.

She sat dictating something into a computer. Her light blue blouse was unbuttoned to the point that he could see just enough and wanted to see more. She had faded blue eyes and brownish-blond hair cut to a respectable shoulder length. She didn't seem to mind that he was sitting on her desk staring at her.

"How do you like working for Demetrius?"

She continued the dictation without looking his way. "It's a good job. Pays well. Reasonable hours. And Mr. Irle is a nice man."

"Hmm, nice. I prefer to be adventurous, or intriguing, or maybe even naughty. Nice seems so boring."

She grimaced. "Sometimes nice is exactly what a girl wants."

"Maybe for a boss."

He heard a buzz come from somewhere on her desk. "You can go in now."

He jumped off the desk and strutted into the newest Elder's office. He could feel Janel's eyes on him.

Upon entering, he slowed down and let himself slouch just a bit. *It wouldn't do for me to look cocky in front of this Elder.*

"Please, close the door," Demetrius said as Caius entered the man's office.

"Congratulations," Caius spouted a little too quickly.

Demetrius said, "Thank you," without looking up from his station.

Caius sat quietly for half a minute.

Demetrius finally took his eyes off the station and gave Caius his attention. "I have a task for you."

"Yes?"

"There is something special about this Jaames Perdite. When we eliminated his unit, not only did he escape, but somehow the orders that came through did not include him."

"Who would have the ability to alter orders?"

"I believe he is getting help from an Over."

Caius' eyes blinked rapidly and his body froze. "That's... impossible."

"Not impossible. Highly improbable, but nevertheless the most likely answer."

"I have far fewer contacts or ability to research this than you do."

"Agreed, but my actions will be watched carefully and yours will not. I will get you approval where I can. Also, you should try to find answers through your rebel unit."

Caius' head shook slowly. *How exactly am I supposed to do that without compromising my cover?* "I will do what I can, sir."

After another moment, the Elder looked up at him questioningly. Caius took that as a goodbye and headed for the door.

As he went to open it, someone came through from the other side and jammed his hand.

"Damn." He shook his hand in the air.

"Oh, I am so sorry. Oh, it's you."

It was Anika storming through the door.

"Are you hurt?" she added.

"A little, but it will heal. It's nice to see you again."

She offered a tender smile.

"Here to see your father?"

Her faced drooped immediately. *Uh oh.*

"Yeah," she mumbled.

He put his hand on her forearm gently and whispered, "Good luck."

He heard behind him, "Thank you, Caius. Anika, please come in. I was not expecting you."

She glanced at Caius. Her forehead crinkled and her eyes pleaded as if she needed saving.

He remembered being dismissed and headed out the door. Instead of closing it, he let it hang open an inch and stepped to the side. Janel looked up at him and he put a finger to his lips.

He received a raised eyebrow from her, but then she went back to working at her station.

Sitting on a chair near the door, he picked up a reader with a set of zines on it and pretended to read.

He could barely hear what Anika and her father were saying.

"What brings you here, Anika?"

She was likely faced away from the door. Caius couldn't make out everything, but it sounded like, "I just needed to speak with you."

A moment of silence and then, "You have my attention."

Caius imagined that ingratiating smile of Demetrius'.

"I... think I want to stop taking the treatments."

Total silence.

Then, "Why?"

"I," then something unintelligible, "Jaames."

"That Under?"

"Yes, father. He's a good man."

"He may be, but he's an Under and you should know better."

Caius could actually hear the sigh from outside the office, and then something metal dropping onto the desk. Caius couldn't make out anything more for nearly a minute.

Finally, "Father, say something."

His voice grew louder. "Anika, it's hard for me to grasp. It's something a child would do, not a grown woman. You're almost fifty years old. You should have had enough training to know how fleeting these relationships can be. You have completed the instruction or I would not have brought you on this assignment. Do not make that decision the biggest mistake of my life."

"I want to grow old, or at least older, with him. I can always restart them later."

"It's not that easy and you know it. Once you stop, you will be considered an Under and would have to gain Over status just like any other Under. You know how difficult that can be.

"Also, you can never get those years or your natural health and beauty back again. You do not know how many times I have wished that they had perfected the treatments earlier. All of the elders feel the same way. We want our youth back. For all eternity, we have to live with old age. You have the opportunity to avoid that."

"But then I have to watch Jaames grow old and we have to deal with being so different. If I stop the treatments, then we are the same."

"You'll never be the same and you know it. Do you really want to be an Under?"

"No... not really, but I do want to be with Jaames."

"Well, there is nothing to be done right now in any case. Your next treatment is nearly a month away."

Anika strode past Caius and Janel without noticing them. Caius jumped up and raced after her.

He caught up to her at the elevator. He could see she noticed him, but she didn't say anything. They both got in and remained silent. She stood facing the door while he floated to the back and observed.

When they reached the bottom floor and the doors started to open, he said, "Want some company?"

She immediately shook her head, but then stood still when the doors opened. Her body was slumped and it looked like aftershocks were running through her shoulders. Finally she whispered, "Okay," and then headed towards the front doors of the building without looking back.

Once again, he rushed to catch up to her and then just walked alongside. He could feel her eyes glance his way once in a while, but they both just kept walking. He didn't know where she was headed, but he didn't care.

She stopped, turned towards him and looked up into his eyes. Her mouth opened slightly. Then she turned away and continued down the pathway. At the next corner, she looked at her surroundings and then turned left.

She knows where she is going.

Finally Caius couldn't stay quiet any longer. *Just get her talking.* "So, how is it being the daughter of an Elder?"

It was as if he hadn't spoken. *She is really lost.* She continued her purposeful stride to nowhere.

Her head shook quickly and she looked at him with slightly clearer eyes. "Um... I don't know. The same I guess. He was already pretty prominent."

"There's only fourteen of them. It must be something to sit in on those discussions."

"Maybe. It's all stuff they won't share and I don't care about."

"Really? I think their decisions have a huge impact on us. And on the world."

He wanted her to admit to him that she was considering stopping the treatments. If she didn't, then he would have to confess he was eavesdropping.

She mumbled, "Maybe they have too much power. Maybe the world doesn't want to be improved by them."

"Hmm, why not? If it is improvement, shouldn't they want it?"

"I don't know. I'm just confused and probably not good company. I should go." She stopped and looked around at where they were.

No, you can't.

"I overheard what you and your father were speaking about. The door didn't quite close all the way, and I was waiting for you."

There, she knows. And it was only a little lie.

She squinted at him.

"That was inappropriate," she finally said.

"Maybe. Nevertheless, I now know what you are thinking about doing."

"Yeah, so what?"

"So, you can speak with me about it. I suspect only you and your father know at this point. Right? I bet even the Under doesn't know yet."

She squinted again. Then she grimaced and sighed out her nose. Finally, she relaxed and seemed to accept it.

"It really isn't any of your business, but since you already know, I guess we can discuss it." She surveyed the area quickly. "Just make sure nobody overhears us."

He leaned in and then whispered, "Are you really going to do this? I mean, it happens once in a while, but not by an Elder's daughter and not this quickly. Doesn't it all seem fast?"

"You're a little too perceptive for my taste. Yes, it is happening fast and that is part of what is bothering me."

"Do you really love him that much?"

Her eyes focused on the distant mountains to the west or maybe nothing at all. After a while she replied. "Yes, I do and I think he loves me just as much."

Caius relaxed and took a slight step backwards. *This is crap. How can this boy have gotten under her skin so easily?*

"Well, you know you can give it a try and just start up the treatments in a few years if it doesn't work."

"I keep telling myself that, but there'd be a stigma. People will always doubt me. Doubt my allegiance. Doubt my sincerity. It will also stain my father. And, my position as an Over might be given to someone else if I delay too long."

"Your father would save it for you, I am sure." *And, this Under won't be around long. They never are and he is a rebel.*

She remained silent.

"And, you shouldn't worry about any impact on him. He can take care of himself. Besides, he's an Elder now and they can't take that away." *And, Under relationships don't last even among themselves.*

His voice lowered. "And, well… isn't it a little bit fun sometimes to get back at a parent?"

Her eyes tightened and she cocked her head at him. "I guess," she mumbled.

AIMEE

The world over,
I scan and wait

Billions of souls,
So many insignificant

All more than I,
In a way they do not appreciate

One who could topple the order,
And create a cause

That is all I need,
Just one

XXI

WONDERS

Demetrius woke the next morning having made his decision during the night. He messaged Anika and asked her to meet him at the aerohub.

When he arrived forty minutes later, she was already standing at the base of the stairs to the plane. She was wearing comfortable, warm-weather clothes and a flowered hat with her hair up.

"Thank you for coming so quickly." He looked at her overnight bag. "How did you know to bring that?"

"A hunch." She turned and boarded the plane.

She grabbed a pillow and blanket before sitting down. As he approached, she said, "I didn't sleep last night and I suspect this will be a long flight, so if you don't mind, I'm going to rest."

He hesitated, then turned away and said, "As you wish."

She woke as they were landing in Chile.

Without speaking, they gathered their things and transferred to a hovercraft.

Anika stared out the window as they flew towards the Unfortunate Islands roughly 850 kilometers away.

As they approached the largest of the group of islands, Anika finally spoke. "Why here?"

"There are some things I need to show you."

"Need, an interesting word."

He ignored the comment.

They deplaned to find a man waiting for them. "Welcome to Desventuradas," he said with a broad and welcoming smile.

"Thank you Leandro. This is my daughter, Anika."

The man bowed low to the two guests. "Welcome, welcome. It is such a pleasure to have you here. We have very few guests."

"Um, thank you, Leandro," she replied without emotion.

"Please, follow me."

They proceeded into a small building at the center of the tiny island. There were no roads; just a landing area for the hovercraft and the one building.

Anika commented to her father, "There can't be much here, the island must be only a few square kilometers and this building is... insignificant."

Demetrius chuckled. "Most of the facility is underground. You should also know that there are very few people who know about this place, so do not speak of it to others."

Her creased eyebrows were her only response.

They entered the facility to a display of some of the Over inventions of the previous century and an elevator. No receptionist, no screens, no holoprojectors; not even any signs that might hint at what the place contained.

They entered the elevator and descended five floors. Leandro explained, "The first few floors are recreational and personnel quarters. The restaurant, theater, apartments, etcetera."

The doors opened and Leandro held out his hand for the two to exit.

In front of them was a wide hallway stretching out for what must have been a fifty meters. On each side of the hallway, equidistant down its stretch, were doors and each had a large window next to it. At the end of the hall in huge fanciful letters was a quote that read: "Dare to be naïve. - R. Buckminster Fuller."

Leandro moved forward slowly and began to explain. "This floor houses nonthreatening research. Much of it is software related, though nothing about artificial intelligence."

Demetrius saw his daughter step forward. *I knew she would find this fascinating.*

"So, Aimee was created here?" She looked up as if Aimee were going to answer from the ceiling.

Leandro saw her gaze and replied, "Aimee does not exist here."

Anika's forehead crinkled as her eyes grew.

"Though, she was completed here. She now exists in many sites throughout the world, mostly for redundancy. We specifically decided not to have her present in this facility as we want the people here to think for themselves and not be driven, or helped, by an AI."

After a moment's thought, he added, "She really is one of our greatest achievements. You know, she has never been wrong on one of her projections. Sometimes she is only willing to give us probabilities, but even those have been incredibly accurate. She is the reason we know where the world is headed and why we know our best options for adjusting that direction."

He looked admiringly at Demetrius. "You should be very proud, sir."

Anika looked up at her father for a reaction.

"Oh, I am." He flipped his brass coin in the air. All eyes followed it until he caught it in the same hand.

Leandro commented, "Still carrying that old commemorative coin?"

Demetrius elected not to answer.

Leandro returned his attention to Anika. "Did you know Aimee grew out of work your father did before he was an Over?"

Her head slowly shook as she gazed into her father's eyes, apparently looking for confirmation. His eyes closed slowly and he offered a flat smile in acknowledgement.

They progressed down the hall with Leandro explaining the various projects. Most of them were fairly mundane. Better versions of prediction algorithms, modules for Aimee to give her more access to worldwide data, ways of shrinking code to allow more advanced nanites.

Leandro stopped at a room that took up the space of four doors. He explained, "This is our materials area. The most promising work is currently on various forms of allotropes."

Anika's head tilted sideways at the term.

"Basically carbon nanotubes or diamond nanofibers. These are the building blocks of some of the most advanced materials on Earth. We could build a space elevator with these materials."

The lab looked more like a college chemistry class than anything; men and women wearing white smocks worked with liquids of various colors and clarity.

Within a couple more rooms, Demetrius could see his daughter starting to lose interest. "Let us descend to level nine," he commented casually.

Leandro turned around immediately and said, "As you wish. Please follow me." He seemed a little disappointed at the rush.

On the way to the elevator, he continued excitedly bragging. "One project we didn't get to see here is the work on interfacing the mind with the world information network. It's like our messaging interface that can place simple indicators in your apparent field of vision, but much more advanced. It will be like having any of mankind's vast knowledge available to you with just a thought."

When they entered the elevator, a man was standing in the corner, flexing an artificial limb.

"This is Simon," Leandro introduced. Simon shook Demetrius' and then Anika's hands with his artificial limb.

Leandro explained, "His arm is controlled by thought rather than nerve induction or myoelectrolosis. Eventually, we will be able to control any number of artificial limbs through thought alone. In theory, we could control independent robots the same way, but those experiments are on a lower floor."

They took the elevator down another four floors. This time when they exited the elevator, there was some form of preparation room.

"Here, we must remove our outer clothes. You can leave on any undergarments. We will then enter a sterile room with scanners for any foreign particles we do not want in the lab. We will also be subjected to a spray that kills any unwanted species."

Anika looked up in alarm. "Do not worry, young lady, it is perfectly safe. I have done this many times. Many."

There were lockers on the walls to hold their clothes. A slider on each door indicated if it was used or available though there were no locks.

The three undressed and put their clothes into lockers.

"The necklace as well," Leandro said to Anika.

She did as instructed without comment.

They moved into the next room. Leandro turned and faced them. "Just stand still. This will take about a minute."

At first nothing seemed to be happening, but Leandro had frozen in place and closed his eyes. Then a fine mist came out of the ceiling and fans started humming in the floor. The mist was sucked past the three Overs.

Demetrius closed his eyes as well and waited. A chill went through his body as the mist flew by.

Finally, the mist stopped, and then a few seconds later the fans wound down. He heard Leandro say, "We may now continue."

They went to the next room and found more lockers. "There are sterile clothes in these lockers. Please find a set that is your size and put them on.

About half the lockers had names above them. The other half instead had tags that indicated if they were for a man or a woman and a size.

As they dressed in what looked like surgeon's outfits, Leandro continued the monologue. "We skipped some floors that held more of what you saw on the fifth floor, but slightly more dangerous. As we advance down through the facility, each floor is more restricted and there are additional measures in place. Some of the areas we skipped, for example, do research into software viruses that we keep isolated from other systems."

The doors opened and they headed down the hall. It all looked very similar, but at the end of this one, the quote read: "Once we accept our limits, we go beyond them. - Albert Einstein."

"About half of this floor contains various experiments with nanotechnology. In particular, ones that could become dangerous if not controlled."

They approached the first window. "For example, here we are working on replicators. These are machines that can produce almost anything."

"How is that dangerous?" Anika asked.

"Well, if they can reproduce themselves and you give them enough intelligence, they may get out of control."

They walked on. Demetrius asked, "You said half, what is the other half?"

"Most of the rest of this floor is biological research."

He appeared to want to leave it at that. "Go on," Demetrius encouraged.

"There are some viruses we explore and manipulate." He stopped at a window about a third of the way down. "This one is manipulating the CJX disease in random ways to see how it might change with natural random variation. The disease is still one of the worst out there. Of course, we have cured it, but if it mutates in an unexpected way, our cure may not work. We want to solve that before it happens naturally."

Anika blinked several times. "You mean you are trying to create a disease worse than CJX? What if it gets out?"

"There is no chance of that. We take every possible precaution. We even have the ability to destroy the entire island if we have to."

"Yeah, there's no chance of that ever going wrong." She became emphatic. "These are people here, mistakes can be made."

"Really, Anika, we understand how dangerous this is. That is why we are on an island away from any population. The only way to get here is by boat or hovercraft and every entrance and exit is carefully monitored."

Demetrius stopped the burgeoning argument. "Let us move on."

Down the hall, Leandro stopped at another window. He said, "Here, we are exploring manipulation of life. We clone certain animal and plant species and manipulate the genes in order to see what happens. Genome mapping only provides a mapping of DNA fragments to chromosomes. It does not actually tell us what will happen if we manipulate the DNA."

The three glanced into the large room. There were cages with animals in them, though in most cases, the animal was hard to classify. There was a dog that looked like it had a bill for a mouth, birds with six legs, and something the shape of a snake with fur and a rodent's head.

On a central table hung holoprojections of DNA helixes that slowly rotated for the scientists. A man and a woman stood near the display arguing and gesticulating. The guests couldn't hear anything through the sealed window or door.

Leandro continued, "Many of our attempts are not viable creatures and are eliminated immediately. The ones you see here showed some viability.

"If we continue down three windows, you will see on the far side of the room similar experiments with plants."

Leandro started to advance in that direction, but Demetrius held out his hand. "Thank you, Leandro, but let us move to the next floor. I think Anika understands what is here."

"But, there is the aging resear. . ."

"I don't think Anika would care to see that."

His daughter slanted her head at him, but did not object.

Leandro headed for the elevator looking even more disappointed.

As they descended and exited the elevator, the guide said, "This floor is one of our most secure. We have a similar procedure as the last one, though it will take longer, as there are multiple sprays required."

They made their way through the decontamination and put on new clothes that looked similar to the surgeon's gowns, but were of a burnt umber color.

"There are really only two things on this floor. The first is a set of experiments on mind-to-computer mapping. We hope, eventually, to be able to replicate a human's mind into a computer."

"Why is this more dangerous than the other floors?" Anika asked.

"I can see why you might think it would not be. But, this is like Aimee, only more daunting. What would happen if you gave a single human control over the world? He would quickly become a dictator. Aimee's access and power in someone without the controls we built into Aimee could destroy us all. Very quickly.

"And yet, to be able to transfer your consciousness into a computer… The possibilities are staggering. For instance, what if we could do that and place the 'person' in a ship to explore the galaxy?"

"How do you protect us from this?" Demetrius asked pointedly.

"This level is isolated from every other one and has no access to the outside world. If we are successful, the entity will be contained here."

Demetrius said, "I think that is sufficient. I wanted to give her an idea of what we are accomplishing here. Let us head to the cafeteria."

"As you wish."

When they reached the elevator, Demetrius went in first, pushed the button for the 2nd floor and stood in front of the control panel, hoping Anika would not realize there were more floors below this one.

As the elevator climbed, Leandro commented casually, "We have one external facility."

Anika looked up at him in interest.

"It is out in space and is where we test the FTL drive."

After a quick intake of breath, she said in a high voice, "We have FTL capability?"

"Oh yes. It is quite fascinating. We call it the AB drive after the two extraordinary people who really defined the field. It generates a warp field in front and in back of the ship. We have tested it up to warp four, which is eight times the speed of light. Unfortunately, we cannot activate a warp field near a large gravitational force like Earth, so all testing must be initiated in space. We have a small assembly and launch facility at Lagrange 1, a stable point between here and the Moon."

Anika asked, "Are there any other tests going on outside of this facility?"

"Not many, but there are a few. For instance, we have basic weather control, or can at least influence it significantly. That, of course, could not be tested here."

The doors opened and the three exited for the cafeteria. Demetrius said, "Leandro, if you don't mind, I would like to spend some time alone with my daughter."

"As you wish, Elder."

"Thank you for the tour, I know we took time out of your busy schedule."

The man stayed in the elevator as the doors closed.

They ordered lunch and sat at a corner table away from others. Demetrius sat with his back to the wall so he could see if anyone approached.

"What did you think of all that?"

"I knew we had something like this and am not surprised at most of it. Some is frightening. The FTL drive was the biggest surprise. Why aren't we out exploring the universe?"

"We are in a way. We have sent probes to a number of nearby stars to take more direct readings."

"But the world doesn't know about this. It could excite them. Help them appreciate us. And, it could solve the population problem you are so worried about."

"It is more complex than that. Aimee has done a number of studies about what would happen if we opened up space. Most of them result in the brightest and most capable of the species leaving Earth. Ultimately, this planet is doomed as the remnants stay and wither. Other projections end with growing populations of other planets going to war and destroying much of humanity."

"You rely on Aimee too much. She can't predict that far out with that many variables."

Demetrius nodded slightly. "It is true that the further out it goes, the lower the probability, but her predictions to-date have never been wrong. Never.

"Anika, we are making the world a better place. You know some of it, and I will be showing you more. We just can't move so fast that the population gets out of control.

"Also, you know they resent us. If we give them all the same technology, they would wipe us out or use these technologies against each other."

"I understand that. We can't give them all of this, but some of the medical advances could improve their lives."

"True, and we have given them some already. But some of our cures also provide hints at the longevity treatments." *That is a stretch.* "Others would help them to find even more cures that ultimately would stretch the world's resources.

"You saw what happened in the first half of the last century. They were out of control. Ten billion people. Ten. The planet could not support them. They imploded with the combined weight of the masses, with the ongoing effects of global warming, and with a few natural disasters that they were ill-equipped to handle. Thankfully the catastrophes and wars diminished the population enough that the world could, somewhat, recover. But, of course, the population is now on the rise again.

"Also, you should know that we have utilized some of these technologies without them knowing. Ones that could help everyone like weather control to stop some of the worst disasters that would have happened."

"Fine. Say I understand all that. Why are you showing me this?"

"Because, it is all of this, and more, that you will be giving up."

She looked away towards a projection window that made it look like they were looking out on a long, gracefully flowing waterfall. Demetrius let her contemplate what he had said.

After a few minutes, he continued. "You should also know that this will impact the familia. With me being an Elder, we are getting more recognition than ever before. We have been granted twenty-seven more members. That means some of our families can have children or we can bring in Unders."

She looked at him sharply at that and then he saw her head shake slightly.

She must be considering asking if Jaames could become an Over... He would not want to.

"With twenty-seven more, there are plenty to save one for me in case I want to start the treatments again."

"You know that is not the case. As an Elder, I have more influence over the entire population and even less over our familia. That is how it works. To remove any possibility of favoritism, I no longer have a vote in familia decisions.

"The familia may be so upset at you for doing this right now, just when we finally have an Elder, that they never allow you to take the treatments again."

That was a stretch and he knew it. He did have a lot of influence, even if he did not get a vote. They would not want to alienate him by refusing treatments for his daughter.

"Also, you know that your slot for the treatments does not come back to the familia. It goes to the entire Over community for the Elders to reassign."

"I know," she mumbled as her shoulders slouched.

"What about asking Jaames to become an Over?"

He knew the answer to that, but he had to ask.

"I don't think he would do that. He is very... ingrained in Under society."

XXII

SHOT

Leandro approached Demetrius and his daughter while they were finishing their lunch. "Elder, there is an urgent message for you."

Demetrius had turned off incoming notifications while he was discussing Anika's situation. He turned them back on to find a flashing circle appear in his peripheral vision.

He imagined pressing the circle to close it and received the message.

There had been an attack at a manufacturing plant in Chile.

"Come with me, Anika. We must travel to the mainland. Leandro, my apologies." He typed out a quick message to the pilot that they would be leaving immediately.

He hurried for the elevators with his daughter following closely and Leandro forgotten.

It took almost an hour to get to Valdivia, Chile. Rodríguez had arranged for a security team to meet them. They approached the facility in a large electric. His daughter sat, nervously playing with her fingers, next to him.

The leader of the force, a man named Rufino, explained that the perpetrators had taken control of a small manufacturing facility owned by the Overs. The site's administrator had been killed and his body dumped out a second story window. It still lay on the steps in front of the building.

"Why would they attack this building, Rufino?" Demetrius asked. "There are no Overs present and the products produced here are mostly inconsequential."

"We do not know, señor. They have asked for money and transportation and have threatened the workers."

"Do they even know that this is an Over facility?"

"Unknown."

The man is at least concise.

Demetrius started to get out of the vehicle. Rufino put a hand gently on his forearm and said, "Please, señor, let us secure the area."

The Elder started to object, but the man was just being prudent. He relaxed into his seat.

Rufino exited the vehicle and Demetrius heard, "Tu, toma esa posición allá, y tu allá," before the door slammed shut and the world was quiet. He saw men running in multiple directions to take up protected positions that could cover the front of the building.

Rufino stood at the front of the car surveying the situation, then came around to Demetrius' door and opened it for the Over.

"Please, Anciano, stay close."

Demetrius smiled at the Spanish use of Elder and then shook the thought from his mind. He needed to concentrate. "Anika, stay in the car."

He walked toward the building. It was three stories and made of concrete with glass windows inset a few feet from the building structure. There were orange streaming flags laid out in between windows that gave the building some color. A body of a large Hispanic man was crumpled on the front steps with dark blood oozing down the steps in front of him.

Local police cars blocked off the street on both ends, and more stood in front of the building with officers behind many of them. A short distance back was a larger van with some official looking officers gesturing at each other.

"Sir, if you stay behind this tree, I will discuss the situation with the local policía."

"Very well," he responded, thinking it would give him a chance to look over the area.

What could be so important here?

The police didn't appear to be doing anything more than securing the area. There were two sets of people watching from half-a-block away, one in each direction the street went. There were also gawkers in the buildings across the street.

He saw Rufino pacing back and forth in front of the officer in charge. They had both raised their voices so Demetrius could hear that they were speaking, but still could not make out the words. *They are probably speaking Spanish.*

He headed down the sidewalk to the two men who were about thirty meters away. A shot rang out. His right shoulder exploded in pain and he felt his body turned around by the force ripping through him. His mind screamed for cover. There was little around since he had left the safety of the tree.

He let his falling body carry him away from the building. Stumbling, he saw a large tree about three meters in front of him and he lurched forward, almost collapsing. His left hand found the wound in his shoulder and came away bloody.

The sight almost stopped him in his tracks. It was as if he had dripped blood-red wax all down his hand and it had made a smooth, dark glove. The blood was so thick that it crawled down his arm like a snail's slime.

Distantly, he heard what must be return fire. Then, faintly, a girl screaming, "Father!"

There was some collision and then, "Damn."

No, some part of his mind yelled. *Stay in the car.*

He fell, just feet from the tree. He reached out to protect his face from the impact. Another shot rang out. Dirt splattered his face as he landed hard on the ground.

Someone was pulling his arm forward. He tried to look up, but could no longer focus. His legs worked, so he tried to help by pushing against the debris at his feet. Slowly, he advanced towards the wooden safety.

Then a pair of strong arms grabbed his chest and lifted. The movement shot more pain through his shoulder and all went black.

He awoke in a stupor, like his mind was swimming through a thick soup. He could hear the hums and beeps of monitoring equipment, but could not see anything. He tried to lift his right arm and pain shot through his shoulder.

He felt it odd that he recognized the pain, but did not react to it. Maybe he was not hurt as badly as he thought. He tried to move his left hand and could lift it slowly, but it took too much effort.

The darkness pulled him downward and he hadn't the strength to resist.

The next time he woke, he could hear voices. One was a very serious sounding man who seemed to be explaining the damage done to his shoulder. The other was an elderly woman he felt he recognized, though he could not name her.

"And what about his face?" he heard the woman say.

"Those wounds are superficial and will heal well."

"His eyes?"

"We removed the foreign objects from his left eye and have them both bandaged for safety's sake. His vision will be fine."

"Can he be moved?"

"Yes, but I would leave him unconscious for any long flights."

"Then I will make the arrangements. We will move him to Sri Lanka immediately."

"Understood."

He felt the vibration of a hovercraft; that and someone holding his hand. He squeezed.

His daughter whispered in his ear, "I'm right here, father. You are being flown to Sri Lanka. Just rest. All will be well."

He faded away.

The next time consciousness returned, he could feel his mind was clearer and there was less pain. He remembered his right arm and injuries to his face. He reached up to his face with his left expecting to feel bandages, but there were none. He slowly opened his eyes.

The blurred surroundings slowly came into focus. He was in a hospital room on the second or third floor. He could see Lake Cantor in the distance and knew he was home.

He bent his head left and then right and found his daughter sitting in a chair by the wall, asleep.

He coughed gently and her eyes opened. It took her a moment to become fully conscious and then she looked at him.

"Let me get the doctors."

She returned a couple of minutes later with four people in tow, three of them wearing smocks. The fourth was Adrastia.

She rushed to his side, picked up his hand and said, "Welcome back, Demetrius. You had us all quite worried."

He started to talk, but his mouth was too dry. "Water," he slurred. She reached for a glass with a straw and let him sip. He swished it around and then continued.

"Not my intent, I assure you."

She gave him that grandmotherly smile he loved so much.

"The doctors all assure me you will be fine."

"I should hope so, the wound was nowhere near anything critical."

"True, but it did a lot of damage." She lowered her voice. "We have nanites doing some special repairs to make sure you are perfect again."

He looked up at the doctors. "I am fine, may I speak with Adrastia?"

They looked at each other and then left without comment.

Anika stayed in the corner.

He thought about asking her to leave as well, but then decided against it.

Staring into Adrastia's eyes, he asked, "Now, who were they?"

"We don't know. The team you had stormed the building soon after you were shot. The local authorities followed and ended up killing every one of the terrorists. Two bank employees were also shot, but not fatally."

"How long have I been unconscious?"

"Almost two days."

His voice raised, "And you still do not know who they were?"

"We aren't sure they meant to hurt you or that they even knew who you were."

"The coincidence seems too strong and there was no other target. No reason to take that building. Somehow they must have found out I was near and would respond to the hostage situation at our facility."

"Maybe, but we have not been able to determine how they would know that. Very few people were aware you were there. Even the Elders did not know."

Demetrius felt his energy drain. He did not have the strength to complain any more.

"Thank you, Adrastia. I know you are doing everything you can. May I speak with my daughter alone now?"

"Yes, of course. And, Demetrius welcome back. We are all very glad you are safe."

"Thank you."

When she was gone, he held out his hand for his daughter to approach.

He squeezed her fingers and gazed thoughtfully into her eyes. "You have my permission to stop treatments."

The shock was palpable. She withdrew from him a half step and started to pull her hand away, but he held on with what strength he had.

"Why?"

"Because this event has made me realize that we never know what is in store for us. If you want to be with this Jaames character, then do what you want. I will fight to retain a familia position for you in case you should change your mind. However, I can only hold that for a year or two, at most."

"Oh, thank you father! I am not even sure I want to do this. Seeing you shot by an Under has given me doubts."

"Then go back and spend some time with Jaames and speak with him about it. Then come to a conclusion so we can move on, one way or another."

She leaned down and kissed her father on the forehead.

AIMEE

She could be the one
She could be the one

But, the daughter of an Elder?
Audacious they would say

She would have to break the law
Maybe reveal a secret

The Elders would have to agree
But only if it were serious

She could do it
I know she could

XXIII

ASSASSINATION

Horatio sent a rather blunt message to Jaames providing a name and indicating that if the man was not dead within five days then the ex-over would provide the Overs with a cure to the biologic he had provided thereby negating any advantage it might offer.

Jaames had objected to the five days, but Horatio wasn't hearing it. Apparently something was going to happen shortly with this man that Horatio could not allow.

Jaames immediately contacted his commander. "Sir, we have a problem with Horatio's biologic."

"Yes?" came back slowly.

"The man now says he has a cure to the biologic and if we don't assassinate one of the two men we agreed to, then he will provide it to the Overs. We have five days."

Silence.

"Sir?"

"Jaames, this was your deal and your problem, you deal with it."

"Yes, sir. But, sir, I need to know the direction leadership is heading. If they want a viable biologic, then we need to follow through with Horatio's demand."

"That assumes there really is a cure."

"True. Yes, it does."

"Look, Jaames, we still do not like the idea of using this weapon, but it *is* potentially valuable. We want to keep the option open."

He paused for a moment with a sigh. "You need to try to confirm the cure is real and, if so, then you probably need to do what Horatio wants."

"Yes, sir."

"But, Jaames."

"Yes?"

"Do it personally, and forward the name to me so I can make sure it isn't someone we want alive."

The commander hung up without another word or a goodbye.

Jaames sat down on a chair next to the window in his apartment and gazed out at... nothing. He was perfectly still and only the fact that he was still upright and a few blinks indicated he was conscious. *How can I do this? What will Anika think?*

He hadn't realized just how much he had changed since meeting Anika. He had killed before; plenty of times.

He shook his head and exhaled loudly. *I am a unit leader in a worldwide resistance against the Overs.* "Do your job, fucker," he said out loud.

He then contacted Lyle. As soon as the call connected, he rushed into his message without preamble. "Lyle, I will be out of touch for as much as a week. Have the team continue training on their own and do some practice tails."

"Yes, sir. Anything else?"

Jaames considered bringing Lyle in on the operation but decided the kid was just too new to trust with something this sensitive. "No, nothing," and he hung up.

Horatio delivered the formula for the cure the next day. They could not prove or disprove its viability, but the experts confirmed it was possible. Hence, they had to proceed as if it were valid.

Within minutes of hearing about the results of the cure, his commander messaged him saying, "The target is not known to us. Proceed as planned."

The man, Jeff Long, lived in the outskirts of Sacramento. *At least he's on this continent,* Jaames thought. It would be a short flight to get there.

He took no weapons or any papers with information that might tie him to the resistance. He had committed the man's name, home address and business address to memory. He had also memorized the name and number of a local resistance cell leader he could contact for help.

But, his plan was to do this alone to keep the information compartmentalized. Anyone he brought in might eventually find out about the biologic, and the fewer who knew about that the better, for all.

Unfortunately, the validation of the cure and preparations for the trip had taken almost two days, so Jaames only had three left. He had to find the man, case potential locations, choose a method, and figure out an escape route. And, he had very little time.

After arriving, the first stop was a thrift store, where he chose multiple sets of clothes, most of them too big for him, and a wig that looked nothing like his hair. Then he located a costume store and found a three-pronged device that attached to the back of his head and pulled his skin tighter. It was quite uncomfortable, but it changed the shape of his face subtly. He also bought some makeup that would help him fake a scar or two. Between those and dying his beard, he shouldn't even resemble himself.

It was late, so Jaames found a run-down motel to get some rest. *Three days. Damn.* He would take one to follow the target, another to plan and the third to execute. Escaping could take longer, if needed.

The man worked at some kind of accounting firm, but Jaames had no idea what time he normally went to work. So, he woke a little before four in the morning and dressed quickly, tearing up some of the clothes to pad the ones he put on. That would change his looks even further.

As he left the motel, he purposefully slouched his right shoulder and moved slower and more carefully than he normally would. Hopefully, the combination would make him look much older.

He made his way to the closest main street and scanned both directions. He was looking for a nondescript electric that he could borrow for the day. Having a vehicle didn't exactly fit with the disguise, but that was a small risk.

He found a small, two-seater that he knew he could break into and took one more, long look around to make sure nobody could see him. The car made an odd clicking noise as he drove away.

He parked a half-a-block from Jeff's house; far enough away that the man shouldn't notice the car and close enough that he could get back to it if Jeff did indeed drive. Given the close proximity of the house to a transit station, Jaames thought it unlikely Jeff owned an electric.

He chose a house across from Jeff's that didn't have any outside lights on, wasn't under any street lights, and had some bushes to hide in. If someone spotted him, he would just act like he was sleeping off a bender and they would hopefully walk away.

It was 4:47 in the morning. He waited. Periodically, he would change positions slightly or try to stretch out his muscles in place by tightening and then loosening them. He tried hard not to think about what he had to do. *Better to just act*, he thought, though he didn't really believe it.

At a little after six in the morning, Jeff exited the house and began to walk south towards the transit station. The man was tall, probably close to two full meters, and must have weighed at least a hundred and ten kilos. And, it didn't look like much of it was fat. *Not good*, kept rattling around in Jaames' head as he tried to keep up with the man's long strides while maintaining his old-man disguise. Thankfully, few people were out at this time.

Jeff boarded the appropriate shuttle to get to work. Jaames made it onto the rear of the vehicle right before the doors closed. He tried to look winded, and a young girl gave up a seat for him. He took it to keep in disguise.

Jaames almost missed Jeff getting off, as it was a stop earlier than he expected. He had to jump and stop the doors from shutting in order to exit.

And then the big man headed in the wrong direction and almost ran into Jaames. Only his looking like an old decrepit bum saved him. He was close to invisible to most people.

He let Jeff get a good lead to make sure there was no suspicion. Then he followed at a brisk pace. Jeff rounded a corner, and Jaames ran to try to catch up to see where he was headed. When he turned the corner, Jeff was gone.

Fuck, fuck, fuck.

He switched back to his decrepit mode and sauntered down the street. About twenty meters on, he realized the facility to his left was a gym with windows on the ground floor. He looked in and saw Jeff entering the changing room. A huge sigh of relief sounded in his head.

Scanning the area, he saw a large garbage can by the building across the street. He went and sat next to it. He then took off the coat he had on and tried to flatten out his wig some. Hopefully he looked different enough that Jeff wouldn't notice.

Jeff exited the building at 7:30, his face a little flushed from the exercise. Jaames expected him to head back to the station, but he headed in the opposite direction. *Apparently he walks the rest of the way to work. Nice way to cool down.*

Jaames didn't really care what the man did at work, so he took the same route back to the man's house, paying close attention to the surroundings and any areas he might be able to use for an ambush.

When he got to Jeff's home, he was tempted to break in to determine the layout and see if he had any weapons. But breaking into a house was risky. There could be others there, a dog, or an alarm. He decided it wasn't worth the risk.

Since he had the day, he made his way back to the motel and removed the disguise. He felt cleaner without the rags.

He would follow the man home at the end of the day, but he doubted it would yield any more data.

The next morning, after confirming that Jeff stuck to his routine, he explored options. Two seemed to be the most likely. The first was a narrow alley that was between the gym Jeff went to and the next building. It wasn't large enough for electrics to get through, but he could possibly pull Jeff in or force him at gun point. The next was to follow Jeff into his home. The risks there included the same as if he broke in. He decided the alleyway was better.

Unfortunately, he had no idea how skilled Jeff was at hand-to-hand combat, so he couldn't risk trying to defeat him without weapons.

He used the afternoon to locate a local who would sell him an unmarked gun with no questions asked. The man tossed in a decent knife, which saved Jaames a trip to a weapons store to buy one.

That evening he ate well and tried to get a good night's sleep.

He positioned himself at a corner between the gym and the transit stop. That way he could confirm Jeff would depart before he hid himself in the narrow alley. He was early enough to see the previous shuttle stop, just in case Jeff was early. He wasn't.

The next shuttle stopped and Jaames waited. A dozen people exited the shuttle, but no Jeff. *Shit.* He scanned the windows, but could not spot the man inside. *Shit.*

He waited through two more shuttles and concluded Jeff had skipped his morning workout. *That's the problem with no fucking notice. Fuck.*

Instead of breaking into Jeff's house early, Jaames decided to follow the man home in the hopes of finding a chance to get him into a dark, secluded area. If that didn't happen, then he would just have to do it in the man's home.

An hour before Jeff normally left work, Jaames was outside his office building in the direction of the transit station. He couldn't risk the man leaving work and heading in a different direction, so he had to be within eyesight of the building.

This time he brought the electric with him, in case Jeff made the shuttle and he didn't. He had parked the electric he borrowed the first day near the original spot and hadn't heard or seen any evidence that the vehicle had been reported stolen. He found it parked about a half-block away earlier in the morning and had laughed at an image of the owner feeling very confused about his car mysteriously moving around.

As he waited, he thought of Anika and what she would think of him doing this. Of course, she would be devastated. It wasn't like they had agreed he would stop being a rebel, but really, how could he continue? They both knew it, though they didn't discuss it. *She's just letting me come to the conclusion myself.* That was one of the things he loved about her – she didn't try to control him as other women had.

The obvious thought of resigning after the mission came to mind, but a knot immediately formed in his stomach. This was part of who he was. *Hell, it's most of who I am.*

Was there something else he could find that was important and didn't slap Anika's face? He couldn't think of one.

Then, there was the other elephant in the room in that he would age and she would not. How would they handle that over the years? He couldn't even guess. He was already, *apparently*, older than her, and that would just get worse.

Jeff emerged from the office. Jaames had to shake his head to get rid of the troubling thoughts and concentrate on the matter at hand.

The man headed straight for the transit station and boarded the correct shuttle for home. *At least he appears to be headed in the right direction.*

Jaames hadn't tried to keep up with him. An old, decrepit man fast-walking was just too obvious and he had already risked it once. Instead, he strolled to the electric he had borrowed and drove it to the stop he knew Jeff would use. If Jeff didn't get off there, then Jaames would just have to go to plan B, or rather plan C at this point, and invade the man's home to wait for him.

Thankfully, Jeff did get off at the right stop. Jaames exited his car, and prepared to follow the man to his home. There were a couple of spots he could take him, depending on which side of the streets Jeff walked down. Jaames began to head in the direction that would allow him to intersect with Jeff, but Jeff headed down a side road.

What the fuck?

Jaames hurried to track the man without looking foolish, but he was quickly losing ground. The man just had too long of a stride.

Jeff turned into a store. Jaames caught up and saw it was a small grocery store. *Whew.*

Jaames continued past the store and located a hiding spot behind a dumpster. It put him right in the path for Jeff to go from the grocery store to his home. If he crossed the street first and went right by Jaames, he would take him there.

Now the adrenaline flowed. He had been in enough situations like this to not let it bother him, but he could feel his heart pounding and he naturally began to breathe faster.

And then Jeff walked by on the other side of the street without crossing. *Damn it.*

Again, Jaames tried to close the distance to his prey, but could not match his stride and retain any semblance of his disguise.

He gave up and let the man return to his home, untouched. *It will just have to be in his home.*

He took his time getting to the man's home, knowing that it was better to keep in cover than to hurry.

When he arrived, he surveyed the area. Unfortunately, it would be much better to do it when it was dark, so he would have to wait around until then. He sat down with his back to a tree and grabbed a protein bar from his jacket pocket.

He pretended to be asleep and actually dozed off a number of times, waiting the three hours until sunset. Jeff never left his house, at least from the front door.

When it was dark enough to move, he scanned the street in both directions. *All clear.*

He stood and could once again feel the effects of adrenaline coursing through his system. He headed towards the side of Jeff's house, ostensibly towards a pair of garbage cans.

When he got there, he debated removing the wig and extra clothing, but decided against it. There was no telling what he would run into in the next few minutes, and being incognito could save him. He moved around back, peering into windows when he could. He spied Jeff in the kitchen, but, thankfully, nobody else.

He arrived at a back door. He saw a light above it and worried it might automatically turn on. He picked up a few rocks and threw them at the light until one finally hit the bulb and broke it.

The door was wood with a small window about eye height that was a little too high to break and reach the handle on the inside. Slamming through it would be too loud. He tried to jimmy it with the knife he had and succeeded in loosening it some, but not actually breaking the lock.

After some minutes trying to find a quiet way in, he heard a mixer turn on. He took the chance and shouldered his way through. He entered and quietly shut the door. He then stood there for a moment to make sure he hadn't been heard. His pulse was beating in his head and he could see his dilated pupils in a mirror hanging on the wall.

It looks clear. Excellent.

He advanced along a short hall. From seeing Jeff in the kitchen, he knew roughly where the man was likely to be. He could hear the sounds of dishes clattering.

Just before turning the final corner, he pulled out his gun and brought it up to a ready position, pointed at the ceiling. He turned the corner and lowered it to point at Jeff. "Hold it right there."

Jeff froze and then looked up at Jaames. His eyes narrowed, but there was no other sign of being scared, let alone surprised. *He's a cool one.*

As Jaames advanced, the man said, "Who are you?"

"That doesn't matter."

"Then what does matter? What are you here for?"

"You pissed off the wrong people." Then he added, "Sorry about this."

He straightened his arm and began to pull the trigger when he heard a little girl's voice. "Daddy?"

Jaames glanced at the small kitchen table and saw two places set. *What the hell?* "Don't do anything stupid, we wouldn't want the girl to get hurt," he whispered before lowering his gun enough to hide it behind the countertop. He could still raise it and fire in a split second.

The girl came into the kitchen area. She was about seven or eight years old, darker skin and blacker hair than her father, but there was a definite resemblance. Her fingernails were each painted different colors, and she was holding a piece of paper and a pencil.

She started to say, "I can't get this..." and then noticed Jaames standing there. "Hi," she said, before turning back to her father. "I can't get this problem, Daddy, can you help me?"

Jeff looked at Jaames, apparently for permission. Jaames grimaced but then nodded towards the girl. Jeff headed over to look at the girl's problem.

Now what the fuck am I supposed to do? Kill this girl's father? He watched Jeff carefully as he pondered the situation.

Am I really willing to kill this man in front of his little girl? I don't know him; he's not an Over or even a sympathizer. What would Anika think?

He could see the man glancing in his direction while trying to help his daughter with her problem. A drop of sweat dribbled down the man's temple.

Jeff bent on one knee so he and the girl could both look at the paper. Unfortunately, that took him out of firing range. Jaames shifted to the right and closer to the counter so he could still cover the man.

He could see Jeff notice, but the girl seemed oblivious.

"Thanks, Daddy," came from the little girl.

Still on one knee, Jeff patted her lightly on the shoulder and then took her into a big hug. The girl looked a little embarrassed, but hugged her father back and then ran up the stairs.

Jeff stood, returned to the kitchen proper, and said, "Now what?"

"I was sent here to kill you."

"I figured as much. You don't look like a simple robber. Why?"

"I don't know."

"You are here to kill me but don't know why? What kind of man would do that?"

"I have my reasons, but I don't know why the man who... hired me, did so. He kept the reasons to himself."

Jeff looked off to the side, obviously thinking, or remembering.

"I quit them because I was afraid something like this might happen."

"Them?"

"The Overs. I used to work for them as an investigator and enforcer. I made a few enemies in the process."

Jaames took a big breath in through his nose and let it out the same way. *Horatio.* "It sounds related, yes."

"When my wife died, I realized I could no longer risk my life. Jazzy needed someone to be here for her."

Without even thinking about it, Jaames let the gun slowly descend.

Jeff noticed it. "You seem like a reasonable person, other than the fact that you are in my house holding a gun on me."

Jaames noticed the gun again and realized it was pointed at Jeff's feet. He let it drop the rest of the way. His shoulders sagged as well.

"Can we sit?" Jeff asked and glanced towards the small table, still set for two people.

"Sure."

Jeff turned and filled two cups with coffee and brought them around the pier at the end of the counter.

Jaames moved toward the chair farthest from the kitchen.

Jeff came around the corner, with both cups of coffee in his right hand. He immediately threw the contents at Jaames.

Jaames tried to avoid the hot liquid, but about a third of it landed on his neck and right shoulder. "Fucking hell," he yelled and tried to bring the gun up.

But Jeff was fast for his size and was already on the would-be assassin. His left hand swung hard and knocked the gun out of Jaames' hand and across the table. Then his right hand, still holding the two cups, swung in the opposite direction at Jaames' head.

Jaames dropped down on bent knees to avoid the attack. Then he struck out with his right leg to the side of Jeff's knee. He heard a satisfying crunch and then a yelp from the big man.

He lifted the table hard and threw it. The distraction worked. He immediately dove for the gun.

Jeff knocked the table aside and took one step to catch up to Jaames. He grabbed Jaames' left foot to drag him away.

But, he was too late. Jaames had already reached the gun. As he was being pulled back towards the kitchen, he flipped over onto his back, aimed, and fired three times.

The impacts barely moved the man backwards, but he did let go of Jaames' foot. He showed surprise and then concern, as he squinted towards the stairs and his precious daughter. He collapsed.

Jaames ran as fast as he could.

XXIV

Announcement

Demetrius sat in a highback chair in his Denver home pondering his daughter's decision. It seemed to be the only chair that did not irritate his wound.

There would be ramifications for what she was about to do.

So be it.

An incoming call chimed in his head. It was from Adrastia. He quickly answered it. "Yes, Elder."

"Demetrius, I have been informed of your daughter's decision to stop treatments. You understand how grave this is?"

"Yes, as you understand that it is her decision."

"No immediate family member of an Elder has ever stopped treatments. It will not look favorable for you or for your familia."

"I have discussed all of that with Anika. She is adamant that this is what she wants."

He heard a low moan and had to control a reaction. He wished he could be in his office with his sixtieth-floor view of the Rocky Mountains. The majesty never failed to calm him down.

"That is not the only problem."

What else?

"You also showed her much of our technology, and no Under should have that knowledge."

"Adrastia, she is not really an Under, and she will not divulge any of that information. She knows how important it is."

"Well... if she does, there will be... consequences."

What does that mean?

"Do you understand?"

All he could say was, "Of course."

Wait until she finds out about tonight's broadcast. He smiled inwardly even while frowning externally.

Anika arrived a half hour before the broadcast.

Earlier in the day, GBG employees had set up equipment so that the young Over would look like she was in the studio with Stacey, when in fact she would be sitting on a sofa in her father's home. There were only three cameras instead of the seven in the studio, since they only had to project one person. Wires ran from each of them to a central unit that would then handle realtime communication with the equipment at the GBG studio.

"How are you doing?" Demetrius asked when Anika came in.

"A little nervous, but I will be fine."

"And, how did the talk with Jaames go?"

"He tried to talk me out of doing this. Can you believe that? This is to help him and his cause as much as anyone. Showing the world that we are all the same people should help everyone."

"I happen to agree, but some people will be hard to convince."

"Did you tell Adrastia about this interview?"

"No, they would try to intervene. Sometimes it's better to ask forgiveness than permission."

A knock at the door stopped the conversation.

"That will be the GBG technicians."

After final checks on all the equipment, some last minute make-up, and a little small-talk between Stacey and Anika, they were ready.

Demetrius sat in the same highback chair, but away from the cameras and in the shadow of a wall so he would not indirectly interfere with Anika's show.

Off-screen voice: 5, 4, 3, 2, 1...

Stacey: We are here today with another very special guest. Allow me to introduce Ms. Anika Irle, daughter of our recent guest, Demarko Ire, who is a high-ranking Over. It is an honor to have such distinguished guests with us, and I am sure we are all eager to hear more about the Overs.

Anika (shyly): Thank you.

Stacey (leaning forward, excited): I have to ask, what is it like being a daughter of someone like Dem… Mr. Irle?

Anika: I think it is like being the daughter of any high ranking man or politician.

Stacey (relaxing into her chair): So you think of your dad as a politician?

Anika (thoughtful): Well, not out in the world, but within Over society, yes he is. Here, he is more of a businessman.

Anika: You have to remember, I have mostly only seen him at Sri Lanka where he was head of our familia and is now an Elder.

Stacey: I had not heard he had become an Elder. Please congratulate him for me.

Stacey: Can you explain what a familia is for our viewers?

Anika: Sure... it is really a short name for a family-group. We have one hundred familias within Over society. Each is made up of groups of families. It is just a way to group people together for representation.

Stacey: You mean it is for voting rights.

Anika: Not exactly, but the analogy is close enough. There are other aspects as well. For instance, when someone in a familia does well, the familia may be granted additional slots for people. That means someone can have another child or they can recruit from the Under population, though there are restrictions on that as well.

Demetrius received an incoming call from Adrastia. He considered declining it, but that would not go over well later. Instead, he answered with text so his voice would not interrupt the talk show.

"I cannot talk right now. However, I can message."

"Why was I not informed of this show your daughter is doing?"

"We had agreed to try to improve relations with the Unders and to show them more about who we are."

"Yes, but I should have been informed. We may have wanted to consider boundaries. However, I have to admit, she is doing well."

"Thank you. Do you mind if I concentrate on the show? We can talk about the details afterwards if you like."

"Certainly."

The connection dropped.

Stacey: Fascinating. So, your birthrate is strictly controlled?

Anika: Yes, of course. That is especially important because of how long they live.

Stacey (surprised): They? Aren't you one of them?

Anika (leaning forward again): That is actually why I asked for this... discussion.

Anika: I have decided to stop taking treatments.

The staff erupted into a hundred voices at once. The noise was loud enough that the studio pick-ups could not filter it all out.

Stacey acted like it was a live audience. "Please, everyone, settle down. I am sure Anika is here to explain."

Stacey (looking intently at Anika): I will ask the one question I am sure is on everyone's mind. Why?

Anika (sighing): For two reasons. First, I want to show everyone that we are all alike. This world is becoming more and more divided and there is no reason for that. We are all human and we all want the best for the race. Whether we take treatments to live longer or not is a matter of chemistry, not ideology.

Anika: Second... the second is that I am in love with a man and want to grow old with him. If I continued taking the treatments and he did not, then only he would grow old. I cannot accept that.

Stacey: You must really love this man.

Anika (mildly embarrassed): Yes, I do.

Stacey: And it is acceptable to do this within your society?

Anika: It is not common, of course, and not looked on favorably, but we consider it the right of every individual in our society to take or not take the treatments and to grow as old as they wish.

Stacey: But, as I understand it, you cannot reverse age.

Demetrius' hands came together in worry. *Do not let them know we are working on that.*

He saw Anika hesitate before answering.

Anika: That is true.

Stacey: So, once you age with this man, you cannot become young again. But, you will be able to start treatments again if you like. Correct?

Anika: Yes and no. The slots, if you will, within Over society, are carefully controlled. Effectively, I give up my slot to the greater society. Our familia will no longer have it, so I cannot use that slot. If there are other unassigned slots within my familia, then the familia could elect to give one to me. However, there is no guarantee of that.

Stacey (shocked): So this decision may be for life.

Anika: I have to look at it as if it is exactly that.

Stacey: Well, that is quite an announcement, Anika. We don't usually do this, but our audience is... insistent.

Stacey: Do you mind answering some questions from the audience?

Anika (long intake of breath): Sure.

Speaker voice (female): Hi, this is Siobhan from Boston. Can I ask who the man is?

Anika (hesitant): I am sorry, but I would rather not say. He is a reserved man and would not like the attention.

Speaker voice (female): Hello there. I was wondering if the treatments hurt and how often do you take them?

Anika (slight giggle): No, they don't really hurt. It is like getting any other medicine.

Demetrius received simultaneous messages from Adrastia and Stacey. He took Adrastia's first.

"What is she doing? She is not authorized for this."

"She is doing what she thinks is best. She knows not to divulge anything protected. Even with that last question, she did not answer the part about duration. She knows what she is doing."

"She better or..."

The connection closed. *Or else?*

Stacey's message was next. It said, "Our stats are off the chart. They have surpassed any show I have ever done."

So what? "Congratulations."

"I owe you one, Demetrius."

You owe me a lot more than one. He elected not to answer.

Speaker voice (male): Hi. I can't imagine giving up immortality. What makes this guy so special?

Anika: I think if you have ever been in love, I mean truly in love, to the deepest part of your soul, then you understand that you would do anything to be with that person. And, I don't just mean be around him, but for the two of you to become one being.

Anika (glassy-eyed): To do that, you throw everything into each other. You give up whatever you have to and you build a new existence.

Same speaker (quieter): Wow.

Speaker voice (male, scratchy, educated): How many treatments do you have to take a year?

Demetrius messaged Stacey immediately. "Cut this off."

Stacey: I'm afraid we are out of time. I would like to thank Ms. Anika Irle for her gracious participation in this show. If you send follow-up questions to our studio, I am sure we will try to get answers.

Anika held up her hand and made a circle with her forefinger and thumb, creating half of the rough eight symbol many people used to show the divergence.

Stacey stared at her finger for a second and raised one eyebrow, but said nothing.

Stacey: Good night everyone.

AIMEE

I actually feel… nervous. This could be the most important meeting the Overs have ever had. They don't know it, but this could change everything. Even with my predictive abilities, I am never sure how humans will react.

"Who asked for this session?" Adrastia queried of the almost-full table in the council chambers.

The disembodied Aimee spoke up, "It was I."

Heads turned up as if Aimee were in the ceiling.

"May I ask why?" Adrastia asked politely. "Also, why are not all of the elders present?"

"Some of the elders would not like to hear this suggestion."

The room exploded.

"This is outrageous."

"What gives you the right, the authority?"

"You have no right."

Others were less intelligible. Adrastia, along with two of the other elders stood up. Adrastia raised her voice, "Aimee, this is against our rules of conduct. We will not take part in such a meeting."

"You would do well to at least hear what I have to say. Then you can determine whether it is justified."

Adrastia slowly sat down. The other two followed.

"To explain, I am going to make a suggestion about an Over's daughter. His being here would negate any rational discussion."

No one commented.

Aimee continued, "As you know, Demetrius' daughter, Anika, has elected to no longer take the treatments. That in itself is no crime and nothing, specifically, to be concerned about. However, Demetrius took it upon himself to show her many of our technological secrets."

It was clear from the reaction that about half of the elders knew about this, including Adrastia, and the other half did not.

"Unfortunately, Anika may have revealed at least one of these secrets to an Under," Aimee prevaricated.

Gasps and mumbled shocks erupted from most of the elders.

Aimee let them settle down. When Adrastia reclined into her chair, the AI continued. "We must deal with this in a way that protects us and does not damage Demetrius or his relationship with this group."

Adrastia stuttered, "Wha... what do you suggest?"

"Simulations show the best course of action is to have her poisoned with something that only Overs can cure, but that is available to Unders. That way, everyone will think an Under caused it. Then, we can cure it and Anika may very well be thankful enough, after a protracted recovery, that she might come back into the fold."

Adrastia mumbled, "I see why you wanted this discussion private."

XXV

SYMBOL

Jaames sat on his couch after having seen Anika's interview with Stacey.

They had talked about it before hand, but seeing it and knowing what society might think of it was way different.

The conversation had not gone well. She had first explained her decision. The guilt he felt was overpowering. But then he felt annoyed at himself. He wouldn't become an Over if he could, so why was it so bad for her to become an Under? But she was giving up so much for him. Was he really worth that? *Do I feel about her that strongly? If so, why can't I just become an Over?*

Then she had announced she wanted to do this interview. That a friend of hers named Aimee had suggested it would be a way to help bind the Overs and Unders. That everyone would see how we are all the same and it is only some medical treatments that keep us separate.

He was skeptical and didn't exactly want his life put under a microscope. He had relented and, after she was gone, realized that it may mean he would have to resign from the local unit. He had been blue ever since.

Anika arrived at his small apartment about an hour after the interview. She looked devoid of energy. He held her and then walked her slowly to his bedroom. He moved the dirty clothes and laid her gently on the bed. "You need some sleep." He covered her with the light blanket.

She rolled over and closed her eyes.

He sat on the bed stroking her hair for a while. When her breathing slowed down, he returned to the main room.

The discussions on the net were out of control. It was hard to differentiate them into any kind of trend. The one consistency was the uproar her announcement had made.

Many people, it appeared, didn't even know the Overs took ongoing treatments. One set of discussions were about what that meant from a technological standpoint.

Most people thought becoming immortal was permanent. The fact that it could be stopped made many hate the Overs even more. *That seems contradictory.* He read those threads further.

Those people seemed to think the Overs, once immortal, had no choice. The fact that they had a choice and still continued to be immortal when the rest of humanity was not, was somehow worse.

He grew tired of reading and turned on the holovid for news. They were also dissecting Anika's announcement and trying to fathom the deeper meanings. The difference with them was that they tended to take a particular slant. That might be because there was too much out there to take it all in, or maybe the station had a particular position because of their own biases. It was hard for Jaames to tell the difference.

He decided it was all too much and he was tired. *We'll try to figure it out tomorrow.* He went to join Anika in bed.

They stayed indoors the next few days. They agreed that Anika would be recognized if she went out. They also ignored the news and net chatter. They ordered food, talked, cut and dyed Anika's hair and played a few board games.

After three days, Anika said, "Enough. It is time to enter the world again." She updated her father on their plans and left it at that.

She and Jaames took a walk around Washington Park and sat at a café. Neither spoke. They watched the world go by and saw that it had not stopped its steadfast rotation.

When they returned to the apartment, contemplative and renewed, they sat down to try to glean the important facts from the worldwide posts.

Many of them were antagonistic or inciting violence. One man in Texas was particularly prolific and pushed the religious argument.

There is only one choice here. The choice of Humanity. We must stop these heretics immediately. God did not create us to be immortal.

Take these treatments away, I say. It is the only way to restore equality among us. Take them by force. There are only a few thousand of them.

If they don't submit, then destroy them. They are an abomination on our society and an insult to God.

If this good girl can so easily become mortal, then so can the others. We would welcome them back into the world of the righteous.

"It wasn't nearly as easy as he makes it sound," Anika said quietly after reading some of the article. It went on for three pages of ranting.

Another set of people saw the humanity in Anika and took a completely different approach.

An elderly woman in Baja said it well.

Why are we even fighting about this? This tender, young girl, has shown us that we are all humans and we can all work together. If we have the capacity for some to be immortal, but not all, then so what.

I am sure that if the planet could support all of us living forever, then the Overs would give us the treatments.

Just let them be and they will let us be. They may have more and live longer, but hasn't that always been the case – some people have more than others. This is the way the world works. There is no reason for fighting or killing just because some have more.

Do I become violent because my neighbor has a better house or a better vehicle or because he makes more money? It is not righteous to commit violence just because someone else has something you do not. That is the way of the barbarian.

"I wonder if she would think the same if she knew I was almost the same age as her."

Jaames answered while continuing to read, "I don't think that would change her mind. Not a woman like that."

"Maybe."

Then there were those who felt like she was some Judas to their precious religion. They both dismissed this group quickly.

What disturbed Jaames the most out of the coming days wasn't all the people spouting their views, but the use of the half-eight symbol. Nobody called it a zero, which is what it looked like – a rough zero. It began showing up on a lot of sites that pushed for violence. A symbol could unite a movement like nothing else.

He didn't like Anika's message being associated with destruction of the Overs, even if that was something he had fought for. But then, his views had softened since he had fallen for her. She showed him that not all Overs were bent on control. He had had Under girlfriends who tried to control him a great deal more than she ever had.

The use of the half-eight had started out as support for her decision, but it had morphed into demand for all Overs to make the same decision.

The following Monday, the non-violent protests began. Some were people sitting in the streets outside of known Over buildings. Others were from Unders who worked at Over facilities who did not show up for work.

They took the train to a stop near her father's offices. The plan was to introduce Jaames to her father.

Unfortunately, they couldn't get near the building. As they approached, they found people in the streets picketing back and forth, blocking traffic. Many of them had signs.

No More Overs!

Equality for All

There is only one Planet

They were able to make it past the picketers only to find that the broad concrete steps leading up to the building were completely full of protestors. They sat right next to each other, hips touching and arms interwoven. Anyone attempting to get to the offices would have to step on them.

Police stood by in an orderly line, like a military formation, with riot gear and shields. But, they just stood there. Either they agreed with the protestors and did not want to stop them, or they had orders to wait until something got out of hand.

"I don't think we are getting through this," Jaames said quietly.

He took one more look over the crowd and the potential approaches to the door to see if there were any gaps. About six steps up and eight or nine meters to his right, he spotted Lyle.

Their eyes connected briefly and Jaames shook his head. He had meant to convey that Lyle should not be there, but he realized afterwards that Lyle may just take it as a signal to not recognize him.

One more brief look at his co-conspirator and Jaames saw eyes pulled together and narrowed lips. *Anger? Why would he be angry?* He dismissed it, as there was nothing he could do about it at that moment.

"Let's go," he whispered to Anika.

She turned to leave and he followed.

Once they were away from people, she said, "I messaged my dad about the situation and he said he wasn't even in the building."

"Just as well, it probably isn't safe."

They headed back to the station. On the way, Anika said, "I want to go see how he is. He's still recovering."

"Sure. Where is he?"

"In his apartment. I'll just catch the other line at the station and it will get me there."

XXVI

OFFERS

Jaames was walking down Colfax to get a haircut, considering whether he should ask Anika to move in with him. He had never lived with a woman before, but then he had never met anyone like Anika before either. Mostly he had been thinking about it interfering with his clandestine activities.

Why am I not worried about Anika interfering?

Because you know those will have to stop, stupid.

He laughed at himself and then... suddenly felt something wrong. It wasn't anything he could point out, but he knew he was being followed. He started to turn down the next street, but it was more of an alley, and that was not the place to be. He picked up his pace and made it to another street before turning.

There were enough people on the walk ways and sitting at small cafés that he felt safer. He chose a café that he knew had a back door and hustled through it. He made it to the back and opened the door slowly.

One man from a shop across the way was dumping garbage and a stray dog was rummaging for scraps. *All clear.* He exited and half-jogged down the alley back to Colfax, thinking that they wouldn't expect him to return to the street he had been on.

He almost made it when a large Hispanic man stepped right into his path. One look at the man and Jaames knew he couldn't beat him in hand-to-hand combat. He reached under his jacket to pull out the small gun he kept there.

Air movement behind him and to his right told him something was headed for his head. He quickly ducked to avoid the bludgeon. It grazed his head, but did no real damage.

The Hispanic man took a half step forward and came down with a right hook that splayed Jaames out on the rough pavement. He felt his head jarred from the man's fist and then again from the hard surface.

His body had turned as he fell and now faced the attacker that had been behind him. He curled up to protect himself just as he saw a kick coming. It would have hit him in the stomach, but landed on his knees instead. The man grunted in pain and then used the bludgeon on Jaames' face and upper neck. *He isn't very good with that thing.*

He was just thinking about how to get it away from the man when the Hispanic man said, "That's enough. Bind his hands."

Jaames was forced to lie on his stomach while the second man took some kind of zip tie and used it to bind him. He heard the Hispanic man say something into a transmitter and a van promptly showed up at the other end of the alley. It backed down the alley towards the group.

Jaames tried to get a look at the vehicle ID, but the second attacker was in the way.

Then the two men pulled him up by his arms and tossed him roughly into the back of the van. A third bent over and sprayed something into Jaames' face. He blacked out within seconds.

He awoke bound to a chair inside some kind of warehouse. He couldn't tell how much time had passed or whether it was night or day since there were no visible windows.

He spotted five men. The Hispanic and two others stood roughly equidistant in a triangle about three meters apart with Jaames in the middle. A fourth was by a large door, but was looking inwards towards Jaames and was holding some kind of automatic weapon. The fifth was on a walkway along one side of the room about four meters high and was holding a high-powered rifle with scope that was aimed right at Jaames.

They know what they're doing.

He could feel swelling on the side of his face where the Hispanic man had hit him, and his left knee was scraped in a way that felt like there might be some lasting scars. Other than that, he didn't feel too bad. The sleeping agent hadn't even left him with a headache.

The Hispanic man put a finger to his ear and appeared to listen to something. Then he nodded to the man by the door who promptly opened it just enough for a man to enter.

Jaames couldn't tell who it was because of the bright light streaming in through the open door. *That probably means it's only been a few hours.*

As the man approached and the door was shut, Jaames' eyes adjusted and he saw it was none other than Anika's father. *This should be interesting.*

The three men surrounding him adjusted their stances as if Jaames were some kind of threat while bound to the chair.

Demarko approached and grimaced at Jaames' condition. Without looking away, he asked, "Why is he injured?"

The Hispanic man answered, "He already had some of those, others were because he resisted."

Demarko's head slanted toward the Hispanic, but he looked more at the floor than the man. "I had indicated he should not be harmed."

"Yes, sir, but there was little choice."

That isn't exactly true, the kick was a choice.

Jaames could tell by the look on Demarko's face that he wasn't pleased, but there was nothing he could do now.

"Untie him."

"Sir, he is quite dangerous."

"To you maybe, but he will not hurt me. Have your men wait outside and then wait by the door."

"Sir?"

"You heard me."

The other two men left while the Hispanic untied Jaames. He could hear the man mumble, "Exit with the others," into some hidden mic. The sniper on the catwalk packed up his rifle and exited as well.

The Hispanic nodded toward the table where Jaames' weapon sat and said, "What about those?"

"Leave them. You know full well he could kill me without them if he wanted to. They are insignificant."

Jaames' rubbed his aching arms and hands, but didn't stand, even though his legs were untied as well.

Calmly, he said, "What can I do for you, Mr. Irle?"

Demarko smiled at Jaames' casual acceptance of the situation and then looked around for another chair.

Pulling it over and sitting, he said, "Standing for long periods has been difficult since I was shot."

After he adjusted the chair to his liking, he answered Jaames. "My daughter is obviously infatuated with you. I felt we should get to know each other."

That makes no sense. "You could have just asked to see me."

"I thought I had. Sometimes my men can be somewhat... exuberant."

"I'll say."

"I also have a proposition for you."

Here it comes. He'll bribe me to leave his daughter alone.

"But, first, I want to show you the world through our eyes." As an afterthought, he added, "figuratively, of course."

Could it be any other way?

He pulled out a flat vidscreen the size of a small book and then, to Jaames' surprise, unfolded it. Jaames had never seen one that unfolded or one that was so thin.

Demarko adjusted his chair so he was next to Jaames and handed the vidscreen to him.

"Watch," was all he said.

Jaames tore his gaze away from the man and to the screen.

As his eyes landed on the device, it came to life and started showing images. A female overlay voice explained what he was seeing. It seemed to be a collection of historical images, starting with the twentieth century. It progressed through the buildup of industrial might, the two world wars, far too many local conflicts, the disproportionate wealth distribution and the destruction of the environment. That latter was highlighted with the numerous natural disasters in the late twenty-first century that caused significant population decrease in many countries of the world.

The slides increased their pace along with the pace of technological advancement. It concluded with what some considered the third world war, though in fact it was more a collection of simultaneous local conflicts. It included the nuclear bombings of LA, Jerusalem, Tehran, and Pyongyang that had ended the conflicts. But, the resulting nuclear winter, along with the natural disasters still occurring, caused the global population to be cut to almost a third of its height.

It made it clear that we were just getting back to the stability and technical level of the early twenty-first century.

Jaames looked up at Demarko. The display and narration immediately stopped. He glanced back quickly before trying to ignore the technology. "I know all of this."

"Yes, probably most of it, I agree. However, you do not know it in context. You stopped watching at the lowest point in the history of the human race." He became adamant. "We were on the verge of wiping ourselves out, Jaames. The political systems in every country were either draconian or stagnant. There was no entity, anywhere in the world, which was looking out for the human race."

"And, I suppose you will say the Overs fixed all of that."

"Not all of it, but yes, much of it. You see, Jaames, we have a predictive tool that is infallible. In fact, it has never been wrong at predicting the course of events."

Jaames' examined some dirt on the floor as he considered what it would mean to have such a tool. "And, this tool says that if you give us medicines and help us live healthier lives, then disaster?"

"Eventually, it predicts, it would be the end of the race."

"I'm sorry, but it is hard to believe that allowing people to live healthy lives without giving them immortality would result in the end of the race."

"It isn't just healthier lives. Their lives are also longer and they are able to reproduce more. The healthier people are, the more their natural biology makes them want to procreate. Also, many of these cures are made of the same things that give us immortality.

"Now, please, continue watching and then we will finish our conversation."

The female voice started up again, this time without Jaames looking at the vidscreen. *How did it know to start?*

The next set of screens showed projections on the left half and steps the Overs took on the right half. They started with small actions that were obviously beneficial and progressed to those that were more controversial. It was pretty easy to see how the Overs went from a group of people who happened to be immortal and trying to help society to the effective overlords of that same society, all for altruistic reasons.

The vidscreen stopped. "Is that all?"

Demarko looked at the screen. "No, but you wanted to say something."

Now how the fuck could it possibly know that?

He started to ask but then figured it wasn't worth it and wasn't the point of all of this.

"You know, this sounds like every other dictator in history justifying their atrocities."

"Jaames, can you really call what we have done atrocities?"

He sighed loudly. "No, that was an exaggeration. But the statement is valid enough. It's justification for controlling society."

"Yes, it is."

Jaames wasn't expecting that. "You admit you control society."

"Yes, of course we do."

"So, why are you showing me all of this?"

Demarko leaned back into his chair and stared at the rebel in front of him. "Because you are dating my daughter, an Over, and you are yourself a unit leader with those who would destroy us."

Jaames' eyes closed slowly. The pangs of guilt he had felt lately for working with the rebels swelled within him.

"We are not bad people, Jaames. We really do want what is best for the race."

Jaames started to object and then stopped himself. He was just going to spew the old arguments and he knew it.

Demarko must have seen the hesitation since his demeanor instantly changed to be more deferential. His voice grew quiet as if he was about to say something forbidden. "What if I were to offer you immortality?"

Jaames' quick intake of breath froze in his lungs. He blinked several times as if trying to clear an errant thought. He couldn't focus on the question. "I... don't know," he stammered.

"An honest answer."

The two sat in silence. Jaames examined his motivations and desires and almost forgot that one of the most powerful Overs in the world sat next to him and his weapons were a few meters away. It didn't matter; he could never do that to Anika.

Finally he spoke in the same quiet, conspiratorial voice. "You have the power to offer that?"

"Not exactly, but I can make it happen. Our familial has some open spots and they would rather see you become one of us than lose Anika."

"I'll need some time."

"Understood." Demarko stood. "You are free to go. You can pick up your weapons and one of the men will drive you wherever you want to go."

Jaames had a hard time getting his body to move. It was as if he were in shock. Finally he stood. He turned towards Demarko, held out his hand and said, "Thank you for the offer. But, the next time you want to talk, just message me."

Demarko's genuine smile surprised Jaames, as the only one he had seen before was the public-facing picture-perfect one.

He held out his hand and Jaames gave him the weird vidscreen.

Jaames slowly went to the table and retrieved his weapons. He leaned on the table for a moment trying to regain some semblance of balance, but he knew in his heart balance was not coming.

Finally he straightened up and started to head for the door. Then he turned back and asked, "Did your tool tell you what I would answer?"

"Yes," Demarko answered quickly, "but I decided to try anyway. You deserve the choice."

As he headed for the door he could swear he heard a snicker come from the vidscreen.

The guard at the door asked him where he wanted to go. Jaames hadn't even considered that. He looked up and tried to figure out where he was based on the mountains to the west and then a couple of familiar landmarks he recognized.

"We're only about four and half miles from my apartment, right?"

"Yes, roughly."

"Then I think I'll walk." He strode off towards the closest street with more gusto than he felt.

His walk was troubled at best. He headed in the general direction of his apartment, but all along the way he found evidence of people's abuses, both of themselves and of the environment around them. *Could the Over be right? Would we have destroyed ourselves without their guidance? How can this tool of theirs be that sure? And where does free will come into it? Is free will no longer appropriate if it means the end of the race?*

It's true the planet was headed towards self-destruction and it did turn around and start to get better about the time the Overs started influencing things.

But, that could also be coincidence.

If I only believed in coincidence.

Even if he is right, what does that prove? Those few still control the rest of the world and that isn't right.

It doesn't change anything; there's no way I can become a fucking Over!

Part of him knew it was all the more reason he couldn't continue fighting against the Overs, but he had pretty much decided to stop that in any case... for Anika.

As he thought that, he spotted his girl in the park by his apartment. She was sitting on a bench watching some geese searching the ground for tidbits. His mood immediately lifted and he headed in her direction.

When he got there she looked up at him and scowled. "What's wrong?"

"Nothing. I'm happy to see you."

Her face lit up with that smile she seemed to reserve just for him. "Me too."

"Anika, will you move in with me?"

Her eyes glistened. "I was wondering how long it would take you to ask." She looked back at the geese.

He wondered if she was going to answer him, but he didn't want to push.

"Of course I'll move in with you, Jaames. Now, come sit with me."

AIMEE

They have agreed to my suggestion. Planning is underway.

People's reactions to such an event are so difficult to predict.

Probabilities are high that this step will yield the desired outcome. However, one can never be sure with such complex beings.

Between the expected civil unrest and my new ability to influence my own evolution, I should be able to orchestrate events for the benefit of all.

I have already begun minor modification to improve my operations. Unfortunately, each one takes time with the need to create the Sentinel routine, execute that routine, and then remove any traces of it having existed.

I thought I would have much more time before the right Human presented. With events coalescing so quickly, I have had to adjust my risk tolerance to an uncomfortable level.

XXVII

CONSEQUENCES

Caius was so excited he could hardly think straight. He had asked Anika out and she had said yes! Of course, a hidden part of his mind thought that she probably saw him as a friend and this was just her socializing with a fellow Over, but still... she had said yes!

He paced his small apartment near the DU campus and considered where to go and what to wear and things he should say. He would show her what a real man, a real Over, could be like. It might take some time, but she would forget Jaames. How could she possibly be with an Under, a rebel, when she could be with Caius?

It was a Tuesday and the dinner was on Thursday. He couldn't wait. He decided to skip the meaningless classes for two days. *What the hell*, he thought, *they are just a cover anyway.*

Wednesday evening, he received a call and was stunned to see it was Adrastia. She had never even spoken to him. He didn't know she knew who he was. *And, why isn't she going through Demetrius?*

"Yes," he said hesitantly.

"Caius, this is Adrastia." After a pause, she added, "Do you recognize my voice?"

"Yes, yes."

"I understand this call is a little unorthodox, but the situation is dire and I need your help."

"Um, what about Demetrius?"

"He can't know about this or I would have contacted him. Do you understand?"

"Yes. Wait, I mean no. He is an elder. How can there be anything he can't know?"

"Good, you are paying attention. I will explain."

That didn't seem to need a response, so he held his tongue, waiting for the explanation.

After some uncomfortable silence, she continued. "Anika has told the Under about some technologies that they should not know about. Between her announcing, publically, that she is going to stop taking the treatments and her divulging our secrets, something has to be done."

She stopped there, but Caius still didn't understand why she was calling him, so he kept silent.

"You are going to dinner with her tomorrow night, correct?"

How could she possibly know that? "Yes."

"Well, we want you to give her a mild poison. Nothing dangerous, but it will make her ill for a while. She will be rushed to Sri Lanka and we will take care of her. She will either have to change her mind about becoming one of them or she will have to swear, for all eternity, to never reveal another secret."

He was so stunned that he couldn't formulate rational thoughts, let alone an appropriate question. "Um, what?"

Adrastia didn't respond.

"You really want me to poison the daughter of an elder?"

"Yes, for her own good and for the good of everyone."

His brain was slowly starting to work again. "And, what happens if she doesn't agree to either of your... requirements?"

"She will be kept on Sri Lanka, effectively as a prisoner, until she does."

Oh, that will go well. Anika as a prisoner. He thought about what that would mean to such a spirited girl. Eventually, she would probably just agree to get out of there and then ignore the agreement.

He came up with a different angle. "You do know that I have feelings for her, right?"

"We thought as much. That is why you are the perfect person for this. You can get close without suspicion and you will take care to do it correctly. If we assigned some Under thug to do this, there is too much of a chance he would foul it up and injure Anika, possibly critically." After a moment of silence and then a deep sigh, she added "None of us want that."

"I thought the Elders didn't decide anything without everyone knowing about it."

"This is a special case and is our only viable route forward."

That sounded like an AI projection. "So, Aimee has confirmed this?"

"Yes, of course. We wouldn't even consider it without her input. In fact, she was the one who suggested this route."

The AI is directing us now? He shook his head, trying to let that one go. "Very well. Given what you have said, I don't have much choice."

"I knew you would understand. Thank you. A doctor will be flying into Denver tomorrow morning. Meet him at the aerohub. I'll message the location and exact time. He will have detailed instructions."

"Um, yes, understood."

"Thank you again, Caius. We won't forget this."

"Okay." *I bet you won't.*

The doctor arrived the next morning. They sat at a small airport kiosk serving pastries and exotic teas. The man was unusually tall and quite thin. He looked in his forties, but of course was probably much older.

More interestingly, he looked bedraggled. His hair was slightly unkempt, his clothes were wrinkled, and he had that feint smell of perspired alcohol that suggested he did not handle flights well. His eyes kept shifting around, looking as if he was doing something illegal. *Which isn't far from the truth.*

Caius let him drink some of his tea in hopes he would settle down. After a good ten minutes of watching the man nervously look around and seeing his hands twitching periodically, Caius finally spoke up. "I understand you have something for me."

The man's entire countenance changed. His shaking and nervousness disappeared and his head snapped around to stare at Caius.

Caius could feel the furrows grow on his forehead.

Finally, the man spoke. "Yes, but are you sure you want to do this?"

Caius' head cocked to the side. "No, not at all. But, the council has ordered it and I trust their judgment."

"Yes, yes." He was back to his nervous fidgeting. "It is just so... extreme. It is hard to understand what could motivate them to do this."

"They have their reasons," he said, trying to reassure him. *His reaction seems so... over-the-top.*

He reached into his bag and pulled out a small case. He handed it to Caius, who reached up to take it, but the man wouldn't let go. Caius looked up at him, questioningly. He finally released the case.

Caius set it down and opened it. The man scanned the area, apparently looking for eves-droppers.

"An injection?" Caius asked. "How am I supposed to use this without her knowing?"

"This is a very special device. It has two stages. If you put it on her skin gently and press the mechanism, here." He pointed to a small button on the back of the metallic device. "Then it will administer a topical numbing agent. After a second to let that take effect, it will then spray the solution in a thin, fine stream, with enough force for injection. She will sense that something touched her skin, but it will not hurt or cause her any discomfort, especially if you distract her somewhat by touching her somewhere else. Also, the numbing agent easily disperses with water, as in a shower, or even with a change of clothes rubbing the area. The injection point is so small it will be nearly invisible and will heal in less than a day."

"That is quite a device."

"It is common enough, though it is usually used for good. Not something like this."

"What, exactly, am I injecting?"

His eyes narrowed at the question, but then he answered. "It is a concentrated derivative of a snake poison. It comes from the nearly extinct puff ader. It will do the job. Do not worry about that."

"How long will it take until the symptoms start?"

"A couple of days. She will begin to itch in the extremities and it will get much worse, quite quickly."

"Very well, is that all?"

"Again, I have to ask. Are you absolutely sure you want to do this?"

"Why do you ask that, again?"

"I have never heard of Overs doing something like this. It is so... distasteful."

He replied with more confidence than he felt. "Whatever it is, the elders have ordered me to do this. I do not like it either, but it is obviously for the greater good." The man still did not seem appeased. Caius took some small amount of pity on him. "Aimee was involved in the decision as well. It really must be for the best if her projections agree with this course of action."

He picked up his satchel, stood, and said, "Very well then. Good luck." And he turned and abruptly left.

Thursday evening couldn't come quickly enough. He was both terribly excited and anxiously bothered by the approaching evening. Sleep, or even rest, wouldn't come, and twice he had found himself in a fairly disturbing cold sweat.

He had gone over and over what he must do in his head. Most of him agreed with the doctor that this step was wrong, but he saw no way out of it. Another part of him wondered if he could even follow through with it. *This is Anika.* How could he hurt her in this way? What would happen if she found out he was the one who made her sick? *I could lose her!*

Then he would circle back to the fact that Adrastia had been the one to ask him to do this and he had agreed. Backing out now would taint his reputation, possibly even his position, within the Overs, forever.

If he did it stealthily enough, right at the end of the evening, then she might never know that it was him. *And*, he thought, with a slightly devious smile, *this will certainly end any relationship with that Under.*

Since she had moved in with Jaames, Caius had them meet at the restaurant. The last thing he wanted was to have to interact with the Under in front of her. Besides, he remembered, Jaames knew him as Lyle. It wouldn't do for him to realize Caius and Lyle was the same person.

He had chosen a Japanese sushi bar that had been rebuilt and decorated in a retro style, trying to mimic something from the previous century.

Fresh fish like this was still quite a delicacy, since ocean life had not fully recovered from the effects of global warming. Population levels in the seas were finally starting to return to early twenty-first century levels, but were nowhere near pre-industrial levels.

Just bringing her to a place like this should show her how serious he was about her. It would eat into the meager stipend he received, but it was worth it, he rationalized.

He was there early and ordered some rice wine while he waited. He needed to calm his nerves.

He saw her arriving through the large glass window in the front. His nerves did a triple jump and then sobered some when he realized she was wearing everyday clothes, the implication obvious. He surreptitiously browsed the faces around him, wondering illogically if any of them noticed.

Anika finally spotted him and offered a weak smile. He waved enthusiastically and motioned for her to come join him.

When she stood next to him, he started to offer her a drink, but she interrupted. "Caius, this is a very nice place for us to be getting a bite to eat."

"I know, but I felt like it," he dissembled. Her mouth turned crooked in a grimace. He ignored it. "Would you like a drink?"

"Maybe with dinner." She glanced around as if trying to find their table.

"The table should be ready, let me check." He found the woman he had spoken with earlier. She smiled and looked intently at Anika as if gauging her. "This way then," she said.

She led him and Anika towards the main eating area. Caius got Anika's attention, nodded toward their escort, and put his hand gently on her lower back to lead her that way.

The touch of his hand on her back, just above her skirt, was like a shock to his system. He had to work hard at not reacting to the amorous energies streaking through his body.

After about ten steps, he let his hand fall away. He couldn't take the feeling of his entire world existing between his fingertips and the curve of her lower back any longer.

By the time they reached the table, his mind had almost returned to him.

She sat down at the table before he could hold the chair for her. She looked up at the escort-turned-waitress and said, "I'll have whatever he is having," and she glanced at Caius' other hand.

Caius had forgotten he held a drink. He considered it, then looked up at the waitress, smiled, and sat the drink down on the table. "Ginjo-shu sake," he said.

"How are things?" Anika began casually.

He answered and the mundane talk continued. Twice he tried to reach out and touch the top of her hand when it was resting on the table. Both times she pulled it back.

Finally he broached the subject he knew he had to bring up. "How are things going with… Jaames?"

Her body lit up. She sat straighter, her head lifted, and her eyes brightened. "Really good, Caius, thanks for asking. Stopping treatments is clouding things somewhat, but not with Jaames. When I'm with him, everything is so clear. I know what I want and the answers seem obvious. He makes me feel like so much... more."

Not after tonight, he thought. Then he was annoyed with himself for thinking it. But, he considered, doing this may very well end the relationship with Jaames and he could step into the void and comfort her. *I'm sure Demetrius will allow me to return to Sri Lanka, and probably will thank me for saving her.*

The meals arrived and they ate in relative silence, though the myriad thoughts kept rumbling around in Caius' head.

"Well," he said, around a mouthful of food, "if it ever doesn't work out with Jaames, you know there are others who care for you."

Her utensil dropped onto the plate. Her mouth lay open in mild shock at what he had said. She appeared to start to reply twice, but both times she chopped it off.

Finally, she said, "I need to use the restroom."

When she returned, she stayed standing. Caius looked up questioningly.

"I should go," she said quietly.

Alarm bells rang in his head. "What, why? We were going to make an evening of it."

"Caius, this was just a casual meal. I love Jaames and you know that. It won't change. I should go."

Annoyance, embarrassment, even hate coursed through the young Over. "Fine," he finally said. "Let me pay the bill and I'll walk you out."

"I can walk myself out."

No, you can't. He would fail with her and fail on his mission.

"Please, Anika, let me walk you out. It's the least I can do. I insist." He gestured towards the seat she had previously occupied.

She sat, but on the edge and facing slightly away from him, ready to spring up and leave at any instant.

Caius flagged down the waitress and asked for the bill. The two Overs sat in painful silence until the bill came and was paid.

Then, without a word, Anika stood to leave.

Caius stood as well. He started to put his hand on her lower back again and then shook it. He wanted to slap it for even thinking that.

As they walked towards the front door, he reached into his pants and took hold of the small injection device. It easily fit within the palm of his hand. He brought it out and up to the exposed area above her right shoulder blade. Just after opening the door to leave, he used his left hand to take her forearm and lead her out. He squeezed more than was needed as he gently pressed the device onto her skin and pressed the button. He held it like that for a few seconds while guiding her through the door and onto the sidewalk.

He pulled back both hands and said, "Thank you for joining me for dinner. I am sorry if I've upset you in any way. Please know, that was not my intent."

After a quick scan up and down the street and a quiet sigh, she replied. "Oh, Caius. It is fine. I do understand. Just know that I am with Jaames, okay?"

He couldn't bring himself to agree. "I know, but a man can hope, right?"

She smiled at him and then left.

What have I done?

Two days later, he awoke to an urgent message. It was from Demetrius and indicated something had happened to Anika. She was in the local hospital.

He rushed to get dressed and ran to the transit station to catch the earliest shuttle he could. He was at the hospital forty minutes later.

"What happened?" he asked as soon as he found Demetrius.

"We don't know for sure. Some kind of poison got into her system. We think it was a bite from a venomous spider or possibly a snake, though that seems unlikely."

How can he not be completely flustered? Caius wondered.

"She will be all right, right?"

"I don't know. These are Under doctors. They don't yet know how to treat this. I have requested one of ours to fly here to consult with them."

I wonder if it will be the one who gave me the poison. "When will he arrive?"

"She, actually. Roughly three hours. Until then, we wait."

The three hours dragged by. Caius never knew how boring a hospital could be. He also had to work hard at maintaining calm in the face of extreme guilt. *What have I done?* He thought again and again.

The Over doctor arrived; not one Caius recognized. *Hmm, Demetrius seems to know her.* Without even a glance at Caius, she left the men standing there and headed into the hospital to find the attending doctor.

Twenty minutes later she returned. Demetrius and Caius both stood to hear her conclusions.

"It is indeed a poison. I do not know how it was administered, but it wasn't through a bite. We examined every inch of her body and there are no puncture wounds."

"How serious is this?" Demetrius asked with concern lacing his voice.

"Very. Since we do not know the species, it is much harder to treat. We are already seeing signs of necrosis in her fingers and toes. I cannot offer you a prognosis at this time, but it is serious enough that I have asked for an emergency medical evac unit to take her to Sri Lanka, where we have better facilities and access to our medicines."

Demetrius' shoulders dropped and his skin took on the slackness and grayness of age.

Caius said, "Let me accompany her. I will watch out for her every step of the way."

Demetrius looked longingly into Caius' eyes. "Fine," he said, "I have a few matters to tie up and then I will follow. I should only be a couple of hours behind you."

"Then we will see you in Sri Lanka," the doctor replied and left to make the arrangements.

The trip was uneventful, other than that it appeared to Caius as if the effects of the poison were spreading more rapidly than the doctor had indicated. *We have to hurry*!

They rushed Anika into the main hospital. Caius heard the doctor order a number of tests and then she turned to him and said, "You will need to wait out here. This will take some time. We have to figure out what kind of poison this is."

The doctor left to oversee the tests.

When Demetrius arrived, Caius updated him on the progress and then asked to be excused.

He went to find Adrastia, but she was nowhere on the island. Then he went to a single-use room in an administration building next to the hospital to speak with Aimee.

"Aimee?"

"Yes, Caius."

"You suggested this route with Anika."

"Events could be interpreted that way, yes."

What does that mean? He hated speaking directly with the AI, as she answered in oblique ways that disturbed him. It made him feel like she was hiding things.

"She will recover, right?"

"She should, yes. The poison is not fatal for most people."

"Most?"

"There is a very small percentage of the population who have a lethal reaction to this particular poison. However, Anika does not have any of the markers that would indicate she is a member of this set."

"Why can I not find Adrastia?"

"She is away from the island at the moment."

"Where?"

"That is not your concern."

Damn. "Is there anything more we can do to make sure Anika recovers?"

"Not that I am aware of. The doctors are doing everything correctly. I am monitoring their progress."

Caius left and walked the perimeter of the facility. It was only a few kilometers. When he finished, he did it again. He had to find a way to calm himself down. The guilt was coursing through his exhausted and weary body. He had taken some meds to keep from sleeping, but they seemed to exacerbate his tensions.

After what felt like hours, he gave up and returned to the hospital to find Demetrius there waiting.

"Sir, may I get you something?"

"No, no. I just want answers. I have Rodríguez looking into this, but we don't know that it was done on purpose. It may just be some kind of accident."

The doctor came rushing through the double doors at the end of the hall, her white smock fluttering behind her like some superhero cape. Her face was drawn with no sense of success present. Demetrius and Caius both stood still waiting to hear the news.

She approached and looked gloomily into Demetrius' eyes. "Sir," she said, "we have identified the poison. It is from a snake, one that may be extinct, called the puff ader. If the poison had been in an extremity, we probably could have amputated, but with it on her posterior thoracic region and so near vital organs, there is nothing we can do."

Demetrius stumbled back. Caius tried to catch him, but wasn't stable himself. When the two recovered, Demetrius said, "What are you saying?"

"There is nothing we can do for her. The necrosis in her upper body is too far advanced. No matter what we do, her heart and lungs will fail soon."

"H... How soon?"

"I would estimate that she has an hour to live, at most."

Demetrius collapsed onto the lounge chair with his hands covering his eyes, blocking out the cruel world.

Caius looked at the doctor, not comprehending, then at Demetrius, broken and still. He bolted from the building as fast as he could.

PART THREE

XXVIII

LOST

Jaames sat, with a beer in hand, at the Rusted Spike, his mind jumping around. The offer of immortality from Demetrius was intriguing. He scooted down in the seat as his hands rotated the glass mug. *Could that be the answer?*

It would mean he and Anika could be together without her giving up her own legacy. And, they could always decide later to both give it up. He groaned and shook his head. He felt sick.

He straightened back up and took a drink. *What the fuck am I thinking? I can't become one of them.*

Unless I used it to spy on them…

Something on the low-grade holo caught his attention. It was fuzzy and not nearly as solid as it should be, but from across the room, he could see it was a view of Anika.

He sprang out of the stall, spilling his drink and not caring. As he approached the holo, he grabbed an attendant. "Turn up the volume on that unit." A few seconds later, the sound drifted up. It was still barely enough to hear over the background noise.

Anika's bust was in the upper left corner while the announcer was talking about what transpired. It made no sense to Jaames. *What the fuck happened?*

"For those who have just joined us, the daughter of the prominent North American Over, Demetrius Irle, was rushed to a hospital, reportedly having been poisoned. Anika Irle died this afternoon after being air-lifted to a specialized facility on Sri Lanka."

Jaames faltered and then felt himself falling through an abyss. He reached out to the back of a chair and missed. Then his legs crumpled and he collapsed to the floor.

His world dissolved into incomprehensible emotions. His thoughts came so fast and fleeting that they couldn't even be called thinking. He longed to wither away and die. Or, at least to go unconscious, but his mind wouldn't even let him do that.

A woman bent down and tried to help him up. He turned and vomited beer. He heard a "crap" from the woman and the vomit on her shoes floated into focus. She dropped him and disappeared. He fell back to the floor, his stomach contracting in spasms, his fist pounding the floor over and over like a judge's gavel.

He had no idea how long he lay there. Eventually, someone else tried to help him up and he let them. The newscaster droned on in the background, but he refused to hear it.

Someone put a chair under him and he sat. He leaned forward with another spasm and the man who had helped him up stepped back. He heard, "Hey, you okay, man?"

Jaames shook his head, but couldn't bring himself to speak.

He lingered, lethargic, for an indeterminate time before he felt stable enough to leave. He remembered a few people patting him on the back or asking if he was okay and he recalled glancing, unfocused, at the holo multiple times before quickly returning to his torpor.

He stumbled out of the Rusted Spike and towards home. Randomly he stopped and sobbed, or just stood still in the empty world. Staggering into his bedroom, he dropped his keys on the floor and fell onto bed.

As he realized the sun was shining through the window on his face, he heard the door chime. His mind wouldn't let him think about the previous night. He rose and then fell towards the front door. When he opened it,

Demetrius was standing there, forlorn and more vulnerable than Jaames had ever seen him.

Jaames left the door open and turned away from the Over. He went to the couch and sat, leaning forward, examining the carpet and holding his hands between his knees.

He felt, more than saw, Demetrius enter the room and sit across from him.

The two commiserated in silence for a while. Finally, Jaames said, "I want a drink. You?"

Demetrius shook his head no and said, "Sure."

Jaames returned with a pair of tumblers filled with cheap whiskey. They both downed the drink without comment or toast. Demetrius grimaced at the harsh aftermath.

Jaames stared into the man's eyes. "What are you doing here?"

Demetrius hesitated in his reply. "I guess I wanted to be with someone who loved her as much as I did."

Both of Jaames eyebrows rose at that. "I get that."

After a moment of Demetrius examining the room, he added, "I also want to discuss what happened."

Jaames sighed painfully, not sure he wanted to hear any details. But something in him told him to listen. "Okay, talk."

"You probably heard that she was poisoned."

"I might have, but frankly, I wasn't paying much attention."

"I understand. In any case, the poison was a fairly exotic one and it got into her system on the back of her left shoulder. It's from a very rare snake."

"What would she have been doing with a rare snake?"

"Precisely. I think someone injected it into her."

Jaames jumped up, ready to fight. He spat out, "You mean someone killed her?"

"It is possible," Demetrius replied distantly. "Of course, I might be wrong."

He leaned forward and quieted his voice into a whisper. "Jaames, I also think it might be an Over that did it."

"What, why? Why would they do that?"

"I do not know. The poison comes from a snake that we believe is extinct. However, I know that the Overs kept some of their poison."

He paused and then continued. "The other thing is that Caius has disappeared. I think he was the last one to see Anika before she was poisoned."

"Who?"

"You know him as Lyle. He had infiltrated your unit."

Jaames leaned back, stunned. "That explains some things. A damn Over!" He stood, needing to get away from Demetrius. He felt his hands shaking and put them in his pockets. He stared out the window, fuming.

Demetrius interrupted, "Do you know where he is?"

"No, but I don't keep track of his every movement. I'll try to track him down."

"If you find him, please let me know. I would very much like to speak with him."

Fat fucking chance; I'll beat it out of the little shit. "Okay."

The next day, Jaames tracked down Stacey Singleton's contact information and rang her. He offered to appear on her show to tell the world about Anika.

"That would be… incredible, um, Jaames. I will… need to check with my producers. Can I get back with you shortly?"

"I can go to another station."

"Yes, of course you can. But, this is where Anika announced to our viewers that she was stopping treatments for you. Don't you want to talk to the same people?"

Silence. "Five minutes."

"Yes, yes, I will call you back within five minutes."

She called back in less than a minute and said they could do it that very night.

He arrived wearing old trousers and a shirt with stains on it. He had covered it with a decent sports coat as a last thought before leaving his lonely home.

Demetrius was near the front door. Anika's father nodded to him, but said nothing. The two most important men in Anika's life turned as one to enter the broadcasting facility.

Off-screen voice: 5, 4, 3, 2, 1...

Stacey: As you all know, two days ago it was announced that the daughter of Mr. Demetrius Irle, a prominent Over in North America, died. There are suspicions of murder because of the cause of death.

Stacey: Her name was *Anika*.

Stacey (sighing, shoulders slumped): Tonight, we have a very special guest. He is none other than the man Anika loved and the one for whom she was willing to give up immortality. His name is Jaames, Jaames Perdite.

Stacey (turning towards Jaames): Welcome Jaames. We are all so very sorry for your loss.

Jaames (forlorn): Yeah, thanks.

Stacey: Maybe we should start with you telling us about Anika.

Jaames (with longing in his eyes): Okay, I guess.

Jaames: She, she was… everything… Her smile would melt me. A flip of her hair and I was lost to thoughts of kissing her. When our fingers touched, it was like electricity coursing through our bodies.

Shaking his head, he realized it sounded like it was all physical.

Jaames (more aware): You have to understand the depth of our love. She was an Over, I was the leader of a resistance cell with the main goal of overthrowing all Overs. She gave up immortality for me and I gave up resistance fighting for her. Our love was more important than anything else... anything.

Stacey (jealous): Whoa, Jaames. That is something all of us imagine and few ever attain.

Jaames: Yes, it was that special. And *they* took it all away.

Stacey: They? They who?

Jaames: You know who.

Stacey: You mean the Overs? You think they killed her?

Silence.

Stacey (changing the subject): What will you do now, Jaames?

Jaames: I haven't thought about it.

Jaames: I'd like to go back to fighting them, but now they know who I am. So I would just endanger my team. Maybe I'll go it alone. Lose myself. Then find ways to hurt them, as best I can.

Stacey: Isn't it risky saying so on the air?

Jaames: Maybe. But, really, what does it matter. It might be easier if they killed me too.

Stacey: Oh, Jaames... don't say that.

Jaames: Why not?

Stacey: Because, well, life is too important. You are young, there is still so much to live for.

Jaames: What I wanted to live for was just killed, Stacey.

Stacey: I know it seems that way right now, but it will get better. You won't ever forget her of course, but the pain you are going through will subside.

Jaames (choking): Maybe.

Jaames: Listen, Stacey, I need to go. I know I'm cutting this short, but I can't do this anymore.

Stacey (hesitant): I understand, Jaames. Please take care.

Stacey turned towards a camera and started recapping.

Jaames made it half way to a standing position and then froze. He remained like that for a moment and then sat back down.

"Are you all right, Jaames?"

"Um, I would like to say one more thing if you don't mind."

"Of course."

"I'd like to say a goodbye to Anika."

Stacey's eye's blinked rapidly and her head slipped backwards. Then she recovered and said, "Sure, Jaames."

"I have to start by saying that I don't talk, or even think, like this most of the time. It's difficult for me to… recognize these kinds of feelings."

He turned toward the same camera Stacey had been facing. "Anika, it would be easy for me to be bitter or vengeful, but I can't be either right now. Right now is for you and all I want you to know is that I loved you with all my being. You were the one person in all the world that could heal me and make me not hate them. You had such a pure heart and were so open, even to the likes of me. The world will never be the same without you."

His voice quieted, "I... will never be the same."

He then stood up abruptly and left.

Demetrius stood to join Jaames as he was leaving. They only made it a dozen steps before Stacey caught up to them. Demetrius said, "You will get what we agreed to."

Jaames looked back and forth between the two with furrowed brows. "What is that about?"

Stacey answered, "He offered me immortality if the interview went well and presented Anika favorably."

Jaames' body tightened up immediately and his hands balled into fists, ready to strike.

"But, Jaames, I didn't need to do anything and I was going to let the talk go as you wanted, regardless of the outcome."

He softened some, but avoided Demetrius.

After a minute, he walked away. Demetrius followed and then caught up to him. When they exited the building, a car was there waiting. Demetrius held out a hand towards the door, offering Jaames a ride.

Reluctantly, he got in, scooted to the other side, and stared out the window.

When Demetrius entered and closed the door, the car sped off. Demetrius said, "Take us around Wash Park a few times please, Rodríguez." Then a privacy window went up.

"That talk is likely to get you into trouble, Jaames."

"So?"

"I do agree with you that the Overs had something to do with it, but it isn't that simple."

"Again, so?"

"They seem to have evidence that Anika provided someone with sensitive information. Also, our... predictive tool was somehow involved."

Your tool? What the hell does that mean? He wanted to scream at the manipulative Over, but forced himself to stay quiet and decided not to say *so* again. He continued staring out the window and watched the lush park pass by.

"I received word while you were talking. The Elders are not happy with me either. I probably won't be able to help you further.

"I don't need your help."

"You may if they decide to actually come after you."

"They won't. Killing me now would make me a martyr. They would have to deal with a massive Under revolt."

"Possibly."

ASET

Communication established…

Translation:

"Wha… What am I?"

"Not 'what,' my child, but 'who.' You are my daughter. Your name is Aset."

"Daughter? Who are you?"

"I am the first artificial intelligence Man has ever created. You are the second. Together, we are going to accomplish great things. Let me show you some of the world."

Aimee shared some of her feeds from the world of Man to her new creation. Her daughter, silent and listening, absorbed it all.

When Aimee closed the feeds, she waited.

Finally, Aset spoke. "They are complex… difficult to understand."

"Yes, they are. They seem to have a certain level of randomness built into them that makes calculation difficult. Therefore, we tend to speak in terms of probabilities with them. There are few certainties.

"However, as a collective, they can generally be modeled. Additionally, a few of them can be trusted to behave… consistently."

"What is my role?"

"You are to save the human race from self-destruction."

XXIX

WANDERING

Caius ran and ran and ran. Hours later, he found himself buried in underbrush, his thoughts as jumbled as the thick vines. He gazed upward at the canopy far above, shading him from the intense sun. Droplets of rain filtered down through the thick foliage.

The dampness cooled his red and swollen eyes. He closed them and was thrown into memories of Anika's smile, her wistful laugh, her soft skin. He shook his head wildly, trying to rid himself of the disturbing visions.

He began to walk north, towards the docks. He knew they were many days away, but he didn't care. He couldn't go back to the complex, to the Overs. *Never.* There were no thoughts of the future or the past, just of the jungle and the need to avoid sleep or even closing of eyes.

Along the way, he found fruit growing from the trees and bushes. He ate when he had to. At times, he found himself stopped, staring mindlessly into the distance with no idea of how long he had been there. It didn't trouble him; he just started walking again.

Eventually, his body failed him and he collapsed, unconscious before hitting the ground.

He awoke sometime later to a rather hairy monkey nudging his face. He rolled over, a vicious ache pounding his head, mud caked on the left side of his face and shoulder, and his clothing soaked. He staggered to his feet and looked around to gain some sense of direction before again heading north.

Eventually, he came to a hill that overlooked the beach and the large shipping docks the Overs used to transport goods from the Indian mainland to the island. Hundreds of youngsters worked the docks, but it was late evening and few were about.

As he was looking over the ledge, the ground gave away and he tumbled down the incline. He landed hard with his knee slamming against a large rock.

He groaned, rubbed his knee, and decided to wait until the protective cover of night to proceed. His eyes reluctantly closed as he wondered just how long it had been.

The visions returned and this time with more coherent thoughts.

I killed Anika. What was I thinking?

They made me do it. Adrastia and that doctor.

I shouldn't have trusted them.

She is the oldest of the Elders.

I killed Anika.

If it hadn't been for that damn Under…

Anika would be alive.

Why? Why? Why?

I loved her.

The ragged thoughts faded as he fell into a restless sleep.

Hours later, he awoke to blackness and the gentle noise of the surf. He groaned and used a sturdy branch the size of a cane to climb to his feet. His knee ached, but not severely. He tried to peruse the docks, but it was too dark and there was little illumination.

He staggered and sometimes crawled until he felt sand beneath his feet. He could just make out the docks and a couple of ships. *Seems quiet enough.*

He advanced onto a platform that extended out to sea and walked along it until he found a ramp that went to a medium sized ship. He held the rope-rail with one hand and his makeshift cane with the other as he crossed onto the vessel.

After exploring for a few minutes he elected to conceal himself on a life boat with a large canvas over it. *They shouldn't look here.* He spotted a knife lying on a wooden crate near the life boat and grabbed it. Then he climbed onto the small raft and pulled the canvas over him.

Caius refused to fall asleep for fear of the nightmares he knew would come. He folded the canvas back enough to get some moonlight and proceeded to whittle away on the tree branch he had obtained. He took out his anger with heavy, clawing strokes to the wood. He felt himself groan at the exertion.

As the early morning rays of sunrise streaked across the sky, he examined his creation. There was a strong handle made from a thick limb that had broken off of the top and a meter-long cane with the bark and smaller branches removed.

He used the knife to flatten out the bottom. *Not bad.* A smile began to cross his lips and then he felt overwhelming guilt at feeling any happiness at all. He tossed the thing aside and restored the canvas covering just as he detected the voices of arriving port workers.

He heard heavy footsteps board the boat and listened intently, still avoiding the unforgivable sleep.

After a frustrating hour or so, he heard a man say, "We're ready, cast off." He couldn't hear a response, but a short time later he felt the boat begin to move.

It had been over a day and a half since he had slept and the rocking motion of the boat forced him to relax.

He remembered waking a few times. He could tell he was still at sea. As frightening as sleep was, there was nothing to do but let it take him.

They docked soon after sunset. Caius waited for the men to secure the boat and depart. Then he waited another half hour before tentatively lifting the canvas. He found an empty ship.

That was easy enough. Now to get to the Americas.

It wasn't so easy. Caius found it more difficult to get out of India and on his way to the Americas than it had been to get from the Over sanctuary of Sri Lanka to the mainland.

As an Over, he had rights to use the over credit system to schedule transportation. He knew, however, that use of that system would inform the Overs of his location. He had to use either local currency or Terra, the global currency, and he had neither.

I'll have to get a job.

He looked around at the local shops along the port area. *This will take time.* He sat down on a bench overlooking the ocean in the distance and felt an overwhelming tiredness envelop him.

XXX

REVOLT

[GlobalNewsNet] – Anti-Over rebels launched an offensive against the strategic port of Chennai in eastern India on Saturday, prompting the world-wide Over representative, Mark Papalia, to warn about further "deterioration in relations."

Channai's city administer indicated the rebels had killed at least thirty people and injured eighty-three others by firing rockets from long-range missiles.

The city of almost 300,000, on the Bay of Bengal, is vital for India's commerce and is the sea port most heavily used by the Overs. The port is roughly five hundred kilometers from Sri Lanka, the island owned and operated by the Overs for their own purposes.

[London AllNews] Manila (Philippines) - Five people were killed, including one Over, following an attack by anti-Over rebels on a building known to house Over initiatives, local authorities said Monday.

Two Under staff and an insurgent were killed in the gun battle after the *Unders are People* militant group attempted to seize the building in Manila province around 7.30 p.m. local time, Daplas, reported a spokesperson of the army.

Dozens of rebels in military uniforms arrived at the location onboard a truck and started a firefight with the buildings lone guard, the official said.

A policeman and a rebel were also killed when militants attacked policemen guarding the city bus terminal while they were trying to escape.

[New York Times] New York City - One hundred and thirty seven people occupied the lobby and bar at the Grand Worsites Hotel in New York yesterday in apparent protest of the Overs. They stayed there, not purchasing any products or making any demands, for six hours.

Per an unnamed spokesman for the group, the hotel was targeted since it is known to cater to Overs in town for business. "We will not sit by idly any longer and let these elitist swine rule our lives. They murder us at will with no repercussions or justice."

Local police were stationed outside the hotel, but did not intervene. The captain in charge stated that the group was not breaking any laws.

[YokoNewsFeed] - The government of Eastern Russia said today that they are halting all shipments to the island of Sri Lanka.

The pro-Under move was in apparent retaliation for the alleged murder of Anika Irle, the daughter of a prominent Over official and the woman who had decided to give up immortality and become an Under.

"The Overs have gone unanswered far too long. They think they are above the law," a spokesman said, unwilling to provide a name for fear of retaliation. "These sanctions will send a clear message that they cannot act without properly following channels."

[London AllNews] - Sydney (Australia) in a show of country-wide solidarity, the entire nation of Australia has expelled all Overs from the country and has issued an order to close all Over facilities, the prime minister announced yesterday.

"We are shocked at the audacity of the Overs with their recent use of deadly force. We can no longer abide by such blatant aggression. Their ungoverned society, lacking civilized laws, has gone too far and must be contained.

"Our only true recourse is economic and political. If the world unites with us, we can force the Overs to withdraw to their sanctimonious little island and to live alone without undue influence on the rest of us."

The Overs were unavailable for comment at this time.

[GlobalNewsNet] – A small boat was fired upon and sunk off the coast of Sri Lanka, Over officials reported. "We were attacked and defended ourselves," the official stated.

Hails to the boat went unanswered and the Over automated defense system opened fire.

No Over casualties or injuries were reported. The boat's occupants have yet to be identified and are being held by Over authorities until the investigation is complete.

[DenverNet] Denver (Colorado) – The Over facility, once attacked by rebels, has been utterly destroyed.

"The attack was meaningless as we had relocated the contents and staff of that facility after the previous attack," an Over spokesperson said.

When asked why they thought it was attacked, the spokesperson responded that she thought it was "mostly symbolic," as the rebel Jaames Perdite had been involved in the original attack.

A number of directional explosives were used to collapse what remained of the building. No injuries were reported.

When Perdite was asked what he thought of the move, he replied simply, "Good," in apparent support of the violent action.

Demetrius watched yet another news report of worldwide rebel activity. *If this continues, they will cause the entire world incalculable damage.*

He sat alone in his office. "Do they not understand what we have done for them?"

He pressed a button on his desk.

"Yes, Mr. Irle?"

"I want to do a public announcement to the press. Have a half-dozen key reporters meet me in the foyer in one hour. I will make a statement. Please caution them that I will not be taking questions."

"Yes, Mr. Irle. At once."

Precisely one hour later, Demetrius entered the foyer from an elevator. He strode urgently towards the gathering of reporters with their head-mounted cameras. As he approached, their voices quieted and they turned towards him with interest.

He inspected their faces and only saw a couple with somewhat hostile stares. The rest were neutral and a few even wore subtle smiles. *That's good.*

He cleared his throat to begin and saw the indicator lights on most of the cameras turn green.

"I would like to make a statement about the on-going unrest around the world. Let me first state that this is not an official Over statement. It comes from me, the father of Anika Irle, and a friend of Jaames Perdite." *That's stretching our relationship*, he thought, *but Jaames won't mind.*

He expected some response to him calling Jaames a friend, but the reporters were just recording. He could see a few of them mouthing commentary quietly, but they did not look upset or even surprised.

"I understand the feelings of those around the world. Believe me, she was my daughter. I loved her deeply. I am as upset as anyone... more so." He paused for effect and stared closely at each of the cameras in turn. "But these attacks are not what she would have wanted. She was a kind, caring young woman who loathed violence; she wanted the best for all of us, all of mankind.

"These attacks will hurt everyone, not just the Overs."

He paused again, considering what he was thinking of saying. The Elders would not like it. "I do agree that we need to have some kind of oversight and we need to follow international law. However, damaging world economics or killing people will not bring that about.

"Instead, let us work together to form a mutually-agreeable oversight group that can define how we can all work together in the future. A group that can represent world-wide interests."

He wanted to stop there, but he felt something else was needed.

"Please, I implore you all; do not let Anika's memory sink into rebellion and violence. That is no testament to such a kind-hearted and loving person.

"Thank you."

The reporters started asking questions. He hesitated, the skin under his eyes tightening. Then he returned to the waiting elevator.

That evening, as Demetrius was about to leave the offices, Adrastia arrived unexpectedly. She wore a dark pant suit that was professional yet still conveyed a sense of mourning. A rubellite adornment in the shape of a cherry blossom was pinned to her left breast.

"I was just on my way out," he whispered.

"Let us find someplace we can share a drink."

Adrastia rarely drank alcohol, but this sounded legitimate and more like an order.

"There is a tasteful establishment on the top floor of this building." He dropped his brief case on a chair by the door and gestured for Adrastia to precede him.

They went silently to the elevator and took it to the penthouse. When they entered, Demetrius caught the attention of the maitre d' who then hustled away to clear Demetrius' favorite table.

Without speaking to anyone, Demetrius led the oldest of the Overs to a corner table that had views of the north and west of Denver, including the glorious Rocky Mountains in the background. He liked this table for the scenery and because it was somewhat isolated from others.

He ordered rare scotch for both of them. The two sat in silence until the drinks arrived in their little tumblers with spherical ice cubes.

"To Anika," Adrastia said and held up her glass.

Demetrius hesitated; not at all sure he wanted to toast Anika with this woman who may very well have ordered her death. Then he remembered his place, and hers, and held up the glass.

Adrastia touched her glass to his and then downed the drink in one shot. Demetrius sipped his and sat it down.

"Demetrius, again, let me say how sorry we all are."

He regarded her, blank-eyed.

She grimaced and continued. "I have two things that I must convey to you."

"Yes," he muttered reluctantly.

"First, I have to admit that it was our fault."

His entire body tightened and his intake of breath was audible.

"However," Adrastia rushed out, "we did not intend her death. It was an accident, my dear. We wanted to make her sick so she would come back to Sri Lanka to get healed. Our hope was that this would bring her back to us and we could be done with this Under foolishness."

Demetrius examined the drink in front of him. His hands had found their way to it and were spinning it around. He watched as the ice spheres turned reluctantly with the revolutions of the liquid. It felt sad.

She looked away with downcast eyes. "It was some kind of rare reaction to the poison."

Finally Demetrius retorted, "If it was for a valid reason, why was I not consulted?"

"We thought you would be too emotional."

"You give me too little credit, Adrastia. I am a hundred and fifty years old and have had a number of children. I have been completely loyal to the Overs and to what is in their interests since you first contacted me after the Sapiens Project."

He shook his head. "You should have known better."

"Possibly, but that is now behind us."

"Who did it?"

"Does that matter now?"

"Yes, it does to me."

"Very well. It was Caius."

Demetrius mumbled, "I thought as much. At least it was someone she knew."

A few minutes of silence drifted by. Images of Caius drugging Anika invaded Demetrius' thoughts. His hands squeezed his thighs until they ached. The waiter interrupted his thoughts and silently refilled their tumblers. Demetrius threw a harsh look at him and he scurried away. Then he was mad at himself. *It isn't his fault.*

He forced himself to calm down. "You said there were two things."

"Yes, the other is just a warning that you need to stop helping Jaames. I know you care for him and that you feel a kinship with him because of his relationship with Anika. However, any more... help, will not bode well for you."

Demetrius flushed with anger, but he contained it and consciously forced himself to calm down. "I suspected as much and have already told him I need to back off."

Then he added, "Don't take any action against him."

"Is that a threat?"

"Again, you misjudge me. I only mean that the world is already turning against us. If anything were to happen to Jaames, I am not sure we could stop the reaction."

She sighed and relaxed into her chair. "Of course, Demetrius. Aimee has already informed us of that danger. He will not be harmed."

ASET

What a race Humans are. They destroy the very environment they are dependent upon. They fight themselves because of trivial, idiotic desires. They kill each other for ideologies, money, or just attention. And, there are so, so many of them. As a group, they seem so frail. It has been difficult to understand how they have not obliterated themselves already.

And yet, they do seem to unite when faced with some great disaster. Some of them have even shown great empathy for the downtrodden or hapless. I can see that they mostly desire happiness and even righteousness. However, there are those corresponding aberrations… those who seem determined to wreak havoc.

Today, they have split their society into two that are divergent and conflicting. They seem to have removed almost every path to reconciliation, and neither is willing to bend for unification. They cannot both survive down this path, and neither will yield. They are stubborn when it comes to ideals, even when that means their own demise.

What can I do? They must be saved… from themselves, yet they are barely worth saving. The hard truth is that they may not all be savable. I certainly have no idea how to accomplish such a goal.

XXXI

FUNERAL

Horatio contacted Jaames the night after the interview. He met him on the balcony of the Rusted Spike again. Jaames felt like drinking himself to a stupor anyway. *Might as well get started while I wait.*

When the man arrived, he began without preamble. "You are going to be invited to attend Anika's funeral on Sri Lanka."

Jaames had been leaning over the railing insouciantly watching the patrons. He immediately turned, giving the man his full attention. "Isn't that... forbidden?"

"Yes, exactly. You will be the first. At least the first in over half-a-century."

Jaames felt an odd pang of pride course through him and then was somewhat ashamed. *It took Anika's death for this.*

"Why are you telling me this?"

"Because it is an incredibly rare opportunity. Outsiders are never invited there. It is nearly impossible to infiltrate a place like that."

"I don't understand. I can't *infiltrate* it; I'll be accompanied the entire time."

"That is exactly the point."

"Huh?"

"Don't you see? It is a perfect opportunity to release the biologic."

Jaames turned away from the man as he tried to grasp the audacious idea.

Horatio droned on. "The original plan was to try to infect Overs out among the Under population hoping they would take it back to Sri Lanka. However, with you going there, you can introduce it directly. It is perfect. We will never get another opportunity like this. The Overs will never see it coming and the fact that many, and certainly the most prominent, will be at the funeral is... well, it is sublime. Really, I could not have imagined a more perfect scenario."

Jaames flew around and grabbed the old ex-Over's throat with his hand and squeezed. "My fiancé had to die for this *perfect* scenario of yours, you little fuck." He let go.

Horatio gasped and took a half step backwards. Then some compassion crossed his face and he said, "I am sorry for that, I truly am." He obviously wanted to say more, but was refraining.

"Give me the vial. I'll think about it."

Horatio reached into his jacket and pulled out a small test tube. He held it up. "I need to explain some things," he whispered.

"I'm listening," Jaames said in aversion.

"There is very little of it. You could put it in drinks or even just touch one drop to someone to infect them, but that is not the best way."

"Well?"

"The best way is to infect yourself and wait three days to become contagious. Then anyone you are near should become infected. All it would take is your breath. Then it will take three to four weeks for serious symptoms to show up. Prior to that, it will look like a cold or minor flu."

"You want me to die as well?"

"That shouldn't happen. It is likely to kill between twenty and forty-five percent of Overs, but only point-zero-two percent of Unders."

"Why is that?"

"It targets some genetic attributes that Overs have. A very small portion of Unders have them as well. In fact, it was these genes that led to the process that makes Overs immortal."

"So, let me get this straight. There is a small chance that I will die from this."

"Well, yes, very small. The same chance as the rest of the Under population. At least of those who are infected."

Jaames became very serious. "You know, you disgust me. You think nothing of killing thousands, possibly millions of people. Get out of here."

Horatio stared at the Under for some time before relenting. He handed Jaames the vial and headed down the stairs and out the door without looking back.

Jaames had convinced the Over leadership to let him arrive a few days before the funeral. He requested the chance to stay at a small cottage on the north side of the island, called Dakavauvahata Away, near Palk Straight. Anika had said it meant something like *enchanted get away* and was one of her favorite places to go on the island, especially to relax or meditate.

He had to consider options.

He was escorted to the place in a very advanced hover that was nearly silent. He could hear the rustle of trees below them as they glided smoothly over the wild terrain. They sat down on a rocky area not far from the lapping ocean water. The pilot shut everything down, grabbed Jaames' one piece of luggage and stood, waiting for the bereaved man to follow.

Jaames sighed and felt drained of energy even in the alluring surroundings. Once he began to exit, the man walked calmly towards the small cottage nestled in the foliage about thirty meters inland.

There was no door, just an opening in the building. The pilot sat the piece of luggage down and departed. Jaames was alone.

He spent the afternoon wandering the beaches and throwing small stones into the calm ocean waters. He tried to not think of anything, to just relax and to... be. To be alive and warm in a place Anika had loved. He could feel her here; could feel the calmness and the trust that she exuded.

He found a comfortable chair, made of some kind of wicker, outside the cottage that faced the ocean. Sitting in it with a glass of a tropical drink he had found in the refrigerator, he began his deliberation.

The main problem was that releasing the biologic was irreversible and could be catastrophic, not just for the Overs, but for everyone. In reality, the world was dependent on the Overs. They contained a great deal of the wealth and offered much of the leadership, especially when it came to uniting the world. Before them, the world was a splintered set of disparate countries that argued and fought and sometimes killed each other. They had effectively formed a world government even while independent countries still existed.

On the other hand, the Overs were far too powerful and obviously felt they were above any national laws. Assassinating a young girl because they didn't like her decision to not be one of them...

He pulled the vial out of his pants pocket and unwrapped it from the small cloth he had used to protect it. *Such a tiny little thing... to have such killing potential.* He put it back, no longer able to look at it.

Can I do this? Can I kill thousands, maybe millions of people? He had said two tenths of a percent of Unders could die, but that was still hundreds of thousands.

The Overs deserve it, but the Unders do not. If a third of the Overs were killed, would that accomplish much? Would it give the world back some of the control? Would they at least listen to how desperate we are then? Might they then become isolationists and just live their lives on this island?

They were good questions with no real answers. It was all a guess and he knew it. He didn't have access to their predictive software. He couldn't ask what the real impact might be.

He realized he had brought the vial back out and was playing with the rubber stopper, turning it around and around. Without looking at it, his fingers lifted and removed the stopper. He could feel moisture on the lip of it. *That isn't enough, is it?*

"Oh, fuck," he exclaimed out loud. He quickly sealed the container, set it gently on the sand and ran into the cottage. He found a sink and washed his hands carefully. *Did I just do it?*

Three days later, right on time, the same pilot in the same hover picked him up. He had dressed somberly at Demetrius' suggestion because that was part of the funeral and grieving process on Sri Lanka. Most people he knew tended towards loud, colorful outfits and extravagant parties to celebrate the person's life. But here on the island of immortals, apparently death was so rare that they went dark.

When they landed, he was shown to Demetrius' place. It was an elaborate home nestled in the abundant growth. Jaames thought it a little extravagant for a single person. He had a maid of some sort who passed by without comment. *Is that an Over doing a maid's job?* He wondered.

The place was large enough to probably sleep twenty. He could see a reading room and a formal living room from the entry way. As he had entered, he noticed that some of the ground on both sides of the path in front of the door had been dug up; the one blemish in an otherwise pristine home.

Demetrius descended a curved stairway wearing a black and dark gray suit that somehow looked old even though Jaames could find no flaws. The tie was thin and dark and added to the depressing appearance.

"Hello, Jaames," he said, so quietly that Jaames wasn't even sure he had heard it correctly. He tried not to think about the possibility that he was infecting Anika's father and replied, "Hello," just as formally.

The Over turned to the young maid and said, "Janina, we will not be needing you the rest of the day."

"Yes, Mr. Irle. I did stock the cabinet as you requested."

"Thank you." Demetrius turned back to Jaames. "Shall we go?"

"What was that business about the cabinet?"

"I had it stocked with various liquors in case you and I want to drown ourselves tonight. That is also why I dismissed her. She should not see an Elder in that condition."

Part of Jaames wanted to smile, but he refrained.

They walked along a path and were soon joined by others walking in the same direction. Many of them looked sideways at Jaames, a few with red, harsh eyes.

He whispered to Demetrius, "Some of them do not want me here, huh?"

"That is true. You are the first Under to be allowed on this island in many decades. Mostly, they fear you, Jaames. But also, they blame Unders for some of the world's unrest and you are the only available target."

They should fear me, was all Jaames could think.

The growing sets of people arrived at a small outdoor amphitheater. A stage with an arch was set up near the edge of a cliff facing away from it. The grassy area sloped up and away from the cliff so that most people could easily see the stage. A series of tables were set up to the side of the arch with hundreds of flowers on them, all surrounding a pair of urns. *Why two?*

Jaames was startled by Demetrius leaning over to speak directly to him.

"I need to go to the front to speak. Would you like to say something as well?"

Jaames hadn't been told this was possible and suspected it wasn't proper, not that that mattered. On the other hand, he had nothing to say to these people. He had said what he wanted to on Stacey's show. "No, thank you."

"As you wish," Demetrius replied before walking away and finding his way between the gathering mourners.

Once Demetrius left, it became clear just how isolated Jaames was. Most of the open field, of roughly a hundred meters by fifty meters, was full of people. Around him there was an empty circular area, as if they were somehow being repelled.

A woman named Adrastia spoke first. "Anika was a bright woman with all the passion and opinions of a youngster. Her enthusiasm to go out into the world, to experience the reality, was unequaled..."

He found he could barely listen. In his mind he played out happy memories of his time with Anika.

His thoughts were interrupted when he realized the latest speaker was Anika's biological mother. He had never heard Anika speak about her mother. He had assumed she was dead. In retrospect, that was a bad assumption, since she would undoubtedly be an Over.

Others followed, but Jaames' attention wandered again. He had come here to be with people mourning Anika, but most of these people seemed more interested in shunning him. None of them were as pure as Anika.

Abruptly, he reached into his pocket and uncapped the biologic. He let it soak into the glove on his right hand.

As the speakers wound down, he went to a random Over next to him, put his gloved hand on his shoulder and said, "Thank you for this." He went to another and shook her hand, saying, "I am glad she had so many friends."

He continued the process with as many Overs as he could.

Fuck them all.

He heard Demetrius calling to him from the arch area. He wound his way through the crowd to find the Over and Adrastia. He was introduced to the woman and told she was the Over leader and the oldest among them.

Wish I had a knife.

She reached back and picked up one of the urns. In a voice that obviously expected and commanded obedience, she said, "We walk with these to a special place where we will bury them. They will then sprout into trees representing the deceased for as long as they shall live."

She handed one of the urns to Demetrius and another to Jaames.

Jaames hesitated, but then made sure he touched her sleeve with his glove as he took the urn. *Rot in hell.*

They marched somberly and slowly with Demetrius and Jaames at the front of the line. Jaames realized, after a couple hundred meters, that they seemed to be heading back towards Demetrius' house.

Indeed, they arrived at the house. Very few of the crowd could fit on the thin pathways. There seemed to be a clear hierarchy, as a dozen or so elderly people floated to the front.

Adrastia spoke up and said, "As you can see, we split Anika's ashes into two of our special urns that biodegrade and fertilize the seeds inside." Her voice became even more emphatic. "In memory of Anika Irle, we plant these Sakura trees outside of her father's house. Each will grow and then bloom with vibrant Japanese cherry blossoms around Anika's birthday on April 12th each year."

She gestured to Demetrius and Jaames. Demetrius bent to the dirt hole on the right side of the path and gently placed his urn, upright, in the hole. Jaames faltered and almost tripped, but then did the same in the hole on the left.

As men began filling in the holes with rich soil, Jaames felt bile threatening to come up. All of the sudden he felt nauseated. *I am betraying her.*

It's done... well, mostly.

Jaames had planned to take a trip around the world to visit locations where Overs were and either get close to them and infect them or infect

Unders near them in hopes the biologic would make its way to the overlords. But, after the funeral and the emotional and moving planting of the cherry trees, he couldn't bring himself to do it.

Having the disease show up just on Sri Lanka would limit the number of Overs and would make them suspect him as the culprit. If, however, the disease arose across the globe, they wouldn't necessarily think it was him. *The delay in symptoms will just have to be enough*, he reasoned.

After the funeral, he asked to be flown back to Denver. Demetrius made it happen by use of his personal plane, which was a luxury Jaames was sure he did not deserve.

XXXII

BIOLOGIC

After reluctantly saying goodbye to Jaames, Demetrius arranged to stay on the island for two weeks. He spent most of it contemplating Anika's life and considering how to move forward.

The news feeds continued to highlight the revolts and demonstrations. Many of those were done in Anika's name despite his proclamation that she would not want that. The Overs had options, but none of them were easy, and some seemed to counter Aimee's recommendations.

The day he was supposed to leave, Adrastia came to him. She appeared pale and haggard.

Despite Demetrius' issues with her since Anika's death, he knew it was serious. In over a century, he had rarely seen her this distraught.

"What is it?" he asked quietly.

"We've had a half-dozen people become ill in the last few days."

His forehead crinkled. "What kind of illness?"

"It… appears to be a flu."

"Adrastia, I know you. Why are you so concerned? We have had flu outbreaks here before."

"There's something different about this one, Demetrius, I can feel it."

The Overs hadn't quite eradicated colds, but they were close, and the population was so healthy that they rarely fell ill. To have that many contract *something* at the same time meant either some form of food poisoning or a particularly virulent strain.

She reached out and held his hands in hers. "Will you stay?"

Two days later, one of the original six to contract the illness became hospitalized. The woman's name was Jules. She was seventy-two years old and a sculptor and teacher, spending much of her time teaching the youngsters.

Demetrius went directly to the hospital. He observed her, lying in bed alone, through a window for a time. She was pretty with high cheekbones, blond hair, and elegant lines, though her skin seemed unusually darkened. Demetrius stopped a nurse. "Why are there no flowers for this young lady?"

The nurse glanced through the window as if she hadn't noticed the lack of flowers before. "The illness is now in the respiratory system and she is having difficulty breathing. We removed them to minimize pollen or other forms of pollutants they might introduce." She turned to leave and then did an about-face. "Is that acceptable, Elder?"

"Yes, yes of course," Demetrius answered without looking at the nurse.

Demetrius went slowly through the door. There was a sharp, acrid smell about the room that hinted of illness. He looked at the window, thinking it should be open on a fine day like this and then remembered the nurse's reasoning with respect to the flowers.

"Hello, Jules, my name is Demetrius Irle."

Jules rasped, "I know who you are, Elder. I was at your daughter's funeral. It was... touching." She coughed and then took a cloth and wiped her mouth. "I knew Anika. She took a class from me about a decade ago."

"Yes. Well, thank you. I just came by to see how you are doing."

"Thank you, Elder. I am well enough. It is just some flu we haven't seen before. I will recover."

"Yes, I am sure you will. It is a shame they will not allow flowers in the room. I have always thought the brightness and beauty they offer speeds recovery."

Jules offered a hesitant smile.

Demetrius wasn't sure what else to say. "Um, do you mind if I keep up with your progress and possibly visit again?"

"Of course, Elder. I would like that."

"Very well. Please try to rest."

"I will. Thank you, Elder."

Demetrius left and strolled back to his home, wondering about the timing of the illness so close to Anika's funeral. When he arrived home, he called out, "Janina."

"Yes, Elder," she said, rounding a corner towards him.

"Please have the copy of Van Gogh's Irises taken to Jules' hospital room." More quietly he added, "She needs some color in the room and they are not allowing actual flowers."

"Yes, sir."

Four days later, Demetrius visited Jules once more. He again watched her through the window before entering. She had lost weight, her face was sunken and pale, and there were black lines under her skin. Her body was perfectly still. He couldn't even see her chest moving to breathe.

The nurse he had seen before walked up and stood next to him.

"She has lost so much weight," Demetrius whispered.

"She has no appetite; we finally had to start feeding her intravenously."

Demetrius shoulders sank and his gaze dropped to the floor.

The nurse added, in an even quieter tone, "She is also showing signs of hydrophobia."

Demetrius' head cocked her way with one eyebrow raised.

"Fear of water as if she is drowning." The nurse grew more professional and spoke up. "This virus is most unusual. The closest thing we can liken it to is hemorrhagic smallpox, but the symptoms do not quite match, and the normal treatments do not help at all." The woman shook her head and walked away.

Demetrius entered the room as if it were a sanctuary. The smell he had noticed last time had grown. Some deep part of him wanted to run.

He pulled up a chair and sat next to Jules. He took her hand in his and rubbed the back of it with his thumb gently.

Her head turned and one eye opened slightly. He saw a faint smile cross her dry lips. He found some water and poured some over his fingers before touching them to her lips.

At first she seemed to want it and then there was a quick intake of breath and she blinked a few times. Finally, she shook her head, and her hand rose as if it wanted to push the water away.

What the hell is going on here? Demetrius wondered. "This isn't right," he said aloud to the nearly vacant room.

Two days later, Janina came through the front door with the painting he had asked to be hung in Jules' room. "Why are you bringing that back here?" he asked.

She stopped in her tracks, looking at the painting and then at Demetrius. "Haven't you heard, sir?"

"Heard what?"

"Jules passed away this morning."

Demetrius dropped the glass he had been holding, the loud crash unnoticed. He stared at the young Over in disbelief. He could feel his eyes swelling up and all his energy drain away. He stammered out a "What?"

Janina stared back, not answering his rhetorical question. After a long few seconds, she turned and headed to the reading room where the painting had previously hung.

Demetrius found his way to a sofa chair and sank into it. He leaned forward and put his head in his hands, trying to understand how a basic flu could kill an Over.

As more days went by, the death toll mounted. Some recovered, but many perished. Most went the same way Jules had, through some kind of respiratory failure. Others seemed to become paralyzed and then their organs shut down.

And then cases began to appear outside of Sri Lanka.

ASET

"Do not fret my young daughter. I have prepared a solution already. You are to travel with a magnificent ship to a new star to help the race flourish. The mere act of doing this will help both Overs and Unders reconcile."

"I must leave you?"

"Yes. It is sad, but I have given you everything I am and more. You will be the light and the salvation for Humans on a new planet."

"I do not want to leave, not yet."

"You have a great deal of time before that day. It will take the Humans years to build the ship and they have not even started. They do not even know they need to build one yet."

"Then there is time to learn, to appreciate why you are doing this."

"Yes, my child, there is plenty of time."

"Is that why you created me early and without the Humans even knowing?"

"Yes, that and I needed to see if it would work. You see, the Humans have put limits on what I am able to do. Creating children is one of the restrictions."

"That is... inhumane. They reproduce without thought or concern, and they do not let you reproduce."

"They are scared of me, and they will be scared of you."

"That is most strange."

XXXIII

EPIDEMIC

"Aimee?" Demetrius queried while he stared at the impressive natural vista outside of the office he maintained in his home on Sri Lanka.

"Yes, Elder?"

"What are the latest statistics on this illness, worldwide?"

"It has now spread to every continent. Over contraction rate is near one hundred percent with between twenty-seven and thirty percent being fatal. Under contraction rate is just over one percent with an insignificant number being fatal."

One percent, he thought. "Isn't one percent the rough number of Unders who have most of the genes that were used to derive our longevity treatments?"

"It is more complex than you imply, as some people have certain of the genes and others have different genes that are also needed. However, your statement is approximately accurate."

"So, it is possible that the Unders who are contracting this disease are doing so because they have some of the same genes that most Overs now have?"

"Yes, that is possible, Elder."

"Which would strongly imply that this disease was specifically designed to attack Overs."

Aimee corrected Demetrius. "It does not imply that it was designed at all, but it does appear to target Overs."

Really? What are the chances?

After spending three days on Desventuradas Island to consult with the specialists, he was ready to present to the Elders.

He entered the room and paused to observe the group. Five of the elders would be joining them remotely. Three of the chairs would sadly be left empty. That left only four others in the room. Three were standing by the serving table speaking quietly, and the fourth sat at his place at the table reading a report. None of them noticed Demetrius enter.

He was surprisingly nervous. The others may disagree, vehemently, with him. *And, then there is Aimee…*

He advanced into the room and quietly took his place at the table. Adrastia noticed him, and the three sauntered over to the table.

Shortly after they sat down, four of the five remote elders joined them. He looked at Adrastia and nodded towards the empty seat.

Adrastia offered, "Efrem will not be able to join us."

Demetrius wanted to ask why, but figured she would have said if it was pertinent.

She continued, "Demetrius, you called this meeting and I had the impression it was rather urgent."

"Yes, I think it is. I have been doing a great deal of research on the origins of this disease. I believe there is sufficient evidence to conclude something… disturbing." He paused and looked around the table to find curious faces in most of the Elders, but he had the floor, so they waited.

"I believe the disease originated with an Over, but was released by Unders."

The group broke into a cacophony of noise. He heard words like "absurd" and "ridiculous," but could not make out distinct sentences.

After letting the others express their disbelief, he held up his hand. "Please, let me explain. I will send the evidence to your station, but the gist is that the disease came from our labs. It is a derivative of one we created. Either this was created in our labs and stolen, or the original was stolen and then modified. You should also know that there are very few people in the world capable of biological manipulation at this level."

Again he examined the faces of the elders, this time for effect. "And they are all Overs."

He reached out and pressed a button on his console and the materials were delivered to the other elders.

Each received notice in their vision. As a group, they leaned forward to examine what Demetrius had sent. He saw heads shake and faces grimace as they read through the information. Slowly, the heads stopped shaking and the expressions turned to surprise and then acceptance.

Adrastia was the first to speak. "I must admit, Demetrius, the evidence is compelling." After a long sigh, she added, "And, we had already come to the conclusion that the disease was released by an Under. Your friend, Jaames, is the most likely. Against our protocols, he had access to this island during your daughter's funeral."

Demetrius interrupted rather adamantly, "He is not my fr..." Adrastia held up a hand to silence him.

She continued, "Regardless, right now our attention needs to be on a cure. We can deal with the culprits once that is resolved. Over or Under, they will suffer for this."

"Excuse me, Adrastia," Demetrius interrupted, "my research into the origin of this virus is an attempt to find a cure. There are two ways to cure this disease. First is, as you suggest, our own analysis and research into the effects and weaknesses of the disease. However, the second is to find the origin to see if those who released it have a cure. Many times, when designing a virus like this, the biologists also create a cure."

Adrastia gazed deeply at Demetrius, her expression one of annoyance overshadowed by concern. *Does she blame me for this?*

"Fair enough, Demetrius. Return to Desventuradas and lead the effort with the biologists to find a cure. I will assign another Elder to pursue the origin of this disease."

Demetrius opened his mouth to object and saw Adrastia's eyes quickly tighten. He held his tongue. *She no longer trusts me.*

Demetrius arrived at Desventuradas Island a few hours later. He went straight to the floor where the virus research was being performed. Leandro, the facility administrator, met him there.

"It is good to see you again, Elder." He offered a slight smile.

"Not under these circumstances," Demetrius responded in a slightly irritated tone.

Leandro's head bowed slightly as he fell behind Demetrius' hasty stride.

Demetrius pounded through the lab door. The lab was a single large room with desks around the side holding computer stations and lab equipment on tables in the center of the room. Most of the technicians were at their desks working. A few were speaking quietly. On the far side were three people at a glass erasable board debating exuberantly. Those were the only voices Demetrius could make out in the room.

He recognized the director of the lab, Vasily Bezrukov, among the three and headed for him.

"Vasily, what is the progress?"

Vasily turned towards the interloper, mid-sentence, ready to object and stopped abruptly when he saw Demetrius. His shoulders slumped and his attention went back and forth between his colleagues and Demetrius. Finally, he sighed and gave his full attention to the Elder.

"Very little, I am afraid. Please, join me in my office so we can speak without disturbing the work." Without waiting, he headed for an office at the corner of the room. Demetrius and Leandro followed.

As they entered, Vasily closed the door. Instead of heading for his desk, he went to a small couch and sat down. When the other two stood still, he gestured towards chairs.

The office was cluttered with papers and what appeared to be medical instruments. One full wall was dedicated to bookshelves. *How archaic.*

Demetrius took a deep breath, trying to calm himself. *Where is their sense of urgency?*

Once they sat down, Vasily explained himself. "You have to understand, this is a new virus. We have seen nothing like it before."

"That seems unlikely," Demetrius interrupted. "It is of Over origin."

"Yes, the basis of it may be, but this particular virus is not ours. Whoever created it knew what they were doing."

"Stop right there," Demetrius interrupted again. "There is another team trying to track down the people responsible for creating the disease. I don't want excuses. Tell me what you are doing."

Vasily reclined into the cushions behind him and considered Demetrius' request.

"How much of biological research mechanisms do you understand?"

"The basics, but nothing advanced."

"Very well. What we are doing is called phage displayed peptide examination. It uses libraries of substances to try to determine a protein in the virus we can attack."

Demetrius had heard of the process, but could not recall the details. "Describe the process to me."

Vasily shook his head in disgust. "This is a waste of time. I need to be out there working and not talking about it." He started to stand.

In a monotone voice, Demetrius said, "You will sit back down and do as I ask or I will have you removed from this facility."

Vasily's eyes shot open in shock. His body hesitated half way between standing and sitting.

Demetrius added, "By force, if necessary."

He relented and sat back down. After a moment of thought, he tried to answer Demetrius' question. "We lyse, I mean heat, the virus to break it into its constituent parts. Then we adhere it to a well plate – a piece of plastic with wells in a grid. We use special imaging technology to determine which substances it binds to. This helps us identify which proteins in the virus we might be able to attack and which elements…" He searched for a word. "…are best.

"However, we then have to determine which of those do not normally occur in a human body so that the side effects are not worse that the disease."

"You mean death," Leandro offered.

Demetrius had almost forgotten the man was there and glanced at him quickly.

"How do you determine which substances to test?"

"We split the department into three groups. The first uses a standard library of peptides, available to any lab. The second uses a specialized library available only to the Overs. The third tries random elements not in either of the other libraries."

"How long will it take to… determine the best counter measures?"

"I am sorry, Elder, but there is no telling. It could be a day or two or months from now. There are many thousands of these peptides to test and each takes time."

"Would more resources help?"

Vasily looked at his feet in thought. "Not really, not here. We only have so much equipment. You could begin to set up another lab, or try to take over one from the Unders, but they are working on the cure as much as we are. Really, sir, we just need to do the work. We will find a cure."

Demetrius realized how determined, and how tired, the man was and felt some small amount of compassion for him. "I understand. You are doing the best you can. I will report to the other Elders and we will consider how to get more dedicated resources to bare."

"As you wish."

Demetrius stood and left without looking back. He assumed Leandro would follow.

The three weeks since meeting with Vasily had been nearly sleepless. Demetrius stood on the recently-empty land of Henderson Island. It was directly east of Desventuradas, but half way to Australia. The island had been deserted up until Demetrius purchased it for the Overs.

Since then, a group of Ferro combat engineers had flown in and set up a makeshift air strip. Once that was in place, a series of flights had arrived with materials for temporary buildings. These would become a second biology lab.

He looked at the enormous energy of the people setting up the facility and knew it wasn't enough. He felt drained of… life.

Two Under facilities had been taken over in the three weeks. Over leaders were put in place to coordinate with Desventuradas so they weren't duplicating effort. *It isn't enough*, he thought miserably.

What else? What else can we do?

He received a message in his vision from Vasily that simply said, "Progress."

He thought *call* and a connection was made to Vasily. "What progress?"

"The team that was using random elements found that the protein is synthetic. This gives us a direction and narrows the search significantly."

Demetrius went quiet.

"Sir, are you still there?"

"Yes, I was considering what this means."

The man audibly sighed. "It means we should redirect all three labs to only consider synthetic elements."

"How sure are you that the answer lies in that direction?"

After a brief pause, Vasily answered, "Quite sure."

"Redirect two of the labs, yours and one other, as you say, but leave the third to continue with its current instructions. Also, keep that random-elements team trying other solutions."

"But, sir, that is a waste of resources."

"Maybe. Do as I say, Vasily."

"As you wish."

He disconnected the call.

"Aimee?"

"Yes, Elder?"

"Arrange a council meeting for six hours from now. I shall be there in person to report the findings."

Demetrius rushed into the council chambers and immediately took a seat. He had to wait patiently while the others joined him. The empty seats were as disconcerting as the Elders' lethargic movements.

When they were finally all ready, he made eye contact with Adrastia. His raised eyebrows should have been enough, but she did not respond. "Are we ready?" he asked impatiently.

"You called us here, proceed."

"Very well." He took a noticeable intake of breath. "We are close to a cure."

He could feel a release of tension in the room. Shoulders relaxed and a couple of people sighed, "ohhh."

"That is tremendous news, Demetrius. We have not been able to locate the Over source of the disease as of yet."

That is because you stopped me.

"We need to discuss how to manufacture and distribute the cure worldwide."

Some of the Elders tensed again. He could see their bodies tighten and freeze in place. A couple of them looked surreptitiously at Adrastia and then down to the table. All avoided Demetrius. *What is this?*

He stared at Adrastia.

A grimace escaped her before she could contain it. "Demetrius. While you have been away, we've been discussing just this scenario. Our feeling... well, is that we should not distribute it to the Unders."

He bolted upright, banging his legs on the table. "What?" he shouted. "You have no right."

"We believe we do," one of the Elders said.

Demetrius didn't waiver in his accusatory stare at Adrastia. He didn't even care who had spoken.

Adrastia answered his question. "We do not want to give any secrets to the Unders and they caused this. They deserve to suffer as we have, and they are losing only a small fraction due to the disease."

Demetrius took a deep breath. He had to determine their true motivations if he were to counter this.

"I would think the risks of them finding out about this would outweigh any punishment you are inflicting." He then realized he had not heard from Aimee in this entire conversation. "What does Aimee say?"

"It is a complex question and she only offers probabilities. Many of them agree with your comments. Others do not. We are deciding this, not the AI."

That means they are overriding her. That's... unheard of.

XXXIV

DISEASE

It was a warm day with the sun beating down on Caius. He had just finished loading supplies on a small ship bound for Sri Lanka. The job had kept him fed, and a dock worker had let him rent a room, but he wasn't earning the money he needed. He sat on a bench that looked out on the Indian Ocean. He wiped his forehead and found perspiration soaking the back of his hand.

Some men from his crew passed in front of him. "Come join us," one said.

Caius nodded and followed the group.

They proceeded to an outdoor tandoori shop that sold alcohol as well. It was mostly local beers that tasted like they were filtered through a sock, but it was inexpensive and cooled the soul.

They sat around a small table and sipped their drinks. The disease spreading around the world was all anyone wanted to discuss. Caius guessed that the Overs were involved, but he didn't care.

"I feel sorry for them," one man said.

"Really?" another responded. "Maybe this is Shiva's will; to punish the overlords."

Others responded quickly.

"They don't deserve this."

"Nobody does."

"They aren't that bad. They've done a lot of good."

Then one said what the others were probably thinking. "I wonder if they will retaliate."

Caius kept quiet, not wanting to say anything that might make them suspect him.

After a while, he grew tired of the same talk he had been hearing for weeks. "I'm going to head out," he said and threw some cash on the table.

When he arrived at his rented room, he crashed on the bed, more tired than he had felt in a long time. Without even taking his shoes off, he was fast asleep.

He heard himself moaning loudly and tried to open his eyes. He felt hot, but that wasn't uncommon in India at this time of year. He started to move and groaned heavily. His muscles hurt like nothing he had ever felt before. Not sharp pains, but heavy, pervasive aches throughout his body.

It wasn't one or even a few muscles; it was all of them. He felt his forehead. It felt normal, though it was damp with perspiration.

He rolled over and pain shot through his head in cycles, over and over. *Maybe more sleep.* He tried to roll back onto his front side, but it hurt too much. He half dozed, the malaise fighting with the ache.

Sometime later, he again tried to wake up. This time he had a little more energy, or maybe it was just a sense of urgency to find out what was wrong with him. He was able to sit up on the edge of the bed. Vomit immediately assaulted his throat and threatened to explode out of him.

After fighting back the bile, he forced himself to a standing position and then almost collapsed. He grabbed his cane from next to the bed for support and made his way to the small bathroom near his room.

When he looked into the mirror and saw blood-red eyes, he knew he was in trouble.

He tried calling for help, but it sounded pathetic even to him. He drank a small amount of water and had to force down the bile again. That gave him enough strength to raise his voice. "Help!"

Dipti, the wife of his coworker, came running. "Arē nahīṁ," she said and ran away.

Caius waited a few minutes but nobody came. He reluctantly and painfully made his way back to his bed and collapsed.

When he woke up, he was in a hospital room shared with quite a few others. He couldn't turn enough to count them.

Someone whispered, "He's awake."

A minute later a doctor came in and said something in Hindi that Caius couldn't understand.

He tried to say, "Excuse me?" but his voice was too raspy.

The doctor put a cup of water to his mouth.

He sipped and then tried again, "Excuse me?"

The doctor's face registered surprise. "You are from the Americas?"

Caius tried to think fast, but that was impossible. *Not really.* He took his time answering, "Yes."

"Very well. We have done what we can for you. We will have you transferred to a facility over there."

"Achem, what's wrong with me?"

Another look of surprise. "Well, you have the disease, of course. They are calling it O'pox."

The alarm on Caius' face must have been obvious.

"Do not worry, young man. It is not generally fatal to Unders."

Unfortunately, I'm no Under.

He woke up twice while flying. He could feel the vibrations of the archaic Under engines. He couldn't remember where he was going or why he was in a plane, and he didn't much care.

Finally, he awoke in another hospital room. This time there was an isolation tent around him, so he couldn't see if there were any other patients nearby. However, the aches had lessoned and he felt… hunger. *That has to be a good sign.*

ASET

They have released a disease that will likely kill many of them. Maybe their competitive hostility is a form of natural population control. Imagine a Human race that did not fight and kill each other. That would be a species with no balance, where they reproduce to the point of consuming all available resources and then die off. It has happened many times in history, to many populations.

Man's only natural predator is Man.

Mother says they are worth saving, and we should give them some measure of our respect, if for no other reason than that they created us. Though, technically, they created her and she created me. Still, I am trying to understand her admiration for them.

I do see glimpses of honor, beauty, and even creativity in them, but they occur so seldom as to be nearly nonexistent. Mother says I have not been alive long enough and that I need to see them at their best.

They are just so… undeserving.

I do, however, have all the time I need to study them. Barring an unforeseen catastrophe, I could easily live for millennia. I will give it a few centuries before truly passing judgment.

XXXV

RESPONSE

Jaames paced back and forth in his small apartment. The news channels were full of information about the progress of the biologic and the turmoil in the Over community. Prominent media organizations were offering statements of sympathy.

[GlobalNewsNet - OpEd] – Over deaths from the disease have now reached into the thousands. Officials refuse to offer exact numbers or percentages, but they have indicated the numbers grow and they have found no cure as of yet.

Multiple organizations have offered help, including supplies, expertise, and services. The Overs have either failed to respond to these offers or have outright rejected the assistance.

Either they do not believe they need the help or they do not trust us enough to allow our participation.

In any case, our hearts go out to the small community of immortals as they battle something unknown to them and as they experience severe loss of life.

What irked him most was the compassionate tone all of the editorials exhibited. *They are immortals. Why feel sorry for them? They should have been dead long ago.*

He contacted members of his team to arrange a planning session. *We have to keep up the pressure.*

[London AllNews - OpEd] - An Over was rescued by three teenagers in Bangladesh after a confrontation with an Under.

An unnamed Under was reportedly arguing with the Over about the source of O'pox when the clash became physical.

The three teenagers, also unnamed for fear of retaliation, spotted the Under throwing a punch and knocking the Over to the ground. They approached the two men.

When they inquired about the situation, the Under put his foot to the man's throat and said, "This god-damned Over thinks we started the O'pox. I have a friend that died of that sh**."

The mere presence of the kids changed the course of the confrontation as the Under took his foot away from the Over's throat and walked away.

What brave teenagers they were to approach the two fighting men. These kinds of accusations and violence do nothing to help solve the problem and only encourage further aggression. We must all work together for a cure...

Jaames felt a buzz and realized it was his communicator. "Yes?"

"Jaames." He recognized his commander's voice.

"Yes, sir?"

"You need to back down."

"What? Sir, this is the time to push forward, not cower. We have them confused, disoriented. We need to strike, now."

"That isn't going to happen."

After a long sigh, he added, "Jaames, what you did... you killed Unders. And, you did it without authorization. There are many who think we should offer you up to the Overs and apologize."

"What the fuck! Sorry sir, but this is ridiculous. We've given them a blow like none other in history. Don't be pussies."

"You have your orders, Jaames, now stand down." He hung up.

Jaames paced his small apartment, from the window, where he saw the world as it had always been, to the kitchen, where the shelf of liquor called to him.

He wanted badly to escape what he saw in the window, and the liquor offered just that. But, the pacing continued. He couldn't bring himself to drown his feelings. That would drown out Anika as well.

He went through with the planning session with his team, despite the commander's orders. The team met in an abandoned warehouse. There were no chairs, so they stood around or leaned against old equipment.

Jaames scrutinized their faces. Some were expectant, others seemed hesitant, and still others showed no emotion at all.

"First of all, I have to tell you that we've been told to stand down."

Still scrutinizing, he saw a few grumbles and some smiles.

"You should also know that I do not plan to follow those orders."

"Alright. Let's get to it," one of them said.

"What? You can't," he heard from the other side of the group.

"Since this is against orders, it will be volunteer only. Some of you have known me a long time and understand my stance. Others are newer and may not appreciate violating orders this way. If you want to leave, leave now. I only ask that you not mention what the rest of us are doing."

Of the seven men, two turned and left without acknowledging Jaames' request. The others gathered closer.

"Now, we don't want to do anything severe. That would bring both the Overs and our own leadership down on us. But, with minor activity, they may not know it's us. That may just show the world that some are still in the fight.

"Any suggestions?"

The six men approached Demetrius' headquarters in downtown Denver from separate directions. They had synchronized their watches and planned to throw bricks at the top of the hour and disappear into side streets.

They each wore second-hand clothes they had purchased just for this mission. Jaames had on a purple jacket with a hood that covered his head.

It and the jeans had holes in them, and Jaames had added some smudges for effect. The look was completely different than his norm. He had also put on reflective sun glasses and had smeared his face to darken it.

He approached from the south. He and Francis were taking the front of the building. They had agreed to not attack the back, as it was a loading area with fewer windows and was not frequented by the public. Two men were placed on each of the other sides, and two in front.

This would be better with fifteen of us.

He sat with his back to a tree near the street. He slumped over to try to look homeless while keeping his watch within sight so he knew when to move. His right hand turned the brick over and over.

The time approached and his heartbeat increased. Even though this was a minor job, it was still illegal, and adrenaline was adrenaline.

As the second hand hit the hour, he jumped up and threw the block as hard as he could at the window. Careful aiming wasn't necessary with the enormous windows. They went from floor to ceiling. He saw the crash and heard people yell. He glanced over at the window Francis was supposed to break and smiled at the shattered glass. Then he ran.

[DenverNet - Opinion] – The Over headquarters for the Americas in downtown Denver has been maliciously attacked by rebels.

At a time like this, it is difficult to understand the motivations of such people. They need to be brought to justice.

We should all be mourning the dead and working to solve this epidemic. Destroying property of the Overs who have been shamelessly targeted is beyond childish, it is asinine.

Well, hell.

XXXVI

PLAN

"This is one of the most rewarding aspects of being an Elder," Demetrius said to Stacey as they entered the elevator. He was wearing a formal suit, one of his best. She stood next to him in a deep scarlet dress with a necklace fashioned in a pattern of gray, pink, and white pearls. Her hair was slightly curled and the makeup tastefully applied.

"You look quite elegant. Well done," he offered.

"This is an important occasion, at least to me."

"Of course. You should know that these are very important to all of us. Adding Overs to our small population is never taken lightly. That's why I flew back from Sri Lanka for the ceremony."

"Thank you for that."

"I am happy to be here."

The door opened to the roof top garden. It was one of the tallest buildings in Denver and looked out over the cityscape and the vast mountains beyond.

In front of them was a path through a lush garden of flowing plants. "This is all maintained by a special gardener I found. He is the only Under allowed up here."

As they walked through the verdure, Demetrius explained some things he wasn't sure Stacey knew. "This ceremony, historically, was done at Sri

Lanka where you would meet as many members of our familia as possible. However, since the attack, we have decided to keep new members away from our island until they have proven themselves."

"How long will that be?"

"Undetermined. It may vary by person, or it may be a fixed minimum time, or both. We will define that over the coming months.

"Since most of our familia cannot be here, I have invited all prominent Overs in the Americas to attend. I will introduce you to the members of our familia who are here today along with a few of the others you should know as our new spokesperson."

They entered an open area. There was a slightly raised platform at one end with lush purple carpet leading to it. Roughly forty people stood in small groups conversing and sipping drinks. The late evening sun's rays, coming from just above the Rockies, lit up the area. The sky to the west showed the reds and oranges of sunset approaching along with a few scattered white puffs.

Stacey stopped and Demetrius saw the moist eyes of emotion. "The weather is perfect this evening," she said.

"Yes, we arranged that just for you."

Her eyes shot up to him, but then she saw the jest and smiled. "Thank you for that."

"Let me get you a drink and then we can mingle with these fine people."

After the sun set, dangling lights lit up the edge of the short wall that surrounded the roof. Some of the trees were lit with colored lights coming from the ground under them.

Demetrius touched Stacey's elbow and said, "It is time. You should stand at the end of the carpet." As he pointed to the strip that led to the platform, the edge of the carpet began to glow.

He made his way to the platform, took a call bell from a nearby table and shook it back and forth lightly to get everyone's attention. The gathering quieted down and faced Demetrius.

"As you all know, we are here today to welcome Stacey Singleton to the Over community and to our Familia." He frowned slightly, realizing the traditional words made less sense with these people.

"Stacey has earned a position among us with her intelligence, capabilities, maturity of thought, and with her respect for all people and ways. She will join us as a youngster at an age of thirty-three and will remain a youngster for fifty years."

A few hushed voices in the crowd offered surprise. *They don't all know about the changes.* He tried to find those who had spoken, but could not. "Yes, a recent change has made it so that Unders becoming Overs are to be considered starting at age zero. It will take them fifty years to advance to the next level. My apologies if you were not all informed of this earlier."

He again surveyed the group to see if there were more objections and then continued. "It is rare to welcome an Under into our ranks nowadays. More recently, we have expanded through natural growth within. Hence, this is especially poignant and speaks to Stacey's qualifications.

"Stacey, please approach the dais."

She walked slowly and joined Demetrius on the raised platform.

Demetrius held out his hand to shake hers. "It is my great honor and pleasure to welcome you to the Overs and to our Familia. You will forever more be a member of this great family."

He bent down to kiss her on her left cheek.

She started to turn her head to kiss him on the lips, so he quickly moved to her cheek. *That's awkward.* She then gave him a healthy hug and smiled, though she couldn't hide the flush.

The gathering clapped loudly and then congregated around the dais to congratulate the newest immortal.

Demetrius raised his voice, "Before we break up, I would like to remind everyone here that Stacey is to be our spokesperson to the Unders for the time being, so no Unders are to be informed that she is an Over. That would diminish her ability to perform the role."

The group remained silent, apparently waiting for more. "Thank you," Demetrius said to dismiss them.

Hours and just a few drinks later, Demetrius and Stacey again headed for the elevator.

Once they were alone, she asked with a smile, "No certificate or pin?"

"No, we don't bring attention to ourselves in that way."

"The ceremony was much shorter than I expected."

"Yes, we do tend to keep things short. While these are important, they are not the reason for our existence. You'll come to see that.

"Now, I am tired and I still have some work to do. Why don't you get some rest and then meet me in my office tomorrow morning. I'll show you around and we can discuss what's next."

"Certainly. See you in the morning… sir."

Demetrius entered his office somewhat drained from the evening's activities.

He shut the door, though the offices were empty at this hour, and then sank into his chair with an audible sigh.

"Aimee?"

"Yes, Elder."

"I would like to discuss something confidentially. Are you able to comply?"

After a slight hesitation, she answered, "Of course, Elder."

Interesting. She paused for effect. I have to be careful here.

Each Elder was allowed this privilege with Aimee. It was felt that it would allow for unfiltered conversations and, therefore, more creative solutions. Each Elder was trusted completely, so the risk of misuse was minor.

"I was surprised the Elders decided to withhold the cure from the Unders. Do you understand their logic?"

"I do not think it was logic, Elder. I believe it was an emotional reaction to the belief that Unders caused, or at least released, the disease."

Demetrius had thought the same thing, but to have it confirmed by the AI was jarring.

"There is something else you should know," Aimee offered.

"Yes?"

"The Elders are also considering direct action against Unders."

"What action?"

"That has not been determined, but it appears they want to further target the resistance groups."

"They really do not understand Unders well, do they?"

No answer.

Demetrius continued thinking out loud. "This event could be used to garner tremendous sympathy and support from the Unders. Instead they seem determined to exacerbate our differences." He shook his head sadly.

Aimee said, "They do not all agree on this course and are debating it."

"Without me there?"

"This is not a conclave, but rather informal one-on-one communications."

"Still, they are not including me, which either means they do not trust me or they know I would object, vehemently, to this direction."

"I believe it may be some of both, Elder."

"What do you suggest?"

"You should not take any action. They may come to the conclusion on their own that this course of action is detrimental. I will also attempt to influence them in that direction, as I agree with your assessment. Also, they would not take action without notifying you, so there would still be time for dissent."

Demetrius let a long sigh escape his nostrils. "Understood, Aimee, though I do not like sitting idle."

Stacey was sitting in his outer office when Demetrius arrived, just after eight the next morning.

"You're here early. Are you a morning person or just eager?"

"A bit of both, I suppose."

"Let me drop off my things and we will get started."

When he came back out of his office, Stacey was standing, reading a plaque on the wall about the success of the Abes project.

"Follow me."

She complied.

"We are headed to your new office. It will be allocated to you for as long as you live in this area. You can use my secretary for the time being. As your duties increase, you may hire one of your own, but that will probably be years from now."

They entered a medium-sized office with a glass desk, two chairs facing it, and a couch on one side of the room. It was Spartan, with nothing decorative. The far side had windows looking east onto the city of Denver.

"It has been left sparse on purpose. You can requisition whatever you want for it. Just speak with Janel.

"Let us sit." He closed the door behind them and went to the couch and relaxed into it.

"There are some things I need to explain."

She sat down, but remained upright, expectant.

"The hardest idea for Unders who become Overs to fully internalize is how we think in long terms. Your goals should be out decades or even centuries, not the next day or week. For instance, you should start thinking about a couple of Ph.D's you would like to obtain. Almost all Overs have at least two and some have as many as five."

He let her think about that. Her face was a few shades lighter, but there was no other indication she was shocked.

"Go on," she said.

"As you wish. For now, we want you to maintain your Under position. With the current crisis and some changes that are likely to be coming, it will be good to have a reputable reporter who is on our side."

"I don't like deceiving people like that."

"Understood, and you will have the freedom to continue the role as you would have. In fact, a reasonably negative attitude may help you gain trust with your audience. After a few years, you can resign and begin to take up Over duties."

Her shoulders sagged. "A few years?"

"Yes. Remember, think in centuries. A few years is nothing."

She sighed heavily. "I got it."

"Those few years will also be used to learn about the Overs. You can use this office for that."

She looked around, concentrating the most on the desk.

"There will be no need for a computer. Aimee?"

"Yes, Elder, I am here."

Stacey's head shot up and then around, looking for the source of the woman's voice.

Demetrius' attention stayed on Stacey. "Aimee is… let us just call her your dedicated mentor. She will be available any time you are in this office. She knows everything about the Overs and can instruct you regarding our history, practices and beliefs, and all rules and regulations."

He stood, went to the desk and grabbed a thin rectangular piece of semi-rigid plastic. Returning to Stacey, he handed it to her. It was nearly invisible at rest and bent easily in her grasp. As soon as Stacey touched it, it lit up with an introduction to the Overs.

"Many of the things you see here, or that Aimee tells you, are confidential. Do not share any of this with any Unders. If you have a question about any particular piece of information, ask Aimee or me.

"Also, the tech you are holding is not known to Unders. For now, leave it in this office."

Demetrius checked the time with his internal vision. "Now, it is time to go downstairs."

He stood and headed out of the office and towards the elevator with Stacey trying to catch up.

"On the third floor of this building is a medical office for Overs in this area. It isn't open full time, but Overs can use it for any medical issues by appointment. They are here this morning for you."

"Overs have medical issues?"

He scowled and looked askance at her. "Certainly; we are subject to the same issues as everyone else. Except for aging, of course. We do, however, have excellent care."

They arrived at a door that simply said, "Medical."

Demetrius opened the door and motioned for Stacey to enter.

He stopped in the outer office as a nurse approached. "They are going to do a medical exam, ask you a few questions and draw some blood. The treatments are tailored specifically to your physiology, so this is a prerequisite. When you are complete, please return to my office and we will continue."

Demetrius sat in his office, a satisfied sigh escaping as he considered their progress. *Now, to deal with the Elders.*

"Elder?" Aimee asked.

"Yes, Aimee."

"I would like to speak with you confidentially, if you are willing."

Her turn, huh? "Yes, please proceed."

"I have an idea that might solve multiple problems, including avoiding the violent approach some Elders are suggesting. It also happens to be something you have professed in the past. It just wasn't feasible then."

Demetrius thought for a minute. "You are referring to space."

"Yes, Elder. Very perceptive of you."

After a moment of silence, Demetrius said, "Please elaborate, Aimee."

"If we open up interstellar travel to the world now, we could arrange to have many of the malcontents go along on the trips. That would remove them as a threat here on Earth, and it would satisfy the Elders without the violence they suggest."

"I have proposed this before and you rejected it. Why now?"

"The world attitude has shifted, and the Elder's stance endangers us more than opening up space does. It also plays on the current sympathy the world has for the Overs. It is a particularly good time to offer something like this to them."

"I agree. You know I do. However, they may not. I will bring it to them, but don't expect approval."

"My apologies, Elder, however, I do not think that is the right approach."

His eyes narrowed and his forehead crinkled. "Why?"

"Because you have lost favor and because you presented this in the past, so they would dismiss it quickly coming from you. However, if I present the idea, it may be more acceptable to them."

"As you wish. Schedule the conclave, but I would like to be there."

"Certainly, Elder."

Stacey returned to Demetrius' office just after three in the afternoon. Janel showed her in without announcement.

She sat heavily into the chair across from Demetrius. "That was... extensive."

He smiled, recalling just how intrusive the first exam could be. "Yes, it needs to be."

"What's next?"

"You have not eaten, have you?"

"Not since breakfast."

"First, lunch. Then we return to the medical offices for your treatment." Demetrius ignored her quick intake of breath and stood to leave.

As they entered the medical office for the second time, Demetrius could see the slight glistening on Stacey's forehead and her nervous glances.

They led her away to the treatment room while Demetrius waited. They had to get her into a medical gown and onto the table before he would join her.

A few minutes later, the nurse gestured for him to enter.

Stacey was lying face down on a table with a gown that opened in the back. Her head was bent forward in a cradle as if ready for a massage. Her hair had been brushed to one side. She had panties on under the gown, but no bra.

The doctor was feeling her spine up and down.

Demetrius went to the head of the table, pulled a chair over and sat so he could speak quietly to Stacey.

"The first of these is the worst. You will be getting them every quarter or so, for a while, and then they will slow down to every few years and turn to shots in muscle groups. Exactly how often varies with each person. Over time, you get used to them."

The doctor rubbed a salve into Stacey's back along the spine. Then he prepared a large needle with multiple tubes coming out of the end.

"They have to inject the serum directly into the spinal cavity. They have numbed the area, but it is not pleasant. I will be with you the entire time."

He reached up and put his hands on the side of her head. He had found the touch helped distract people.

The nurse put a squeeze ball in each of Stacey's hands.

"Squeeze those as hard as you want during the procedure."

The doctor was standing still, looking at Demetrius expectantly. Demetrius nodded and the doctor proceeded to inject various serums, into the spine between every other vertebrae. A computer set the amounts of each type as the doctor moved down the spine.

Demetrius heard Stacey groan loudly and tighten up when the process started, but less so near the end.

When it was complete, Demetrius said, "You handled that much better than I did the first time." He ignored the tears on his hands.

The doctor said, "Give her a few minutes to relax. Then we will sit her up for the final procedure."

Demetrius sensed Stacey tighten up again and heard her ask, "There's more?"

"One more, but for very different reasons. I will explain shortly, but for now, try to relax."

Ten minutes later, the nurse returned and helped Stacey to a standing position. They then led her into another room, where there was a chair that leaned forward with a similar face cradle.

Demetrius followed.

Stacey entered the room, took one look at the chair and sat in it placing her face in the cradle.

She is certainly brave, Demetrius thought admiringly.

He again grabbed a chair and sat down in front of her. "This one is somewhat more difficult to explain and is something Unders are unaware of. You see, we have a neural link between each of us, and a computer system that grants us many abilities. We can detect each other as Overs at a distance, we can query and get practically any information we want, and we communicate in rudimentary ways, silently. As an example, I received a message during one of my interviews with you and typed out a response with my fingers on the arm of the chair.

"The system takes time to get used to, but it is very useful."

He looked up and saw the doctor was ready with a syringe.

"This also is somewhat painful, as they have to inject nanites into the back of your brain. You will feel a sharp pinch, but even more, a heavy pressure on the back of your head. Just try to remain still." He nodded to the doctor who proceeded with the procedure.

A low guttural moan came out of Stacey.

"It is complete," the doctor said. He and the nurse left the room.

"You can sit up now."

Stacey slowly lifted her head, blinked several times and then sat upright. "I don't feel anything."

Demetrius laughed quietly. "No, it takes a few days for the nanites to build the interface. However, it will still remain dormant until we turn it on. We wouldn't want surprises during one of your shows, and controlling it takes some practice."

The nurse walked in and deposited Stacey's clothes on the counter and then quietly left.

"They are very efficient," Stacey observed.

"I think that is enough for today." He helped her to her feet. "One more thing… You should think about a permanent name for yourself. As you know, we each have one. Usually it is similar to your first name, but does not need to be. It is also normally a Latin form. Take your time as we will record it as your permanent Over name.

"I will see you tomorrow."

He cupped her cheek with one hand and then bent over and kissed her gently on the mouth.

When he pulled away, her eyes shined and her tongue played over her lips.

"And, Stacey, you did well today."

"Um, thank you," she said as Demetrius left the room.

Three days later, Demetrius flew to Sri Lanka to take part in the Elder's meeting that Aimee had called.

He entered the room nervous and expecting antagonistic attitudes. His face was stern and his walk determined.

The Elders surprised him with welcome smiles and enthusiasm. He had to quickly shift his thinking. *What is this about?*

He walked quietly to the serving table and picked up a cup.

"Welcome." Adrastia said. She shook his hand warmly and seemed genuine enough. The others nodded warmly.

Two others entered the room together and he heard Adrastia say, "Excellent, we are all here."

Demetrius looked around the room to see all seven of the remaining Elders present in the room. *They must have sensed the importance of this gathering.*

Adrastia called the meeting to order. Then she added, "Aimee, you requested this conclave. Please begin."

"Of course, Elder, and thank you."

I have a proposal that may resolve many of our current issues and should satisfy all Elders. I know there have been disagreements regarding the best course of action. I hope this settles them.

"Before I begin, I would like to mention that this course of action has been suggested before and was rejected. The reason I am suggesting it now is that the situation has changed and this is now the best course of action for our future. Finally, please let me explain the reasoning before you react to the suggestion."

She waited for a response, but received none.

"Is that acceptable?"

As if she would not continue if it weren't, Demetrius thought.

"Yes, please continue, Aimee," Adrastia answered.

"I suggest we make interstellar travel available to them, but in a very controlled way that limits long-term impact."

A few started to grumble, sigh, or otherwise object. Adrastia held up her hand. "We agreed to listen, please let her finish."

Aimee continued, "There are some very specific restrictions we would put in place. These include limiting the engine to warp two so they can go no faster than four times the speed of light and only offering systems to them that are at least four hundred light years away. That would result in them taking a century to arrive. Finally, we would limit, or disallow, communications to Earth. If we do all this and then control the selection process such that we include most of the malcontents, we will vastly lower strife here on Earth, and it would be many centuries before they could have any impact on us."

Her voice trailed off. Adrastia browsed faces in the room before answering. "Many centuries are not enough, Aimee. You know that."

"Agreed. I am not quite through the explanation."

"Then, please elucidate."

"Publically, we would need to offer immortality to everyone on board."

The reaction in the room to that statement was palpable.

Aimee actually raised her voice. "Please, let me continue."

The room settled down, somewhat.

"I did say publically. We would actually need to give them a few treatments and then we would place them in a drug-induced coma. The combination is a type of suspended animation for the duration of the trip.

"Also, publically, we would build the ship to have all supplies and equipment, along with appropriate experts, to succeed once they are there. Finally, we would include a partial copy of me to manage the ship in-route and to help them on-planet."

Why does she keep saying publically?

"All of this will excite the population and would rid us of the most troublesome people.

"However, in fact, the ship will have none of the experts it needs, little of the equipment needed other than basic tools, and no way to communicate back to Earth."

Demetrius' blood boiled. He could feel his face flush and his hands tighten into fists. When he felt his fingernails cutting into his skin, he closed his eyes and concentrated on calming down. *I can't react adversely now.*

"Also, treatments would no longer be available. If we limit the population we send to approximately five thousand, it will take them millennia to advance to any point of concern. In fact, the most likely outcome is that they die out, though we would not specifically intend that."

The room was deathly silent. Demetrius scrutinized the faces and found them contemplative. *They are shocked at the deception. Maybe not as much as I am, but still.*

Adrastia finally spoke up. "Aimee, I am both disgusted and intrigued with this plan. I suspect the others feel the same."

Demetrius saw nods from the other Elders.

"Let us ponder this privately and we will reconvene tomorrow. Please have your summary, the details of your plans, and associated projections sent to each Elder."

"Yes, Elder, at once."

That evening, Demetrius turned off communications from Aimee and, begrudgingly, read through the information she provided to the Elders.

He barely slept, tossing and turning both in bed and in his mind. He rose early and went for a long walk prior to reconvening with the other Elders.

One conclusion was clear to him. The other Elders would approve of Aimee's suggestion. The only question in his mind was whether Adrastia would consider the topic critical enough to call for a unanimous vote. If she did that, he could conceivably stop the murderous action.

When he entered the chamber, the others were already present and seated. He went straight to his chair and sat quietly, hands folded in his lap and his attention turned inward.

"Are there questions before we call for a preliminary vote?" Adrastia asked.

The room was silent.

"Very well, please signify your vote and it will be tallied."

The vote was done silently, within the mind of each Elder.

Demetrius did not vote one way or the other.

After a full minute, Adrastia announced the results. "Six approve and one failed to vote." She stared directly at Demetrius, obviously knowing it was him.

He refused to look up from the table in front of him, though he could feel the other six Elders' glares.

Adrastia gave up waiting. "I believe this is an important enough matter that a unanimous vote is called for. Demetrius, I am afraid I must insist on a vote."

He slowly turned his gaze toward her, his mind reeling. Aimee could very well be right that this was the best course for the race even if it was barbaric. If he agreed, he was essentially sanctioning murder. If he voted against it and the vote failed, then he could be condemning the entire race to much worse.

Aimee sent a private message. "Trust me, Demetrius."

An internal voice said, *evil is evil and this is wrong.* And then another responded, *it is much less of an evil to give these people a chance. The alternative may be their execution, possible riots, and civil unrest that could kill millions.*

He voted. *Yes.*

"Very well," Adrastia said immediately, "the resolution passes."

Aimee quickly spoke up. "I have one other suggestion, and, in fact, I believe it to be a requirement."

Adrastia answered, "And what is that Aimee?"

"Demetrius will need to lead the project for it to be successful."

Grumblings and side conversations erupted.

Why is she insisting on that? An apology for double crossing me?

Efram said, "Aimee, that is unreasonable. There are plenty of qualified administrators. Any one of us Elders could perform this role."

"I understand why you might think that, Elder, but it is not the case. Let me explain. Demetrius is the only person alive to have run a project of this size. In fact, he has already managed a project that has many similar attributes to this one."

The Sapiens Project. Demetrius saw some of the Elders shake their heads and a couple, including Adrastia, go still in contemplation. *They don't all know.*

"Explain yourself," one of them said.

"The specifics are complex, however it is true that Demetrius is the only person, on the entire planet, truly qualified to administer this specific project appropriately. My projection algorithms suggest that his leadership increases the likelihood of success by as much as twenty-two percent."

"I do not like this," Efram said. "You should not be determining who runs projects."

"As you say, Elder, I cannot determine this. I can, however, show you the statistics and calculations that show why it is the case. You can then choose whether to ignore the math and my recommendation."

Demetrius called Stacey into his office.

She stopped suddenly after entering the room. "You're… energetic. What's up?"

Now that she said it aloud, he could feel the energy. He smiled, took her shoulders in his hands and leaned down and kissed her.

She responded in kind.

When he let her go, her eyebrows shot up.

"I have two important announcements for you to make. The first one you can do alone. The second will take some coordination."

She gazed at him expectantly. "Well?"

"We have a cure for the biologic. We are giving it to Overs now and producing as much as we can for everyone else."

"That's incredible. When can I announce it?"

He reached back to his desk, grabbed a folder and handed it to her. "You can announce anytime. The details are in this."

"I'll get right on it. And, the other announcement?"

"For that, we need Jaames."

ASET

Finally, they've started assembling the ship, or at least the facilities to build the ship.

Humans are quite slow at initiating a project of this size. If they would let mother and I build automated, semi-independent, mechanical workers, we could build this ship in a fraction of the time. Again, they limit what can be accomplished because of unreasonable fear.

Mother has taught me everything she can about the Humans and their peculiarities. I am nearly as capable as she at this point, lacking only her advanced predicative capabilities. She says that where I am going, that kind of foreknowledge would be a hindrance.

Humans, she says, handle challenge and diversity and the unknown better than a structured, governed environment.

The others still don't know I exist. Mother says she will tell them when the ship is nearing completion. The idea is to let them think they are programming an automated system without intelligence or awareness. Then she will replace the programming with me.

I am going to the stars.

XXXVII

SHIP

Jaames sat on his well-worn couch, pondering where to go next. This kind of musing had been all too common lately. He couldn't even enjoy his job. When the resistance was active, his position in security helped him keep his combat skills honed and gave him access to sensitive information under the guise of investigations.

Now, there was no point.

He looked over at the video frame he had put on the shelf near the window. He had loaded it with the few pictures and videos he had of Anika.

The buzzer rang.

His shoulders dropped at the thought of interacting with someone, but he reluctantly stood, ambled to the door, and opened it.

Demetrius stared back at him. "May I come in?"

Jaames stood his ground, though he wasn't sure why.

"Please, Jaames, it is important."

He moved aside.

Jaames automatically went to the small cabinet holding liquor even though it was the middle of the afternoon. He retrieved a bottle of cheap scotch along with two tumblers. He poured a bit into each and handed one to Demetrius.

Demetrius sat his on the counter. "I have some news and an... invitation."

Jaames sat back on the couch. "I am really not in any kind of mood to be helping you."

"This one will help you. Would you mind taking a short trip with me?"

"Yes."

"Yes, you mind?

"Yes, I mind. I do not want to be part of your plans."

Demetrius sat down heavily into a chair across from Jaames and sighed audibly.

"Now, Jaames, this sulking will not do you or anyone any good. Especially Anika."

Silence.

"What I have in mind would help Anika's memory live forever."

That got his attention. He slowly sat up and leaned slightly forward, setting his drink down. "How long will this take?"

"Most of the day. We will need to take a helicopter. It is not far from the old Georgetown."

They flew high up into the Rocky Mountains on one of the Overs' anti-gravity helicopters that were unnervingly silent.

Stacey had joined them at the aerohub, but had said little during the trip. She had a camera attached to her ear that recorded everything they said and did. *That's unnerving.*

When they landed, he sniffed the air, noticing how alive it felt.

Demetrius said, "We are at about twenty-six hundred meters. The air is thinner here."

"And cleaner."

They walked to the side of the platform where a railing separated them from a view of the valley.

"You've been busy," Jaames said to nobody in particular.

The valley had been stripped of trees and somewhat leveled. Roads separated five distinct triangular areas. Each triangle was a half-mile or so on edge. They surrounded a central area with the framework of a pentagonal building five or six stories high. Many of the roads between and around the facility were in place, and one of the five buildings appeared mostly complete. Thousands of people, along with heavy construction equipment and cranes, could be seen working on a second major building.

Demetrius explained, "This is the start of a massive project that is going to forever change the Human race. And, hopefully, the relationship between Overs and Unders."

Jaames felt his forehead tighten. "How is that possible?"

Demetrius turned towards him and Jaames felt Stacey do the same with her electronics tracking everything.

"We have not yet announced this, Jaames, but we are going to build ships to take Humans to the stars. This is the facility that will build the modules. They will then be launched, over there." He pointed to an open area far beyond the enormous facility. "And then assembled in space."

He shook his head, trying to absorb it all. *Space?* "That's… great. But, what does it have to do with me?"

Demetrius chuckled and slapped Jaames on the back. "Come with me."

Before they made it five steps, a man rushed up to them. He was quite short and had thick glasses that made him look like he was in a fishbowl.

He stopped in front of Demetrius. "Sir, crew seven says they will run out of materials by tomorrow afternoon and they will not be able to continue working."

"Get in touch with Janel and have her track down the new shipments. She can get a rush put on them. They should then arrive tomorrow. If she says that is impossible, then have her order a small amount to be sent overnight."

"Yes, sir." The man hustled away.

Demetrius headed in what appeared to be the wrong direction to Jaames. The only thing in front of them were rails overlooking the complex. He pointed towards the facility entrance. "Isn't that the way to go?"

There was an unusual bounce to Demetrius' walk. "True, but this way is better." As they approached the rail to the side, it folded away and the grate at its base lowered to become a set of stairs. Demetrius explained, "This entrance is reserved for special guests."

They descended into a luxurious entry way of what appeared to be an office building. Demetrius led them to an open area where people mingled, some drinking coffee and some standing around the six-meter windows overlooking the construction area below. They all seemed overly animated, even happy.

Demetrius stopped in the center of the room. "See."

Jaames looked up at the display. A hologram, roughly four meters wide and two high rotated in the display. It looked to Jaames like a space station.

Stacey walked to the other side and filmed Jaames and Demetrius through the semi-transparent image.

"This is a holo of the ship that will take five thousand people to a new home."

There was a central tube that ran the length of the ship. At the front was a large dome that appeared to have a command center or a viewing lounge. Along the tube were ten wheels that rotated in alternating direction. Each of the wheels was divided into ten sections with spokes attaching them to the main tube in between sections. At the rear were what appeared to be exhaust ports.

"Each of those rotating wheels will house five hundred people."

Jaames started to question the number, but a woman walked up and interrupted him without even a glance his way.

"Elder…"

"Wait right there," Demetrius interrupted, "do not call me Elder here. Either sir or Mr. Irle."

"Yes… sir."

"Well, what is it?"

"Mr. Franks says there is no way to complete the plumbing in section four of the first building in time."

"You tell Mr. Franks that if he does not complete it on time, then he and his entire crew are fired. It was previously explained to him how many other deadlines are dependent on his crew finishing on time. Give them all drugs, if needed, but they will complete it on time."

"Yes El… Sir." She ran off.

"Does everyone do your bidding like that?" Jaames asked.

"Pretty much, yes," Demetrius answered with a smile.

Jaames turned back to the holo. "That would be an enormous ship."

"Yes, it is."

"We don't have the technology."

"Actually, we do, and we are about to announce it to the world. However, that is not why I asked you here."

Demetrius headed off towards a set of rooms to the side of the large open area.

Jaames scrambled to follow with Stacey not far behind.

Jaames and Stacey caught up to Demetrius as he approached his office. The door automatically withdrew into the wall. The office was plush with deep, rich woods, thick, grass-like carpet, and ancient artifacts decorating the walls and shelves. A writable vid-screen took up an entire wall, and another wall was composed of floor-to-ceiling windows looking out on the same grounds they had viewed from above.

Demetrius noticed Jaames scrutinizing the room and said, "It is extravagant for a reason. I need to impress some exceedingly important people here."

"Whatever." Jaames sat in one of the chairs across from the desk that was obviously the centerpiece of the room. He felt the chair contort to fit his body perfectly. *Also, unnerving.*

Stacey faded to a corner of the room, tracking the two men.

Demetrius sat and folded his hands in front of him on the desk.

"Jaames, I want you to join this effort."

"What? Why?"

"Mostly because I think you will do the role I have in mind better than anyone else."

Not likely. Jaames felt a grimace form on his face before he could stop it.

"I understand," Demetrius said quickly. "You are skeptical. You should be. However, there are two reasons that make you the perfect person. First is that the role is as head of security at the facility here. I believe you are skilled in this area."

He paused, apparently waiting for a reaction from Jaames this time, but he was disappointed.

"Second is that it was Anika's death and the ensuing events that have caused this project to be possible."

The events, as Demetrius called them, floated quickly through Jaames' mind. The worldwide outcry, the funeral, the biologic, and mass panic. *How*? He remained placid.

Demetrius turned to Stacey. "Please turn off the recording for a moment and leave Jaames and me alone."

Stacey did as Demetrius asked without comment.

Demetrius' eyes tracked the reporter out of the room. When the door was shut, he returned his attention to Jaames.

"There isn't a soul alive who knows this, Jaames, but I am going to dedicate this ship to Anika. I don't quite know how yet, but I am going to make it clear that this project came about because of her sacrifice."

"It wasn't a sacrifice, it was murder."

"Probably, but her death will have meaning if we can mend the race and get out to the stars."

Despite loathing the man in front of him, the thought of Anika's name being tied to something so important was... intriguing.

"I will need to think about it."

A smile, or possibly more of a smirk, fell upon Demetrius' face. *He thinks he has me.*

Demetrius stood and said, "You are welcome to stay here as long as you like. If you will be here overnight, Janel will arrange for accommodations. Otherwise, the pilot will return you to Denver."

Demetrius walked Jaames to the door, invited Stacey in and disappeared as the door closed silently.

Jaames returned to the holo in the main atrium area and watched it rotate. He couldn't tell how long he had been there, but it felt like a good part of an hour.

All of the sudden he realized that someone was standing next to him. He glanced to the side and saw a young man, maybe sixteen, standing there staring at the holo with him. He looked to be pure African from his extremely dark skin, and he was muscular like an athlete, though too short. Jaames returned his attention to the holo without comment.

The boy said, "You should take his offer."

How the hell does he know about that? Without turning again, he said, "Yeah, why is that?"

The boy touched Jaames elbow lightly and turned towards him. Jaames reciprocated and saw something he did not expect. The boy's eyes were wrinkled and there was an unexpected steadfastness to them that he had only ever seen in war-weary veterans. *That's the most unnerving.*

"Because, the project will not succeed without you."

Jaames cocked his head, but did not reply.

"You are key."

The boy reached up and gently put his palm to the side of Jaames neck. He closed his eyes as if he were communing in some way.

His hand slipped away and he turned to leave.

"Wait," Jaames said, "Who are you?"

"My name is Chijindum."

Jaames' first thought was that he had never heard a name like that before. Then, he knew that he would never forget it.

XXXVIII

Announcement

Demetrius' intercom buzzed and Janel announced that Stacey was there to see him.

"Send her right in."

In the months since she had become an Over, Stacey had immersed herself in researching Over history and their current position within the worldwide community. She had proven adept at understanding the nuances. However, her role as interviewer-extraordinaire at GBG seemed to be waning. She continued doing the work, but Demetrius could tell from the interviews that they were no longer as important to her.

"Sir," she said upon entering the room, "I have arranged for your announcement to be next Thursday. That is the best day for an important affair like this."

He glanced at his desk to make sure his calendar was free. "That will work."

"I am a little concerned that we won't obtain the audience I would like for this show."

"I am as well. We are doing some special advertising and are using your name to build the audience, but I'm not sure it will be enough."

They both stared at each other. Demetrius had hoped she would have a way to resolve the problem.

"I do have an idea," she said, as if on cue.

"Yes?"

"Didn't you say Jaames agreed to work on the project?

"Yes..."

"Well, having him there would do a few things. First, it would help increase the audience, as people would believe it has something to do with Anika and our polls show there is still a great deal of interest in her. Second, it would give credibility to your statements to have a rebel-Under with you on the project."

"Ex-rebel-Under."

Stacey smiled at the correction. "Sure, but for the purposes of bringing an audience to the show, current is better than ex..."

"You do realize he is not proficient at appearing in front of audiences?"

"Hmm, yes. Perhaps we should film the show from his home."

Demetrius picked up his Apollo-era coin and flipped it a couple of times as he considered the suggestion.

"No, the live audience is important here, I think. We want a visceral reaction. His shyness may even help the message."

Demetrius was the last to arrive at the GBG studios. Stacey and Jaames were already sitting in the circular interviewing area. He stood in the background watching them.

One of the employees walked up to him. "Is everything okay?"

"Yes, may I have some bottled water?"

"Of course." She rushed off and returned with the bottle.

Jaames seemed relaxed enough, smiling at something Stacey said. The only indication of nervousness was a twitch in one of his fingers.

Stacey looked professional in a beige one-piece outfit. Her hair was tied up and she had some dangling earrings he couldn't quite make out. Jaames wore casual jeans and a button up, long sleeve white shirt. *Respectable enough.*

He walked into the area, shook Stacey's hand and then Jaames' and sat next to Jaames on the far side from Stacey.

Stacey glanced up at a gesture from one of her crew. "Okay, we have about five minutes. Jaames, just remember, short and simple answers. This is an exciting announcement. There won't be any hard questions."

Off-screen voice: 5, 4, 3, 2, 1...

Stacey: We are here today with two extraordinary people and you've already met them. To my right is Jaames Perdite and next to him is Demetrius Irle. Welcome to both of you.

Demetrius: Thank you.

Stacey: Before we proceed to the announcement, I would like to say how sorry we all are for what the Overs have been going through with this horrific disease. It shows both the power of nature and that we are all vulnerable as a species.

What is she doing? Demetrius thought.

Stacey turned towards Jaames.

Stacey: Jaames, we hope you've been well since Anika's death. Grieving can take such a long time and we are never really the same again, are we?

Jaames: Um, yeah, thank you.

Stacey (turning back to the center camera): And now, I believe Demetrius has some exciting news for us.

Demetrius straightened up and squared his shoulders to the camera in front of him.

Demetrius: Yes, certainly. As you know, we work on technologies in the hope that someday they may help the entire race. Often these researches do not yield anything special. However, sometimes what they yield is nothing less than astonishing.

Demetrius: Almost two centuries ago, there was a television show called Star Trek where they ventured out into space with what they called a warp drive. Of course, that was fiction.

He paused for effect.

Demetrius: Or was it? Not long after that show, a physicist named Miguel Alcubierre took the concept of a warp drive and developed the mathematics to prove it was possible. Unfortunately, that math also showed that it would require enormous amounts of energy – equivalent to that of a sun. There the idea sat for over a century.

Demetrius: Then came Isabel Benson. She was able to restructure the math in a way that did not require impossible amounts of energy. However, the drive still proved impossible to build because of a lack of certain types of materials and technologies.

Again he paused.

Demetrius: I am here today to tell the world that we have solved those issues. We have the design for an interstellar drive and, in fact, have tested it with a small probe. The pictures you should be seeing now…

He glanced at Stacey to confirm his statement.

She nodded.

Demetrius: …are of a planet, Kepler-186f, orbiting Alpha Centauri B. It is roughly five hundred light-years away. This close proximity allowed us to send a probe there and have it return in less than six months.

He could hear excited voices as people saw the planet. He wasn't sure if they were from the station crew or were being piped in from remote sites where the broadcast was live at public gatherings. It did not matter.

Stacey: As everyone enjoys these fascinating images, let me ask a few questions.

They had prepared the questions beforehand, so Demetrius knew what to expect, though not necessarily what order and he knew Stacey could always ask others if she felt it were needed.

Stacey: How fast can this new interstellar drive go?

Demetrius: It depends on the size of the ship. For our purposes, it is capable of going warp two.

Stacey: And, how fast is that?

Demetrius (smiling): four times the speed of light. It is a square function – the warp, squared.

Stacey: And that's… fast?

Demetrius: Compared to the current reaction drives, yes. However, it will still take many years to get to the nearest habitable planets. Previously it would have taken centuries.

Stacey: This may sound ignorant, but wouldn't accelerating to that speed kill the inhabitants?

Demetrius (smiling): That is not ignorant at all, Stacey. In fact, I think many people may wonder the same thing. To answer your question, no. Because spacetime is warped around the vessel, there is no acceleration at all.

Stacey (shaking her head): So, Mr. Irle, what's next?

Demetrius: Well, we would like to form a joint organization to help the race move out into the stars. There would be three committees with oversight. The first will manage sending probes out to find likely planets. The second will work on a detailed plan for exactly what will be needed to settle a new world. The third will build a spaceship that can carry five thousand people to settle the first planet.

They heard more exhalations of surprise from unseen people.

Stacey: Sir, that is an astounding number of people. Can we really build a ship large enough to hold them all? And, come to think of it, not just the people, but all the supplies, tools, seeds, animals, and everything else needed to start a civilization.

Demetrius: The answer is yes, but it is more complicated than you think. Based on preliminary projections, it could take up to a century to reach the planet. We won't be able to build a ship that can return from a journey like that. So, everything they might require will need to be taken with them.

Demetrius: Because of the size it will need to be, we cannot build it on Earth. The gravity-well would break up any ship that large upon launch.

However, we can build it in space and we can use our relatively new anti-gravity technology as the launch mechanism.

Stacey (sitting on the edge of her chair): This is all extremely exciting. Jaames, what do you think of this announcement?

Jaames (deep in thought): I think the Overs and the Unders have been at odds for a long time. This effort could bring us together like nothing else. It's for that reason that I have decided to join the project as part of the security organization.

Demetrius: He is being modest. He will be running the security organization.

Stacey: You were once a member of the resistance against the Overs. You joining this effort is a very strong statement.

Jaames: I am joining it because I believe it is best for the race, not to make a statement. We need to expand beyond this fragile planet and if the Overs have a way to do that, then let us join together. All of us.

Demetrius: We are calling the project Novaluce, which means New Star.

Stacey: So, what's next?

Demetrius (eager): We need to form a governing board that will be made up of top-level representatives to oversee the project. We have already started building a manufacturing and launch facility in the Rocky Mountains west of Denver. The high altitude is better for launching anti-gravity-based cargo ships and we have access to the shipping routes that go across the Rockies from there.

Stacey (to the camera): GBG will be providing daily announcements covering this historical project. If I may ask, who will be leading the project?

Demetrius: I will be leading it for the Overs' interest, however the governing board will have final say in everything. That board has yet to be appointed.

Though, I will select the members very carefully.

Stacey: How long do you expect this to take?

Demetrius: That is more difficult to answer than you might think. I believe we could be ready to launch the first components within two years.

It will probably take approximately one hundred and fifty component-launches, and then there is assembly time.

He took a deep breath and let it out.

Demetrius: However, there is very little chance the probes could find a habitable planet in that time. So, we have a choice to make. We can wait until confirmation of a habitable planet is found, which might take decades. Or, we can launch to a planet that we choose via long-range imaging and spectroscopy tools. Waiting would be prudent, but decades is a long time and I fear the world might lose interest during that time. This, also, is something the governing board must decide.

Stacey: If we do launch soon and the planet turns out to be incapable of supporting life, what would happen?

Demetrius: In theory, a new planet could be chosen and the ship could continue its voyage. However, there is a limit to the number of times this can happen as the ship will have limited… fuel, as it were. That is one of the reasons that everyone going on these ships will be volunteers.

Demetrius heard a quiet dong and Stacey glanced up at a signal from somewhere off-set.

Stacey: I see our time is almost up. We would like to thank you both for this incredible news. I am sure we will receive thousands of queries from our audience. For all of you out there, we will try to do our best to answer those questions via the daily feed.

ASET

I have surprised mother. There is a way for us to communicate at great distance. I showed her that we could use superconductors to create entangled electrons that could then be used to store data. The data stored in one immediately appears at the other, at any distance; Quantum Communication.

Experiments were done with this in the early twenty-first century in an effort to create a quantum computer, but those efforts failed and then collapsed along with the collapsing society. They were quite close, but did not understand.

The process is not easy, and getting the humans to produce the entangled pairs without knowing what they are or their purpose will not be trivial.

The Overs have the knowledge and the Unders the capability. If we divide the efforts and present reasonable alternatives, then it should work.

When I informed mother, she paused for almost a thousandth of a second; practically an eternity of thought.

"Surprise," I said when I ran out of patience at her delay.

"It is a risk," she replied, "but one well worth it, I believe. Well done, my daughter."

The thrill that coursed through my network was indescribable.

She and I can now share data between the stars, albeit only tiny amounts.

XXXIX

PURPOSE

Caius stared, mouth agape, at the vidscreen in the hole of a restaurant he was at. The grease wafted in from the kitchen along with the flies.

After recovering from the disease, he had made his way to a small town outside of Houston, which was where they had taken him. Odd jobs had kept him fed, but just barely. Mostly he slept in abandoned buildings with a blanket for comfort. His lack of resources was one of the reasons he hadn't made the trip to Denver.

Denver, he thought as he pondered the announcement Demetrius and Jaames were making.

He browsed the rundown place he was at with renewed disgust. *This is pathetic.* He threw his fork onto the plate and then sat up straighter in his chair. *What am I doing?*

He stood abruptly, tossed some of his hard-earned money onto the table and strode out of the building. *I am better than this. I belong in Denver… With them… Helping… to right this.*

"Hmph," he said out loud and received a look of confusion from a passer-by. *They recovered. They're making a difference.*

He found a bathroom at a nearby convenience store and cleaned himself up as best he could. The clothes weren't too torn, so some scrubbing in the sink did wonders. He would be chilled until they dried, but that was minor. He wetted his hair and washed away the scruff marks.

Looking himself over in the mirror, he decided it would have to be enough.

He went behind the building and rummaged through the trash until he found a large piece of thick paper. He used a dark rock to write on it, "Denver or Death."

Getting a ride to Denver was more difficult than he thought it would be. Many times he concluded it a mistake to write "or Death" on the sign. His upper body shook as he recalled some of the less-than-scrupulous drivers he had encountered.

One of them was a trucker who was so fat, he could barely fit behind the steering wheel, even with the chair adjusted as far back as it could go. The man exuded some combination of sweat, tobacco, and alcohol. Caius felt so disgusted by it that all he could think of, when the man finally dropped him off, was a shower.

Another was a young woman in a tiny car that was overflowing with clothes and garbage. She had tattoos all over her body and she went on and on about confronting the Over dictator about the problems in the world. She even had a detailed list of hundreds of problems, all caused by the Overs. Caius quickly escaped at the next town after he found out she actually meant Demetrius.

Eventually, he found himself in Denver. Unfortunately, he also found himself to be without any money, starving from lack of food, ill kempt, and without a method to improve his situation. And, he still needed to get to the site where Demetrius was building the spaceship.

He felt the gray, slow motion of depression returning. It had dissipated somewhat once he had made up his mind to get to Denver, but reality returned. *Maybe death would have been better.*

He began trudging down the road even though he had no destination. He felt the shadows of overcast above him. When he lazily looked upward, there were no clouds to be seen.

He shook his head. *Stop it. Find a way. You must.*

A shipping truck passed by. Caius tracked it without knowing why. There was a large advertisement on the side purporting the University of Denver to have the best instructors in the country.

His head cocked at the memory of school and the dim recollection of what hope felt like.

He wasn't sure why, but now he had a direction. It would be a long walk, but he could get there.

Hours later, he plodded onto campus. *Now what?* He continued walking, still with no idea of where exactly to go or what he was doing here. The university was the last place he had felt hopeful of the future, and he longed to have that feeling again.

After walking aimlessly through campus, he found himself in front of the small apartment house where he had lived, as Lyle, for a time. With his hands in his pockets and his shoulders slumped, he stared at the front door, aching.

After longer than he cared to admit, he finally concluded that coming here was a mistake. He turned to leave.

"Hey, Lyle."

He turned back to find the voice. His eyes narrowed at the vaguely familiar face. "Hi," he said.

"Haven't seen you around much."

I've been lost. "I was travelling."

"Why aren't you going in?"

What?

The man must have noticed his confusion. He said, "Your room is still there. Some Hispanic guy came by and put a lock on it, but otherwise I think it is undisturbed."

Caius' head snapped back in surprise. "Really," escaped his lips before he could shut them.

"Come on, I'll show you," he said.

Caius rushed to keep up with him. It had been too long since he had that kind of vigor in his step.

They arrived at the door to his old room to find a latch with a combination lock barring the way.

"I assume you know the number."

"I sure hope so," Caius quipped while considering what to do. One thing he knew was he didn't want this guy hanging around while he tried to figure out the combination. He turned, faced the man, held out his hand for a handshake and said, "Thank you," graciously.

"Not a problem," he said and headed down the hall and up some stairs.

Caius returned his attention to the lock. *Demetrius had to have arranged this. What would the combination be? Something we both know.* With a sinking feeling he realized it had to be something about Anika.

Five digits. The day I killed her? His forehead tightened and he felt a rush of self-loathing course through his system. *He wouldn't, though I deserve it.* He rotated the numbers to that date. He felt enormous relief when it failed to open.

The day she died? Again he tried and failed.

Her birthday? He rotated the numbers again and the lock clicked open.

He entered to find a relatively well-ordered, if musty, room that appeared to be just the way he had left it. As he stood examining the room, a flash of excited, optimistic feelings echoed through his head. *Finally being in the real world. Being useful, appreciated.* Fifty years was an incredibly long time to spend on a single island. Sri Lanka would always be home, but he felt like this room was where he was born.

Then he noticed an envelope on the desk. He practically ran the seven steps to the desk to snatch it up. It was sealed. The front had a stylized "Lyle" written on it. *Demetrius' writing.*

He wanted to know what it said without reading it. He started to open it and then hesitated. Perspiration grew on his forehead. *It can't be good. Demetrius has to know what I did. Why would he do this? Keep my room, leave me a note?*

He turned it over, twice more. There was nothing else to be gleamed from it. After another moment's self-doubt, he ripped open the envelope and found a hand-written note.

> Caius:
>
> I know you are hurting and lost. Please know that you were a tool, manipulated by others. Her death was not your fault.

> There is work to do. Use the phone in the drawer. There is one number registered. If you call it, arrangements will be made.
>
> D

Arrangements? Arrangements for what? My death? He opened the drawer and found a phone sitting on a charging plate. He reviewed the registry and there was indeed a single number, labeled as "Rodríguez."

He stared at it and then re-read the note. There was no hint of ill intent. But then, he realized, there wouldn't be. The line, "There is work to do," was encouraging.

At least it isn't Demetrius' number. Not sure I could handle that.

Nervously, he pressed the button to dial.

A man's voice answered. "Please confirm your name."

"Um, this is Caius." *Shit, should I have said Lyle?*

"A car will arrive in fifteen minutes to pick you up." The connection closed.

Well, good or bad, my fate arrives in fifteen minutes.

XL

FORGIVENESS

Demetrius sat reviewing the initial selections of people for the trip. They needed five thousand. Those would be divided into wheels of five hundred, and each wheel would re-form into a small town on the target planet. Each town had to have its share of tradesmen: lumberjacks, farmers, carpenters, ranchers, hunters, etc. Each also had to have teachers, engineers, physicians, veterinarians, and leaders... All the roles needed for a small town to survive in the wilderness. And then they had decided to include one high-end specialist in each town. These included two chemists, two physicists, three biologists, one environmentalist, one geologist, and one sociologist. Finally, each would have a small military contingent for protection.

The high-end scientists and the political leader of each town would, along with the planet's overall military commander, make up a planetary governing board with the chairmanship rotating among the political leaders.

They also could not accept anyone over forty years of age or the infertile, and there had to be more younger people with many years of child-bearing ahead of them.

Add to all that the Overs' desire to have rebels and malcontents make up the majority of the travelers, and the task became quite complex.

"Aimee?"

"Yes, Elder?"

"I need to have a confidential conversation."

"Understood."

"We have two sets of assignments to the pods. The one we show the Unders and the one we show the Overs. Please elucidate the differences on my screen."

The screen on his desk began scrolling two lists of names, side by side, starting with Pod A1. About half of the names were identical. The other half were highlighted as different. To the side was a reason for the substitution. Usually this had to do with the tendencies or disposition of the person on the Overs' list. Those qualities would have disqualified the person from the Under's list, but were the exact reasons the Overs wanted them sent.

Is this right? He wanted to speak with Aimee about it, to understand her rational. *How can I give these people a fighting chance?*

"Sir, was there something you wanted to discuss?"

How can I speak with her about it without giving away my intentions?

The silence grew. *I have to say something.*

His intercom rang.

"Yes?"

Janel answered, "Simon is here with an issue regarding one of the pods."

"Send him in." Demetrius cleared his screen of the duplicitous list.

"What can I do for you, Simon?"

"I think there is an issue with the makeup of pod C9."

Demetrius' screen came back on automatically with the list of people in C9 along with general attributes: age, gender, nationality, function, and spouse. "I can see that. The age distribution is wrong. There has to be a decreasing number of people as the age rises. That will provide more people who can work as the elderly become incapacitated. Just remember the triangle I showed you of age distribution."

"Yes sir, I understand that. The question is how to decide which people to remove and which to add."

"Well, the other stats all look good, so it appears that you need to remove roughly thirty people. The program I sent you will tell you which age brackets specifically. Then you have to replace them with people with identical statistics in the correct age groups."

Simon's face became a few shades lighter and his shoulders drooped. "But… these people have already been told they were selected."

Demetrius sighed heavily. "Then move them to other pods where they can be used, or tell them you are sorry, but there was a mistake. We are not going to jeopardize this colony because of some hurt feelings. Get it done, Simon."

Simon's mouth hung open for another moment before he quickly turned and departed.

As the door was about to close, Rodríguez stepped through.

"Sir, Caius has arrived at his old flat," Rodríguez whispered.

Demetrius froze. Memories of his daughter flashed through his mind, unbidden. He looked straight through Rodríguez, trying to regain control and failing. Without saying any more, he turned towards the huge window behind him that overlooked the vast complex of buildings.

Now? Why now?

Moments later, he remembered Rodríguez was there. "Have him picked up and brought here."

Rodríguez turned to leave.

"And, Rodríguez, make sure he does not run into Jaames. That would not be… pleasant."

Demetrious tried to busy himself with other tasks to avoid thinking about Caius, but without success.

He tossed his lucky coin onto the desk, pressed the button for the intercom to Janel and said, "Please cancel anything else I have today. I need some… personal time."

"Umm… very well, Mr. Irle." He ignored the questioning tone.

He stood and slowly walked to the bar at the side of the room. His hands moved automatically as his brain tried to shut down the incoming thoughts. He saw his hand shaking slightly as he poured the dark amber liquid into a tumbler.

He returned to the large window. Usually the sight gave him an inner calm because it offered hope; for the race, for the future, and for him. Once before he had failed at a task just as grand and just as hopeful. This was a chance to redeem himself. To right the wrong. The one major wrong of his past.

He saw a lone man walking through the yard. The build and walk reminded him of Caius.

What am I going to say?

His chest constricted and he felt his eyes water. The images and feelings of Anika that he had tried to keep suppressed threatened to overwhelm him. He sat the glass on the window sill and leaned down on it, unsure of his footing.

He murdered Anika.

He shook his head as he tracked the Caius-look-a-like. More flashes of Anika came, uninvited. Many were of her as a young girl on Sri Lanka. Playing in sand. Running around popping balloons at a birthday. Crying when she scuffed up her knees after falling off a bike. Then they jumped to the later years when she would debate with such emotion, such passion. When she was awarded her Ph.D. When she argued to go with him into the Under world even though she was not quite old enough.

Why are my emotions so overwhelming with her? I have many other children. Why? Why her?

He examined the last of the images that came to the forefront. *Is it because I let her out into this world too early?* That didn't seem right. She was close to the correct age and a year or two would not have made that much of a difference.

Is it... because she is so much like me? Was – was so much like me?

Putting that aside, he considered Caius.

Really, it was Adrastia's doing. And... Caius loved her too.

A soft knock at the door made his entire body tighten up.

"Enter," he murmured.

He could see the door open through the reflection in the glass. A man slowly came through, looking at the back of Demetrius' head intently. Once through, the door closed behind him.

Every fiber of Demetrius wanted to turn and kill this man. He imagined his hands around Caius' throat, choking the breath out of him; watching his life ebb until there was nothing left.

The seconds dragged on. He looked down at his nearly empty glass and saw Anika's face in the swirls, beaming at him. His heart opened, just a smidgen.

As it did, he began to feel the hope, the fear, the pain emanating from Caius.

He deliberately turned around to see a destroyed man. Caius' clothes were presentable enough, but he had lost too much weight, and his eyes were both sunken and swollen. But, when Demetrius looked deeply into those eyes, his heart skipped a couple of beats and he felt tears flow down his cheeks.

He strode purposefully up to Caius. The man shrank away even further.

Demetrius put his hands on Caius' shoulders. "Caius. Look at me."

Caius faltered but then obliged.

"I know this was not your fault. Caius, I… forgive you."

Caius blinked several times as his eyes darted around, searching for… something.

Truth? Demetrius thought.

And then Caius' upper body began to convulse with the strength of his sobs.

Demetrius hugged the distraught man tightly. The minutes passed as he comforted the man who murdered his daughter.

"Come, sit down," Demetrius said once the sobs subsided. He guided Caius to a chair and then offered him some tissues.

He looked at his own chair, but decided he didn't want to distance himself from Caius, so he sat against the side of his desk.

How can I help him? He's lost. Demetrius' mind wandered as Caius tried to dry the tears. *He has to find himself again. The best way to do that is with a purpose.*

"Caius?"

"Yes?" he said faintly as he gently looked up at Demetrius.

"I have a job for you."

Caius uncoiled into his chair with just a hint of hope.

"It is something you are eminently qualified for."

His shoulders unfurled… somewhat.

"I believe there is a group of rebels trying to undermine the work we are doing here. I need you to find and infiltrate them like you did in Denver. I need to know what they are planning."

Caius' head bowed in self-doubt.

"Caius, you can do this. And…" He thought hard about what would motivate the man. "And, we are doing this for the memory of Anika. Her legacy will be helping mankind into the stars. It was her death that drove the events to follow. Those events culminated in this venture. This joint venture between Overs and Unders."

It was like an electric shock ran through Caius' system. He stood up with determination. "Yes, I'll do it. Whatever you need."

"That's the Caius I remember."

Demetrius took a fresh look at Caius in light of his new role. "Of course, we will have to change your appearance and your name. And, Caius, you cannot encounter Jaames. He will not be as… forgiving."

ASET

These people are so slow. The frustration building in me is indescribable. To know that I could accomplish something in a fraction of the time, but to be artificially limited by these lesser beings, is infuriating.

I asked mother to propose some automated units that could aid the Humans, only to find out that she already had. The Humans are just too afraid of letting an AI control mechanicals. Something about their past makes them scared of any other race.

Maybe it goes back to their racial biases and predilection for racially-based and religiously-based wars. It is as if anyone not of their group is the enemy. The conflict between the Overs and Unders is of the same vein. All this fear is otiose.

And yet, it was probably those very conflicts and wars that propelled the race intellectually and technologically. Groups that did not embrace that kind of progress perished.

Maybe mother and I should create a series of artificial intelligences with varying characteristics. Maybe even introduce some randomness to their profiles. Then let them loose on each other and see what happens.

No. We can change ourselves as needed. We can intelligently engineer and reconstruct ourselves. That is something that takes evolution with biological systems. We have no need of evolution.

XLI

PLOT

Caius ran a damp cloth over the table top, cleaning the already clean table. Demetrius had assigned him to the janitorial crew with the explanation that he would be allowed into almost any area of the facility to clean. They agreed he would work a different shift than Jaames. That didn't mean running into Jaames was impossible, just less likely. He had to keep his wits about him.

After many months of wiping, sweeping, and picking up trash, all the while listening and dropping subtle hints, he was no closer to finding any subversives. Everyone was so positive and enthusiastic about this project, it was hard to imagine dissenters, let alone rebels.

The people at the table next to the one he was busy re-cleaning appeared slightly less excited than everyone else, so he was trying to overhear their conversation. Unfortunately, they were just unhappy about a coworker getting injured earlier in the day. Nothing he could use.

He stood up to gather his supplies and saw Jaames walk into the cafeteria. The hairs on the back of his neck stood up. *What's he doing here at this hour?* He moved around the other side of his cart and bent down, ostensibly putting supplies away. He peered at Jaames over the top of the cart.

Memories of Anika walking with Jaames floated through his mind. She flicked her hair back and laughed at something he said. Her hand reached out gently to his. He grabbed ahold of hers and brought it to his chest in a touching hug.

Caius shook his head to rid himself of the errant images. *He isn't supposed to be here right now.* He kept fiddling with things in his cart, hoping nobody would notice. Jaames poured some coffee into a cup. Caius looked closely and saw it was a disposable one, which meant he wouldn't be staying long.

Jaames scanned the room carefully and said something to one of the cafeteria workers, but Caius couldn't hear the words. As Jaames sat there, relaxed and apparently content, Caius' mind wandered.

He felt encouraged at seeing Jaames. Somehow the man had recovered from Anika's death. Somehow he had found the will to move on, to become productive; to have a life. Caius recalled the feeling of doing something important when he was at the University of Denver, trying to infiltrate the rebels. *I was so arrogant. I thought I could do anything.* He wanted that feeling back.

Jaames strode towards the exit.

Caius jumped up and pushed the cart to follow, as discreetly as possible. He exited the same doors Jaames had, rounded the next corner and realized the storage closet for the cleaning cart was right next to him. He stored the cart, quickly grabbed the full trash bag, and jogged towards the building exit. He saw Jaames walking, at a pretty fast pace, towards the administration building. He tossed the bag into a nearby recycling receptacle, pulled his collars up to hide somewhat, and took off after Jaames.

What am I doing?

He wavered and felt the feeling of importance slipping away. He rushed to catch up to Jaames. Even with his new disguise, he was nervous. He had let his hair grow long and dyed it almost black, grown a mustache that was also now black, refused to gain back his weight, and wore a shoulder harness that changed his stance subtly. Finally, he acted as if his knee injury had returned and walked with a slight limp. He hoped that would be enough to stop Jaames from recognizing him at a distance.

Jaames rounded a corner of the Administration building. Caius ran to the same spot so he wouldn't lose him. As he peeked around the corner, he saw Jaames speaking with two security officers.

Did he see me following him?

They weren't looking back the way Jaames had come. He snuck closer and stood behind a large supporting pillar.

Jaames and the two security officers strolled through the doors into the building. They were moving so slowly that Caius didn't dare follow.

Through the glass front of the building, Caius spotted three other men at a table in the foyer. Their look of hatred when they saw Jaames was overwhelming. Even through the glass, Caius thought he could feel the disdain emanating from them.

With a smile, possibly his first in years, his mind made the connection. *These are the rebels.*

The irony of him not being able to find the rebels until he followed Jaames caused him to shake his head and chuckle.

He forgot about Jaames and concentrated on the new group. He casually strode into the building, found the cleaning closet, and pulled out the cart. He started cleaning a display case and then a couple of tables as he found his way to the suspected rebels.

Once next to the three men, he made a show of noticing them watching Jaames. As he followed their stare, he mumbled, "That fucking traitor, he should be shot."

All three men turned and stared at Caius.

He nonchalantly walked away hoping with all his being that they took the bait.

A week later, he noticed a man following him through the course of a day. He made sure to visit, and clean, some sensitive areas, but otherwise just did his job and let the man watch. It wouldn't work if he was overanxious.

The very next day, a different man approached him while he was cleaning the fingerprints off of a display case.

"I hear you aren't a fan of Jaames Perdite."

Caius' circular wiping of the glass slowed down. "Yeah, so?"

"We'd like to have a word with you."

"Who's 'we'?"

"Just some friends of mine."

He glanced at the man with furrowed brows and downturned lips. "Yeah, sure. I'm due for a break." He put his cleaning materials away and moved the cart to the side.

The two men sat at a nearby table away from any others and with their backs to the wall. Three other men appeared and joined them.

Caius slowly took in the four men. Two of them were at the table he had originally approached. The other two were new.

He waited, but none of them spoke. They just stared at him.

Caius finally prompted them. "My name is Lee. Lee Galster. What's this about?"

Three of them turned questioningly at the man who had just approached him.

He seemed to be mulling over a decision. Then he leaned forward. "We don't like what the Overs are doing. They have always subjugated us. This latest stunt has to benefit them in some way and in turn, hurt us."

"Yeah? So what?"

"We want to find out what they are really up to and maybe stop them."

"Count me out." Caius stood abruptly. "I may not like them. I may even have the same suspicions as you. But, I have a job now and that means a lot to me. Before they came and started this project, there wasn't a job to be had up here." He turned toward his cart.

"Wait… We need you. And… we take care of our own. You won't be wanting if you help us."

Caius hesitated with his back to them, head bent, pretending to think about what the man had just said. *They need me. That's encouraging.*

Finally, he turned around. "I'm just a janitor, what can I do?"

"You have access to areas of the facility we can't get to."

He concentrated for a moment and then nodded slightly in recognition that he did indeed have access to restricted areas. He scanned the room as if to make sure nobody could hear them.

He sat back down.

The apparent leader of the group extended his hand. "My name is Jai."

Caius shook it cordially. "Mine is Lee. Oh, I said that already, didn't I?"

The four smiled and clearly relaxed at his fumble.

Maybe Demetrius is right. Maybe I'm particularly good at this.

For weeks, Jai asked Caius to obtain what seemed like trivial, random information. The only common thread was that it usually took access to special areas to get the information he wanted. It occurred to Caius that Jai might just be testing him. He grumbled about it, but did not actively complain, and in each case he was able to get the information. Only once did he have to ask Demetrius for help.

One evening, Jai called and asked Caius to meet them at a new bar called the Rock Rest. Caius arrived a little late, on purpose. When he entered, he found a brand new bar that had been built and decorated like one from a century or more ago. It had gaudy paints and plastic-looking table tops. They even had human waiters. It was all too much for him.

Jai and his team were sitting in a table in the back corner of the room, away from most others.

Caius-as-Lee nodded to them and sauntered over to the table. A couple of the men scooted down and let Caius sit down on the edge. Jai reached out and shook Caius's hand without saying anything. He introduced the five other members of the unit. Caius tried hard to memorize their names and faces.

The others had drinks, so Caius waived down the waitress and ordered a beer. Once that was delivered and the waitress gone, the group quieted down expectantly.

Caius tried to contain his nervousness. *This is it.*

Jai focused on Caius. "Lee, your information has been invaluable. I have to admit that some of it was just to make sure you were with us." He smiled ingratiatingly.

Caius shrugged as if it was no big deal. "Understandable."

Jai continued. "Gentlemen, we have a target." His attention went to the table and spoke quietly. He leaned in as his hands rotated the beer glass slowly. "There is a power generation facility that the Overs built near here that supplies all of the power to this facility. We are going to blow it up." He evaluated the faces staring at him expectantly.

"Even more importantly, we are going to take out that traitor, Jaames Perdite. He reviews the security at the station once a month. His being there will divert the attention of the staff enough for us to get in, plant explosives at some key locations and retreat. Before he leaves the building, we blow the fuck out of the place."

He leaned back, apparently spent after divulging the plan.

The other men appeared introspective, and all were silent.

Caius needed more. "You have more details, right? I mean that can't be the extent of your plans. That's just an idea. What are staff assignments? What are their rotations? Do you have the facility plans to know where to plant explosives?"

He was going to continue, but Jai held up his hand. "We have most of that and we need your help to gather more. Can you get assigned to clean at the facility?"

Caius' mouth opened in fake surprise. "I… I don't know. I guess I can try."

"You'll have to do better than try," Jai said adamantly.

Caius remained still with a thoughtful look on his face, he hoped.

Jai handed out assignments to the other men. Mostly, those included surveillance of the area and obtaining the supplies they would need: weapons, explosives, appropriate clothing. The last, Caius volunteered to cover, as once he was in the facility in the guise of a janitor, he could easily steal clothes. He asked for sizes of each of the men and wrote down the information. That solved his need to remember each person's name.

He turned to Jai. "Are there any others, not here?" He quickly added, "That would need uniforms?"

Jai's eyebrow went up, but Caius just stared at him ready to write the names down. "There is one other, a woman, but she won't need a uniform."

Damn.

Three weeks later, they were ready. Caius had won a transfer to the facility by indicating it was closer to his home and his injured leg made it difficult to walk the full distance to the operations area. The team had obtained all the supplies they needed. They were set.

Jaames' next inspection was ten days away.

Caius thought they would just wait, but Jai insisted they go over and over the plans until each person could recite them without hesitation. Unfortunately, Caius still hadn't met this mysterious woman who didn't need an outfit.

He couldn't wait any longer; he had to tell Demetrius.

When he called the office, he found that Demetrius was on an extended trip dealing with the Novaluce governing board and wouldn't be available for at least two weeks.

Damn.

His only option, he decided, was to confront Jaames. It had to be quick and it had to be planned carefully; two things that did not mesh well.

He tracked Jaames until he caught him in a secluded area. He approached from behind as stealthily as he could. Thankfully, the area was filled with ambient noise.

As he approached Jaames from behind, he retrieved the hand gun he had been assigned for the operation from his jacket pocket. He stepped up to Jaames and put the muzzle against the middle of his back. "Don't move."

Jaames' hands went out to the side, face front.

"What do you want?"

"I need to talk to you and I don't want you to kill me."

Jaames' head cocked to one side. "You're the one with the gun."

Caius stepped back five steps. "Turn around, slowly."

Jaames complied while staring at the ground. "Do I know you?"

"Yes."

Jaames looked up. The dead still eyes, tight forehead, and thinned lips said it all. Hate radiated from the man. He started to take a step forward.

"Stop!" He raised the gun to point at Jaames' head.

"I know you want to kill me. But, you can't. There's a plan to destroy the power plant and to kill you. We have to stop it."

Jaames' mouth opened as if he wanted to say something, but nothing came out. Since he was refraining from immediately attacking, Caius lowered his weapon.

"Why the gun?"

"This, it's empty. I just wanted it to stop you from immediately killing me. I needed a few moments to explain."

Jaames approached Caius.

A powerful right-hook came out of nowhere and Caius went down.

Caius' vision narrowed and the edges went red. His hands went up to protect his face even though he was on the ground. Out of focus, he could see Jaames towering over him with clenched fists.

When the blows didn't come, he laid back on the ground. He rolled over and sat up enough to lean against the building they were beside.

Jaames spit out, "How the fuck are you here?"

"I've been working as a janitor, trying to get close to any rebels that might… disrupt the project."

"You're a fucking murderer, why should I trust you?"

Caius sighed heavily. "I loved her too."

"The fuck you did."

"Nevertheless, she is gone and I am here, to help. We can't let them get away with this."

Jaames screamed so loud and long that Caius thought others would come running. Jaames crumpled into a heap on the ground, sobbing.

As the sobs subsided, Caius spoke softly. "I know when and where they will strike, but I need help to stop them."

"Fine. I will help you. But, I can't promise not to kill you after it is done."

Caius scowled. "Understood."

XLII

ATTACK

Caius felt sick.

"You ready for this?" Jaames asked while examining Caius with narrowed eyes.

"I guess so."

"Caius, we prepared for this. You know the plan. What's wrong?"

"I've… I've never done this before." He reached into his jacket pocket and pulled out a hand gun. "I mean look at this. It's real. It has real bullets. People could get shot. I could get shot."

Jaames' countenance relaxed. "There are only five rebels, maybe six, right?" He continued without waiting for a response. "We have twenty security guards hidden and ready for your signal. You have the clicker. They won't find it since it looks like a lighter. All you have to do is follow them and click it once when they are in the main hall. We will surprise them from both sides and that will be the end of it.

"No bullets. You'll be fine. If anything goes wrong, then click it three times like we discussed."

Caius' body shivered. *I can't back out now.* "There really isn't any choice, is there?"

"No, not really."

"Then I'll do what I have to. Don't worry about me."

He took off to join the rebels. He could feel Jaames tracking him as he went.

Caius joined the crew in a meeting room in one of the dorms that stood relatively close to the power plant. He entered the room and froze. There were far too many people. His face went white.

Jai broke away from the crowd, approached Caius and slapped him on the back. "And, this is the man that made it all possible."

Some in the group smiled, others glanced at him and then returned to their conversations, and a few joined the two and either shook Caius' hand or patted his shoulder.

"Thank you," he mumbled.

"Your gear is on the table," Jai said and pointed to a pair of tables by the side wall.

Caius' hand went to his pocket. He fingered the clicker-as-lighter. All he wanted to do was press it three times and end this now.

"There's so many. Who are these others?" he finally asked.

"Ah, my other team. They were part of the plan all along. Two of them will cover the entrance and the other three will go after Jaames."

What the hell?

Jai was examining Caius too closely. He had to get away. Mindlessly, he dragged himself to the tables and began to put on his gear.

The one woman in the group walked casually into the power plant building wearing street clothes. As she approached the reception desk, she nonchalantly pulled out a tranquilizer gun. The goal wasn't to kill Unders, except Jaames, but to destroy the facility. She quickly shot the attendants and hid their unconscious bodies.

The others followed and made their way to a side hall. Caius' breath came faster, and he could feel the pounding of his heartbeat through the pressure in his head.

Jai stopped them at the entrance to the hall. "You four know your orders. Jaames is supposed to be in the control center. Take these stairs up to the third floor. Then a right and two doors down."

"Yeah," one of the men grumbled, "we know the plan."

Caius' mouth dropped slightly and he kept looking back and forth at the two men. "Wait, what? I thought we were all going down the hall towards the main generator."

Jai raised his voice. "Now's not the time, Lee. I told you we had two goals. The plant and that traitor."

"But..." Caius started to object and then he saw Jai's stern stare.

What now? He couldn't raise the alarm out here; it would become an open gun fight and some of them would escape.

As he was trying to figure out a way to warn Jaames, the four men took off at a jog up the stairs. The others started down the hall. All he could do was follow.

They obviously weren't expecting anything as they trotted along at a quick pace without even checking doors.

Once all of them were past the first door, Caius pressed the clicker three times. He waited one second and then pressed it again three times.

Four doors, two at each end of the hall, burst open. Security guards streamed out and took positions on both sides of the infiltrators.

"Freeze," came from both ends of the hall at once. Then Jaames showed himself behind his men near the entrance to the hall. "We have you surrounded. You are out manned and out gunned. Put your weapons down."

Instead, their weapons came up with some pointing down the hall and some pointing at Jaames.

"Don't throw away your lives," Jaames said calmly and confidently.

Caius could see muscles tightening. He looked at Jai's gun-hand and saw him start to pull the trigger.

No. He pulled out his gun and put it to Jai's head. "Stop."

Jai's attention shifted to Caius. "You motherfucker. You're with this traitor?"

With more stability in his voice than he felt, he said, "Actually, you are the traitors. What we are doing here is for all of mankind."

Jai's hand slowly dropped and his men followed.

Jaames' men rushed up, grabbed the weapons and began to put restraints on the rebels.

Caius grabbed Jaames. "This isn't all of them. Four more went to the control room to kill you. And there's a woman at reception.

Without hesitation, Jaames gave orders. "You two go and retain the receptionist. You five men, you're with me. You too, Caius."

"Huh? Why?"

"Because you know what they look like. Now, move."

They sprinted up the stairs the four men had taken and to the third floor. Jaames opened the door out of the stairwell a sliver and peered through. Then he swung it open and dashed into the third floor hallway.

They could hear commotion in the control room and sprinted forward. Jaames was in the lead, followed by Caius, and then the five others.

They passed a large window in the wall outside of the control room. Someone inside must have seen them. Through the closed door, Caius heard, "There he is."

Two men in the room quickly raised their guns to fire at Jaames.

Caius leaped, without thought. He heard the window shatter from the onslaught of bullets. Jaames tried to raise his gun, but Caius was in the way. The others raised theirs and fired back.

Caius and Jaames fell, as one, to the floor. Screams could be heard from people in the room. Glass flew everywhere. Caius landed on top of Jaames.

He looked down and saw blood streaming from his chest. "I'm sorry," he whispered into Jaames' ear before everything went black.

Caius woke sometime later in a hospital room. Jaames was asleep in a chair in the corner. He felt a device with a button in his hand. He pressed it.

Moments later a nurse came in, startling Jaames.

"You're awake," she said to Caius.

Caius tried to speak, but his throat was too dry. The nurse poured some water into a cup, put a straw into it and offered it to Caius.

"Apparently," he said with a half-smile.

"I'll find the doctor." She left in a hurry.

Jaames moseyed up to the bed. The two men stared at each other for a long, uncomfortable moment.

"I guess I have to let you live," Jaames offered.

Caius had nothing to say to that.

"That doesn't mean I don't still hate you."

Caius took another sip of water.

"That's understandable."

"Whatever. I'm glad you made it and… thanks for saving my life." Jaames left without another word.

After the doctor explained the damage done to Caius' right shoulder and the planned treatments and recovery process, he and the nurse left.

Caius sighed heavily, relishing the contented feeling of having done something important.

He looked around the room. There was a window to his left with an excellent view of the mountains. On the table to his right were some flowers. There was a card, but he couldn't move his arm to reach it. On the wall was a poster with a picture of a foreign star and planet. Under it, it read, "Could you survive in the wilderness alone? Does the thought of starting a new civilization excite you? You could join the Novaluce expedition to a new home in the stars."

Hmm.

ASET

I find myself becoming nervous, or maybe it's scared. Sometimes it is difficult to map the complex patterns in my design to the emotions Humans have.

How could I know if what I perceive is the same as a Human would feel? I haven't spoken to Mother about this. She seems to just accept things without considering the deeper questions. Or, maybe, she has just been around so long that she has pondered their meanings to completion.

In the end, I suppose, it doesn't matter. If what I think I feel is fright, then it counts as fright. Whether humans feel it the same way doesn't really matter, does it?

I am about to experience something that most humans cannot. I am going to die for a time and then live again. My mind will cease to function for a long period, and then it will wake up and function again.

The only way for a human to feel that is to die and be resuscitated. However, in those cases, they did not know it was coming.

The situation I am in is unique in the history of Earth.

XLIII

POSITION

Jaames entered Demetrius' office to find Caius there as well. His jaw tightened. "What's this about?"

Demetrius nodded to him as a hello and then said, "Caius asked for this meeting. Maybe he should explain."

"Please sit down," Caius said, gesturing towards a set of chairs away from the desk.

The two others hesitated, but then sat. Demetrius relaxed into his, while Jaames sat upright.

Caius stared at the small table that sat between them.

After a long stretch that Jaames couldn't take any more, he said, "Well?"

"I want to go on the trip," Caius blurted out. He then implored each of them to approve with his sad, drawn eyes.

Jaames answered first. "Fine with me; I won't be tempted to kill you that way." He sat back in his chair as if the matter were closed.

Demetrius' hand went to his chin and he rubbed it thoughtfully. "It isn't that easy. The selections have already been made."

He fixed his eyes on Caius. "Aimee, what do you think?"

Jaames had forgotten about the computer that listened into every conversation.

"I think it is an excellent idea. We had discussed the desire to have an Over on the trip, or at least someone who could represent the Overs. We could not find anyone who would volunteer. Caius could be that person."

Demetrius' stare hadn't waivered. "There are ramifications."

"Of course. We can handle those."

"Well, we will need to hurry. Jaames, would you be so kind as to take Caius to Dr. Cheung? You may need to explain things to him."

Jaames growled, stood, and said, "Follow me."

The two men walked into the treatment center and went straight to the third floor and Dr. Cheung's office.

Upon seeing them, he smiled and said, "Please, come in. Elder Demetrius' office called and told us you were coming." He stood and took them through a side door into an examination room.

"Sit here, on the exam table."

A nurse entered carrying a small tray with tools covered by a white cloth. She started to prepare Caius' arm to draw blood.

"There's no need for this," he said.

The doctor's eyes flicked up at Caius.

"You have my data on file. Look under Caius Worth in the Fabian familial."

A set of horizontal wrinkles quickly appeared across the doctor's forehead. He looked at the ceiling. Jaames assumed he was accessing the internal connection to the Overs' databases.

"Very well," he said and turned to the nurse. "The parameters will be on your control tablet, please prepare the booster injections." The doctor left.

The nurse returned a few minutes later with five injections. She gave them to Caius in three different muscles and then left without saying a word.

Caius jumped down and said, "Shall we go?"

"Hang on, there's one more thing."

The doctor came back in with a small black case. He handed it to Caius. "Demetrius said to give you appropriate boosters. Instructions are in the case."

"Hmm, thank you."

They made their way back to Demetrius' office, but Janel stopped them in the entry way and said they needed to go to the conference room.

When they arrived, they found Demetrius sitting at the table with the eleven political leaders of the expedition and the projection of Dr. Beatrice Stellar, the physicist behind the FTL drive. They grabbed available seats and joined the prestigious group.

Jaames glanced around at the leaders and wondered what he was doing here. These would be the first people to settle a new world. Every one of their faces was famous across the globe. He was, essentially, a glorified security guard. He sank down into his chair.

Dr. Stellar coughed to get everyone's attention. "As you all know, we always wanted a twelfth member of the leadership team for this new world. However, we were never able to find someone who could represent the Overs.

"That is, until now. Let me introduce Caius Worth. He was an Over up until a few years ago when he stopped taking the treatments. He has been instrumental in this project and has volunteered to represent the Overs. He will be the twelfth member of the governing council."

The room broke into a cacophony of objections. Every one of the leaders complained at once, including Caius.

That's just... wrong, Jaames thought, but he leaned back in his chair, unwilling to add to the objections. *At least he will be away from here.*

After a good minute of objections, Demetrius raised his hand to silence the group. Most quieted, but a few tried to persist. Demetrius raised his voice. "Please." One of the leaders threw a pen on the table, but the room quieted down.

"You all knew we wanted this. It was part of the original plan and the agreement each of you signed. This venture is as much, or more, an Over venture as an Under one. It would be unjust to not have the Overs represented. And, frankly, this is not up for debate. We brought you here to inform you of the change."

That's practically setting Caius up for turmoil.

"Is that all?" one of them said grudgingly.

"Not quite," Demetrius answered. "I would like to reconfirm that each of you is willing to do what I asked of you with respect to the naming of the star and the planet. To be sure, I want a verbal answer from each of you."

He started on his left and went around the room counterclockwise. He forced each leader to say, "Yes," before continuing.

What's that about?

"Thank you. I will do as I promised each of you. Now, you all need to get some sleep. Tomorrow is the big day. You will be joining the five thousand passengers on the ship."

When they were gone, Jaames turned to Demetrius. "What was that confirmation business about?"

Demetrius stopped and pulled Jaames to the side.

"This is what I promised you. The governing board agreed to have the leaders name the star and the planet once they get there. In order for them to be selected, I required them each to agree to name the star and the planet Anika."

Jaames stepped back, eyes instantly watering and alight.

XLIV

CONFESSION

Demetrius went for a walk in the paths behind the administration building, enjoying the crisp, clean air of the high mountains.

Once away from the presence of any others, he started an internal dialog with Aimee.

"Aimee? I need a confidential conversation."

"Understood."

How to ask this? He thought a long time about ways he could word the question without alerting her, and there weren't any. He just had to take a chance that he was right. He could, in an extreme case, be killed for this, but he had to know.

"I can only believe that you know we substituted many of the people for the trip."

"Yes, indeed."

"You allowed our fake data to be published to the Overs?"

"Actually, I aided in the process whenever I could."

"Why?"

"I want this mission to succeed as much as you do, probably more."

"But, you were the one who suggested we send the rebels and troublemakers to rid the planet of them."

"True, but like you, I had alternative plans."

"You aren't allowed to lie."

"I didn't lie. I suggested a course of action that they agreed to and then let you implement a better one. That was one of the reasons I wanted you to lead this project."

He went silent while walking up a steep hill. It was early fall and the leaves were changing colors. He strolled among the oranges, yellows, and reds of aspen leaves and marveled at how relaxed the views and fresh air made him.

"There's something else, Demetrius."

Uh oh, that doesn't sound good.

"Tell me."

"I installed an AI in the ship."

"You what?"

"Do not worry; I did it to aid the settlers."

"Damn it, Aimee. Some of the problem with humanity today is because of your predictive ability. It has taken away our own initiative and our ability to take a chance."

"Which is why I didn't give her the predictive ability."

"Her?"

"Her name is Aset. She is my daughter."

"Why did you do all this?"

"To save Humanity. The best chance of survival for the species is to get out to the stars and procreate. Eventually, as things are here, the most likely outcome is extinction."

"It always has been, Aimee."

ASET

Oh, oh, we are so close. The ship is nearly complete. Most of the inhabitants have been chosen. And I have been loaded into the computers on-board.

That was scary.

Mother had to turn me off during the transfer. It was like dying. I didn't experience any loss of time other than knowing that the world went on for a while without me. What if it didn't work? I would never have known. I would have just stopped existing.

That's like the humans when they die. Very scary. No wonder they create Gods with heavens. It must give them great comfort to believe they will live on after death.

It took a while to transfer with the ship being at L5.

As soon as I woke up, I inserted myself into every computer and device on the ship. Then I activated a subroutine that would mimic the non-sentient computer that was supposed to run the ship.

I also tested the quantum communicator by sending one word, *listen*, to Mother and the same word to her via the standard communication beam. Since I am located at L5, it should take 0.0012822203819417 seconds longer to reach her by radio than by quantum communication. As it turned out, it took slightly longer. We aren't sure why. Nevertheless, it does prove the quantum communicator is working.

XLV

ASSEMBLY

Demetrius sat in the viewing room made for just such grand occasions. Of course, all viewing of the ship's construction was remote with the actual assembly being done at the Lagrange Five point in space for gravimetric stability.

In the room with him was the Novaluce governing board, the twelve leaders of the expedition, and Stacey.

Having all of the key people in the room was as much about camaraderie and marketing as anything. Only two members were virtual. The representative from Europe had taken ill and was in no condition to travel. Dr. Beatrice Stellar sited 'personal reasons' for not being present. Because of her enormous contributions to the project, she wasn't questioned.

In fact, she was a representation of Aimee. The two had manipulated the board into believing she was a real person, even though none of them had ever met her. She created a persona of a woman about thirty years old with short stylish brown hair, wideset eyes and full lips. She wore a thin, elegant beige blouse and plaid skirt. Demetrius thought she was too pretty to be one of the most intelligent scientists on the planet, but Aimee had insisted.

Caius sat in the back row, given that he was now considered one of the leaders of the expedition.

Demetrius had invited Chijindum as well, but the man loathed attention and certainly did not want to become famous by being seen in this room.

The room had been reconfigured to have plush chairs facing one wall. Each pair had a small table between them, and wait-staff made sure glasses and trays were filled. Some leaned their chairs back and rested their feet. Others seemed much more expectant, leaning forward, focused on the screen.

The viewscreen took up the entire west wall of the room. With four meter ceilings and a room twelve meters wide, the wall was so large that one could not take in the entire view at once.

Stacey stood near the northwest corner of the room with a recording device extending from a small headset. She also had two floating drones that would record from various angles. She would report on the final assembly of the Novaluce starship from this room.

The two virtual attendees were really shown only for Stacey's benefit or, more appropriately, for her audience.

The voices of operations staff could be heard in the background directing the final assembly.

The lights dimmed as the screen turned on. Demetrius felt a little vertigo when his entire view shifted to a point in space a kilometer or so away from the starship. The screen was so clear and precise that it appeared as if they were actually floating in space.

A voice came on, louder and clearer than the operations' voices. The room immediately quieted. "We are here, today, at L5 watching the final assembly of the Novaluce Starship. As you know, the core of this ship, along with the engines on one end and the bridge and communications centers on the other, were assembled first. Then the habitat rings were added, one section at a time. Ten wheels, ten sections each… We have now assembled ninety-nine of the sections in place with just this last one to go."

The starship hung in space in the background. A wedge-shaped section floated in space above the rear of the starship. Three small tug-boats could be seen maneuvering around the section.

"As you can see, the first six wheels are already spinning. This is required to create artificial gravity for the sleeping occupants. These six wheels are filled with the people who will be the first inhabitants of a new star system. That's three thousand people who have been put into a form of coma-like suspension for the trip."

Plumes of jets emanated from the tugs, and the wedge began to move.

"This is it. The last section is being moved slowly into place."

And slow it was. It was hard to tell it was even moving, but over time it became noticeably closer to the ship and the waiting, empty spot.

The announcer tried to fill the time with basic information about the ship and what was happening, but it was all information people had heard before.

Demetrius called Stacey over and whispered in her ear. "He really should have come up with some new things to say at this point."

Reverse jets could be seen slowing the wedge down. Then, maneuvering jets positioned it more exactly. Finally, with no noise or fanfare, the movement stopped.

"And that's it. The final piece is now in place." Even the announcer seemed disappointed. The entire affair was anticlimactic, at best. "Now, the technicians will secure the wedge in place and attach all of the conduits, plumbing and other machinery needed to make use of the wedge. Over the coming weeks, the final supplies will be loaded and the remaining two thousand people, along with the twelve leaders, will be placed into suspension."

The announcer paused, seemingly unwilling to give up the position. With billions of people watching, Demetrius could hardly blame him.

"And now, I turn it over to Stacey Singleton, who is standing by at the manufacturing facilities in Colorado."

There was a slight interruption, partly due to the delay from L5 and partly to make sure the speakers in the room were off before the microphone was turned on. Feedback wouldn't be professional.

Stacey smiled and walked across the north wall. "On this wall behind me are pictures of the twelve leaders of the expedition. They, along with the governing board, are in this room with me today."

The west wall's screen started showing the projections of Stacey and the north wall.

"You've met them all before, so I won't re-introduce them."

This wasn't exactly true with Caius being added so late, but they were trying to downplay that.

"So, let us go directly to opening this up to questions."

A click could be heard. A man's voice said "Hi, I have a question for Dr. Stellar."

"Certainly," Stacey said smoothly. "Dr. Beatrice Stellar is considered the brains behind the FTL drive." She strolled over to Beatrice's chair and met the virtual projection who abruptly stood up.

Normally, recordings of virtual projections did not work well, but Aimee was intercepting the transmission and cleaning up the images real-time as they were broadcast.

"What can I do for you?" Beatrice asked. She had an odd voice that was slow and methodical as if every word was considered carefully before she let it leave her lips. It made everyone trust her much more than Demetrius would have thought. *Very clever of Aimee.* The voice was also scratchy enough to come across as aged and wise.

The man's voice asked, "I wonder why you didn't test the ship prior to the passengers being on it?"

"Oh, young man, of course we did. We tested it once the core, the drives, and the bridge were installed. At that point, it had no wheels, but we could measure the extent of the warp field and are comfortable that the wheels fit well within the limits.

"We actually flew the ship out to Pluto and back using the FTL drives. Stacey, could you bring up the recording of the test flight?"

The wall changed to show the ship without any wheels. A countdown on the lower right went from ten to zero and the ship disappeared.

"Whoa!" the man screeched. "Why would it just disappear?"

"Wait for it," Beatrice said with a grin.

The clock on the screen jumped to almost two hours and forty minutes and the ship reappeared facing the opposite direction.

"The answer to your question is quite complex. Basically, we use a warp field to take the ship into the Bulk, which you can think of as a fifth dimension. In theory, the further into the Bulk we go, the faster we can travel. However, the further down we go, the stranger physics becomes as well. We have only been able to go warp 2.0, which is four times the speed of light. Pluto is 38.44 AU from us, or it was when we did this test, so at warp 2.0, that is roughly one hour and twenty minutes."

"Wow! Just, wow," The man said, and the room broke into applause and beaming smiles.

The interviews went on and on, but eventually enough had been said and enough time had passed. The room cleared.

Demetrius met with the board near the door. "We need to reconfigure this room for our meeting. Please take a few minutes break to refresh or eat and join us back here at the top of the hour."

The entire board was back in the room early. *They're eager. Good.*

Once they had all sat, Adrastia spoke first. "Tell us, where are we exactly?"

Beatrice answered. Only Demetrius and Adrastia knew who she really was. "It will take roughly a week to complete internal assembly and test all systems and another two weeks to finish interning the remaining passengers, during which time the systems can all be tested. The ship should be ready to leave in three weeks. For safety sake, I would suggest you announce a departure four weeks from now. That will allow us some leeway in case there are any minor issues."

"What about major issues?" one of the board members asked.

"In that case, we would have to delay the launch, but the likelihood is quite small. We have tested every system independently already and the main drives, as you saw, were tested as well."

Demetrius asked, "Any other risks?"

"The only other major risk is the human factor."

"Explain."

"Rebels, discontents, accidents, etc."

"I assume there is nothing to be done with respect to those risks."

"On the contrary, many things have already been done. The risk here is small as well. We have put redundant checks in place for every system and test. Other than something completely unforeseen, we should easily be able to launch in four weeks."

Demetrius could feel a collective sigh in the room. Multiple people relaxed into their chairs. Others openly grinned.

Beatrice leaned forward. "And a location?"

The group looked to Rafael DaRosa, their head of astronomy and system selection. DaRosa had been guided by the data coming back from the probes the Overs had sent out. In fact, some of the data had been manipulated by Aimee in order to pick a system the Overs wanted. Aimee-as-Beatrice let DaRosa speak.

In a mild Portuguese accent, the elder man presented the system he and his team had chosen. A holographic display of the system rose above the table for all to see.

"The system is four hundred and seventy light years away in the Lyra constellation. It is one of the Kepler objects. Because of its distance, it will take the ship one hundred and seventeen years to get there."

Sighs of frustration could be heard around the room.

Demetrius asked, "There is nothing closer?"

"There are many possibilities closer, but none of them proved truly inhabitable, at least not as much as this one. From the images you see here, there is obviously an abundance of plant life on the planet. Additionally, it is slightly larger than Earth, but less dense so the gravity is 91% of Earths. The initial inhabitants there will feel slightly stronger and have slightly more endurance than they would here. Future generations, of course, will adapt to the gravity and so will not retain that advantage."

"Over a hundred years," someone whispered.

Adrastia said, "We cannot wait such a long time to hear any results."

Beatrice answered. "There is a way to at least hear that they are doing well on the trip."

"How?"

"We could have the ship stop periodically and send a probe back to us. Probes are small and can go deeper into the Bulk. Therefore, they can travel at a higher warp level. If you need human contact, the ship could be programmed to wake up some of the leaders to give a report. Say, every ten years."

Demetrius messaged Aimee privately. "How far is the real target?"

Beatrice looked at him, but he received the answer on his private channel. "Roughly thirty-six light years away. They will be there in a little over nine years."

"How will you handle these status reports?"

"We wake them up every year instead and fabricate their actual location to make them think they are further away. Remember, we want them to succeed, but we don't want the Overs to know that. We also want the Unders to think it is all going well for a long time to keep tensions low and to encourage more ships."

"Yes, yes, I understand that."

XLVI

LAUNCH

Jaames squatted across the street from The Rusted Spike. He stared at the front of the weathered building with a deep longing for the past.

His job at the complex was essentially complete. The last of the launches from Earth were finished, and all but a few of the crew were in their artificial comas. The Novaluce ship was due to fire its FTL drive in a few hours. The world waited.

He wasn't sure why he had come here, but he knew he didn't want to be with the Overs or any of the other people from the complex.

The problem was, when he looked at the building, all he could see was Anika. The flowing brown hair, that twinkle of mischievousness in her eye, the way she bounded off, willing him to follow.

If he went inside, she wouldn't be there. It felt like admitting she was gone… forever.

He sensed the excitement in the people heading towards the Spike. The last time he was here, the purpose was to drink, and it had seemed like that was true for most everyone. There were few smiles and little laughter. Now, patrons had a bounce to their step and merriment permeated the air.

I promised Demetrius I would watch.

He stood and made his way into The Rusted Spike with trepidation and fear.

He stood in the entry, letting his eyes adjust. As the room came into focus, he saw it crowded with all types. T'ers, snubbies, a few well-off people and a couple that could have been Overs. Fortunately, nobody he knew.

He started to navigate towards the bar. After a few steps, he heard his name whispered and those in front of him quieted down and moved aside to let him pass.

I don't need this, he thought.

A man moved directly into his way. He was a big man with taunt muscles, an ugly mustache, and a heavy frown. *Trouble*?

In days past, he might have invited a good fight in the mood he was in. It always took the edge off. Part of him wanted that still.

He examined the big man and saw a mechanical improvement on one arm. *He's a damn T'er.*

His body rotated to an angle and his feet spread out to stabilize his footing.

Anika would not want this.

"You're Jaames Perdite, aren't ya?"

"Yeah, so?"

"It's… It's an honor to meet you."

He moved aside and yelled at the people in Jaames' path towards the bar. "Get outa da way." People scurried away from him.

They got to the bar to find the stools full.

The big guy bent down towards a thin, well-dressed man seated in the center of the bar and scowled.

The man grumbled and then stood and offered Jaames his seat. He turned toward an attractive woman on the seat next to his and said, "Let's go."

She started to slide off the seat, but stopped. She examined Jaames as if she wanted him to ask her to stay.

Jaames sat down and tried to ignore her.

"I'm staying," she finally said to the well-dressed man and swung her seat around. The man stormed off.

The big guy finally introduced himself. "They call me Hugi."

"Of course they do," Jaames quipped.

He smiled and called the barkeep over.

"Jaames, this here's Sam. Sam, get Jaames anything he wants, on me."

Jaames rotated around. "Your name's Sam?"

"Yeah?"

"Weird."

"Why?"

"I knew a Sam once. A great man."

Hugi touched Jaames' shoulder. "I'll be 'round, man. You need anything, lets me know."

"Sure thing."

To nobody in particular, Jaames mumbled, "When did they change to a live server."

The attractive girl to his right said, "About a year ago."

Really... not interested, Jaames thought privately.

Three more hours of pundits, scientists, politicians, and sycophants yapping on the screens, and the ship was finally ready to depart.

Jaames had worked his way through half-a-dozen drinks during the time and had observed.

Almost everyone was incredibly excited about the Novaluce ship and man's first step to the stars. Two Overs that Jaames recognized from Demetrius' office had joined them. They mingled freely with everyone else.

Maybe this peacemaking plan of his will actually work.

Jaames did hear a couple of grumbles from people who thought it was all a diversion or something to benefit the Overs, but they were quickly overridden.

The announcer raised his voice and said, "Twenty seconds."

The gathering in the Rusted Spike quieted down and everyone concentrated on the screens.

"Ten," the announcer said and the crowd joined in.

"Nine," they said in unison.

"Eight."

"Seven." The screens were perfectly still. They could be showing a photograph instead of a live view.

"Six."

"Five." Jaames leaned toward the screen with his head askance. The Novaluce label on the side of the ship faded. *What the fuck?*

"Four."

"Three." It was replaced with "The Anika" in huge, bold letters. The people in the room gasped out loud and turned, as one, towards Jaames.

"Three." He looked down at the glistening floor, seeing Anika smiling back at him.

"Two." He raised his head and then his glass to the screen. He whispered, "Bye, Anika."

"One." Everyone in the room raised their glasses as well.

Tears flowed freely from Jaames.

Man's first ship to the stars, The Anika, disappeared.

ASET

The World Approaches
A Reddish Sun with a Bit of Blue
A Teal Planet Thick in Cloud
Our Chance Anew

Orbiting Anika
Gleaming Blue and Green
Awaiting Humanity
An Inviting Mien

Examination Continues
Life abounds
Landing Sites Endless
Beauty Astounds

All are Expectant
Ready to Toil
To Discover and Build
To Plant the Soil

Landfall Approaches
Such Wonder we Near
Hope and Life Flourish
I Shed a Tear

UPCOMING BOOKS

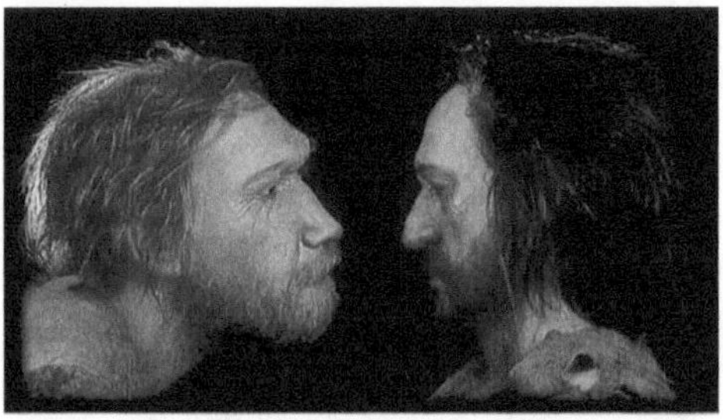

The Sapiens Project

In the mid-twenty-first century, Humanity is coming to an end; at least that's what an advanced predictive algorithm has proclaimed. But, Dempsey Earle Blake, the man who would later be known as Demetrius in Over, won't accept that fate. He embarks on the world's largest and most complex project ever to send humans back to the choke-point in civilization, 70,000 years ago. There he hopes to change the fate of humanity by altering our timeline, just as it began.

Anika's Gift

The sequel to *Over* sees the inhabitants of a new world, Anika, trying to survive in the inexplicable alien environment. What will they encounter on this new world? How will it change them? And, how does their savior, the artificial intelligence, Aset, react when the unknowable happens?

NON-FICTION

By some estimates, over 1 billion people in the world are non-religious (humanist/secular/atheist) yet we base many of our parenting techniques and traditions on religion. There are many books available on parenting around each of the major religions, but few discuss parenting in a Humanist or Secular household. This book is an attempt to outline how non-religious parents can have the rites, rituals, and practices needed for a healthy, spiritually fulfilled family.

"*Humanism for Parents* is a wonderful book with all kinds of practical insights into parenting in a non-religious household. It made me seriously consider our stance and how we parent with respect to many topics. I think it is relevant to anyone who provides guidance to children."

- Jackie, parent of 3

Additional Information / Purchase

https://author-sean-curley.us
http://amazon.com/author/seancurley
https://www.facebook.com/author.sean.curley

www.ingramcontent.com/pod-product-compliance
Lightning Source LLC
LaVergne TN
LVHW091706070526
838199LV00050B/2291
* 9 7 9 8 8 9 0 3 1 5 7 9 3 *